P.N. Elrod

Lunch Time Reading

Omnibus

Also by P.N. Elrod

The Vampire Files
Bloodlist
Lifeblood
Bloodcircle
Art in the Blood
Fire in the Blood
Blood on the Water
Chill in the Blood
Dark Sleep
Lady Crymsyn
Cold Streets
Song in the Dark
Dark Road Rising
The Devil You Know

Jonathan Barrett: Gentleman Vampire
Red Death
Death and the Maiden
Death Masque
Dance of Death

Quincey Morris, Vampire
Quincey Morris and the West End Ripper (2013)
The Adventures of Myhr
I, Strahd: The Memoirs of a Vampire
I, Strahd: The War Against Azalin

Co-written with Nigel Bennett
Keeper of the King
His Father's Son
Siege Perilous

Editor/co-editor
Time of the Vampires
Dracula in London
Stepping Through the Stargate
My Big Fat Supernatural Wedding
My Big Fat Supernatural Honeymoon
Strange Brew
Dark and Stormy Knights
P.N. Elrod Lunchtime Reading Omnibus
Hex Symbols (Pending)

On Her Majesty's Psychic Service (2012)
The Hanged Man
The Tower
The Empress

P.N. Elrod

Lunch Time Reading

Omnibus

Written and edited
by P.N. Elrod

VAMPWRITER BOOKS
2011

Published by Vampwriter Books
Fort Worth, TX USA
www.vampwriter.com

Printed in the United States of America

ISBN-13: 978-1463776633
ISBN-10: 1463776632

CONTENTS

P.N. Elrod

Lunch Time Reading

Omnibus

A NIGHT AT THE (HORSE) OPERA

Author's Note: *I was asked to do a story for a collection called* CELEBRITY VAMPIRES for DAW *and being a fan of the Marx Brothers, it was a no-brainer write about one of them crossing paths with my Depression era vampire PI. It's still one of my favorites.*

Chicago, Autumn, 1936

The smell of buttered popcorn was distracting until I settled in my seat and stopped pretending to breathe. I wasn't able to drink soda pop anymore, and the darkness wasn't really dark anymore, but a movie was still a movie, and it was rare that I didn't drop in on one of Chicago's shadow palaces two or three times a week take in the latest show.

This particular one wasn't especially new; *The Plainsman* had been out for a while, but I'd somehow missed it until now, a sad lapse for a Gary Cooper fan. Of course, I also liked Jean Arthur, who was mighty eye-catching done up in Hollywood cowgirl style. I lost track of the dialog at one point, speculating how my girlfriend, Bobbi, might look in a similar outfit of made of buckskins. Probably very good, I thought; then things started happening in the plot I couldn't follow because of my internal wandering.

"I fell asleep—what's going on?" I whispered to the man next to me. Not looking away from the screen, he obligingly leaned over and filled me in, speaking low and with a decided New York accent. I'd lived there for a long time before moving to Chicago and was mildly curious to find out why he'd left, but it could wait until after the feature.

De Mille's epic danced over the screen with enough thrills and drama to keep the most jaded Western lover satisfied, myself included. If it was still playing here tomorrow, which was Bobbi's night off, I'd ask her out. She wouldn't need much persuading; she liked Gary Cooper, too.

The movie rolled to its end, and the lights came up. Other people rose to leave, uniformed ushers appeared to clean up the trash, and the rest of the audience remained seated to wait for the next feature to start. Bobbi's last show at the night club where she sang wouldn't be over for another couple of hours; I was in no hurry to leave. The same apparently went for my seat mate, who pulled out a crumpled sack of peanuts from somewhere and began shelling and eating them in a leisurely manner.

"Thanks," I said.

His bright eyes clouded slightly as he tried to recall why I was thanking him, then comprehension dawned. "Don't mention it."

"New York?" I asked.

"Ninety-third Streeter," he promptly replied. He had a sloping nose, wide at the base, a wide, expressive mouth, receding hair, and enough mischief packed into his mug for a dozen Christmas elves. He looked as though he ought to be somebody, and I had a nagging feeling that I knew him. "You from there, too?" he asked.

"Not since last August. You ever hang out at a place called Rosie's? Across from the *Dispatch*?"

He shook his head solemnly.

"Thought I might have seen you there."

"You probably saw me here, is what I'm thinking." He tossed a peanut high and caught it in his mouth with the easy skill of long practice. "Want some?" He shook the bag, open end toward me.

"No, but thanks anyway." Maybe I'd seen him here before and just hadn't noticed him among the hundreds of other movie watchers. "Been away from New York long?"

"Long enough. California's home now, least when we're not on the road."

"Salesman?" But that didn't seem quite right for him. Another peanut shot high and dropped in. He chewed it slowly while his eyes, his whole expression, turned steady and serious. "Yeah. I'm a salesman, all right. I sell money."

"You what?"

"I sell money. You never heard of the business?"

"No . . ." I'd either stumbled across a counterfeiter or a lunatic. Now might be a good time to find another seat.

The guy put away his bag of peanuts. "I know what you must be thinking, but it's perfectly legal. I really do sell money."

Okay. He'd hooked me. I had to hear the punch line. "What is it? Like coin collecting or something?"

"Nah, this stuff." He pulled out his wallet and fished for a five dollar bill, holding it up. "Take a look. It's real, right?"

As far as I could tell it looked just like any other used bill. "Right. . ."

"Okay, I'll sell you this five for four dollars and fifty cents."

I shook my head, chuckling. "Ah. No, thanks."

"It's not a fiddle," he earnestly assured me. "Think of the profit."

"What do you get out of it?"

"A sale."

"Maybe not this time, but thanks all the same."

"You sure? It's a great bargain you're passing up." At this point he looked too innocent to be believed. He read that I wasn't going to fall for whatever gag he had in mind, gave a good-natured shrug, and put away the bill and wallet. He brought out the peanuts again.

The nagging set in again with a vengeance. "I *know* you from somewhere."

"Go to the movies a lot?" he asked.

"All the time."

"You really don't know?"

"You're gonna have to tell me."

He grinned, his whole face going into it.

"Wait a second. . ."

He dropped his chin a bit and letting his mobile mouth hang slack in an exaggerated anticipation.

"Oh, jeez, you're—"

A hand clamped down on his shoulder from behind and made him jump. He looked around in irritation to the source of the interruption. The man looming over us was big even by Chicago standards, and he had company: two large friends waiting in the aisle. The three of them looked as though they could take on the Wrigley Building and win. Their hundred-dollar suits were not well-tailored enough to hide ominous bulges under their left arms.

The man's hand flexed and lifted, and my seat mate rose like a puppet.

"Oh, hell," he said, irritation suddenly changing to fear. The smell of it fairly leaped off him.

"You don't know the half of it yet," the man told him.

"Wait a minute . . " I began, not thinking. "You're Guns Thompson, aren't you?" I'd heard he was working as muscle for a West Side mob these days.

One of his goons sidled into the row behind me and dropped a meaty hand on my shoulder. "Or maybe not. I could be mistaken."

"Shhh!" someone down the row advised us severely.

"Out of here," said Thompson, and abruptly the five of us were marching toward the lobby just as the next show began. The noisy barrage of a newsreel theme was enough to drown any protests we might have. I could have made an issue at this point, but I'd heard that Thompson was a rough customer and wouldn't put it past him to open up with his heater right then and there. Better I go along and put a few walls between the other theater patrons and whatever caliber of bullets he and his cronies were packing.

We threaded past ushers with flashlights guiding latecomers in; no one noticed us. If they did, they were going to mind their own business and watch the movie. We were urged through doors into the lush lobby. The popcorn smell hit me again with a brief wave of nausea as they hustled us past the front exit. I'd been expecting a car ride or at least a short walk to the nearest dark alley; Thompson headed for the men's room.

We trooped in. A couple of guys were washing up, and some instinct told them to hurry the job and leave. The last one bolted before drying his hands.

Couldn't blame him, the brightly lighted background of patterned tile did nothing to improve Thompson's looks. Despite their flashy clothes, he and his friends were as out of place as a trio of gorillas at a Sunday School picnic. It showed in their hard, impassive faces and the way they moved like intelligent bulldozers.

"You've got the wrong man," protested my seat mate. "You're after Chico, aren't you?"

"Not anymore," said one of the goons. He went to stand by the door, jamming his foot against the base to keep out interruptions.

"I'm his brother—Harpo. You've got the wrong man!"

Thompson stared, eyes so narrow you couldn't read them.

"It's true," I put in. "This is Harpo Marx."

"Oh, yeah, then how come he's talking?" demanded Thompson.

"Yeah," said the goon at the door, suddenly giggling. "An' if you're Harpo, where's your harp?"

"Back in my hotel room," came Harpo's logical answer, but his voice was thin and nervous. He still clutched his forgotten bag of peanuts in one fist. They rattled against the paper because he was trembling.

"Everyone knows Harpo is a dummy. Dummies don't talk."

"That's just a character I play!"

"Stop wasting time," Thompson growled and pulled out a forty-five that looked like it could drop King Kong in one shot.

He wasn't pointing it at anyone just yet, so I thought I'd try once more. "C'mon, Guns, give the man a real look. He's not the one you want."

Thompson did but couldn't see any difference. Then he focused on me for the first time and started pointing the gun. I must have the kind of face that sets off alarms for crazy debt collectors. "Where the hell do you know me? I never seen you before."

"Hey, everyone in town knows Guns Thompson." I tried to make it sound like he was a respected celebrity. "You're like Big Al—"

"Shut up."

I shut up. Maybe he had a grudge against the long gone Capone. I didn't know squat about Chicago mob politics, though I could recognize a few faces. All you had to do was study the Post Office portraits. There were plenty of local bad guys the FBI hadn't gotten around to collecting yet. This one had gotten his nickname during the Prohibition gang wars with his talent for handling a Thompson machine gun. It was about his only asset, since he and his friends apparently didn't have enough brains between them to fill a whiskey jigger.

"Who the hell are you, anyway?"

"My name's Fleming and I'm nobody special, honest."

"Fleming?" Thompson's face screwed up in an effort to think. "Where do I know him from, Higgs?" he asked the guy by the door.

Higgs shook his head.

"Rinky?" This was directed to the thug guarding Harpo. Rinky shrugged.

Since my arrival in this town I'd been reluctantly bumping heads with its criminal element, so it wasn't too surprising that Thompson had heard of me from somewhere. Most of the time I do whatever's needed to cover my tracks and kept my head down. Apparently not well enough.

"Where do I know you from?"

I didn't meet his eye and acted scared, only it wasn't an act.

He growled and dismissed me as annoying but not worth the effort, turning his attention and gun on Harpo.

"Okay, Marx, you ran up a bill with Big Joey, and it's past due. I can take it out of your pocket or your hide."

"This is a pretty public place for that kind of business," I said. I wasn't crazy about putting myself forward but had a better chance of surviving than Harpo. "We should take this elsewhere."

Higgs giggled again. "Big Joey owns this joint, bo'. Make noise if you want. Ain't no one gonna come in to see why."

Which made for a pretty disgusting situation, I thought, as the three of them enjoyed my reaction. I checked to see how Harpo was doing, but he'd frozen in place, staring at something behind me, his mouth sagging. In no wise was that comical mugging. My nape prickled as I realized what he saw. Hells bells, why couldn't these jerks have taken us into a dark alley?

"Marx?" Thompson said, moving a step closer and raising his gun an inch.

Harpo continued to stare until Rinky gave him a shake, then he looked vaguely at Thompson.

"Stop playing the dope. Pay up, and we'll let you go back to the movie."

"H-how much?"

"Five grand."

The mention of such an enormous sum got Harpo's attention as nothing else could, given his circumstances. He gulped. "My God, how long was he playing?"

"Who?"

"Chico."

"You're Chico, you dope!"

"Sorry, I forgot."

Thompson tapped him lightly on the side of the head with the barrel of his gun, just enough to jar him. "Pay up, or get busted up. I don't want no more shit from you, sheenie."

Harpo had been drained of color up to this point; now he flushed a deep red. There was a lot playing over his face; anger, resentment, and outrage were mixed in with his fear. I'd seen hilarious exaggerations on the screen, but he'd been acting then, working hard to make people laugh. I'd been one of them. This took only a second, maybe less than a second, and then he exploded.

It was foolish and almost too fast to follow. Harpo's fist came up, connected, and Thompson staggered away, clutching a suddenly broken and bloody nose.

Rinky surged forward, slamming Harpo back into one of the stall doors. They were designed to open out; this one's hinges gave and it crashed inward, stopping abruptly when it struck the toilet inside. His bag of peanuts scattering, Harpo fell against it and dropped, but he was still mad and scrapping. From the floor he kicked at Rinky's ankles. Rinky danced out of the way, reaching for his gun.

Before he could haul it out, I was on him. I grabbed handfuls of Rinky's coat and some skin under it; he yelped loud enough. One solid pull, turn, and shove and he was flying across the length of the room, crashing into the tiled wall. He dropped and stayed dropped.

Then something roared, a horrendous explosion, stunning in the confined space. The sound was as solid as a bowling ball, and struck me high in the back. I saw a burst of blood leap from the middle of my chest, then the floor flew up too fast to dodge.

I couldn't tell if the silence that followed was a result of their shock at what had happened or my inability to hear. My ears felt stuffed and when the stuffiness wore off, it was replaced by a hot, unpleasant ringing.

Couldn't move. The pain crashing in was searingly familiar, which did not make it easier to bear. My initial, involuntary reaction to getting shot is to vanish. Once incorporeal I would be free of the pain, floating in a unique pocket of existence that's always given me healing and comfort.

Great stuff, but the drawback is that it always scares the hell out of anyone who sees me doing it. I wasn't about to give away my real nature to these creeps, so I grimly hung on, gritting my teeth as flesh, bone, muscle, and finally outraged nerves began to painfully knit back together again.

"Oh, my God." whispered Harpo somewhere behind me. I wasn't moving and, if necessary, I can lie very, very still indeed. It was a necessity now, if only to allow myself time to get over the worst of the shock. That moment came and thankfully went, but I stayed where I was, straining to listen, trying to figure out some way of helping Harpo that wouldn't get him killed.

Someone shifted, his shoe soles crushing and crunching the peanuts on the floor. It was Higgs, walking over to check out Rinky.

"He's out cold, Guns," he reported.

"Throw water on him." Thompson snarled nasally. I hoped his nose hurt worse than my bullet wound. It would last him longer.

Higgs complied, running water in one of the sinks. He cupped his hands together to carry it over to his friend. I could see only that much from the corner of one open eye, having fallen at an inconvenient angle. Higgs never bothered to glance at me. I was just another mess, like the peanuts.

Someone was having a hard time breathing, probably Harpo. I heard a series of little gasps, then a sudden scrabble of movement. The next thing I heard was him throwing up in one of the stalls.

Thompson thought it was funny, "The little sheenie shit can't take it, Higgs."

Higgs grunted agreement and made a second trip for water.

"Jeez, that puke stinks. Flush it, Marx."

After a moment, the toilet was flushed.

Rinky began to revive. He groaned, swatted at the latest delivery of water, and was hauled to his feet by Higgs.

"Go wait in the car," Thompson ordered. "I'll finish here."

Rinky made an unsteady exit. Just as he got to the door, someone must have poked his head in.

"Hey! What's going on h—"

"Never you mind, bo'," said Higgs. He followed Rinky, keeping up a patter of tough talk to convince the newcomer to butt out. It left Thompson alone with Harpo. . .and me.

"Come outta there, sheenie."

Footsteps dragged reluctantly over the floor as Harpo emerged from the stall.

"You see what happens when I get pissed? You come up with the money, or you end up just like him."

"Okay." Harpo's voice had dropped lower than a whisper, as though he had no air left.

"So fork over."

"But I—" Harpo broke off.

"Don't tell me you don't have it. You movie people always carry a wad with you."

He'd be concentrating on Harpo now, as good a time as any to make a move, the odds were better with Higgs and Rinky out of the way. I stopped being me for an instant, slipping into that non-place where I had no body, no weight, no sight, only mind and will. I sensed the hardness of the floor and, as I drifted over it toward them, could determine just how close they were to each other.

Close. Thompson had Harpo backed up against the stall doors and I could guess he had his gun square in the poor guy's face.

"C'mon, fork over."

If Harpo came up short Thompson was crazy enough to scrag him as casually as he'd scragged me. I had to break things up now and figure out how to cover my tracks later.

Thompson never knew what hit him. I materialized with my hands already reaching, one to push his gun out of the way and the other flowing smoothly into a solid sock to his jaw. He reeled back, eyes rolling up, and careened off a urinal before making friends with the peanuts on the floor.

I turned to check on Harpo. He was a pale, pale green. If he hadn't been braced against the stall dividers, his legs might have given out. His eyes were wider than they'd ever been in the movies as his gaze traveled from me to Thompson and back to me again, finally resting on the hole in my shirt and its surrounding bloodstain. It was a mess and it was real. No movie fakery here.

A hundred questions raced over Harpo's face, not one of them getting out. He was too damned scared.

I'd seen the reaction before on others, but like getting shot, the familiarity never made it less painful. Backing away, I said something stupid about taking it easy and that everything was all right. I could hear his heart pounding fit to bust and felt a stab of worry about giving him a heart attack. His green tint turned ashy in a matter of seconds.

"You okay?" I asked, hoping he'd respond.

He stared.

I repeated my question.

He gulped, grimacing perhaps, on the vomit taste left in his mouth. "I'm . . . fine," he squeaked.

"You sure? You don't look so hot."

His mouth twitched. "Dead. I saw. You."

I gently put a little more distance between us. "Yeah, I know. I'm sorry."

Now he seemed to twitch all over. "*Sorry?*"

"I don't mean to scare you. I really don't." I'd backed as far as I could. He could run out the door if he wanted. I wouldn't stop him or try hypnotizing him into forgetting his fear or into accepting me or anything like that. It's a dangerous thing to mess around inside people's minds in that way. I never did it unless at the time it seemed more dangerous not to; this wasn't one of those times. Besides, who'd believe him?

"Is it some kind of a trick?" He looked so damned hollow and lost.

"No trick. Houdini I ain't. Nothing up my sleeve but arm."

"Then how?"

I considered how to answer. Even a short lecture on Romanian folklore and how it differs from actuality would take time to get through, and I couldn't deliver it in a men's room with peanuts and Guns Thompson all over the floor.

I said, "You ever see that Bela Lugosi movie couple of years back? The one where he was a vampire?"

Maybe Harpo had seen it or not, but he suddenly understood.

"It's like that. . .only I'm a. . .a much nicer person." I gave a little shrug.

"No kiddin'?"

"No kiddin'. Except for a couple quirks" —I touched where the wound had been— "I'm just like you. I like movies and hate bullies."

Harpo stared, then his gaze flicked to the bank of mirrors on the wall over the sinks. They'd given him his first clue the world was a much stranger place than he'd thought. From where I stood, I could see his reflection. It peered hard at the spot where I should have been, but nothing was there, of course. After a time, it looked down to where Thompson lay.

Then Harpo straightened to look directly at me. "Yeah, you're right. You are nicer than some people I could name."

Life's tough, but every now and then it hands you something you want more than anything else, even if you didn't know you wanted it. Harpo Marx gave me what I'd hoped for, wanted, needed.

Acceptance.

Just like that. No fanfare, no conditions.

"Thanks," I whispered.

"Doesn't that hurt?" he asked, cautiously pointing to my chest.

I shook my head, too full to talk just yet.

"What are you going to do with him?" He pointed at Thompson.

I coughed to clear my clogged throat. "Damned if I know. Got any ideas?"

Harpo's face relaxed into more normal lines as the tension melted, and I saw a ghost of his character's elfin mischief flit past. He walked over to Thompson and studied him, then stepped to one of the sinks, turning on the tap. Cupping his hands like Higgs before him, he slopped water onto Thompson, who jerked and jumped and rumbled an obscene protest.

Harpo stooped and solicitously helped Thompson to his feet.

Thompson was awake just enough to see and vaguely understand something was wrong. He was to the point of snarling at his benefactor, but Harpo cut him off by landing as neat and as forceful a gut punch as had ever been my privilege to see. He all but buried his arm to the elbow in Thompson's middle, and the man immediately folded. His breath whooshed out.

Harpo stood over him, waiting. After a minute, Thompson, being fairly tough, recovered enough to straighten again. The second he was up, though, Harpo let him have it once more. Thompson grunted and dropped to his knees. It took awhile before he could breathe regularly, and even longer for him to find his feet.

Harpo helped him.

Thompson should have known better.

This time Harpo's gut punch was followed up by a hard, crisp left with just enough force in it to finish the job. No gasping for air for Thompson. He simply dropped. Next Christmas was about ten months away. Maybe he'd wake up by then.

Harpo shook his hand, blowing on it, then returned to the sink to let the cold water run over his bruised knuckles.

He grinned. "I shouldn't have done that. Any more and I couldn't play the harp for our show. We're touring, you know, trying out gags we're going to use in a new movie." he explained.

"We? Your brothers?"

"They're back at the hotel."

"Where'd you learn to sock like that?" I asked.

"Benny Leonard." he answered, dropping the name of the lightweight champion of the world. "We did a tour with him once, used to take turns sparring with him. Great guy. Taught me a lot." Harpo cut the water and toweled off. "Wish he could have seen this. He'd a been proud of me."

I picked up Thompson's .45 which had fallen when I'd hit him. It probably wouldn't hurt to call up a homicide cop I knew and ask if he was interested in an easy collar. Lieutenant Blair didn't like or trust me much, but he wasn't above accepting a favor when it was offered. Putting the gun in my overcoat pocket to give to him later, I buttoned the front together to hide the bullet hole in my bloodied shirt. I'd have to remember to keep my back to the walls to hide the corresponding entry hole there.

The first cold tickle of hunger plucked at my belly and throat. It wasn't critical, but I'd have to make time tonight to stop at the Stockyards to feed, to replace what had been lost. Some of it still smeared the floor. Frowning. I went to a stall, ripped away toilet paper, and swabbed my blood from the tiles, tossing the waste and flushing it away.

Harpo watched without comment, his face solemn.

"I know you've been through a lot," I said, "but would you mind doing me a favor?"

"Anything you want."

I got out my notebook and scribbled a name and number on a page and gave it to him. "Could you call this guy for me? Tell him Jack Fleming is babysitting Guns Thompson here and for him to come over right away."

He looked dubious. "This a cop?"

"Yeah, but you can leave your name out of it if you want." That made him happy.

"What about his friends?"

Higgs and Rinky. The ones in the car outside. "Wait back in the theater office until it's over. They'll clear out the moment a patrol car pulls up. They're dumb, but not that dumb."

"I owe you."

"Let's call it even if I can have an autograph."

Harpo shook his head and laughed in a big way. "How 'bout I take you to meet my brothers?"

This was almost as much of a shock as catching that bullet, but without the pain. "Really? You mean it?"

"Yeah. I'd want them to meet the guy who saved my life."

I sagged a little. "You won't tell 'em how, will you?"

He pulled in his lower lip, considering. "Noooo, I don't think that would be a good idea. We'll talk around it somehow."

"That'd be great, then. Just great." I was suddenly grinning.

He grinned back. "Grouch'll be there and he might know where Chico is. I think," he added darkly, "I have to talk with Chico. When we were kids we were always being mistaken for one another, like twins. I never imagined anything like this would happen because of it, though."

"Maybe you should wear the wig and raincoat—at least while you're still in Chicago."

He nodded. "There's an idea. I'll go make that call. Will the cops take long?"

"I'll make sure they don't." I promised. "One more thing—"

He paused at the door.

"That stuff you were giving me about selling money—is that part of your stage show?"

His eyes twinkled—they really did. "Nah, that's just a gag Chico and I do for the hell of it. People try to figure out the catch, only there isn't one. It drives 'em crazy."

"Was I crazy enough for you?"

He flashed another broad grin. "Brother, you were a pip!"

I looked at the gently closing door and decided that I'd been handed the privilege of a lifetime. The Marxes worked their butts off to give people like me a good laugh, and the chance had fallen my way to give one back in return.

And that felt pretty damned good.

THE BREATH OF BAST

Author's Note: *I'm not cat owner (allergies) but am fond of the beasts. My vampire PI's human partner was an easy choice to deliver a wholly non-supernatural case for* KITTENS CATS AND CRIME *from Five Star. My thanks to author, editor and friend Carole Nelson Douglas for inviting me to write this one!*

Chicago, 1937

Charles Escott smiled across his uncluttered desk at a potential client. "May I inquire as to who referred you to me, Miss Selk?"

Cassandra Selk was what his part-time partner in the Escott Agency would have called "a knockout in heels." Possessed of raven-black hair and expressive eyes so brown as to be black as well, Escott's first thought when he ushered her into his office was that she was an artist's model. As it turned out, she was herself an artist, a famous one. He was chagrinned that he'd never heard of her, but she didn't seem to mind; apparently few outside of certain rarified circles were familiar with her name. Her area of expertise was sculpture; her favorite subject was cats, and she sold them all over the world.

Miss Selk's remarkable eyes seemed to shimmer. "Mrs. Wasserman spoke highly of your efficiency and attention to detail—and your sympathy toward animals."

Mrs. Wasserman's business was still fresh in Escott's mind. He'd agreed to kidnap her dog from her estranged husband. Hardly a case to test one's intellectual talents, but that sort of mundane job paid the bills.

Besides, Escott liked dogs. "Yes, the little canine was a most agreeable travel-companion. Have you a similar task in mind?"

Miss Selk shook her head. "I require a dropping-off, not a picking-up."

"May I have more details?" He hoped she would take her time; he wanted to extend his enjoyment of her altogether entrancing face.

"Hm?" She blinked. "Yes, of course. I've completed a commission for a local collector. I need you to deliver it, then return to tell me her reaction to my work."

His smile faltered. "Why not employ a regular delivery service?"

"I want someone with an eye for detail and a good memory to make a full and complete report."

"Of the collector's reaction? I see." He didn't, but would never admit it aloud. "Why not go yourself?"

Her bewitching smile melted into one of rueful sadness. "It's impossible because of my severe allergy to cats. This collector has at least a dozen running about her house, and I dare not set foot to the threshold. It's terrible for me because I absolutely adore them. They're such beautiful, graceful, noble creatures, don't you think?"

"Oh, yes, I've always thought so. You say they are your specialty? What do you do for models?"

"I rely on photographs; many artists do so. The difference for me is making a three-dimensional creation from a two-dimensional image. The dynamics are fascinating."

"Is it not frustrating being unable to work from a live model?"

Her eyes shimmered again, as though she'd heard that question many times. "Not really. From conversations I've had with photographers, it's very difficult to get a cat to hold still for anything. On the other hand, I've been compared to Beethoven. I'm unable to be in the same room with my favorite animal just as he was unable to hear his own music."

"That is ironic."

"I've had years to consider the irony and concluded that if I did not have this allergy, then I would have a house full of cats and not one piece of sculpture. Without what some would call a defect, I should be leading quite a bit different life, perhaps not as fulfilling."

Escott found himself warming nicely to her turn of mind, which he found as interesting as her looks. However, this was a business transaction, so he gently asked a few more questions and said he would be delighted to take on the errand. Miss Selk—she asked him to please call her Cassandra—signed his standard contract and they shook hands.

"The sculpture is in my car," she said. "It's not large, if you. . ."

He assured her he would be happy to fetch it.

On this humble Chicago street close to the Stockyards there was no question about which car was hers. The 1937 Cadillacs were barely off the assembly line, but she had one. That, combined with Cassandra's expensive fur coat and silk dress, belied any doubt Escott harbored about whether she could afford his standard fee. He retrieved a small, heavy wooden box and carried it up to his second floor office, placing it carefully on his desk.

"Would you like to see it?" she asked, eyes bright with pride.

"Very much." After she left he'd planned to open it to answer his own curiosity and as a precaution. In his line of business, which required that he undertake odd and frequently unpleasant errands between parties in disagreement, it was only prudent. So far he'd not been employed to deliver a bomb for some crazed anarchist, but there was a first time for everything.

The box was just over a foot tall, the top not nailed in place, but fitting snugly like a humidor lid. Cassandra lifted it off, revealing a tangled nest of excelsior.

"I'm afraid it will make a mess," she said.

"Easily cleaned." He pulled out handfuls of the stuff until encountering something hard. Cold metal, with dulled points, he thought.

"Just take it out by the head. It won't break."

He did so, brushing away more excelsior. "My heavens."

He reverently set the object on his desk. He was no expert in the field, but possessed an instinct for genius, and that was what shone before him. The metal statue was of a proudly seated feline done in the Egyptian style. For all he could tell, it might have come right from some ancient temple. Hieroglyphs were incised into the cat's body and along the base upon which it rested.

"Is it silver?" he asked, eyeing its regal head. The points he'd felt had been the ears.

"Yes." She seemed pleased with his obvious awe of her work. "I normally cast in other metals when I use them as my medium, but this was a special commission, and I'm sure you're aware that the client is always right."

"Indeed." On visits to Chicago's museums Escott often found himself mesmerized by certain pieces. He was aware of his own artistic streak, expressed, once upon a time, by being on the stage in his youth. In those early years of knocking around with a traveling repertory company he learned how to create a realistic illusion out of next to nothing. Those illusions lasted only for the duration of the performance, though. Such work gave him a sharp appreciation for individuals whose talent could make a lasting creation. "This is exquisite. Perhaps sometime you could let me see more of—"

"Yes, of course. Tonight, if you'd like—after you make the delivery."

He looked at her, slightly startled at this display of repressed eagerness. Certainly he found her attractive, but was this a reciprocation of a like feeling on her part or merely a desire to show off to an appreciative audience? He was not inexperienced when it came to artists and their egos. The fact that she wanted a full description of her client's reaction indicated that Cassandra possessed a sizable vanity concerning her work. But then this cat sculpture was evidence enough that its creator had earned the right to indulge.

Well, he would find out later tonight.

* * *

The delivery went smoothly. A somber butler took Escott into the depths of an enormous house where he met the client and several of her cats in a lush drawing room. With a flourish—for he understood the importance of a proper presentation—Escott placed the Egyptian-style work on a central table and duly observed every nuance of reaction. The woman waxed long in her praise for Cassandra Selk.

"It's perfect, exactly what I wanted," she said. "I've commissioned similar works from others, but only Cassandra truly understands. The hieroglyphs are all real, you know. I wrote them out for her to copy, and she got them right! Every last one of them. I think I shall get rid of the others, now. I shan't allow lesser works to share the same room with this piece."

"Indeed," he said. Three of her cats busily wound themselves in a friendly way around Escott's legs, their tails straight up with a small crook at the end.

"Goodness, they do seem to like you."

He smiled good-naturedly down at his furry worshippers. "I like them."

The client turned back to her acquisition, a dreamy look on her soft features. "Cassandra has a remarkable perception about this period, though that's hardly a surprise, as you know."

Escott realized she did not understand he was a hired agent, and had taken him for one of Cassandra's friends. Curiosity led him to encourage the misapprehension. "I'm amazed by it," he said agreeably.

"Her past life during that time must have been marvelous. She retains so much memory of it. Such a strong soul."

"Indeed?" This was an odd turn.

"But then one would have to be for the gods to choose her for one of their high priestesses. It's a great responsibility. What a pity she wavered in her vows by falling in love with a priest of Ra and he with her. Such a punishment to live this life allergic to these dear ones." She stroked the silver cat as though it were one of the live specimens loafing and prowling about the room.

Escott read a lot, including a certain amount on esoteric topics, so he wasn't wholly at sea but he did not know what sort of response was expected to this revelation. He settled for making a sympathetic noise.

"Yes," she continued with a sigh. "We ordinary mortals are allowed our little mistakes and can obtain forgiveness, but those chosen by the gods are not let off so easily. I think Cassandra has dealt marvelously with her punishment, though. Surely by such an outpouring of work in this life she will have proved to them her sincere atonement, don't you think?"

"Oh, absolutely," he said, with much confidence. He wondered if this was the client's own fancy or if Cassandra also shared it. He suspected this lady had seen that film—what was it?—*The Mummy*, one too many times.

A cat of the Abyssinian breed leapt lightly up on the table, nosed the sculpture, then jumped on Escott, who was just quick enough to catch the lithe animal in his arms.

His hostess gaped. "I'm sorry. That's Ma'at. She's usually very reserved with guests."

He managed to keep Ma'at from mauling his suit in her endeavor to burrow inside his coat. She purred like an idling car. "How flattering. I hope she doesn't expect to go home with me."

"Oh, you won't budge her from the house, but I've never seen her take to anyone so quickly before. It's quite astonishing."

Escott noted that Ma'at's claws were dug deep into his nearly new single-breasted coat. He refrained from pulling her off since forcing a cat to do something was always unwise; she would let go when she was ready. It seemed prudent to continue holding her for the rest of his brief visit. And anyway, the purring was pleasant.

* * *

Miss Cassandra Selk lived in another large house halfway across Chicago. Escott knew he had the right place; a dozen identical terracotta lions in the Egyptian style guarded the walkway from the street, and two uncannily realistic life-sized ceramic leopards crouched on either side of the entry.

Cassandra had changed from her furs and silk dress into a pearl gray silk lounging outfit. It was diaphanous, but cunningly pleated so the many layers concealed everything, yet at the same time revealed much. Rather too much for a formal interview, he thought. As the sole owner of his agency Escott could dictate whether or not fraternization with clients was appropriate on any given case. This commission was all but completed, though. Escott thought he knew what she was doing, and composed himself to agree with everything. After all, the client was always right.

Her home reflected her inner creative drive; cats were everywhere. When he asked, she replied with pride that yes, she had sculpted all of them.

"There are so many different artistic styles," he said. "My understanding is that an artist strives to perfect his or her own expression."

"I do that, but I also enjoy exploring the various modes of the past. Each age looked on cats in their own way, and it helps me to understand those lost worlds better when I create something that could have come from a long dead time. Of course, my modern efforts are signed and dated so I'm in no danger of being accused of forgery."

"You display an amazing range." Escott compared an elongated Celtic-style carving to one with a distinct Chinese ancestry. "I could swear that these were done by two different artists."

"It took years of study and experimentation." She invited him to sit on her couch, and he accepted her offer of sherry. "What I have here are my best efforts, the ones I can't bear to sell. As you can see, Egyptian is my favorite. It's clean and pure in form, but can be both staid and playful, depending on one's approach. . . ." Her enthusiasm for her craft made her pale face light up, creating a hypnotic contrast to her dark hair and eyes.

Eventually they took a tour of her home. It was better than a museum, for she was able to tell exactly how she'd made each of her works, pointing out details he might otherwise have missed. By the time they'd returned to her parlor she sat next to him in a most cozy and unaffected manner.

Cassandra plied him with more sherry and finally asked about her client's reaction to the statue. Escott gave her a full report.

He concluded: "She told me that you must phone tomorrow so she may express her pleasure personally."

"Of course. I'm relieved I got the hieroglyphics right. Sometimes taking a commission is a thankless task. A client's vision is often totally different from what's in my mind. They are rarely able to describe what they want, and more than once I've had pieces rejected because of the client's own confusion—for which I would get the blame. When an acceptance like this happens it's something to celebrate."

Escott congratulated her and privately wondered if she would mind very much if he kissed her. They were seated quite close on her couch. Not quite yet, his inner instinct told him. He expected she would let him know when she was ready.

"Would you like to see my studio?" she asked.

"Very much."

Standing up was almost embarrassing, but he managed not to sway from a wave of dizziness. Normally two small sherries wouldn't faze him, but he'd forgotten to eat again. Perhaps that was a good thing. He could ask Cassandra to a late dinner. It shouldn't take her long to change from her outfit. It looked as though an easy tug on one of the ties would have the whole thing off in a trice.

Happy thought, that.

Cassandra led him down to what would be a basement in any other house. This one had been reconstructed to her needs, though. The ceiling was twelve feet high and decoratively painted. This time the Egyptian influence was undiluted. Birds, flowers, rushes, palm trees, and papyrus plants brought the smooth plaster walls to startling life.

"This is no studio," he said, entranced. "It is art itself."

"I knew you would feel it, too," she said. "Let me show you where I work."

But as she led him in he saw no sculpting tools, no kiln, no boxes of supplies, no piles of raw clay kept damp under protective cloth, no works in progress, not even a sketch book. This broad room was more like an extravagant film set. Rows of torches marched along its walls. Though their light was obviously electrical, the anachronistic bulbs were carefully concealed by yellow and red tinted glass shaped to look like flames. Some mechanism for the current made them flicker, giving the effect of fire.

At the far end of the chamber stood two tall guardian cats of painted terracotta, larger yet still-elegant versions of the silver one he'd delivered. Between them, standing on its end was a—oh, God, that couldn't be right—a mummy case? It was open, and within lay a shrunken man-shaped form wrapped with dusty gray bandages.

"You look a little overwhelmed," said Cassandra. "Here. . .sit a moment." She eased him onto a low, wide bench covered with hieroglyphics, many of them picked out in gold leaf.

"I-I might mar the finish."

"It's all right," she assured him. "There, that's much better."

He had to admit that his dizziness was turning into a great nuisance. Unless he could get it under control this evening would conclude with an ignominious finish. What would she think, him getting drunk on just two—

No, impossible. Even on an empty stomach.

His inner alarm bells rang loud and long, yet he felt strangely distanced from them, strangely slowed. There was a terrific emergency he had to see to, but it seemed miles away. Someone else would deal with it, he was sure.

Smiling down at him beatifically, Cassandra persuaded him to stretch full length upon that low bench. She really was quite breathtaking in the flickering light. For a moment he thought she would kiss him, but she moved out of his rapidly blurring view.

He called after her, futilely. She didn't come back.

God, he was so tired.

The drink, Hamlet, the drink. . .

Queen Gertrude's words as she succumbed to poison drifted through his mind. That had always been a hard scene to pull off well. The audience was focused on the excitement of the duel, and then Gertrude had to shift their attention and sympathy over to her. Not easy, but with the right actress. . .

Escott shook his head violently. It made him more dizzy, but woke him up a bit. Right. He had to get out of here. Find some fresh air. He'd send Miss Selk a bill, and that would be the end of it.

But when he tried to sit up, he found his arms to be snugly bound to. . .to. . .he wasn't sure what, but it wasn't allowing him much movement.

Oh, dear. This was bad.

His surge of panic helped clear his muzzy head enough to stay awake. He had a presentiment that sleeping in this place would prove fatal. Where was Cassandra?

Escott shoved his immediate terror down deep and concentrated on getting loose from the bench or altar or whatever it was. He didn't want to think of it as an altar, for that implied a sacrifice of some sort.

Bloody hell. . .

He struggled to slip free, and when that didn't work, he tried to make slack instead. That tightened his bonds, but allowed him movement. By some hard and painful twisting, he was able to get a hand inside his waistcoat pocket where he always kept a pen knife. No longer used to cut quill pens, it served to open his mail, and hopefully the blade would be sharp enough to sever these. . .bandages?

His guts swooped at the sight of so many layers of narrow, wheat-colored linen wrapping his wrists. He looked like a recovering suicide. Careful not to drop the knife, he got the blade open using his thumbnail and began awkwardly sawing away. He couldn't see what he was cutting or feel much. His hand was numb. Had to work fast, before he lost all feeling, before Cassandra—

He froze at the soft sound of a door opening. Should he pretend to be unconscious? No, better to try talking to her.

She glided close, bare feet whispering against the floor. They darted in and out from the long hem of her gown like shy doves. She wore the same pleated silk garment, but had added wrist cuffs covered with glittering stones, a jeweled belt, and a wide pectoral collar rested on her shoulders.

She'd arranged her black hair so that it hung straight, held back from her face by a gold forehead band. He wasn't sure how historically accurate it might be, but she did look impressive.

Please, God, don't let her notice the knife. He thought his fingers were closed over it, but couldn't tell.

"Hello," he said, as though nothing was amiss. He was surprised at how calm he sounded. All that stage training helped.

"Hello," she responded, her tone warm and loving. "Don't be afraid."

"Oh, not at all." Improvisation had never been his strong suit on stage, but it seemed to work well enough here. Desperation turning to inspiration, that had to be it. "Is everything going well?"

She caught her breath, fingers to her red-painted mouth. "I knew, I just *knew* you were the one."

"Of course I must be. Your insight is uncanny."

"But I've been misled before. Those who have tried to keep us apart interfered, but I have at last been guided to the clear path. Oh, my love, it's been such a long and terrible wait."

"It has. But it's over now. Please, raise me up that I might embrace you." He hoped this was what she wanted to hear.

Her eyes blazed with exultation. "Yes, oh, yes! Soon, my love. Soon we will join. Bast has forgiven our transgression. She knows that the world is changed and her chosen ones must change with it. In this life we can be together. That which was once forbidden now has her blessing."

"How glad I am. My heart sings from it, but I'm not sure I remember everything." He'd begun sawing at the linen bindings again. If he could keep her talking long enough, distracted. . .

Cassandra seemed as fixed on her delusion as she was about her art. "My poor love, of course you can't remember, not until you are made whole again. In his rage Ra struck with his sword of gold and sundered your ka in twain. Only part of you lives on in this body, your other half was preserved until such time as Bast could persuade Ra to forgive you as she forgave me."

Just who or what does she think is in that mummy case? "I deserved mighty Ra's wrath, did I not?"

"It's followed you through many lifetimes. Bast revealed them to me, but your suffering is about to end."

He didn't care for the sound of that. "What glad news. How will you—ah—heal me?"

"You shall see, my dearest of all dear hearts. You'll have but the briefest moment of darkness. In that moment your ka will return, and you'll wake again whole and well."

"I'm looking forward to it. Each word you speak seems to open my memory. But these bindings are too tight and quite unnecessary. Please, take them away that I may give my ka a proper welcome."

She stroked his brow with cool fingers. "Soon. Your hold on this life may overpower your willingness to surrender to the next. There are vast forces at work against us. This time we will prevail. This time I will get the ceremony right. There is nothing to fear."

He held to a brave loving face until she walked from view, then fought another swift jolt of panic. He doubled his sawing efforts, but couldn't feel anything of his fingers; for all he could tell he could be cutting the wrong bit of fabric.

Cassandra was somewhere by the mummy case, half-chanting, half-singing words he couldn't understand. Occasionally the name Bast cropped up, and twice he heard Ra mentioned. Their latter-day priestess began pacing around the chamber, carrying a shallow bowl filled with aromatic incense. Clouds of the stuff filled every corner. He hoped it would obscure her vision, for now he was being anything but subtle at trying to cut the bandaging.

Then Cassandra appeared next to him. Her eyes watered freely from the smoke, but she seemed elated. "They have heard my prayers."

"Good," he said, resisting the urge to cough. "I feel my ka approaching across the darkness."

"Not yet. Just one more moment of darkness. . ."

She bent and pulled up a thick and heavy cushion. It was embroidered with more Egyptian motifs. She raised it high like an offering, and called for Bast and Ra to bless what she was about to do.

Abrupt comprehension as to what that would be flooded him. He threw all his strength into tearing his arm free, but though there was some give, the bindings remained fast.

"Cassandra!"

She looked down.

He spoke quickly, trying to keep up with a burst of an idea engendered by her watering eyes. "I beg of you a boon. Something to give me courage in the darkness, for my fear is great." No lie in that.

"What? The gods won't be put off."

"They will for this, they understand. Please, love, let me kiss you on this side of the veil."

She hesitated. "But why? Soon we will—"

"It's for *you!* Once I have passed through the darkness, once my ka has returned, I will kiss you again, and then you will be certain my sundering has been healed. You will know!"

Cassandra lowered the cushion. "Oh, if I had doubts before they flee from me now. You are the one!"

With that, she fairly flung herself upon him. In turn, he managed to summon up an illusion of feeling for her. He hoped she would mistake it for sincere passion rather than shuddering terror. It helped that she helped. Her anticipation for his soul's restoration had apparently gotten her well into a state of arousal.

He put everything he had into their kiss, and prayed it would be enough. Eventually she collapsed breathless onto his chest, holding him tight. Better and better.

"Soon," she muttered into his coat, which still bore a liberal coating of Ma'at's fur. "Very, very soon."

After a moment, she dragged away, wiping her wet cheeks. Her eyes streamed tears, yet she smiled through them. She sneezed, messily, and grabbed his breast pocket handkerchief. Repairs took a little time and didn't seem to help. Her kohl-outlined eyes were red and puffy.

"How sweet it will be for us both." Her voice had grown thick with emotion, but her arms were steady as she picked the cushion up. She raised it again, then brought it down hard on Escott's face.

He struggled, wrenching to one side, trying to draw air, but his mouth and nose were wholly covered. There was no escape. If he could just hold his breath long enough, she might take him for dead, if he could just—

The terrible smothering weight suddenly lifted. He gasped, filling his starved lungs while he could.ut no second assault came. He could hear Cassandra wheezing like an asthma victim.

Escott dislodged the cushion. It dropped away, but he couldn't see Cassandra. She was over by the mummy case, panting, trying to speak to her gods. He worked the knife blade. Quickly now, while she was—

Then came the awful gagging sounds, followed by a thump and thrashing.

He frantically hurried to cut free.

By the time he succeeded, it was long over. Cassandra lay curled at the foot of the case, her face rounded like an apple and just as red. Her lips were distended, her swollen tongue showing between them, huge and purple. He hastily turned away and staggered upstairs.

* * *

A few nights later, after he'd had enough to drink, Escott sat in his living room and told his partner what had happened.

Jack Fleming remained quiet through the whole story, moving his long lanky form only once to pour Escott another shot of gin. "Tough spot to be in," he said. "I don't know how you could have done things different."

Escott lifted one hand in a hopeless gesture. The red marks on his wrists were nearly faded. "I thought she would only suffer a sneezing fit, and that would buy me enough time to get free. I had no idea her allergy was so deadly."

"Is that why you wiped up all your prints and never called the cops?"

"I phoned the police. Once I was well away. Couldn't just leave her there. But nothing good would come of my involvement. They can draw their own conclusions about how she died—after they're done digging up her garden. The paper said three bodies have been found so far, and they expect more to follow. Dear God."

"They couldn't have nailed you on murder one," Fleming speculated. "Involuntary manslaughter at the most."

"Self-defense, I should think."

"Self-defense? After you let that cat climb all over you?"

"The climbing all over me was the cat's idea, not mine. I just went along with it." Escott fell silent, thankful he made the delivery in Cassandra's name, not his own. With any luck he would remain forever anonymous.

Fleming picked up a book next to Escott's chair. "Reading up on Egypt? Haven't you had enough of it?"

Escott shrugged. "Knowledge is power. Perhaps if I'd known more I could have talked the woman out of her twisted ceremony. She had an extraordinary talent. Gone now."

"Learn anything?"

"Nothing relevant to what I went through. I think Miss Selk made up most of it to fit her delusion. However, that cat, the way it took to me. . .I can't help but think the influence of Bast was indeed involved in some way, and that she used me to stop her erstwhile and misguided priestess. Either Bast or some other goddess."

Fleming flipped through the book, stopping on a page. "You underlined this name, but the picture's not a cat, but a woman with a feather. Maat? Is that how you say it?"

"Ma'at, the goddess of order and justice." Escott grimaced. "What a dread and terrible lady she must be."

BOSSMAN

Author's Note: *I was thrilled to get a call asking to trib a story to a collection edited by bestselling author Anne Perry. This one sold to* HOROSCOPE MURDER, *and while locations and some of the people are real, everything else, happily, is not!*

Dallas, Texas, The Present

Elbows on the table, Caitlin read from a new paperback with a gaudy cover. "It says you're headstrong, you like challenge, conquest, and pursuit, but bore easily once your objective is achieved. That sounds about right."

"Only because it means I've finished my drink," said Nick Tarrant, suiting action to word. He polished off his Guinness with relish. "Let's boogie, chickadee."

She shoved the book in her coat pocket and scooped up her shoulder bag. Tarrant left cash on the table and led the way out of the restaurant, holding the door for her. The Texas sun was bright with the promise of a brutal summer to come, but the early spring air tempered things for the present.

"We're still in the lion part of March, dammit," Caitlin grumbled, shrinking into her coat against the chill wind.

They got into Tarrant's car, a non-descript American product, neutral in color. He drove fast, the pint of beer he'd had with his burger and fries not showing in his reflexes. He felt as mellow as he would ever allow himself to be while more or less "on duty." Taking Caitlin to lunch (for him it was breakfast) had served to settle him into the right mindset for working. He was now fully awake and professionally curious about the interview ahead.

"What's this job you're on?" she asked, struggling with her seat belt, trying to get it around her bulging shoulder bag.

"I'm not on it yet, but it's a Highland Park address, so I can probably charge more."

Caitlin snorted. "Rich people don't get rich by spending it like the rest of us think they do." She finally snapped the belt into place.

"We'll size her up first."

"You'll size her up. I'm not sure what my role is."

"You're along to provide reassurance in case she's skittish. Another gal in the room will do that, and she's into astrology."

"So?"

"You are, too."

"Not that much. I just read what's on the 'Net when I bother to remember."

"That's why I got you the book." He referred to the one in her pocket. The cover featured a stylized moon and sun combination favored by New Age shops and garden centers.

"I'd wondered. If this client is really into astrology she'll know a ringer. I only look when it's flattering or funny. Casting horoscopes is too damn complicated. Tarot cards are better, more focused."

Tarrant nodded once, respecting her eccentricity, which wasn't as annoying as some he'd dealt with. "Doesn't matter," he said. "If the topic comes up all you do is look interested. The book's just background research. Half the work for landing a commission is knowing what makes the client tick. Before she set the appointment she wanted to know my sign. I think the answer was important to her."

"But all that stuff on the stars has been debunked." Caitlin had won the fight with her seat belt and pulled out the book again. "The rules were set down back in ancient times; they're all a month out of sync these days."

"What do you mean?"

"I read somewhere that they're a month late or early, I forget which. So instead of me being an Aquarius, I'm really either a Capricorn or a Pisces. Instead of being Aries, you're either a Pisces or a Taurus."

"Now that's funny."

"The problem is. . ." Caitlin peered at the pages. "You act like an Aries, and I seem to act like an Aquarian. Some of the personality traits for the signs are so general as to apply to anyone, though. On the other hand, maybe we grow into what's described for us. The problem with that is people like you who aren't into this kind of stuff still seem to run to type.

You've got this leadership thing going, and as for your love life, you like to chase and catch, but sooner or later the heat fizzles out of the affair."

"Not all of them. One or two have exploded quite spectacularly. I was lucky to make it clear with my life."

"True, but was that because you're an Aries, a son-of-a-bitch, or just overloaded with testosterone?"

Tarrant smirked, aware of his faults and proud of them. "All three."

She snorted, putting the book away. "You don't need me on this."

"Sure I do. While I interview the client, you pretend to take notes like a personal assistant."

"I won't be pretending."

"Good, then I won't have to pretend to pay you."

Tarrant consulted scribbled directions he'd stuffed into the dash clipboard, negotiating turns and counting off house numbers. He had a GPS unit, but liked doing things old school to keep in practice. The houses and grounds in this section of Highland Park were very large, the low end of the real estate scale starting at a million and a half. When he pulled into the right driveway, he estimated the place as being easily in the three million range.

"Wow," said Caitlin. "People really live like this, it's not just something made up for movies?"

"Yup."

"How'd you come to know them?"

"I didn't, she had my pager number. Said I'd been recommended." It was the only way he worked on a blind commission. Safer.

"By whom?"

Tarrant had an idea, but wasn't certain. "If I told you I'd have to kill you."

"You terrify me, did you know that?" she deadpanned, half-serious.

"Go with what you're good at."

The house was a southern-mansion, post-World-War II, but pre-central air-conditioning era with its long windows. To his eyes it looked like an overgrown version of a small-town Texas funeral home.

Caitlin said *wow* again, under her breath, then shut up and squared herself, assuming a cool, friendly face. He could trust her to stay in that mode until they were finished. Her awe was understandable; he felt its tug himself here on the threshold of a place that represented Real Money. He also understood what it took to obtain that kind of wonderfully filthy lucre.

"Sure we're supposed to use the front door?" Caitlin muttered. "I delivered flowers to get through college. A joint half this size got snotty when I knocked with my basket of posies. They made me go around to the side. It didn't sit well with my ego."

Tarrant grunted and rang the bell, assuming his own game face. He wore one of his better suits, a quietly expensive tie, his Rolex peeking discretely from beneath an Egyptian linen cuff. He would make a reasonably good impression to anyone used to GQ-style wealth. Caitlin had on new designer jeans, boots, and an oversized olive-colored sweater that played nicely off her redhead's pale complexion. Her leather coat added the right kind of flair for this job; she'd invested well in that. His instinct to ask her along had been right once again; like a good nurse she radiated cheerful competence. Safe-looking.

Caitlin stood straighter at the sound of approaching footsteps within. "It's show time," she whispered.

The door was opened by a Hispanic maid who apparently knew to expect them. She smiled and led them into expensively decorated depths.

Tarrant made an accurate gauge of the surroundings, concluding it was old money, at least three generation's worth. The woman who'd set the appointment gave no name, only an address which he'd checked using a reverse directory on the Internet. He'd turned up the name of Pangford as the property owner. The family had something to do with textile manufacturing. That was all he'd managed to get by the time Caitlin arrived at his condo for a short briefing over lunch. Normally he'd be more cautious over new business, but the bills were piling up. If this interview went well he could score enough to float for a considerable period without having to dip into savings.

The indoor hike ended at a lavish home office with a wall of French windows opening onto a garden. Clumps of gold daffodils dominated the perfectly kept beds. The room was also colorful, with phalanxes of books, paintings, and appropriately matched furnishings. There were too many pillows and doilies scattered around for it to be a man's office, though it might have been one once. Tarrant saw no horoscope symbols lurking in the décor.

A small woman in her young forties came in from a side door and nodded to the maid, who left. "I'm Mrs. Dolly Pangford," she said, extending a delicate hand. A peach blond, she wore a simple dress that was nearly the same color as her creamy skin.

"Nick Tarrant," he responded. "My associate, Caitlin McGill."

Caitlin shook hands, murmuring a soft greeting in a mid-Atlantic non-accent she'd picked up in her drama major days. She wouldn't revert to her Texas drawl until they were back in the car.

Mrs. Pangford went through the social ritual of getting them seated and offering refreshments. With a tray of coffee delivered from a distant kitchen—she'd used the house intercom to call for it—Tarrant thought she'd be ready to settle down and talk.

"What seems to be the problem, Mrs. Pangford?" he asked.

She glanced at Caitlin, who pulled out a small note pad and pen. "I shall want absolute privacy about this."

"You'll get it."

Caitlin nodded, smiling sympathetically, projecting more confidence with her silence than if she'd seconded his assurance aloud.

"Very well." Pangford took a deep breath, lifting her chin. "This is about my stepdaughter, Amanda. She doesn't know that I'm interfering in her life, and she's not to find out. I'm sure you'll have heard this before: she's taken up with the wrong sort of man."

"Go on."

"Amanda met him at one of those clubs she's been sneaking out to since she was fifteen and got her first fake ID. She's nearly twenty-one now and not past her wild oats yet. I've not been the best mother for her; we don't get along, especially since her father died and left the bulk of the estate to me. We have horrible fights, but I don't want her walking off a cliff. . .or being pushed off."

"How so?"

"She ran away to Las Vegas a few months ago with a loser named Kyle Deacon and married him. I made sure that her trust money was tied up in such a way so he couldn't get to it even after she turns twenty-one, which endeared me to them both. Since then I've discovered he's put several insurance policies on her life. You don't have to be a rocket scientist to figure out where that might lead."

"You think he's planning to kill her?"

"I do. He'll have to do it in such a way as to make it seem like natural causes or an accident. I think he's just smart enough to succeed. He runs with a rough crowd. I'm sure he knows people who can arrange such things."

"Your stepdaughter suspects nothing?"

"She's in love and it's made her stupid. He's her ally against her wicked stepmother, after all. The more I disapprove, the more she clings to him. He's garbage, but clever. I know his type and how they work their game. When I was her age I had a similar parasite turning my head with charm and an offer of shelter from a family that didn't understand me. I emerged with only a bruised ego once I figured out the truth. I don't think Amanda will be so lucky. She's a Gemini, but not one of the brainy ones. He's a Scorpio with a mean streak and a rat's cunning. Their marriage will never work anyway, but I doubt he'll let it go on much longer."

"What is it you want me to do?"

Dolly Pangford's beautifully-preserved pale face went still, her gray eyes hardening. "I want you to do whatever it takes to keep Amanda alive."

"That could involve any number of possibilities, ma'am."

"I will leave the means and manner to your choice, then. You've more expertise than I, though in my opinion it's best to keep things simple. I was told by Doc Jessup that you were very good at your job."

At the mention of that name Tarrant's own face went still. "May I ask how you know him?"

"Through my late husband's business dealings. Henry had a wide range of acquaintances, with many, shall we say, forceful sorts. I'd hoped Doc might take care of this, but he's retired. He said he had every confidence in your abilities, though, and gave me your number."

"Did you discuss this on a phone or by E-mail with him?"

"No, face-to-face over dinner in a noisy restaurant. He said you should see this." She drew forth a business card from her sleeve and handed it over.

Tarrant recognized the embossed lettering and phone number. Those could be faked, but on the flip side, in Doc's distinct scrawl, was a short note, addressed to him. *Syko, this one's ok. Come over and buy me a beer later*. Tarrant's mouth twitched. Only a handful of his old fight-kill-and-die-for-you cronies were alive to call him Syko these days. The job would be safe enough to take with Doc's seal of approval.

Of course, Doc would want to meet afterward and hear the details. He loved post-game quarterbacking.

Tarrant smiled, not showing his teeth. "All right, Mrs. Pangford. I think I can come up with some kind of agreeable solution to your problem."

"Without Amanda finding out my involvement?"

"No, ma'am. I'll have to get some basic information from you, quite a lot of it."

"Whatever you need."

The coffee was fragrant and perfectly brewed and accompanied by home-baked cookies, which got past Caitlin's professional facade. She helped herself to two. He sucked hot caffeine to be sociable, wishing for a Pepsi instead. As soon as the maid left Tarrant began asking questions. Caitlin wrote down the replies.

He got the names, numbers and addresses he'd need, a general idea of schedules, and photos.

Neither Amanda or Kyle Deacon worked; Amanda received enough from her trust fund each month to afford a loft in Deep Ellum, utility bills, and groceries. If either or both of them had a regular job they could live very well indeed. Deacon called himself a musician, Amanda was an artist.

God save us from liberal art degrees, Tarrant thought, wondering what academic idiot ever imagined those to be a good idea.

According to an earlier inquiry, Dolly Pangford had initiated with a legitimate private investigator, the young and carefree couple each had five credit cards, all ten hovering near their maximum limit.

Amanda frequently demanded loans against her trust to pay them off. Dolly just as frequently refused, suggesting a job search and using scissors on the cards as the obvious solution to debt.

"I am then called foul names and treated to the sound of the phone slamming down," she told Tarrant. "After a week, or until the next collection agency calls, she starts all over again. Sometimes it's tears, other times she's honey-sweet and apologetic. It worked on Henry, but not on me. I don't know why her father didn't teach her how to be responsible about life and money. By the time I came into the picture she was spoiled rotten and out of control. I was the first person who ever said no to her, and it was an ugly shock for her to find out she was no longer the center of the universe. I should have brought in professional help for our family. Too late now. All I want is for her to survive this and live to grow some brains."

Tarrant's own keep-it-simple solution for spoiled kids began with a good spanking followed by a lengthy stay at a boot camp. Perhaps after this was settled, he'd suggest it to Mrs. Pangford. Maybe if she got Amanda declared mentally incompetent. . .there was probably enough cash lying around lost in the mansion's sofas to buy off all kinds of doctors.

Not my problem today.

"I think that should do it," he said. Caitlin had filled several pages. He'd memorize it, then destroy the notes. He had no worry about Caitlin; hers was a selective memory with a convenient ability for forgetting data when it was no longer needed or too dangerous to recall.

"What about your fee?" asked Mrs. Pangford.

Tarrant quoted her a price based on what he'd learned in the last hour, factoring in anticipated difficulties. It was fair, the average rate in the more rarified circles of his trade.

Mrs. Pangford didn't blink. Either she deemed it a bargain for what she wanted or Doc had warned her what to expect. "You'll want that in cash?"

"If you don't mind. Small bills, nothing over a hundred. I'll need half as a retainer, and we can arrange later to pay over the balance when the job is done. All incidental expenses are included, by the way."

He'd learned in the course of business that clients didn't mind forking over a flat fee even if it was huge, but most balked when presented with the chicken-change of an itemized expense account.

"I can manage that now," she said. "It will take a few days to get the rest."

"I trust you," he said, and almost meant it. He'd dealt with occasional hold-outs who thought they could get away with not paying the balance. Fortunately those were an infrequent annoyance. Other people were smarter.

"If you need any other information, just phone," she added.

Her hand was cool and dry when he took it. That was good. The lady was no wimp. He thought he could trust her to see things through.

"You're absolutely sure about this?" he asked. "Doc mentioned all the possibilities?"

Her gray eyes reminded him of polished granite. "I am absolutely certain, Mr. Tarrant. Doc told me everything. I will be comfortable with whatever measures you judge necessary to keep Amanda safe from harm."

"So long as we're clear on that."

She smiled. "Crystalline."

* * *

"Jeeze-Loueeze," said Caitlin, once they'd left the driveway. She heaved a huge sigh of relief, resuming her native drawl. "That was one hell of a learning experience. Are they all like that?"

"Every job's different." For instance he'd not expected Mrs. Pangford to have the first half of his fee ready and in the house. The usual thing was to wait however long it took for a client to get hold of the required funds, then make a drop. Doc Jessup must have given her one hell of an earful.

"You didn't need me along to take notes." Caitlin tapped the shoulder bag on her lap, which held the pad and its possibly incriminating information. Mrs. Pangford had supplied an envelope with copies of her private investigator's detailed report on her stepdaughter's life. It also held Tarrant's down payment money and was now quite heavy. He would work out Caitlin's percentage when they got back to his condo.

"You put her at ease," he said. "She glanced at you a few times."

"I noticed. I tried to look intelligent and poised."

"You did and it worked. It helped having another woman there so I wouldn't scare her so much. She's the old-school sorority-sister type."

"As in never wears white shoes before Easter?"

"Bulls-eye."

"She didn't look scared."

"No, but it was there. She covered it well, I'll hand her that. The lady's also got plenty on the ball in the brains department, so I wonder why she goes in for astrology. You're a smart chick, why do you go in for Tarot cards?"

"I use them as psychological tools. Their images spark a response in my sub-conscious that allows me to make decisions or draw conclusions to my own best advantage. Though once in a while they've predicted events that I never saw coming. Or maybe I just fit the events to the cards, but that doesn't always work. Like that guy I went nuts over last summer? No matter how many times I shuffled and asked about my future with him the results were all dismal. Not the answer I wanted to see, so I tried to make things turn out different, but they never did. You remember?"

"Yup." He'd kept his mouth diplomatically shut while Caitlin had been in the throes of her brief romance, though he could have told her it was doomed. You didn't need a deck of cards to see that. He was glad when she'd finally smarted up and broke things off. He'd been ready to kill them both on the distraction factor alone, the guy for making her cry, and Caitlin because he couldn't stand a crying dame.

Caitlin shrugged, cocking her head in thought. "Maybe astrology works for Mrs. Pangford in the same way on a psychological level. It allows people to place order and structure into an otherwise chaotic world. One can have a weird sense of security knowing that some life events and personality traits are beyond our best efforts at control and that we're at the mercy of a pre-determined stellar destiny. If it's in the stars that something nasty will happen, then we have to shrug and accept it, for what can we do about it? Mrs. Pangford can then excuse her faults and those of others by blaming them on outside forces over which she has no command."

"Or maybe it's a lot of horse hockey."

"There's that," Caitlin agreed, amiably.

One long drive later he pulled into his assigned parking space, and they decanted for a short walk to his condo. The gate to his small walled porch screeched as he pulled it open for her. In the years since he'd moved in he made a point of never greasing the hinges. Their noise was too good a burglar alarm.

Inside, Caitlin dumped her purse on his long leather couch and rubbed her shoulder. "So—what's your next move on the case?"

"Tonight I do a little checking up on Mr. and Mrs. Deacon in their stately Deep Ellum manor. Won't need you along, it's scut-work."

"And you think slaving over a computer chasing down obscure data for you ain't?"

"You're in a nice, warm indoor environment, free to use the toilet any time you feel the urge and have a supply of drinks and snacks. I shall probably be confined to my mobile prison disguised as wheels for an indeterminate time as I check out the field."

"Okay, you win. You'll change clothes, of course?"

"Of course." He made a start, loosening his tie and undoing the collar button. Nothing he had on was right for what lay ahead, especially the Rolex. He retreated to his bedroom to complete the transformation, while

Caitlin fired up his computer. He emerged wearing a faded black polo shirt with dark cargo pants stuffed into boots. With a baseball cap and a loose pocket vest to finish things, he expected to go unnoticed in the eclectic atmosphere of Deep Ellum.

"You'll need an earring," said Caitlin, peering at her screen, comparing search engine results with her notes.

Sometime ago he'd had one ear pierced. "You think?"

"Oh, yeah. Anyone without metal hanging off them is the exception there, not the rule. That's why I don't fit into those artsy-fartsy circles." Caitlin was so squeamish she'd been known to faint when taking her pets in for their shots. Her earlobes were quite virginal.

He went back, dug around on his dresser, and found a plain silver earring, fitting it into place.

"That's better," she said, giving him a brief once-over. "You look nice and rakish."

"I need to be nice and anonymous."

"Okay, rakish in Highland Park, but Mr. Ordinary in Deep Ellum."

He looked over her shoulder while she did magic with the computer and its wide range of special search programs. Everything she found confirmed Dolly Pangford's story. Kyle Deacon had a police record, minor skirmishes for being drunk, and a slap on the wrist for selling pot. His juvenal files were sealed, but that was no hindrance to Caitlin's hacker talents.

"My, but wasn't he Peck's Bad Boy way back when?" she muttered. "We got us a little joy-riding vandal, some assault, some shop-lifting, some drug dealing, now didn't he have fun? But it's still a long jump from murdering your wife."

"That's what I'm checking out later." Tarrant wished he'd not had the coffee or stared at the computer screen for so long; he felt a headache coming on. Of all the lousy times to get a migraine. "I need to rest until it's dark. Tell the kids to keep hush."

One of his five cats meowed at him, looking innocent. The others sprawled around as though they owned the place and didn't care much for the fact. He picked up the opinionated one, turned her on her back and rubbed her fat belly.

"Don't go bitching at me, you freeloading leech," he advised her, until she grabbed his hand in both paws and pretended to bite. He ignored the assault, his knuckles could stand it. "Make a funny noise for daddy. Make a funny noise." She emitted a cross between a muted yowl and an irritated purr, which satisfied him, and he put her back on her resting place, which happened to be atop Caitlin's purse. Her dogs would just love the smell of outraged cat.

The distraction didn't work. His head began pounding. Damn. It would build into a volcano with an attitude if he didn't nip it in the bud.

He got a bottle of Stoli from the freezer to wash down a couple prescription pills. An unwise combination, but it would put him out right away and maybe halt the headache before it took too firm a hold. He gave Caitlin a wake-up time and after removing his boots, rolled into bed. As a distraction he flipped through the astrology book, reading up on his own sign, finding amusement at what it got right and wrong about him. It did seem to have nailed it square about his craving for challenge and boredom with achievement.

Just as he drifted off, he remembered that they'd not divided the money up yet.

Later.

* * *

He had a good four-hour nap, waking when it was full dark, about five minutes before Caitlin was due to come in. His mouth tasted bad, but the pain that had threatened to squeeze his skull to mush was thankfully gone. He was set for the evening, no matter how long it might prove.

Caitlin was still at the computer. "I was about to give a yell. Did you sleep?"

"Yup. I just got an accurate body clock. What's this?" On what had been a clear coffee table newspaper pages were now spread wide over something lumpy. One of the cats lounged on top. He scooped the animal out of the way. The payment money was underneath, neatly stacked and sorted. There was a lot of it.

"I raided my purse for a candy bar and had to get the cash out of the way," Caitlin explained. "Then once started I couldn't stop. Counting that was almost as good as sex. It's all there. She didn't short you."

"No one does and lives," he intoned, dropping the papers back. He went to the fridge and pulled out a big bottle of Pepsi, taking hits off it to fully wake up. The cold carbonation burn made him wince, but it felt great. Tarrant did a quick calculation, returned to the money, and set aside a portion. "There's your percentage, chickadee."

"Thanks. I think I earned it." She slowly stood and stretched, audible popping noises coming from her neck and spine. "My butt's gone dead. Why don't you invest in a comfortable chair?"

He peeled five hundred from his side and put it on her pile. "Go pick out one you like, but no leather or vinyl. Make sure it fits my color scheme." That wouldn't be difficult. His condo was dominated by blacks and whites. "What did you find out?"

"Exactly how much those two owe on their cards and the last time they made payments. But something odd is going on. Last month they brought in enough to catch up on all ten. I couldn't find a source for the windfall. Maybe Kyle's band cut a recording contract or Amanda sold a painting to the Met and they paid her in cash."

Tarrant frowned. "Or he's dealing again. Only way to get that kind of money is being lucky in Vegas or selling drugs."

"I can believe that. I've read through the file Mrs. Pangford got from her investigator—little Amanda has a will. She leaves everything she's got—including her trust fund—to her beloved husband. He'll have to wait until she's twenty-one to get it, though, or it reverts to the estate. That's less than four months away. It's like the poor bimbo has a death wish."

"Does he have a will?"

"Yeah. He leaves her all his worldly goods, which at present includes four guitars, an electronic keyboard, and a 1986 Ford Escort."

"Good God, and she thinks he loves her?"

"It's grounds for divorce for me," Caitlin sniffed. "Only I'd never have married the loser in the first place."

"I'm gonna boogie. Put that in the safe?" He gestured at the money. Despite her predilection for Tarot cards, Caitlin was sensible and prudent on practical matters, like never cheating the boss man, but was also hard-wired with a sense of honor. Funny trait to have in their business, but he understood it and trusted her with the safe combination.

"Don't worry, I'll lock everything up. Have fun, but don't get caught."

"Never."

* * *

The drive to Kyle and Amanda's Deep Ellum loft, which was on the east side of downtown Dallas, took about an hour. Being Saturday night, the streets were jammed with a mixed crowd determined to have fun. Some of the wilder clubs were overflowing, yet still trying to attract more inside. One place had a line of new Harleys out front, each draped with a shapely young thing in leather posing for anyone with a camera. Tarrant considered the pros and cons of making the choice between having the wheels or one of the girls. He concluded that the machine would draw the attention of any number of females to it and thus to himself. If he chose one of the girls, the encounter would last a weekend, if that long.

He liked women just fine, but enjoyed their company more when they didn't talk much. He'd long grown bored with the no-win "Do I look fat?" discussion and the disastrous "Why were you looking at *her*?" salvo. Caitlin was one of the few with whom he could hold a decent conversation, but out of unspoken mutual consent they were each off the other's menu. Caitlin was too smart to get involved with him and Tarrant's policy was to never shop at the company store. Too many complications. Women he could get easily enough, but trustworthy hackers for his line of work were rare.

The outsides of the Deacon's loft was not as depressed as he expected from the look of the rest of the neighborhood, but far from the level of Bohemian sophistication as seen in countless films and TV shows.

The Arctic-cool heroes who lived in those fantasies never had trouble finding a parking space, either. Tarrant was a full three blocks from the main action and the curbs were still clogged. At least he was getting paid nearly enough for the annoyance.

Four blocks down he found a spot and gratefully pried out of the driver's seat. Without hurry, he locked up and strolled back, eyes raking the dim areas between streetlights. He located one parked cop car and counted three more cruising past, each with two officers inside. That was a lot of muscle even for a party night, but Ellum was long-infamous for problems. The patrol car occupants gave him the hairy eyeball, but he just smiled and sent them a friendly wave. Cops were his friends, after all, there to keep him and other honest citizens safe from the dregs of society.

He trotted up the metal exterior stairs and knocked on the Deacon's door. No reply, but he'd expected that. Kyle usually played with a club band on weekends and Amanda went with him. That detail seen to, Tarrant pulled on surgical gloves and got out his collection of lock picks and skeleton keys, entering the loft about thirty seconds later.

The place smelled heavily of incense and mildew; the housekeeping exceeded his most pessimistic prediction. Without a maid to look after things, they both proved to be slobs. Clothing, booze bottles, empty beer and diet drink containers littered the floor. Flipping on a light was unnecessary; they'd left several burning, indication of an after-dark departure.

He made a quick search of the more obvious hiding holes, turning up a wad of fifties and twenties under the futon along with a loaded Glock. Tarrant had never warmed up to the brand. They got the job done, but just didn't feel right in his hand. He decided this one would work better for him if he took the bullets out of the magazine and did so, dropping them into one of his vest pockets, not forgetting the round in the chamber. He slipped the pistol back into place, wondering if Kyle would notice the weight change. Probably not.

Along with another Glock (which he also neutered) under the unmade bed, and a third (the owner must be a real fan) in the kitchen, Tarrant found a fine variety of pharmaceuticals: pot, some possible Ecstasy, and bags of small oblong blue pills that might be Xanax. A party-hearty starter set. His roughest estimate put them at a street value close to twenty grand, and these were just what he'd turned up on a surface search. It would be easy enough to make a phone call to have a couple of DEA types waiting there for the Deacons to return, but that would land Amanda in jail. Mrs. Pangford would not be pleased, though time in a lockup might do her step-brat some good.

How had Kyle gotten the seed money for this kind of stash? Suppliers only sold in bulk, leaving the piss-ant sales to the small fry dealers. He'd need at least five figures to start with, then keep buying more stock with the profit money to build up the trade. Maybe he'd borrowed from a mob shark against his wife's trust fund without mentioning the down side, like the wife being unable to touch the money. They might get mad at him if they learned the truth. Or they might not care and off them both if anything went wrong.

Tarrant had an idea about how to turn that to his advantage, but first he had to close the store and dump the inventory.

He now made a thorough search of the place, finding more illegal chemicals. Strips of LSD blotters lay in plain sight in the freezer. Kyle Deacon might possess a rat's instinctive cunning, but he was dumb as a brick.

Tarrant found a metal wastebasket and, after removing the battery from the fire alarm, made a little blaze of the blotters. The pot and pills he ground to oblivion in the kitchen garbage disposal, using gallons of hot water to dissolve everything. After putting the alarm battery back, he left, politely relocking the front door.

The outside air was sweet and cold. He breathed deep to clear his lungs of the upstairs stuffiness and checked his watch. He'd been at work for over an hour. Not bad. He walked down the street as though he owned it, until he reached the Iguana's Cave Club. According to regular charges on their cards, it was the couple's favorite hangout.

On Saturday nights after ten it changed its name to The Temple, and Goths in the area converged there to see who was the most groveling fashion slave. A slim girl walked past him as he checked the area. She wore a transparent black body suit, only just legal in public by the use of a G-string beneath and a few strips of electrician's tape criss-crossed over her nipples.

He grinned. *And I'm getting paid to do this.*

He followed her toward the entrance. Though he was obviously of an age to drink, the bouncers asked for ID. He good-naturedly presented one that looked real and was passed in quick so he could pay the cover charge and get his hand stamped. He smiled at the girl ahead of him and wondered where the hell she kept her money.

Techno music boomed loud in the lobby and grew deafening once he found his way inside. The main dance floor was an oblong pit with platforms at each end for the more extroverted types to show off their physical coordination skills. Both sexes and a few genders in between filled the place. Nearly all were head-to-toe in black with matching dyed hair, lipstick, nail polish, and bits of silver-plated hardware piercing various parts of their bodies. More often than not some of them sported fangs. A round-faced girl flashed hers at him in a teasing way, flicking her studded tongue, trying to look both dangerous and seductive. All he saw was jail-bait. Tattoos, once a male's rite of passage to prove his toughness or to advertise a military affiliation, were now regulated to being a cliché fashion statement.

Girls who wanted to be noticed as such were in paint-tight outfits, breasts pushed prominently high by corseting; the boys were either in equally tight jeans or pants so baggy and low on the hips as to make walking difficult and wedgies easy. One male slouched by in a black skirt and combat boots, his too-thin chest and nipple rings on display beneath a net T-shirt. Obviously from the peculiar end of the gene pool.

Drugs were present. Tarrant didn't have to see them; as a matter of course he simply noticed their effect on the crowd. There was an artificial quality to their body movements, like actors who'd played the same part too often. What a shame to be so young and world-weary.

He looked for Kyle Deacon, but the platform where a live band should have been was thick with dancers, not instruments and players. He'd be difficult to spot in this mix of darkness and flashing lights. By the time Tarrant's night vision adjusted the light show would change or a muffled faux explosion would take place. Then special effects smoke roiled across the flailing dancers and curled up to the ceiling. He'd seen real hell before in combat once upon a time; this was the fantasy version, dramatic enough for the inexperienced, just plain silly to one who knew.

The music changed to a slower tempo, the driving bass vanishing for an extended phrase of electronic whooshing, like jets taking off. It made a change from the techno beat, which sounded like a breathing exercise for women in the last stages of labor. Amazingly, the kids were still dancing to it, if one could call it that. A tall girl with a too-black curtain of hair swayed in the middle of the pit. She appeared to be tossing invisible pizza dough the way she waved her arms over her head. It did show off her lack of a bra. Nice figure. She might make for a good weekend, providing she didn't talk.

Then with gratification he realized that under the dead white make-up she was Amanda Deacon, nèe Pangford. Now that was convenient. So where was Kyle? She didn't seem to be dancing with anyone.

None of them did.

Time to gain a little altitude. Tarrant found stairs that took him to the upper level where a long balcony overlooked the pit. It was lined with tables, the patrons drinking, watching the dancers, or attempting to converse by means of shouting directly into one anothers' ears. The lighting was a little better. He found a free space next to the rail and searched the shifting faces below. Amanda remained in place, her patience sometimes rewarded when the center spotlight picked her out. He wasn't sure if she was on drugs or not, but decided it was safer to assume she'd indulged for the evening.

He didn't spot Kyle on the floor. The place was big, with a whole second dance area and a deck outside for people to catch fresh air and talk. Tarrant was glad of his nap; this could take all night.

He made a casual cruise of the upper floor, his gaze not resting too long on any one person. He wanted to look like a someone trying to hook up with misplaced friends, not a man on the hunt.

Toward the back, seated at a table for two, was Kyle. Finally. Tarrant didn't miss a step as he passed close on his way to the bar. They served Coke, not Pepsi, overfilled the squat plastic airline cup with ice, and wanted three dollars for it plus a tip.

God, I hate these joints.

At the table, Kyle faced an older, white-bearded man who was dramatically out-of-place in this determinedly funereal setting. He wore a red fedora hat, a well-fitted light brown suit with a shiny yellow brocade vest, polished wing-tips, and had a cane under one hand. His beard was carefully trimmed; reflections off his wire-rimmed glasses hid his eyes. Too classy to be a pimp, he looked like he'd been hired to lend quaint atmosphere to a place already flooded with it. He might have been part of the music business or a misplaced queen who'd wandered in from the Oak Lawn area by mistake.

Kyle spoke earnestly with him; his body language trying hard to show self-assurance and presenting exactly the opposite. He was nervous, possibly afraid, but attempting to put himself on an equal footing with the fancy-pants. The man in the fedora held to a calm face, a bored sovereign hearing yet another a plea for favor from a supplicant peasant. That was interesting, and considering all the junk Kyle had had stashed in the loft, highly suggestive. Whatever was going on was important. Maybe this was the seed-money source. Tarrant shifted his focus to the hat-man.

Was he confident enough to hide in plain sight, or a gaudy front for the real entrepreneur? Conspicuously posing was not a healthy way to run a drug business. It could be meant to impress the natives. It seemed to work on Kyle.

They took their time. The music noise made talking difficult and eavesdropping attempts impossible. Tarrant went back to interpreting body language.

The man had two guards, big and little. One for raw physical intimidation, the other for martial arts. They looked alert, and were smart enough not to hover too close. They noticed Tarrant. A couple of predators recognizing one of their own. He didn't want to be mistaken for a cop or a rival supplier; he finished his watery Coke and moved on. No one followed.

Tarrant found the other dance area. He sat at a table with a view of the front door, but out of view of the upper gallery. He pulled out a pen and wrote lines on a cocktail napkin. They didn't serve Guinness here, so he settled for an overpriced Shiner and sat back to wait.

About an hour later Kyle and Amanda walked past. He looked nervously smug; she looked half asleep and staggered against him every other step. Tarrant gave them a two-minute start, then rolled a twenty around his note and went up to one of the door bouncers.

"Hey, bud, you know that old guy who sits in the back by the upstairs balcony? The one with the red hat?"

The bouncer only shrugged. "I see 'em, I don't know 'em."

I just bet you don't. Tarrant held up the bill and the note. "Do me a favor and see that he gets this. I got a fire to put out or I'd go myself."

"Must be some fire." But he took the money. He'd probably read the note, but there was nothing on it that would mean anything to him.

Tarrant escaped from the noise and smoke. Kyle and Amanda were well ahead of him, but walking slow. Amanda was in a giggling, playful mood, bumping her hip against Kyle and pretending to trip so he had to catch her. He visibly snarled, not in the mood. Tarrant went one block over to the next street, going at a brisk walk until he was way in the lead, then cutting back again.

His car was unscathed where he'd left it, but alone. Most of the fun seekers had had their fill and departed, freeing up parking spaces. He drove back toward the loft and found a spot close in. Before getting out, he slipped a semi-auto from its concealed bracket under the dash into one of his pockets, hoping he wouldn't need it. He left the doors unlocked, but that was okay as he'd be within sight.

Going behind the loft building he went up metal stairs to a fire exit that served as the Deacon's back door. He picked the lock and left the door ajar. Just in case.

Back on the street, Tarrant located an alcove between buildings and melded into its shadow. From here he commanded a view of the loft and the parking lot next to it.

Things were much quieter now. The bars would be closing soon, their patrons either going home or seeking an after-hours club to round off the night. Only one patrol car crept past. As soon as it was gone a tan SUV rolled up not thirty feet away and parked, dousing its lights. His mouth tightened when the smaller of the bodyguards emerged and went up to the loft, entering without trouble. He returned soon after, walking fast, limbs stiff with anger. It looked like Tarrant's note, helpfully suggesting that Kyle Deacon's inventory had gone missing, had been taken seriously.

What the fancy-pants boss's reaction was remained a mystery, but Tarrant felt the satisfaction that comes from having made the right call. The larger guy came out next. Both bruisers stood ready by the loft building, waiting. Anyone within fifty yards could see they were loaded for bear; Tarrant was considerably closer. He swapped his ball cap out for a Balaclava from a cargo pocket and pulled it on. Running around Dallas looking like an urban ninja would get him arrested, but only if the cops saw him. Tarrant could trust the party in the SUV would be on the alert, telling him if he needed to duck.

Neither of the Deacons noticed the gathered company until it was too late. Big grabbed Kyle; Little grabbed Amanda. The men knew their job, making sure it was done with a minimum of noise and movement. It helped that their victims were too flatfooted with surprise to make a fuss. Kyle knew better than to try and Amanda was still stoned.

Both were dragged toward the vehicle, and the rear passenger window slid down. Tarrant got a glimpse of a red fedora. Kyle shook his head a lot, firmly denying whatever he heard from within. He gestured toward the loft, insistent.

This was the tricky part, waiting for what fedora would do next. Take both kids in the car and drive off or settle things here and now? Tarrant's hand drifted toward his pistol.

The bruisers took the couple toward the loft. Tarrant faded from his shadow and sprinted across behind the building. He was up the fire escape and through back door while the unsteady foursome negotiated the stairs. Pulling on his surgeon's gloves, he doused lights, scanning for a decent weapon. He lucked out, finding a nearly full bottle of vodka. It pleased him that it was a brand he hated.

Tarrant was in time to get behind the front door just as it swung inward for Little and Amanda. She was whining and cursing and crying all at once, demanding to know what was going on, trying to shake off Little's grip.

Kyle was shoved in so hard he skidded and tripped. He didn't have time to curse as he fell. Neither did Big once he was past the door. Tarrant smashed the heavy bottle in just the right spot on the temple.

The man may have been of a size, but damn few were tough enough to ignore that kind of greeting. He went sprawling with a grunt.

Before Little could react, Tarrant gave him a double punch in the back under the ribcage, one for each kidney. He also ceased to be an immediate problem.

Amanda was just beginning to realize there was another player in the game. She got a clout in the jaw, just enough to ring her bells but not so hard that Tarrant couldn't use his hand. She dropped. He pulled a small bottle and a fist-sized wad of cotton from another pocket. In moments she was out completely, chloroformed into dreamland. She might be sick later, but better that than dead.

"Who the fuck are you?" Kyle demanded. He had a gun in hand and it wasn't a Glock. Big's coat tail had been yanked up, and if he'd kept a gun in the small of his back it wasn't there now.

Tarrant went still, arms out away from his body. "I'm the guy who just saved your life."

Kyle got to his feet. "What the fuck are you doing in my place?"

"Saving you from bad guys," said Tarrant, leaving out the word "asshole." He pointed to Big and Little. "They're here to snuff you and your old lady."

"What'd you do to her?"

There was no good reply to that. Tarrant's gaze went to something behind Kyle. "Oh, *shit!*"

The kid was just dumb enough to fall for that one, and jerked his head in reaction. The wrong end of the gun ceased to point at Tarrant for half a second, which was all he needed. He slammed the bottle of chloroform at Kyle's face, and dove forward, tackling him. They hit the floor with a solid *whump*, Kyle on the bottom with all the breath knocked out. Tarrant wrested the gun away and slapped the still wet wad of cotton against the man's nose and mouth. He didn't have much fight left and went limp, but Tarrant kept the pressure up until he felt dizzy from the fumes himself.

He got up, unsteady, and made for the kitchen sink, pulling the Balaklava clear of his mouth just in time. Caramel-colored spit gushed from him, followed by the dry heaves. He ran water and washed the stink from his gloved hands. The place reeked of chloroform. He staggered to the back door, yanked it wide, and gulped air, his head pounding.

No time for this.

Fancy-pants might get curious and come check on his troops.

Doc will laugh himself silly if I get popped by an old man in a red fedora.

Can't have that.

Still wobbly, Tarrant went back for the girl, hoisted her over one shoulder and took her down the back stairs. He gave himself points for not falling and killing them both.

With her belted into his car's passenger seat, he shifted to reverse and backed down the empty block, then cut a U-turn. He headed south until reaching I-30, then north on I-35 until he found a suitable cheap chain motel. There he checked in using his false ID and paying in cash. The night clerk noted down his car tag numbers anyway, but those were false as well.

Tarrant carried Amanda into their allotted room, easing her down on the bed. She looked better unconscious, and cleaning off the white makeup would have made her pretty, but that wasn't in his job description. She'd been removed from the line of fire for the time being, and that's what mattered. He took off her shoes, tucked her still-dressed under the covers, and adjusted the room's heater to circulate in some fresh from outside.

He block-printed a note to her on motel paper.

Don't go back to the loft. Cops are after you. If you want help, call.

He then wrote out a number for a disposable phone. He made sure she had cab fare, dropped the room key on the nightstand, and left.

Tarrant returned to Deep Ellum, but there was no sign of Kyle, the bruisers, or the SUV. The loft doors were wide open, the interior even more of a wreck than before, which he'd thought impossible. He departed, not touching anything.

He felt a little gut-sick on the long drive back to his condo, but it was only reaction to the lengthy adrenalin high and the chloroform. It was good to have cleared the job away in such short order, but Kyle had been of great help there; he'd done everything but paint a target on his chest.

For the luckless Kyle Tarrant had no pity. Some people were fish and others were sharks; that's just the way it was in the big food chain. Bad luck when you're born a minnow and don't know it.

Every job was different, he had told Caitlin. Especially so for this one. For once he'd completed a hit and not had to pull the trigger himself. It made a nice change. They should all be so easy.

But that would take the fun out of the game.

Challenge versus achievement.

Tarrant knew what he liked best.

SLAUGHTER

Author's Note: *Again, editor Martin H. Greenberg sold the collection* THE REPENTANT *to DAW and asked me to trib a story. And again, given the opportunity, I tweaked the original to present this expanded version of Gordy and Jack teaming up for fresh mayhem.*

Chicago, 1937

"He calls himself Slaughter. None of the guys knows his real name," said Gordy.

The self-named Slaughter had a booth to himself a few yards from where Gordy and I were seated in the dimly lighted nightclub. More than half in shadows, Slaughter had his back to a wall, but in Chicago that was just a healthy habit for certain guys. He'd popped up out of nowhere, and had apparently, without any fuss, taken over the running of one of the more active businesses under Gordy's protective eye. Well, it had something to do with protection. I rarely asked for details about his work. If he wanted me to know something, he'd say.

"What's the story?" I asked, pretending to sip coffee. It was only coffee, too; Prohibition being a not-so fond memory meant you could now order the best from Brazil without getting something routinely added in the cup. Coffee and booze were the same for me: undrinkable. Thrift and principle dictated I not waste booze. The bonus with plain coffee was that it still smelled good to me.

Gordy was slow to reply, being a man careful with words, never using many and often given to understatement. He frowned slightly over his drink, which was also free of alcohol. When on a business call he never had so much as a short beer. "Sent some boys here last night to collect the usual cut. They came back empty. None of 'em's talking much, and it's what they don't say makes me think he's like you."

He had my full attention. Another vampire?

We're a rare breed. It takes a deliberate conscious effort to pass the potential on to another person, and the effort doesn't always work.

The buzz from a dozen conversations surrounding us faded to nothing as I studied Slaughter, trying to detect any sign of kinship. That would be impossible, not until I got close enough to discern the absence of a heartbeat or unless he chanced to walk in front of a mirror.

"Can't tell from here," I said, anticipating the question.

"Time for a word. I'll lead, you watch him," Gordy wore caution like his tailored suit, which was why he'd lasted so long in his ruthless line of work, and tonight I was his insurance. If Slaughter was like me, no ordinary human bodyguard would be enough.

We left our table; Gordy's broad back blocked my view of a sizable portion of the club for a few moments. He was taller than me and a lot wider, all of it muscle. Through restless clouds of cigarette smoke people stared and some whispered recognition. No one noticed me, which was exactly how I preferred it.

Slaughter watched our approach. He was young, reasonably handsome, on the good side of his twenties, dark eyes, tight mouth, and pale skin, but lots of guys were like that. His suit was sharp, expensive, and so painfully new it looked like it was wearing him. I tried to pick up his heartbeat, but the general noise prevented anything so subtle.

"Slaughter," said Gordy from his height. "You know who I am." It was not a question. "We need to talk."

Slaughter gave a half-smile to show he was amused, not intimidated. Wise men were respectful to Gordy; the rest tended to disappear. "Do we?"

"Find a place."

More smile. Slaughter's gaze flicked my way. He'd see a tall, lean man in a flashy double-breasted dark suit and silk shirt, fedora pulled low: probably the boss's pilot fish, errand-runner, bodyguard, or all three. No one important, easily dismissed. When his attention returned to Gordy, I could tell I'd conned another one. "Okay, come to the back."

We threaded past the tables, drawing a share of attention from the dance music and couples drifting around the floor in front of the band. The ripples we made subsided along with the hubbub as Slaughter preceded us into the manager's office behind the stage.

Gordy paused at the door. "Where's Herm?" Until last week Herm Foster had been running things here.

"He left," Slaughter answered with a straight face. "Greener pastures."

We went in. The room had the usual office stuff, plus a long couch. A large-busted blonde girl was sprawled on it, fast asleep, one arm thrown across her eyes against the glaring overhead light. She wore a shiny red evening dress, cut low, and it looked like she'd been wearing it for at least three days without a break. Slaughter went over and tapped the back of his hand against her hip. She woke slow, pitifully hung over.

"Out," he ordered. "Go clean up. Come back tomorrow." Then he sat behind the desk, flopping back in the chair and putting his feet up, making it clear that she was of no further concern to him.

She blinked, her sunken eyes smudged and disoriented. It took her a moment to stand, and then she tottered like a drunk. I put a hand out to steady her. Her eyes blank, she stumbled, arms falling heavily over my shoulders, half-turning us around. She sighed, pressed the length of her body against mine, and tilted her head back, smiling. I sniffed and got a whiff of stale sleep-sodden breath. She wasn't drunk.

Gordy caught my glance over her shoulder. Yeah, he'd also spotted the clumsy bruising and red marks on her throat. Under her ghost-pale skin, her heart raced too fast, trying to pump blood that she didn't have.

Proof enough. It told me all I needed to know about Slaughter.

I focused hard on her but the effort was unnecessary; she was still under his influence and shifted loyalties easily enough. "Take it easy, you're going home, now." I could have said she was going for a swim in Lake Michigan in January and gotten the same lack of comprehension.

I gently peeled her off and made her sit.

Gordy and I looked at Slaughter.

He put on that half-smile and twitched some fingers in a self-deprecating gesture. "You know how it is, boys. They like me to tire 'em out."

Gordy had the most poker of poker faces, but I could tell he was pissed as hell. That wasn't even close to how I felt, but tempting as it was to take two steps and punch Slaughter's nose out the other side of his head, I held off. This wasn't my show for the present.

While I kept the girl from falling over, Gordy left and returned with the club's hostess in tow. He could move and talk fast when necessary.

"You know her?" he asked the hostess, indicating the lady in red.

"That's Penny. Is she drunk?"

"She's sick. I want you to look after her. You know a doctor?"

"Uh. . .yeah. . ."

"Give him a call. You know who I am?"

"Uh-huh, Northside Gordy, you run the Nightcrawler Club—unless you want me to forget all that."

"Have the doctor call my club after he sees Penny." He gave her a C-note. "That's for expenses."

"Golly!" Her eyes popped.

"You get another if you take care of her good."

"Just call me Florence Nightiebird," she said, quickly stuffing the money down the front of her dress.

I looked hard at Penny again, trying to reach whatever lay dozing behind her glazed eyes. "You rest up, get yourself well again. Don't come back." I handed her over to the hostess, who guided Penny out the door. The poor girl chose her steps slowly, one at a time, an old woman's walk.

Slaughter had a narrow eye on us during the exchange, but I didn't think I'd tipped my hand. If he saw us as mugs with a soft spot for dames, all the better. He seemed to be at ease with himself and what should have been dangerous company. Gordy took a chair, and I shut the door so we wouldn't be disturbed. I remained on my feet, still playing bodyguard.

Slaughter shot me another dismissive once-over and beamed a smirk at Gordy. "You wanna talk? What about?"

"This club is run by Herm. I picked him. Who picked you?"

"I did. It was a sweet setup, so I moved in. Herm decided he should leave. He told me to expect you to notice."

"He was right."

"You got nothing to worry about. I run it the same, maybe better. No fights, no problems with the cops. Everything's copasetic."

"Except for the weekly payment."

Slaughter flashed teeth. They were very white, but otherwise normal appearing, as were mine. "Yeah, I decided I don't need your kind of insurance after all. I'm glad you came by so we could straighten this out."

Gordy studied him a long time. He could take the spine out of most men when he gave them the cold eye, but this one seemed immune. "You are not being wise."

"Maybe, but I'm getting rich."

He really wants to die, I thought. Of course it's easy to take risks when you know you're damned-near impossible to kill. In the brief silence to follow I heard one heart beating, one set of lungs pumping: Gordy's. Given the situation he was almost relaxed. It seemed to be a good example to follow.

"If you want to keep the club, you have to pay for the privilege. That's how things run in this town."

I worked to not show surprise. Gordy was open to leaving things as is? I'd expected he'd want this gatecrasher pitched out on his ear. Maybe he was considering the advantages of having another vampire as an ally. I couldn't blame him. I'd turned out to be damned useful when occasion demanded.

Slaughter shrugged. “Those rules don’t apply to me.”

“To you more than most.”

“Uh-uh. You’re gonna listen to me from now on.” Slaughter took his feet off the desk and leaned forward, fixing Gordy with a good hard stare. He had emotional strength behind it, had worked himself into a little anger, which was dangerous. Though it helped to hammer a point home, too much rage can shatter minds. I should know.

Gordy’s expression had gone as blank as the girl’s.

I stepped in before things went over the edge, slipping a .38 revolver from my coat pocket and standing between them. “Lay off,” I ordered, my voice calm.

The unwelcome reminder of my presence startled Slaughter. He rocked back, eyes blazing. “Hey!”

“Fleming?” began Gordy, puzzled. I spared him a glance. He made a vague movement toward the gun he packed under his left arm, then stopped.

“It’s all right,” I said. “He’s covered. He was working a persuasion move on you. Might be better if you let me take it from here.”

He bit off further questions, trusting my judgment. That’s why he’d asked me along. He quit his chair and got out of my way.

Slowly standing to bring us even, Slaughter turned his persuasive stare full on me. “You’re gonna to listen to me, punk. You have to listen, understand? From now on I’m the only voice you can hear.”

I felt pressure inside my skull, like the air gets when there’s a sudden weather change. Nothing I couldn’t ignore.

“You are gonna listen and do everything I say. . .”

Familiar words. I’d used the same ones countless times. It’s a great way to get out of speeding tickets.

“You must listen—”

And it doesn’t work on another vampire.

“The hell I will. Sit down and shut up.” I pushed him hard enough to knock him back into his chair, then cocked the gun and brought the muzzle level with his left eye.

That broke his concentration. His mouth dropped open with shock. I wondered how experienced he was, if he knew he could survive a bullet. I had, but getting shot hurts. Slaughter’s hands went palm-out in sudden placation. The keystone of his confidence was quite gone.

An intake of breath from him, a sniff. He was checking me for booze. He knew how that could interfere with hypnosis. What else had he figured out?

“You can’t do this,” he said, dumbfounded, maybe a little hurt. It’s a tough moment, that awful one when you realize you're not all-powerful. Usually it happens on the first day of school when the teacher isn't looking. Slaughter must have forgotten that lesson.

"How old are you?" I asked.

"Huh?"

"Your age. I won't ask again."

"Uh. Twenty-five."

"You got this dumb in just twenty-five years? Amazing."

"Who the hell are you?"

"To you, kid, I am Mr. Fleming."

"Don't call me kid!"

"How old do you think I am?"

"Who the hell cares?"

"This dumb with bad manners. What a world."

"You—"

But he didn't get a chance to finish. I vanished first, cocked gun and all. Though invisible to Gordy, Slaughter would be able to see me in this state—as an amorphous gray shadow—and if this was his first experience, it would startle the hell out of him. I wasted no time sweeping through the bulk of the desk. When I reappeared, I was behind him, leaning over his shoulder, my mouth close to his ear and the revolver's cold muzzle pressed to his temple hard enough to leave a bruise.

"You will be quiet now, new boy," I whispered, trying to be as scary as possible. It didn't take much; I was in the mood and had seen enough movies to know how it was done.

Though he no longer used his lungs regularly, Slaughter caught his breath. "Oh, shit, you're—"

"Yeah, I'm in the same club, and you screwed up on the secret handshake."

His lips moved, but nothing came out. He looked a lot younger without the self-importance.

"You've been putting your foot wrong ever since you crawled out of the woodwork. You're making certain people unhappy." A pause to let it sink in. I straightened enough to check on Gordy. His slab of a face was impassive, but I got that he was highly amused by my act.

Slaughter tried to twist toward me. "Jeeze, I didn't mean anything—"

"Shuddup, kid. This piece has a hair-trigger and lead hurts just as much as a wooden stake. You can't vanish faster than I can shoot."

He made like a statue. Maybe he did not know about our relative immunity to bullets.

I eased back, giving him an opening to jump me. He didn't take it. Going around the desk in the normal way, I hitched a hip on the front, taking the gun off cock, but keeping it aimed at him. Used to be I didn't bother carrying, but Chicago's a tough place, even for a vampire, as Slaughter was beginning to learn. I looked him over, the same as he had for me, only I didn't make the mistake of underestimation. He was inexperienced, but every bit as physically dangerous as I when it came to supernatural abilities like strength, speed, and vanishing. What he'd done to the collection boys and the blonde girl indicated he knew how to cloud minds better than Lamont Cranston.

If Slaughter was smart—I had no confidence in that—he would listen to sense before he went too far and really hurt anyone.

"You made a messy start, kid, nothing that can't be fixed, but only if you decide to get wise. You begin by apologizing to Gordy. Tell him you're sorry for being such a rude son-of-a-bitch."

Too off-balance to argue, Slaughter made a handsome, word-for-word apology. He didn't mean it, but was obeying orders. Just what I wanted. "That's good. So—how long since you died?"

Wall-eyed, he glanced at Gordy.

"He's wise about this stuff," I added. "Answer."

"About a month."

"How'd it happen?"

"I don't wanna say. It was in a fight, that's all."

One's death is a very personal experience. For me, it was singularly unpleasant and violent, and even after a year I could still get a case of lockjaw when the topic came up. "Okay, never mind. Who made you?"

"Nobody made me, it just happened."

I gave a short laugh. "And the stork finds babies under cabbage leaves. Come on and spill, we're all grown-ups here. Who was she?"

"No one."

"Was it a he, then?"

That made him sputter. "You son-of-a—"

He saw my expression and a twitch of my hand reminded him about the revolver. He thought better about finishing and settled back. "It was some girl."

"Where?"

"Here in town, the south side. Saw her in an alley, thought she was whoring a drunk. Looked like she was kissing him, then she—there was blood on her mouth. It was sick. I tried to chase her off, but that didn't happen."

"What did?"

"She came after me instead. When she looked at me. . .I wanted her to, so she did. We did. I don't wanna say any more." He'd gone beet red.

"No need. But sometime during this enchanting encounter you

exchanged blood, right?"

He nodded.

That was disturbing. What kind of vampire runs around doing a blood exchange with a stranger? Was she ignorant or just reckless?

"And then you got killed sometime after. And then you woke up."

"Yeah. That's how it was."

If his story was true, I had to find this careless girl. Vampires are damned rare, and the few that I knew were levelheaded and conscientious about their second chance at living, particularly when it came to bestowing the possibility on others. They didn't just leap out of alleys and attack people for blood, nor casually exchange it. Stupid behavior like that can get you permanently killed. Even in these days of electricity and skepticism you might run into a would-be Van Helsing who's more than happy to rid the world of a medieval kind of bloodsucker. It had nearly happened to me once.

On the other hand, not everyone in the world is a sane, sensible, law-abiding citizen. Why should a vampire be different? I had a prime example right in front of me.

"What about you? She do you, too?" he asked.

"No. The lady I was with had a better sense of responsibility. What's her name and where does she live?"

"I don't know where she is. That was months back. I forgot about it until the night I woke up. I guess she made me forget."

"She didn't tell you what to expect, what to do?"

"I figured it out. I remembered what she did and how she did it. It wasn't hard. I read that book about Dracula, but it was fulla crap. I can't turn into a bat or a wolf."

I snorted. "You do more than enough as it is. You've been abusing the privilege, taking this place over."

"It beats rolling drunks."

Thus did I get an idea of why Slaughter had been in that particular alley.

"How else am I supposed to make money? The guys in the bread lines can work days, I can't. I'm flat on my keister the whole time. You want I should rob a bank?"

"You've got options, but stealing isn't one of them. It annoys people."

"That's what *he* does." He pointed at Gordy. "Why do I have to be any different?"

"Use your common sense. Get noticed and get dead. You think we're the only ones watching you?" That, so far as I knew, was a lie, but maybe a little paranoia would keep this idiot in line.

"There's others? Like us? Where?"

I just smiled. "They can turn up at the damnedest times—and you won't know until it's too late. There's plenty who would have staked you on sight. It's just your good luck I'm willing to give you a chance to clean up your act before they come calling."

"Why should they bother? Or you? I'm not hurting you. Who the hell do you think you are to march in my place and tell me how to live? You some kind of king vampire around here?"

"Only when it comes to the dumb ones. Don't be dumb, kid. You've got a lot of great years ahead so long as you wise up fast. Gordy might not mind you running this place, but you have to follow the rules and show respect just like everyone else."

"Huh. What can he do to me if I don't?"

"He just waits for the sun to come up—you work out the rest."

Gordy played it through with an appropriate cold-faced stare. I knew him to be a good egg when it suited, but he was also a killer. He showed that side now.

Slaughter scowled, sullen. He only half-understood, half-believed. "So just like any other mug, I pay him and he doesn't kill me?"

"Unless you tell Herm to come back, that's all there is to it."

"But—"

"Taking over a club ain't the same as stealing apples from a sidewalk cart. Every boss has his boss."

"Not me."

"Especially you. I know how you feel. You got something that puts you on top of the world, but you let yourself get noticed by that world and suddenly you're having a bad night. You read the book. What did they do to Dracula at the end?"

"I'm too smart for that."

"You think so? Gordy, what happened to the last vampire who went wrong in these parts?"

"You don't want him to know."

"Yeah, I do."

Gordy surprised me and shook his head.

Was he being careful about admitting to killing someone or was the memory that bad for him? Could be a bit of both.

Slaughter couldn't miss this exchange. "What'd you do?"

I tried to read Gordy, but he gave nothing away. He had more experience with intimidation. Sometimes keeping shut was more frightening than being up front; this was one of those times. So be it. I turned back to Slaughter. "Use your imagination. Suffice to say it was ugly and the party involved did not survive. You sure you want to be stubborn just when things are going good for you?"

"What do you want from me?"

"Pay your dues on this club, same as Herm. Beyond that, you live like a normal human being and keep your nose clean."

"How am I supposed to be normal? I'm not!"

"If I can get away with it, so can you."

"Why should I?"

"Figure it out. Your answer will tell you how long you'll live. Lay off the hypnosis until and unless you really need it to stay alive, the headache ain't worth the trouble. And you stop feeding from people like you've been doing."

"I gotta eat!"

"Then go to the Stockyards."

"What?"

"Plenty of cattle there, or hadn't you figured that out yet?"

"She didn't."

"The one who made you was careless. And I will find her, don't kid yourself."

"Animal blood? You nuts?"

"They were good enough eating before your change, what's so different now?"

"But—"

"Just try it. They've got blood to spare. You can have all you want then."

He clammed up, hopefully thinking it over.

I hooked a thumb toward the door, indicating where Penny had left. "What about the twist? You exchange blood with her? With anyone else?"

"No."

"I don't believe you. Think you can live forever with just one eye?" I raised my gun again.

"Hey! I didn't!" He half-rose from the chair, hands out, trying to back away. "I didn't! Swear to God!" The chair crashed over. He pressed against the wall and seemed to fade to an overall gray tone, about to fully vanish.

I put the gun away. "All right, get off your hind legs. I had to ask."

He grew more solid looking, but was still shaken. "Who the hell are you?"

"The nearest thing you'll see to a teacher for this kind of life. Right now you need me. I'll play square with you, that's a promise."

"What do you get out of it?"

"A quiet town to live in."

"What's in it for me?"

"A quiet town to live in—where you don't have to watch your back."

"I do okay on my own."

"Yeah, that's why I was able to put a gun in your face. Wise up, Slaughter, you're getting a hell of a chance here. Is that your real name?"

"It is now."

"All right. For now think how vulnerable you are and how much you don't know. In the meantime, if you ever use another person for food, I'll twist your head off. And you know I can do it."

* * *

The interview wasn't exactly satisfying to everyone, but Slaughter looked like he'd behave himself for a while. He grudgingly provided a general location for the vampire who'd used and made him. Gordy and I left the club, climbed into his armored car, and drove to his own place, the Nightcrawler Club.

"Don't trust that weasel," I said. I went over things in memory, thinking up all the stuff I should have said.

"Never," he agreed. "I see his kind plenty. He'll go along until he thinks he's got my number, then watch out. I'll have people keep tabs on him in case he gets cute."

"Or at least until he's broken in on this new life he's got. The change is a hell of a thing for anyone to handle. It still gets to me sometimes."

"No excuse. He's trouble. His type don't learn easy. Maybe never."

"Yeah. But I have to give him a chance. He didn't ask to be changed. Who the hell could have done that to him?"

"Wasn't in my territory, but I can ask."

"Without mentioning vampires?"

"If there's a dame biting drunks on the south side maybe some cop or a doctor noticed. More than one person shows up with a blood on his throat, someone will remember."

"Check the morgues, too. If she's using people for food. . .it can get out of hand. Like we saw back there."

"That girl was half-dead, Fleming. If we hadn't come in tonight he'd have finished her. You've given him a chance to do that to another girl."

"Or a chance to not to."

"Why risk it?"

"I see myself in him. If things had gone different, I'd have needed someone like me to knock some sense into my skull."

"You're too tough on yourself and too easy on Slaughter. You were never that dumb."

"I might have been if I'd lived in his shoes. What is he? Some poor schmuck who never had anything and now he's got everything for the asking. The world's in his hands, but he doesn't know how heavy it is."

"And you did when it happened to you?"

I shook my head. "It hit me different. I made a choice, knowing what I was in for, but I made mistakes I'm still wincing over. I want to stop Slaughter before he trips."

"He's already tripped. You're just trying to stop him from landing too hard."

"What do you want to do, Gordy? Go back and kill him? Just like that?"

"I can live with it. So can a bunch of others, the people he could end up hurting."

I couldn't argue with that and found it ironic that Gordy, who had participated in more cold-blooded killings than I ever wanted to know about, was playing the part of my conscience.

* * *

We spent the rest of the evening in Gordy's office while he made phone calls trying to find the mystery lady. Not having a name, coupled with a second-hand description made the task fairly hopeless, but Gordy had more eyes in this town than Argus. If he hadn't been a gang boss, he'd have made a hell of a detective.

There were some calls even I couldn't listen in on, though. Respecting that, I quit his office and went downstairs to the gambling room to pass the time.

Most of his boys knew me by sight, if not always by name, and they kept their distance. I didn't go out of my way to make friends, but would give a nod here and there just to be sociable and maybe offset whatever bad reputation I'd gotten. Parking at an empty table, I accepted a glass of water from a waitress in a short spangled skirt, and asked her to send one of the guys over.

She read me right and picked one of Gordy's mugs, not one of the gambling operation employees.

"What you need?" the guy asked, standing over me, his stony face guarded. He was one of the ones who thought I was a creep, and that didn't bother me. I prefer an honest reaction.

"Couple of the boys went over to Herm Foster's the other night. They here?"

"Why do you want 'em?"

"Gordy said to say a word."

"What word?"

"You'll have to ask Gordy. I'm just doing what I'm told, same as anyone."

He had to think that over, but must have worked out that I was somehow on the payroll. I wasn't, but it didn't hurt to give that impression. What would really bother him was the pecking order. Was I above, below, or an equal? Details like that are important. I didn't care myself, but no need to broadcast it. Was there a pecking order to cover a neutral friend of the boss? Probably.

He gave a grunt and, without answering my original question, left the room, taking the door to the back hall, the fastest way to Gordy's office. If he wanted to bother his boss about me, that was his business and no skin off my nose.

I wasn't sure how long to wait before deciding that I'd been slighted, but a minute later two large guys came through the same door, spotted me, and strolled over. I motioned for them to sit and asked if I could buy them a drink. They were unopposed to that, and the waitress delivered a couple beers. The alcohol would make my job harder, but I judged these two would be more inclined to cooperate with a man running a tab.

After they each washed down some city dust with a sample of brew, I let them know Gordy wanted me to hear what had happened at Herm's club. They hesitated and went vague. They'd gone there, but beyond that all I got was head shaking, shrugs, and strange looks. They were uncomfortable, but didn't know why.

Where Slaughter tripped up was ordering them to obey a suggestion contrary to what was normal for them. They wanted to talk, but couldn't remember the topic. I got through by using their inclinations—and buying five minutes worth of friendship with the beer.

As Slaughter had done earlier, I leaned forward and focused on one at a time, turn on turn. Trying to put two under at once was risky. I didn't make a big noticeable deal out of it, else one or the other would get wise and perhaps interrupt.

Without them being stone cold sober it took longer and brought on the usual headache for the extended effort, but eventually my evil-eye whammy had them asleep with their eyes open. I gave myself a breather, so to speak, pinching the bridge of my nose even though that never worked. This was more of a mental throat clearing.

I told them to relax and to trust me, and finally cracked open the barriers Slaughter had put on their memories.

What a bright boy he was, too.

He could have ordered them to think they'd collected the week's take, business as usual, but had intentionally primed them to be forgetful, knowing full well that a bigger fish would show up to check on things. He'd have influenced his way to the top man easy enough. Slaughter didn't strike me as being especially smart when it came to consequences, but his acquisitive instincts were good.

It was his bad luck I'd come along.

The two strong arms woke up on their own, having no memory of being questioned. I bought another round, we talked about this and that. They liked me now, my suggestion of trust still fresh in their unconscious minds. It would fade, but for the moment things were fine.

The first man I'd talked to watched from one of the tables, letting me know he was watching.

"I think your pal wants you," I said to my guests.

"That's Strome," one told me. "You've got him worried."

"Oh, yeah?"

"He thinks you want his spot."

Not knowing what that was in the organization, it seemed unlikely. "Once in a blue moon Gordy tells me to do a chore, and I'm in no position to say no. That's as far as it goes. Your pal can relax. I've got my own fish to fry."

They took that as a sign our talk was over and moved on. Not surprisingly they went to Strome's table to finish their beers and probably pass on the newly minted rumor that Gordy had something on me. I didn't mind if mugs here thought I was a reluctant volunteer; it was better than the truth.

I did some thinking.

Gordy's men had done their jobs by the book, so to speak. They'd asked for Herm, got Slaughter instead, and he'd taken them back to the office for some hypnosis.

Only he'd not just changed their minds about getting that week's cut, he'd pumped them dry for information about Gordy and his operation.

They knew plenty. If they'd spoke that freely to a DA, Gordy would be under arrest by now.

So, was Slaughter just nosy or was he planning something? If I told Gordy about this, Slaughter wouldn't see another sunset.

* * *

"Anything?" I asked, walking into the upstairs office again. I'd put some time at one of the blackjack tables. I was down two bucks, but I'd enjoyed the game. Sooner or later I'd win it back with interest, but on another night when my luck was fresher.

Gordy lifted one large hand an inch to indicate frustration. "Bupkis. She could be in a different state by now. Or Slaughter made her up."

"Maybe he killed her."

"No reason to think that yet."

"No," I said. "No reason at all."

I hung around until the wee hours, but nothing new came in via the ringing phone. Wishing him better luck in the coming day, I left and drove to the Stockyards.

The Yards are dirty and when the wind direction and heat are in cahoots the stink is past imagining, but I don't have to breathe regularly. The blood from all those doomed animals is plentiful and free for the taking, fresh on the hoof. I fed well, and I fed deep.

When I straightened from my crouch over the flowing vein I'd opened in a cow's leg, I saw Slaughter on the other side of the enclosure fence. I'd not heard him; he must have gone invisible and floated in.

He looked disgusted. "How can you do that?"

"Because it tastes good." I wiped my mouth with a handkerchief.

"There's better stuff than that for guys like us."

"And we need too much of it too often. You'd kill the girl."

"Then take a little from a lot of girls."

"That's rape."

He smirked. "Not if you make them want it."

"It's still rape. You're not a real man doing that."

"Don't tell me you've never tried. You ever kill anyone? Don't tell me you haven't."

"I've never killed. . .for blood."

He snorted and spat into the mud. It was always muddy here.

"Slaughter, why do you set yourself up to make people want to punch your nose into the back of your head?"

"A fancy-pants like you wouldn't last a minute with me."

He'd missed the point of the question. I'd halfway expected that. "Appearances are deceptive."

"Prove it."

Much as I wanted to turn his smug face inside out, obliging him would do neither of us any good. We were evenly matched; it could go either way, though I knew some tricks that gave me an edge. No matter who won, I'd lose any chance to straighten him out.

"We're not enemies, Slaughter."

"I think we are. . .because of *what* we are."

"We're a couple of guys standing around in cow shit."

"We're goddamn *vampires*, you son-of-a-bitch!"

"So?"

"You nuts or something? The things we can do—I can own this town! Didn't you see that?"

"Yeah. From the first night I woke up, then I decided I didn't want the worry. I've got my piece of the world, and I keep my nose clean. You need to do the same."

"Or Gordy the goon comes after me?"

"You're starting to get it." I vanished from within the cattle pen and reappeared only a pace or so from Slaughter. He was less surprised this time, but still scowled, with a hint of jealousy behind his eyes. Maybe he thought I was showing off.

"Gordy has to find me first," he said, as though trying to convince himself. "No one knows where I hide during the day."

I chuckled a little. "You sure about that? Your life could depend on it. In fact, it does already. Just give us an excuse."

"Goddamn cow-sucker."

"Don't knock it till you've tried it."

"You can't make me."

"The idea is you do it on your own. Playing wet nurse ain't in my line. You think I couldn't force the issue? I'm older and stronger—"

A lie, but plausible to anyone who'd read Dracula.

"—I wouldn't even break a sweat. . .but I'm trying to give you some respect."

A flash from his eyes. Had I finally touched the right nerve? If he had the kind of upbringing that went with his tough guy manners, then he'd be starved for respect and acceptance. On the other hand, he was also scornful of anyone bestowing it. Bad enough if he started out with a general contempt for humanity, his change to something physically superior would tend to bolster that view. I had to get him to see farther than his own nose.

"You've been through the wringer and had it tough," I continued. "I'm not talking about your life before your change, but what happened after you woke up dead. You were smart enough to figure things out and survive. That tells me you've got the smarts to get along without hurting others."

"What's it to you?"

"There aren't a lot of us walking around. We look out for each other. I'm willing to teach you the rest of the stuff you need to know. Think it over. If you decide you're better than the regular kind of mug you see, look me up. I'm usually at the Nightcrawler Club. Just ask for Jack Fleming."

Slaughter made no reply, but he wasn't sneering, so that was some progress. He needed me more than I wanted to deal with him, but no good would come of mentioning that fact. He'd have to think coming around to my view was his own idea.

I wasn't especially excited about playing the mentor, either. He might be picking up on that. I didn't like him. Sure, I saw myself in him, but those were the pieces of me that I'd outgrown and left behind. Having him hanging around would be a reminder of past mistakes and how much I still had to learn.

But balanced against that was something very basic and human: loneliness. We're all alone, but there's a lot more of it when you've got a condition that sets you even farther apart from others. We search for commonalities as a cure for that isolation. Like it or not, Slaughter and I had the vampirism in common. If not for that, I wouldn't spare him two seconds of my time, and it wasn't as though I wanted a new friend. I had to be altruistic to keep him from abusing the privilege.

"I'll see you around," I said. He was in the way. If I walked past, he'd bump my shoulder or try something equally stupid to provoke a fight. Schoolyard stuff: step across that line, I double-dare you. I'll show you who's the toughest kid in town.

Entertaining as that might be, it was late, and my suit had seen enough wear for one evening. I vanished again and floated high above him, moving swiftly away, not reappearing until I was clear of the pens and well onto the sidewalk. Now I was showing off, but I'd had a lot of practice and could make it look good.

He followed. A gray cloud that only I could see sieved through the fence near the ground, hovered a moment, then solidified into his shape. By then, I was in my car and driving off. I didn't wave good-bye; always leave 'em wanting more.

* * *

At exactly sunset I woke as usual, but not in the usual spot at home. There, I had a well-hidden sanctuary in the basement of my partner Escott's house. Because of Slaughter, I'd steered clear of its shelter in favor of an even better bolt hole in a tobacco shop. It was in a seldom-visited upstairs storage room that backed the office where Escott ran his not-too-busy detective agency. In a long box hidden beneath a lot of other boxes I was safe for the day. The only access was through the shop below and through a concealed panel in the common wall of Escott's back room. Only he and I knew about it.

I didn't use the box often. It was too reminiscent of a damned coffin. I'd never been in one, but hated the sight of them.

Leaving it and the small bag of my home earth behind, I dematerialized and pushed through the common wall, going solid again in the back room, which was dark. Ingrained caution made me pause and listen before moving another inch. It paid off; someone was in the outer office. He was quiet, but when I concentrate I can hear a gnat belch.

It wouldn't be Escott; he was out of town running an errand for a client, nor would it be another client. I'd made a point of locking the door before turning in. Next time I'd buy a heavy bolt to beef things up. It could not be Slaughter; he had no heartbeat.

Wary, I vanished and eased my way through the next wall until I was just behind the visitor. Serve him right if I gave him a heart attack.

The general grayness of my perception took on form and color as I gradually went solid. The office light was on. After being in the box, I squinted against the brightness.

The man turned out to be Gordy. His back was to me, his massive frame seated in one of the fortunately sturdy chairs in front of Escott's desk. Something must have come up for him to be here waiting for me. Normally, he'd just phone at sunset.

And he'd phone me at home. He didn't know I'd be here. He knew nothing about the box above the shop.

But Slaughter might have followed me from the Yards. I'd checked for tails, but he could have managed and tracked me as far as the office. My car was right out front.

"Gordy?"

No jump of surprise. Gordy stood and turned like a machine, raising his gun to my chest level. His eyes were empty; his whole face was empty. I dove in fast and grabbed his arm. The big .45 boomed twice, blasting craters in the plaster before I could wrest it from him, He tried to get it back, but I gave him a hefty gut punch to distract him, shouting his name right in his ear.

He didn't quite double over. I had to pop him again, harder. That did the trick. His knees hit the floor, but he still made a single-minded reaching motion for the gun. I shouted at him again, this time making eye contact.

"Listen to me, goddammit!"

He halted in mid-motion, then wavered. I took a breath to calm myself, backing away from my anger and fear, then:

"Wake up, Gordy! Come out of it. You don't hear him anymore."

He blinked and shook his head like a drunk, but awareness flooded back. "Jeeze, Fleming—what the hell. . . ?"

I sagged. "That goddamn little son-of-a—" The sudden shock of adrenaline trying to pound a hole in the top of my skull vented itself in multi-colored phrase. Gone was every shred of sympathy for Slaughter. If he'd been in front of me I'd have killed him then and there. Gordy was right; I was wrong, almost fatally wrong.

When coherency returned, I apologized to Gordy for getting rough.

"No problem," he said, slowly boosting into the chair. "But you didn't have to use a sledge hammer on me. I just wanna know why. How come I'm here?"

"Weasel-boy got to you."

"Who?"

"Slaughter sent you over to drill me." I held out the gun. He gingerly took it and sniffed the muzzle. He looked at the holes in the wall.

"Who's Slaughter?" Gordy asked.

I wasted a moment gaping at him.

Oh, crap. "You know what day it is?"

"Wednesday."

"Try Thursday night."

"I lost a whole damn day?" He never raised his voice. Any other man would be smashing furniture. "How the hell—"

"Hypnosis."

He was fighting to believe me, looking around the office, unable to explain how else he'd gotten here. "Like what you do?"

"Exactly like what I do. There's another vampire in town, and he made you forget all about him. I can find out more, but I'll have to put you under myself."

He thought about it. Taking his time. "Then I'd remember this guy?"

"Yeah. It would come back to you normal in a week or two—if he lets you live that long. You need to remember him."

"You won't make me quack like a duck? I saw a guy on stage do that."

That caught me off-guard. "Uh—no, promise, scout's honor."

His head wobbled, indication that I'd amused him, and he marginally relaxed. "Okay. What do I do?"

This was a hell of a lot of trust on his part. I was strangely uncomfortable with that. "Just sit there. . ."

It didn't take long to jog the whole business from Gordy's memory.

After our cozy chat over the Stockyards fence Slaughter had turned up at the Nightcrawler not long before dawn. He'd located Gordy and put him under, then gave him careful instructions to go to a place called the Escott Agency. There he was to wait and shoot me as soon as I showed myself in the evening. Afterward, he was to return to the Nightcrawler as though nothing had happened.

I made sure Gordy remembered everything when I woke him up.

"Little son-of-a-bitch," he muttered.

It was unanimous. "Simple but effective. If you got caught for my murder, you'd take the fall, and never know why."

"If I'd shot you, you wouldn't have died. Ain't that right?"

"A metal bullet hurts, but isn't enough. Slaughter doesn't know how hard we are to kill or what weapons really do the job. Good thing he didn't ask you."

"Then we show him how it's done."

I was all for it.

"Is that yours?" He indicated something on the desk.

I'd left my fedora there in case Escott returned early from his trip so he'd know I was using the tobacco shop bolt hole. On the blotter next to my hat lay a shiny new hunting knife, the big one made famous by Jim Bowie. Some ancient Roman could have used it for a sword, the damned thing was of a similar size. It was out of its scabbard, ready to hand for. . .

"I think we can reasonably assume Slaughter knows how it's done," I said, feeling sick. "That's not yours? You sure?"

Gordy frowned at it. "I would never bring a knife to a gun fight."

True. He knew better. "Then Slaughter got it for you to. . .what, full dismemberment or just cut my head off?"

"Either way, you're out of the picture."

"But he doesn't know I'd just vanish and heal if shot with a metal bullet. You wanna check what's in your piece?"

He removed the magazine and ejected the round in the chamber. We examined the bullets. They were normal, straight from the factory. No tampering and not a sliver of wood in sight.

"He doesn't know everything," I said. "I can thank Bram Stoker for getting it wrong."

"How's that?"

"At the end of the book they stabbed Dracula with metal, and he turned to dust. Slaughter must have thought shooting would do the same for me, but if there was anything left—"

"Let's skip that part." Gordy checked his watch. "I've been here all day. Derner's gonna be nuts."

Derner was one of his office lieutenants. He answered the phones when Gordy was away, which almost never happened.

"Fleming. . ."

I correctly read the tension on Gordy's face and pointed toward the back. He trundled off to use the washroom. The toilet was flushed and water ran. When he came back the sweat was off his face and he seemed more alert. He rubbed his stubbled chin, looking annoyed. He invariably presented a clean-shaved face to the world.

"Damn, I need coffee," he said.

He never made offhand remarks like that. It told me just how shaken he was inside.

But his hand was steady as he used a handkerchief to polish prints off the rounds and put his gun back together. While he did that I found the two empty casings and pocketed them. Escott liked a neat office. I glanced at the bullet holes; those would have to be patched before he got back. I had a feeling this was not an incident I'd want him to know about.

I was itching to look outside, but didn't dare and stopped Gordy from having a gander. "Slaughter might be watching."

"Hell."

It wasn't likely, being so soon after sundown, but neither of us wanted to risk that he had found a temporary resting place in some nearby attic or cellar. He'd have gotten up at the same time as I and could be watching from the street to see how things progressed for his puppet.

"Wanna bet that he's going to be all set to give you fresh orders? Maybe take over your operation?"

Gordy shook his head. He went into the back room, which was still dark. His shadow wouldn't show against the blind as he checked the street from there, lifting a slat by only a fraction.

"Don't see nothing, for what that's worth."

"Not a red cent. We'll have to play this out, just in case."

"Why bother? Let's just go after him."

"He's too hard to catch. He finds out we're onto his game, he vanishes—literally—and leaves town to set up someplace else. He'll kill, if he hasn't already. His next target could be you. He might hypnotize you again. He seems to like controlling people."

Gordy nodded, accepting the possibility. "Then he'll be at my club. Can you do anything?"

"I got an idea. . ."

* * *

Gordy drove himself back to the Nightcrawler. That he'd left behind his usual driver and strong arm again indicated Slaughter's not-too-subtle influence. I made a more clandestine exit via the tobacco shop in the next street, wafting invisibly past the last customers. One of them shivered when I brushed too close and joked that someone must be walking over his grave.

I have never thought that observation to be particularly funny.

Outside, I streamed down the sidewalk until I found what seemed to be an alley at least a block away and there went solid. I felt naked without my hat, but had left it behind in case Slaughter dropped in to check on things. The idea was to make him think Gordy had succeeded.

As extra insurance, I'd put Gordy under again, priming him with the story that I'd turned to dust upon expiring. Dracula had done so, after all. Never thought I'd be grateful for such inspired misinformation.

Hailing a cab, I got a ride to the Nightcrawler and had the driver drop me in the building's rear alley. I paid him off and vanished, aiming for Gordy's private suite, ghosting up the side of the building to ease through the wall. I didn't like how it felt going through bricks and mortar, lathe and plaster, but it beat the brittle resistance of glass.

If Slaughter saw me in this state, the game was up. There was no way I could tell where he might be, either, whether he'd been watching Escott's street or gone on to the club. Gordy was of the opinion that Slaughter would swagger in by the front door and park himself in the big chair behind the desk all set to take over. I had no reason to disagree.

It struck me that Slaughter could have mistaken my position in the scheme of things, thinking that I was really in charge of the Northside territory. It would never enter his head that I'd be hanging around out of friendship. Slaughter would judge me by his limits; he sure as hell wouldn't have any friends: only enemies and people he could control.

Feeling the general shape of the area around me, I thought myself home safe. Materializing, I sagged with relief. It was where I'd been aiming to wind up: a large, pitch-dark closet. Without even a faint outside source of light I was as blind as anyone else given the circumstance and struck a match, careful to hold it clear. If I singed any of Gordy's custom-made suits, he would not be happy.

In the seconds before the match burned down, I found what I wanted: a sawed-off shotgun high on a back shelf. Gordy assured me it was still loaded with some special shells he'd made up. We'd used it once before to deal with a vampire, and the memory was anything but pleasant. My fingers shook as they closed over its chill weight.

Wood can truly damage us or guarantee a kill. You just have to know to use it, whether it's a stake in the heart, a club to the skull, or small beads loaded into a shotgun shell. On a normal human, the latter would probably do less damage than rock salt, but for guys like Slaughter and me, it's a slow, ugly death. Press both barrels against the chest and pull the trigger. Messy, but effective.

Maybe I wouldn't be able to do it. I'd killed before: by accident, in cold blood, and in the madness of rage. I wasn't proud of myself, and on those rare, awful days when I was stupid enough to get caught away from the protection of my home earth, the bad dreams ate through my helpless brain like acid.

Slaughter was bad news, but was he worth another dent in my already battered conscience? Perhaps all he needed was an almighty scare and some sense beaten into him. That I could do and no problem.

However, Gordy would want him dead.

In such matters Gordy was usually right.

* * *

Ears flapping, I eased open the closet door. It was clear and quiet, but the next room over was Gordy's palatial office, and there I heard activity, but not conversation. I pressed against the wall. At least three people, two of them breathing: Slaughter, Gordy, and one of the strong arms? That wasn't right. We'd agreed to keep this party exclusive. Slaughter may have added a third guest.

Then one of the breathing persons released a long, delicious moan of gratification. The timbre was female, and I thought I understood what was going on, having enjoyed the pleasure myself, both giving and receiving.

Hugging the shotgun close, I bulled invisibly through the wall. When I went solid, pure shock froze me for an instant.

One of the cigarette girls lay on the couch with Slaughter sprawling over her. He'd pawed the top half of her brief costume away, and buried his mouth deeply, greedily in the soft part of her throat. She moaned again, turning it into a sigh. Her face was toward me, eyelids squeezed shut, her arms wrapped tight around him. She was glowing, absolutely glowing from the pleasure of being murdered.

Across the room stood Gordy, hands to his sides like a soldier at silent attention. He should have been oblivious to the scene, but there was a terrible awareness in his expression. He'd been ordered to watch; he'd been ordered to do nothing. He looked at me, hope and fury in his white-rimmed eyes.

I couldn't shoot Slaughter without risking the girl. Had to move fast, he was draining her dry. I had to hold him in place to keep him from vanishing. On Gordy's desk lay a metal letter opener, thin bladed, fragile, not too sharp, but effective with enough force behind it.

Swiftly swapping the shotgun for the letter opener, I closed on Slaughter just as he began to rise to see the source of the noise. Blood smeared his lower face. The whites of his eyes were gone, suffused with blood from his feeding. They flashed scarlet in flat-footed surprise.

I drove hard with the blade, slamming it into his side as far as it would go, then broke off the handle.

Shrieking fury and pain, he staggered to his feet, clawing at it. I grabbed his arms above the wrists and tried to twist them behind him. The metal imbedded in his body kept him from vanishing, but he was still capable of a hellish fight. We danced around the room, wrecking furniture. I kept him busy, waiting for Gordy to snap out of his spell and grab the gun. I yelled his name hoping that might work. He was still rooted in place the next time I spun around.

Slaughter clawed at the letter opener, but the metal stub left sticking from his flesh was too short to grab. I punched a fist against the side of his skull. Any other man would have dropped, the bones caved in, not this guy. It slowed him, but he didn't stop trying to break free.

I dragged him toward the desk, toward the shotgun.

Roaring, he threw himself in the same direction, trying to get me off balance. I was too used to dealing with ordinary humans, not anyone with strength equal to mine. He tore one arm free and managed a solid, gut-bruising punch that made me grunt, then went for the gun, falling bodily on it.

His other arm wrenched from my grasp. He had the gun. I tried to lock him up in a full nelson, but he shifted us in a clumsy waltz until he faced Gordy.

"Lay off or I scrag him!" Slaughter snarled, the barrels centered on my friend.

He'd follow through. Gordy's eyes told me as much. I broke off the wrestling hold and slapped both hands around Slaughter's skull. Then I twisted hard and sharp. I'd never done it before, wasn't sure if I even got it right.

But I heard and felt the awful wet cracking of bone and cartilage giving way to brute force. Slaughter made a sick gagging noise and abruptly turned into dead weight. I let him fall. He dropped straight down like a brick, his only sound now a grunt as the air left his lungs. He lay on his belly, but his head was turned halfway around, blood red eyes staring at me.

I slumped relief, but for only an instant, hurriedly pulling the gun from under Slaughter's body, then checked on Gordy.

He was still stuck in place, the hypnotic influence unbroken. I went over, not sure what to do, and settled for looking him square in the eye. "You can move again. It's okay." I didn't think I'd gotten through but he rocked back a step, then shook into his normal posture, then seemed to swell.

"Jeeze," He whispered staring past me. "Jeeze, that *bastard*. . ."

I'd never seen him truly angry. He always held it in behind a stone face. I anticipated an explosion. God knows he was entitled. I got out of the way and went to check on the girl. He glared down at Slaughter for what seemed a long moment, then straightened and turned toward me.

"She okay?" His voice was calm as always, but I heard his heart booming, almost filling the room.

I pressed a clean handkerchief against her neck wounds. They were larger than they had to be and still freely bleeding. Slaughter had missed tearing fatally wide anything major in his greed, but it was likely more a matter of luck than care. "She needs a doctor."

"I know someone," said Gordy. "This shit. Is he dead? All the way dead?"

With no heart or lungs working, there was no way for me to tell. I'd played possum a few times and gotten away with being taken for a corpse. Slaughter might be doing the same. Or he could be immobile from his injuries, unable to move, and—with the letter opener in him—unable to vanish and heal. I'd been in that position as well, and its dire helplessness was the worst. All you can do is scream within your mind until insanity brings a kind of ease, until death finally comes.

We don't die fast. Maybe it's the price we pay for the life we get after cheating death the first time.

"I don't know," I said. "There're ways to make sure."

Gordy reached behind and pulled out the Bowie knife in its scabbard. He'd tucked it under his belt before leaving Escott's office. He placed it carefully on his desk and shot me a look. "Then we make sure."

* * *

While I trussed Slaughter up in another room, Gordy saw to a doctor, who wanted to know the cause of the girl's strange injury. Gordy told him a crazed customer went nuts and bit her, which was close enough to reality. He said the customer had been dealt with and would not be returning and the man wisely left it at that. Later, I'd have to have a private talk with the girl and make sure she only remembered what we wanted her to know; for now, Gordy and I had other things to do.

He knew how to dispose of inconvenient bodies. I'd been with him on only one such expedition, taking care of another vampire's corpse. We would do the same again, with me along to make sure there was no sudden revival of the body. About an hour later, after a brief phone call to arrange a truck and a boat, we were on our way. Slaughter's corpse was to be dumped so far out in the lake that even the fish would have trouble finding him.

Gordy and I rode in the back of the paneled truck, a blanket-wrapped bundle between us. His men would wrap a couple of hundred pounds of chains and weights to it. I wouldn't be going out onto the lake. Vampires have a problem with bodies of free running water.

Dim light filtered in from the small windows set in the truck doors, not much for Gordy, but plenty for me. He looked a calmer now, almost satisfied.

"Just realized something," he said.

"Oh, yeah?"

"You told Slaughter you'd twist his head off if he used another girl for food. I didn't know you meant it."

"Me neither."

"We'll take his head off the rest of the way. Just to be sure."

My pragmatic reply surprised me. "Wait till you're on the water. Easier to clean up."

Gordy took awhile before replying. He must have been surprised, too. "I'll see to it. I'm thinkin'. . ."

"Yeah?"

"That there should be some distance in between 'em. The body and the head. You know?"

I considered that for more time than was really needed and nodded. "Couldn't hurt. You been reading up on the subject?"

"Maybe."

"You had this ready to hand." I had the shotgun, playing bodyguard. "Wood in the shells, all that."

"Yeah."

"Why?"

"In case you ever got stupid," he said without apology.

"Okay." Well, he was honest. "I don't blame you. Idiots like Slaughter give vampires a bad name."

Gordy's head wobbled. Laughter. Then he sobered. "There's still another one out there. The one who made him, if he was telling the truth."

"Yeah," I said. I puffed air, and stared out the small windows in the doors. No moon. It was dark even for me. "So. . .what're you doing the rest of the night?"

THE DEVIL'S MARK

Author's Note: *This story went into an anthology I edited with Marty Greenberg for DAW, called* TIME OF THE VAMPIRES. *Try as I might I could not come up with a Jack Fleming story for it—but I had watched a bit of an old movie that dealt with a "Witch-Finder General" who swanned around England murdering innocent people in the 1600s. I began to wonder: "What if one of those wankers had wandered into the wrong village to ply his trade?" The opening was totally inspired by a Monty Python film.*

England, 1646

"She's a witch! Burn her!"

"What if she's not a witch?"

"Burn her anyway, it's cold!"

"Mr. Bainbridge! If you please!"

Belatedly realizing that his enthusiasm and dark humor were out of place—for the moment—Bainbridge got firm control of himself an presented his audience with a chagrined smile and a respectful bow. "Your pardon, gentle sirs, but when one is doing the Good Work, one may easily be carried away by the nobility of the task."

The audience—that is to say the men who made up the leadership of the town of Little Evesham-on-the-Wash made forgiving noises. Lucky for him, that. There was a proper way of going about these things, but Bainbridge had allowed his mind to be distracted by his pending reward, and he'd gotten ahead of himself. The time would come for the people to indulge themselves in a good bit of fire and riot, but one had to build them up to it first, get them used to the idea.

Their mayor—or whatever he was in this rustic hellhole—Mr. Percy, cleared his throat. "Indeed, Mr. Bainbridge, but my question still stands: What if the female you have accused is *not* a witch?

"Why then, she will suffer no harm, but," his gaze swept over the lot of them in such a manner as to indicate he understood his responsibilities perfectly well, "I know that once you are made acquainted with the evidence, you will not hesitate to deliver her to soul-cleansing flames and thus rid your beleaguered village of the Devil's vile influence."

Little Evesham-on-the-Wash was no more beleaguered than any other place had been in the last few years since King Charles and Parliament had gotten down to serious fighting. But each little hamlet Bainbridge had swept through when he began the lucrative work of witch-finding always thought its troubles to be unique to itself. He had but to ask if some oaf suffered mysterious fits or if farms were plagued by sickly livestock to start it all; there was always something wrong somewhere that he could seize upon as evidence of devilish doings. It had been an excellent day for him when he began to emulate the glorious work of the great Witch-Finder General, Matthew Hopkins.

The men conferred briefly, their voices low, but Bainbridge knew what they'd be thinking and discussing. Upon his arrival in town that winter's afternoon he'd made sure to get a few timid souls at the local tavern worked up about the dangers of witchcraft, and as darkness fell they'd carried their worries straight to their leaders.

Forced by the demand for action to hold a council meeting, those learned men in charge of a fearful flock would be afraid themselves. If they forbade Bainbridge's witch-finding, might that be taken to mean they were in fellowship with the Devil as well? If, on the other hand, they hired him to dig out the evil, they'd be short some trifling pounds from the town treasury and no harm done except to the witches, and what were a few old men and women more or less to them?

They reluctantly consented, Bainbridge went to work, and promptly found a witch.

Mr. Percy looked worried, almost morose, at this turn, but some of the others had a gleam of expectation in their eyes. Certainly the news of witch trials taking place in nearby towns had aroused their curiosity. Now it seemed they'd have the chance to see one at first hand.

This was just the start, though. Something entertaining to whet the appetite for the blood-letting to come. Bainbridge had accurately summed up just how much he could pocket from this little village.

Soon would come the real work: the sorting of gossip as hidden jealousies surfaced, as old grievances were recalled, then the searching of houses, discovery, the triumph of good as the flames burned away the evil. Every town in England was bursting with such opportunities, and it was a dull man who could not turn them to his own profit. Bainbridge fully intended to give them their money's worth.

"Very well," said Percy with an air of resignation. "Have the accused brought before us."

Two strong young men standing by the council chamber's door obliged him. They returned almost immediately with their charge; the others, seated judge-like at the long table, leaned forward with interest.

" 'Swounds!" one of them muttered.

The soft exclamation was justified. No aged crone for tonight's event—the sweet-faced young girl that stood before them had the figure of a temptress, with or without the help of stays. For the present she was without, being clad only in a plain chemise of thin and revealing weave. Her cap was gone as well, exposing an abundant crown of dark hair that tumbled over her shoulders and down her back. The flesh of her bared arms and a fair length of leg was a pleasing white and unblemished.

"Why, it's Gweneth Skye," said another man.

Bainbridge knew her name. He knew all about her, or as much as he could pick up from the tavern gossips. The spinster Skye made her way in the world tending sheep like most of the others living here, but she lived alone in her humble croft. Alone, except for a few cats. How Bainbridge *loved* cats, especially when combined with a solitary female. Usually the women he picked out for accusation were old, but this one's youth and beauty would work in his favor just as well, if not better. There was always a contingent of respectable harpies—goodwives, that is to say—in any town ready to think the worst of any well-favored, unmarried, and therefore threatening female. They'd nag their husbands into lighting the first fire. Once that milestone was reached, the real frolic would begin.

Gweneth rubbed her arms as though cold and glanced at the row of men gaping at her.

"See, but she's a bold and shameless wench," said Bainbridge, planting his favorite and most fruitful seed. "Given is to the chance she'd gladly seduce any one of you goodly souls to the service of her dark master, if she hasn't been doing so already in the town."

Oh, but that always gave them something to think about. Once he'd introduced the idea of her lustfully preying on their weak physical natures, the men would have her tied to the stake quick as spit before their wives could think to suspect them.

"It has yet to be proved that she is in league with the devil, sir," Percy reminded him.

"Then I will delay no longer." Bainbridge turned full upon the girl, thrusting his face at her. "What is your name?" he roared.

She regarded him with calm eyes, showing not the slightest hint of alarm. "Gweneth Skye," she answered in a clear, church-cool voice. "What's yours?"

Bainbridge blinked. She should have at least flinched at such a vocal assault. "I am," he announced loudly so any villagers with ears pressed to the chamber door could hear without strain, "the Witch-Pricker Bainbridge."

She favored him with a stony face. "Meaning you run about the countryside pricking witches when the fancy takes you? What do you do with all the brats that come of it?"

He rounded on the mayor and his men in time to see their sniggering reaction. That was bad. If he lost control of things at this early point, he never would see his fee of twenty shillings per head.

"Are you very *good* at pricking, Mr. Bainbridge?" she inquired innocently.

"Honest sirs," he said keeping his gaze steadily on his restive audience to better regain his hold of them, "You have just heard for yourselves that this female not only has a lewd mind, lacks the natural womanly virtue of modesty, but she also holds absolutely no respect for authority."

Gweneth Skye made an audible yawn.

"She's ever been modest, sir," said one of them, Cameron by name. "As you've taken away her clothes, it makes that virtue impossible."

"Ah, but there is a good reason, sir. The most infallible way to prove anyone is in the service of the Devil is to find the mark of his filthy claw upon their body, so it was necessary to make the woman ready for just such a search. Since I have much experience at this, I will conduct my query here and now—with your permission, of course."

"With *our* permission, eh? How do you feel about it, Gweneth?"

That was unexpected. Bainbridge hadn't thought she'd have a friend here. Perhaps later, when the time was ripe for it, he could bring an accusation against this Cameron and remove his sympathetic influence. He was a handsome, well-set young bravo, though, and men like that always had friends. It would be a nimble trick, but just possible to play if Bainbridge worked things right. Once the panic had firm hold of them, the hunt took on a life and course of its own.

When that happened, he'd leave this place with full pockets and another tale of success to add to his growing reputation.

"I suppose so," Gweneth replied with an indifferent shrug. "I've nothing to hide."

More laughter. Percy cast a sour glance at the others to quell it, then nodded. "Very well, permission is granted."

Bainbridge swung upon Gweneth and reached toward and her, but she was too quick for him. Her chemise was off this her shoulders and in a crumpled ring at her feet fast as lightning, inspiring a collective gasp from the men and a snarl of baffled annoyance from Bainbridge.

"So there, witch-pricker," she said feet apart and hands on her bare hips. "Are you content now?"

Guffaws and hooting now, but Bainbridge wasn't worried; he'd found what he needed. This smirking wench was headed straight for the flames. First she'd be given the opportunity to name others in her coven, and once that was out of the way then perhaps a jolly barrel roll to finish her off. Yes, pound a few knives between the staves so the sharp points are on the inside, shove her in, hammer the lid shut, then roll her merry-o down a nice, long hill, to burn barrel and all at the bottom. That was *fine* sport, never failed but to rouse up the young fellows of a town, to make trying them want more of the same, the shillings adding up for each witch that they found. . .

Percy cleared his throat. "Mr. Bainbridge? Does the girl bear the Devil's mark?"

"She does, sir."

"Indeed? Are you ready to prove that to the rest of us?"

From his doublet, Bainbridge drew out a small, elongated box. "In a trice, sir, in a very small trice." He opened the box and plucked from it a slender silver object. "As everyone knows, witches cannot abide the touch of silver. Some squeal at the very sight of it."

Gweneth gave no sign she was one of that number. "But it is also well known that the part of the body branded with the devil's mark is wholly without feeling and may be deeply pierced without the witch giving the least cry of pain or bleeding so much as a single drop of blood."

Those gentlemen not still distracted by Gweneth's ample charms managed to nod sagely at this bit of information.

"You will see that when I pierce the Devil's mark on the wench with this silver pin that she will neither give outcry nor will she bleed, providing unquestionable proof of her guilt."

"Let us see the mark first."

Gweneth, disdaining Bainbridge's touch, stepped forward and pointed out a small red patch on her left forearm. "If this is what all the bother is about, then have a close look, sirs. It's no devil's sign, but merely a strawberry blemish I've had since birth. 'Tis likely you've seen such before on others if not on your own selves."

"Do not try to deceive us with your foul master's lies!" cried Bainbridge, clamping one huge hand hard around her arm. Startled, she struggled a moment, then held still, glaring defiance at him. His fingers pinched tightly on her flesh, hard enough to cut off all blood and all feeling. After a moment, when he judged her limb to be suitably numbed, he gently eased the silver pin into the spot.

Gweneth very unexpectedly said, "Ow!" and tore herself violently away. She gave Bainbridge a slap so resounding that it knocked his hat off, then pulled the pin from her arm and threw it on the floor. "You clod-pate bastard!" she snarled, trying to staunch the blood flow.

"It would seem," said Percy, raising his voice to be heard over the robust amusement of his fellows, "that she is not a witch after all, sir."

Bainbridge hadn't quite recovered from the blow—his ears were still ringing—but he wasn't about to give up yet. "She is a witch, and puts on a false show to trick you. 'Twas the silver pin that—"

"The false show I believe, sir, is what *you* are doing. You come into our town, get everyone all frothed up—which is very bad for the liver—about witch-hunting, repeatedly insist you won't take money until you smell out a witch, but as soon as may be, you do manage to accuse someone: an obviously innocent woman."

"Not innocent, I say! But mayhap *you* are bewitched by her, sir. She is a comely wench, after all."

Percy made no reaction to this accusation. Odd. Usually when Bainbridge called *that* one out, the respectable element would go either huffy or fearful, vigorously deny everything, and hurry the proceedings along their normal path, meaning Bainbridge could get on with the business, take his earnings, and leave.

"Oh, bumfay and nonsense," said Cameron impatiently. "Come, Percy, we'll have to do something about him. Can't hang about all night with this."

"I suppose not," Percy said with a sigh. "Well, Mr. Bainbridge, we of Little Evesham-on-the-Wash do judge that the accused, Gweneth Skye, is not a witch and may go free. Your services are no longer welcome here; you may leave as soon as you will."

Bainbridge saw his fee slipping away faster than an oiled snake. "But you cannot make such a judgment!"

"Why not? It's our town."

"Aye, but there're others who'll not be so quick to deny the presence of the Devil in their midst. Word will get out of your laxness in seeking out and punishing heresy—"

"Perhaps it would be best for you to just—"

"If I have to go to the Witch-Finder General himself, I shall. There *is* evil in this place, and if you're not going to purge it, then he will!"

"There's no reasoning with his sort, Percy, and you know it," said

Cameron. "Things have gone too far already."

Percy, rather mournful of countenance, looked at the others. "Are the rest of you in agreement?"

They all nodded, including, surprisingly, Gweneth. She'd not bothered to pull her chemise back on, but for all her base nakedness she didn't look or act in the leastwise vulnerable or shamed.

"One last chance to forget about all this and be on your way, Mr. Bainbridge," said Percy, in a tone of appeal.

"Oh, aye, but I'll be going straight to the Witch-Finder Gen—"

"Yes, yes. Well, you can't say I didn't try." He looked up to the men acting as guards by the door. "Call in the others."

Bainbridge suddenly found himself close surrounded by several of the townspeople. Closest of all, to his shock, was Gweneth, who regarded him with a strange hot gleam in her remarkable eyes.

"I'll go first if you please, Mr. Percy," she said.

"Seeing what he did to your arm, it's only fair."

Bainbridge's world went all soft as her gaze locked onto his. He heard her clear melodious voice speaking right into his mind, telling him all kinds of interesting things, strange things, imparting a feeling of absolute contentment and safety such as he'd never known in all his hard life. She opened the top of his doublet, undid the ties of the shirt beneath, pushed back the small collar. It was wanton, utterly improper, and in front of all these people terribly embarrassing, but he held still for her, so lost in her words of comfort that the presence of the others did not matter.

Then her sweet face went out of view as she leaned close. He felt a profound leap of pleasure in his privy parts as her mouth fastened on his throat. The people behind him held him fast, but he wasn't about to move, not even when her long corner teeth began to grind away at his flesh. He groaned with delight as she broke his skin and started to suck.

" 'Ow is 'e, Gwen?" someone inquired a few moments later.

"Tolerable," she replied, lifting away. The whites of her eyes were gone, flushed blood-red now. "Likes his ale too well for me. Someone else want a turn?"

"Ale, eh? No, thank you, my girl. Used to love the stuff, but now. . ."

"I'll have a try," said Cameron, coming forward.

Gweneth stepped aside for him. To his shame and horror, Bainbridge again offered no struggle as that handsome young man now suckled at the wound she'd made. It was shameful to him because the bliss that seized him was just the same, just as intense, so much so that he soon altogether forgot himself and gave over to the joyance again, moaning.

One by one the others gathered around him had their turn until Bainbridge could no longer stand by himself, and with much kind consideration from his hosts, he was gently carried to the council table and stretched upon it. The room tilted—no, *he* was tilted. Two of them had lifted the end of the table by his feet. A feeble rush of blood went to his head.

"That's better," said Percy, after he'd finished taking his own drink. He did not appear to be quite so morose as before. Blinking hard, Bainbridge could just see them looking down at him like toothy, red-eyed angels at the Last Judgment and finally began to understand the true nature of his mistake.

"If this goes on much longer it's going to get noticed," Percy remarked to Cameron. "*We're* going to get noticed."

"Then perhaps we should do something about this Witch-Finder General person. He's the one behind this mischief."

"I agree with you, and I know we could. The question is *should* we?" Percy shook his head. "The last thing we want is to draw any sort of attention to ourselves."

"It might be worth the risk. If he's made to retire from the field, then perhaps this nonsense will stop, and things will settle down again."

"I wouldn't care to wager on that. You know how people are once they start killing." There was an object in Percy's hands now. It was a sturdy length of wood, charred and fashioned into a sharp point at one end. He idly turned it over and over, his mind obviously on other things. When he noticed Bainbridge staring at it, he whisked it from sight with an apologetic smile. "Best if we let things happen as they should in the rest of the world and just pay mind to our own matters."

"You're usually right about that, but," Cameron gestured at Bainbridge, who was finding it hard to keep his eyes open, "this greedy clot's our third one this year. I think we should make an exception about the Witch-Finder General, He stirs people up and in the wrong way."

"Agreed, but we'll have to be very careful about it if we do anything. Danger of discovery and all that, you know."

"I know." Cameron licked a stray blood drop from his very red lips. "But mind you, danger of discovery aside, they are such a *tasty* lot!"

* * *

Matthew Hopkins of England, the Witch-Finder General, as he liked to call himself, was directly responsible for the torture and deaths of hundreds of men and women in the years 1644-1646. He had many imitators who brought suffering and death to thousands more. There is a story he was finally discovered to be a witch himself when forced to submit to his own swimming test and floated before finally drowning.

However, one of his associates recorded that he died untroubled of conscience in his bed in the summer of 1647 "after a long sickness of Consumption." (Sic) Most scholars of folklore understand that the disease of consumption (tuberculosis) was often seen in past eras as evidence of a vampire preying upon the sufferer.

YOU'LL CATCH YOUR DEATH

Author's Note: *This is the first Vampire Files short, sold to VAMPIRE DETECTIVES from DAW Books, edited by Martin H. Greenberg. Like many of the works in this new collection I've done a rewrite and polish on the original. No writer ever stops tinkering! It takes place a short time after book 5,* FIRE IN THE BLOOD, *and vampire PI Jack Fleming is in a dark, introspective mood. Nothing like a bit of homicide and assault to snap him out of it!*

Chicago, February 1937

I met a terrified girl named Susan at three in the morning on a barren stretch of beach during an ice storm. The isolated location, late hour, and arctic agony blasting off Lake Michigan gave me the reasonable expectation of having the place to myself.

I'd was there to figure out how to live; she was there to die.

* * *

Black water roared against the shore, spray flying and merging with the sleet, stinging my face. Frozen sand cracked under my shoes as I walked. It was made to order for my bleak mood. I'd planned to do this last night, but delayed when the forecast of a storm came over the radio. The worse the weather, the better so far as I was concerned. A good dose of physical misery would shake me up, maybe help me shed the emotional pain.

Things had been rough for the last few nights. Not far from this spot I had killed, again, had come close to being killed, again, and in that damned lake, again. Each day's dose of dreamless oblivion helped distance me from the bad memories, but only an inch at a time. The creeping pace felt like failure.

I'd been the same after the War. Getting shot at, losing friends in an instant when a bullet found them, seeing the influenza murdering more men than the bullets, and countless other horrors taught me all there was to know about cruelty, suffering, stupidity, and senseless death.

Since arriving in Chicago last August I'd wised up to the disturbing fact there's always more where that came from.

In a remarkably brief time I'd been murdered, returned from a watery grave, and delivered payback with interest to my killers. In the months to follow I'd been subjected to and committed even worse crimes. I'd learned that when someone pushed me I could and would push back ten times harder. Literally. A few never got up again.

Like the man who'd had gone into that freezing black lake, never to return. I'd done that.

It didn't bother me as much as I thought it should.

Apparently a chunk of ice had formed in my soul sometime when I'd not been looking. It had nothing to do with my being a vampire. If I thought that to be true then it was time to give up and find some way of bumping myself off. This inner chill was wholly human—and scary.

I could not ignore it: I was *glad* to still be walking around and just might be able to live with the fact that yet another man was dead at my hands. I'd done the world a service with that death. He could stay at the bottom forever with the rest of the slime and good riddance.

I wanted to not know such things about myself, but too late, I was stuck with it.

Now what?

When I'd come back from the War it had been simple: find enough work to support getting a few years of college into my head, get a real job, meet a nice girl. That had worked at the time. I was with other young men in the same situation. We told our stories, mourned our dead, and got drunk. The camaraderie kept most of the nightmares at bay.

I didn't have that now. Yes, I had friends ready to help, but they didn't know what I was going through, not really. It's a hell of a change to wake up dead: no need to breathe except to talk, no heart thumping stolidly away, trapped in a dead body while the sun made its round.

And overshadowing it all was the exquisite physical joy of drinking blood. Not even those closest to me could fully understand that one. Hell, even I found it hard to accept, and I'd had months to get used to it.

As far as I knew, I was the only vampire in Chicago. We're a rare breed. I kept an eye out for others who might also haunt the Stockyards to feed, but without luck. They were either better at keeping their heads down or didn't exist.

You're on your own, Mr. Jack Fleming of Chicago.

Strangely, I found that to be more annoying than intimidating. If I could get knocked flat and come back pissed as hell and swinging, then there was hope. That part was also wholly human, a part I could respect.

Maybe you shouldn't think too hard about this crap.

True. It didn't make me feel better.

It's not like I'd wanted to kill anyone. If—God forbid—I ever got to that point. . .no. Human or vampire, that just wasn't going to happen to me.

Of course I knew better. You just can't anticipate what bad choices lie in the future, but for the present, this would keep me from putting a wooden bullet in my head.

Turning into the slicing wind, I was now able to savor the solitude and the noisy black water. That restless lake was my vast and ignorant ally, enemy, murderer, and midwife, and a great keeper of secrets. It was comfortable with mine.

I'd come to confront demons, hoping a stormy walk where they'd been born would shake them loose, and it had worked. Perhaps some shred of crippling guilt might sneak up on me later, but not tonight.

Drinking a lungful of damp air sharp enough to cut iron, I held it until the edge was gone. Releasing, the wind whisked it from my lips into the endless sky to grow clean and cold once more. I could do the same, spreading my arms, fading from the world until the wind swept my invisible and formless self away.

In this gale I'd soar up the low bluff to the road like a lost balloon and blunder into my car parked on the shoulder. That would send me solid fast enough. Nuts to that. And nuts to standing out here courting frostbite. The harsh weather and lonely location had worked. I'd needed something bigger and stronger than myself to put my life and hard times in perspective. I was going to be all right…or close to it.

Time to head home.

I glanced up and down the wide stretch of beach a last time as though crossing a street. It didn't seem so bleak now. The high restless clouds reflected back pale glow from the city, not that I needed much to see well at night. My changed condition had its compensations, otherwise I'd have missed the figure struggling along the shoreline from the north.

Fisherman? Not at three in the morning in this weather. Fresh air fiend out for a walk? What a crackpot.

Yeah. I know. I should talk.

The distant figure hobbled closer: a woman, on the small side, looking done in as she stumbled over the uneven sand. She wore a simple dark dress and shoes and nothing more. No coat, hat, or gloves. She was hunched forward, arms folded tight to hoard what warmth remained in her slight body.

A dame alone on a beach in this murderous cold—of course something was wrong. Whatever problems I thought I had, hers were worse. I moved toward her.

"Hey, lady, can I help?"

She didn't hear. Distance, roaring wind, and water masked my voice.

Stepping up my pace, I yelled again. She stopped, swaying a little, and looked behind her. The wild wind grabbed her brown hair as she turned, creating a vertical part along the back of her unprotected head.

"Over here," I shouted, waving, moving closer.

She snapped around, clawing hair from her eyes, and stiffened when she caught sight of me. I glimpsed a young face burned white by the cold. Terror and torment flashed in those wide eyes, then she whirled to her right, away from the lake, toward the road, and tried to run. She didn't get far; the sand slowed her too much. I caught up easily, but kept a couple yards between us so as not to scare her more than necessary.

Blocking her path, I called again, my hands palm out and angled down the way you do to calm a spooked animal. She stopped as abruptly as she'd started, gaping at me. She looked crazy, but fear can do that to you.

"Who…?" was all she gasped. She didn't have enough breath to finish the question.

"My name's Jack. Can I help?" I spread my empty hands, trying to look harmless. It seemed to work; she took a half step toward me with an expression like a lost soul who'd just gotten a reprieve from hell. Then a small, hopeless shriek twisted her mouth and made it ugly.

What the—

In utter silence she and the rest of the beach flared into a blaze of hot silver light. The earth bucked once as though to get rid of me and damn near succeeded; I sprawled on its lurching surface.

My hearing swooped back. There was a grunt that might have come from me as I hit the ground, I wasn't sure.

The silver light focused down to an excruciating spot on the back of my skull, pinning me to the sand.

She screamed again, full-throated, anguished. Behind and above me, a man snarled at her to shut up.

"Move, you dumb bitch!" There was raw venom in his tone.

Footfalls, clumsy in the sand. Fading.

He turned me over, cursing under his breath the way other people nervously whistle. He was big and young with a tough jaw in a lean, jaded face. He wore an red plaid hunting jacket and hat that weren't enough to protect him from this kind of cold, but were more than the girl had on.

I'd been struck by wood, recognizing its vivid agony all too well. If he'd hit me with something metal or a rock, I wouldn't be lying paralyzed at his feet, but he'd used wood—probably the stock of the rifle he carried. While I'd been concentrating on the girl, he'd slipped up behind and—

Mugs unused to dishing out violence hit too hard or not hard enough. This large lad slammed down with enough force to kill an ordinary man and yet seemed surprised by the results. My fixed and staring gaze alarmed him.

He didn't know I was different, still awake and aware.

With his teeth, he tore off a glove to feel for a pulse in my neck and swore again when he couldn't find one. I wanted to swear, too. Pain is always worse when you can't give it verbal expression. My head hurt like New Year's morning in hell. Jesus, what had I done to deserve this?

I'd recover. Eventually. Being a night-stalking blood-drinking vampire had some advantages, and healing fast was one of them. Before dawn came this idiot was in for the shock of his life.

Only he wasn't hanging around. The bastard took off, not after the girl, but up toward the road. I moaned inwardly with disgust and tried to move.

Silver light lanced through my brain. Molten pain on the back of my head swelled, threatening to open my skull.

Too soon. Much too soon.

The wind plucked sand from my cheeks; some grains lodged in my eyes. I couldn't even blink. Shit…that burned. Tears clouded my vision, trickling past my temples into my hair; I imagined threads of ice clinging to my skin.

There was nothing I could do until the shock wore off. I'd have to wait it out, unpleasant but—

The man returned. First I heard the air rasping in his throat, then his awkward, irregular footfalls as he came down the rise from the road. He must still have the rifle; its weight would throw off his balance. I picked up the sound of another person with him.

"Here," he said. "He's right here." His voice was high and taut with near-panic. They reached the bottom, stopping a few paces outside my field of view. The bright beam of a flashlight played erratically over me.

"Give me that thing," ordered the newcomer. A woman. She had a more mature voice than the girl I'd encountered. The light jumped as it transferred to a more steady hand.

"I think he's dead," the man told her unhappily.

"Shut up, Lloyd. Cover him," she said.

The woman drew near, cautiously, as though my apparently final stillness might somehow be catching. After a moment she knelt within my limited range, though I couldn't focus well because of the sand and tears. She had the same general look as the man, big and tough. Family resemblance, I thought, the hard jaw softer, but just as distinct. She wore a heavy cloth coat with a fur collar, with a thick scarf tied firmly under her chin. Her expression was as cold as the wind booming off the lake.

She stretched out a hand as though to caress my face. Her fingertips brushed at the tear tracks from my smarting eyes. I wanted to flinch away, but could not. She aimed the flashlight's beam into them again, blinding me.

"Ellie?" His voice was thin. "Is he…?"

She sought the big vein in my throat, pressing hard. My heart beat its last months ago, churning wildly in a final berserk denial of fate before a bullet ripped through it and stopped everything, changed everything.

Ellie withdrew after a few seconds, then worked on the buttons of my overcoat.

"What're you doing?" Lloyd demanded.

A question I might reasonably ask if I'd not guessed. She opened the coat wide and pawed at the clothes beneath. Her head ducked from my dazzled view and lay heavily on my chest, ear flat to my cold skin. She listened for what seemed an excessively long time before straightening.

"You killed him," she concluded. She sounded matter-of-fact, and I wondered at her choice of words. She could have used a more neutral, "He's dead," but had chosen to keep the blame squarely on Lloyd.

He was anything but contrite, to judge by his language. "What'll we do?"

"We don't do anything."

"But he's *dead*."

"You wanta call a cop?"

"You know what I mean."

"Yeah, so think about it. That's probably his car up there off the road. When someone finds him, they'll figure he stopped to pee, slipped on something, and cracked his head. There's nothing to tie him to what we're doing."

"But what about Susan?"

"We go on as before. This could be the last winter storm, we have to use it and finish the job."

"But this guy, suppose the cops—"

"Lloyd, shut the hell up. There's nothing between us and him. He slipped on a rock in the wrong place."

"But—"

"We don't need no witness."

"El—"

"You did the right thing when you hit him."

Like hell, I thought through the pain.

"Now pull yourself together and g—"

"*Will you listen to me?*" he roared. That bought him a moment. "One body on a beach is one thing, but two on the same beach and the cops will know something's wrong. They won't buy two accidents the same night in the same place, dammit."

Ellie must have thought it through. "Okay, I can see that. You got me nervous with all your jumpin' around, so it's hard to think clear. You settle down, and I'll figure out what to do."

"I *know* what to do. We put him in that car and drive him some other place."

"Drive him where?"

"Don't matter. Why's he out here, anyway?"

"How the hell would I know?"

"Did he follow us from the bar? A couple guys were givin' you the eye."

"He wasn't any of them," said Ellie. She snapped off the flashlight. "No one there was this fancy."

"That's a nice coat he's got." He bent to finger my lapels.

She slapped his hand away. "Get it later."

Grunting, he bent to grab my ankles.

"I can do that," she said. "Go find that idiot wife of yours."

"What?"

"Go get Susan before she runs into somebody else!"

Evidently used to taking orders, Lloyd loped away. Ellie glared down at me with scowling displeasure.

She possessed a big, hearty body, strong enough to drag me over the sand and up to the road. With effort she might even hoist me into the car.

She leaned closer; more of her face came into swimming focus: wide-set eyes, narrow nose, shapely lips parted enough to show the edges of her teeth. If she noticed this dead man was making involuntary tears I was a goner. I couldn't take another slam in the skull.

Her bare fingers touched my face again, cold, tickling as she lightly brushed at the sand on my cheeks.

What are you up to, lady? I wondered uncomfortably. Who gets this close to a corpse?

As though she'd heard my thought, she paused, head up for a furtive look in Lloyd's direction. She stood, going out of my range, pacing one way, another, as though searching. Over the wind, I could hear her breath begin to quicken. Maybe a car was coming. Maybe even a cop. A cop would come in handy about now.

No such luck. She returned, kneeling close by my side. The clean line of her neck escaped her coat collar; I was aware of the blood pounding within that healthy, forceful body, the suppressed excitement. With a terrible sinking horror I abruptly understood what drove her heart to such a pitch, what inspired the intense concentration in her expression.

Her gaze dropped to me again, her eyes bright and wicked. If she'd not had a heartbeat I'd have thought she was a vampire herself working up to feeding on a dead man.

One more flick of her nail on my still face. Deliberate.

She smiled and with a deep sigh lay down on me. She stretched full length over me.

Oh, God.

I tried to recoil, to push her away, and could not move. Blinding pain shot through my skull for the effort. Ellie settled firmly into place, pulling her skirt out of the way, legs straddling me.

She licked her lips, wetting them thoroughly. Then she lowered her head. Our mouths touched, sliding over one another, cold as shards of ice on the lake. Her tongue eased in and leisurely worked against mine. It probed and curled and raked over my teeth. It forced itself deeper until I should have gagged; only I couldn't.

I was inert flesh. Dead flesh. Safe to play with, safe to—

The probing turned to suction. She drew hard on my tongue, taking it in her mouth, sucking it like a piece of sweet fruit. She teased and nipped and pulled it out as far as she could before releasing. It dropped free, bulging as though I'd been strangled.

Her hips ground against mine, leg muscles taut with building tension, breasts rubbing my chest. I felt her warmth through our clothes and was revolted.

A soft, gasping moan escaped her; her fingers clawed my shoulders. Her teeth clamped together, turning the moan to a sharp sibilant. Then, with an exaggerated sigh, she emptied her lungs completely and her full weight collapsed on me.

Her returning breath sawed the air. Eyelids drooping, face flushed from the release, she might have been beautiful under different circumstances. With a cold fingertip, she pressed my tongue back where it belonged and kissed me again to seal my lips shut.

"We have a secret," she whispered, ending with a strange little breathy giggle.

I wanted to vomit.

I wanted to tear things apart.

I wanted to goddamn *move*.

Getting off me, Ellie pulled my clothes together and buttoned my coat to make things look right. That finished, she rose, straightened her own clothes and brushed sand from her legs, peering down the beach where Lloyd had gone.

She called his name in an absolutely normal tone. I didn't catch the reply, but she did, and must have found it exasperating. Snarling ripe language, she went after him.

Tears of rage seeped from my gritty eyes. Ellie might have at least closed them, too. Clouds, racing high above my little concerns, swam in and out of focus. The stinging eased, the sand finally washing away. Ages crawled past before I was at last able to blink. I was pathetically grateful for the progress, and at the same time despairing at how long took.

Who were these lunatics? A violator of corpses giving orders, a not too bright lug with a rifle, a half-frozen terrified girl named Susan—apparently his wife—tearing around a supposedly deserted beach at three in the morning. Lloyd and Ellie might not be intending murder, but until I found out otherwise, it seemed a solid assumption. What could the girl have done that made her death necessary?

My guess was nothing. She was some kind of inconvenience and had to be gotten rid of, and they were using the weather to do the dirty work. People always died when winter storms swept through, the cold cutting down the weak and vulnerable the same as any predator. It was no bother to me, but that poor girl wouldn't last. She might already be gone.

My arms suddenly twitched with returning life. Muscles in my legs flexed, a promise of full recovery to come, but I couldn't wait; I had to push things.

Awkward and queasy, I twisted onto my belly, wanting to scream. The world kept spinning after I'd stopped. Silver lights flared, full of pain. Vanishing would have instantly healed me, but it was too soon to try. I was already hovering on the edge of blacking out. Damned wood.

Blood would have helped. It always did when I was hurt. Why the hell hadn't I stopped at the Stockyards on the way over? With my body flushed full of hot red life, the wallop I'd taken might not have affected me as much, and then that sick bitch Ellie wouldn't have—

On the other hand, I'd have missed Susan. A moment either way and I'd be driving home, oblivious to her dying alone in the cold.

I kept seeing her walking, head down, the hope in her eyes when she saw me, that awful fear replacing it—

Come on, it's just a bump on the noggin. You've had worse. Get moving.

Slowly, I bellied over the frozen sand toward the lake. Wounded animals are drawn to water. That described me well enough. Halfway there, I progressed to a crawl, but collapsed just at the shore's edge, dizzy, half-blind, and trying not to whimper. I dipped a hand into the searing cold of free-running water and splashed the last sand from my eyes, swearing with violent sincerity. My face burned as the wind dried it, but I could see again.

Very gently, I slopped water against the swelling lump on the back of my head.

That woke me up—like a five-alarm fire with the bells going off between my ears.

I hissed at the jolt and for a long moment was in too much shock to move. The cure was worse than the injury.

A few eternities later the crippling agony abated in microscopic increments. When the ringing died down, I cautiously peered around. No sign of the others. I managed to get vertical, unsteady but it would serve.

Lloyd had payback coming. I plotted a number of destructive things once I got my hands on him. Topping the list was a new use for that damned wooden rifle stock in relation to his ass. After that, I could toss him in the lake to find out if he knew how to swim.

As for Ellie. . .

I wasn't responsible for her bizarre appetite for private gratification, but she sure as hell could have kept it to herself.

There was a vile taint in my mouth from her kiss. It was imaginary, but I had to get rid of it.

Though absolutely unable to drink anything but blood, I stooped and swilled a huge gulp of lake water and swallowed, knowing what would happen.

The stuff struck the bottom of my gut like a sword. I took another gulp and forced it down. The sword jumped as though alive. Another drink, and it started cutting. I closed my throat off to keep it down.

The sword sliced and twisted, doubling me over with cramp. Then everything came spewing out. I'd wanted to vomit; it was this or carry along the slimy touch of Ellie's lips forever. I needed a physical rejection of what she'd done to me.

I spat the last drops into the lake, regarding the endless stretch of shifting waves. Sky, earth, and water, ancient, but alive. A different kind of life from mine, but wise and tolerant of one man's little troubles. I should hate this place, but couldn't. It was too big for such nonsense.

Rubbing my mouth on my sleeve, I wiped away the last trace of Ellie.

Time to go to work.

Woozy but full of terrible purpose, I trudged toward higher ground, gaining enough height to check the beach. Lloyd was a small figure far, far down the northern end. He moved fast, but erratically, circling and doubling in his tracks. Ellie stood on the road in a spot where she could overlook most of the area. She had the flashlight on and helpfully stabbed its pale beam in Lloyd's direction.

Susan was nowhere in sight. The sickening thought that she'd dropped in her tracks someplace to curl up for a last, freezing sleep kept me going.

I plodded unsteadily back to where I'd fallen. My crumpled and forgotten hat marked the spot. Punching out the dents and sand, I put myself in the girl's place, trying to guess where she might have gone while Ellie and Lloyd had been distracted with me. How much time had that taken? Had it been enough for her to get to the road? It was something I might have tried in hope of flagging down a car or finding cover on the other side.

The city glow reflecting from the clouds was enough that Ellie might spot me crossing the road. She wouldn't see details, but a dark figure in her peripheral view would set her off and bring Lloyd running.

Vanishing was out of the question for the present; my head buzzed painfully. I'd been through this kind of thing before. Too soon and the attempt could injure me further, even knock me unconscious.

I'd have to do things the hard way and wait for the right opportunity.

Lloyd was an unintentional help as his search for Susan took him farther along the beach. Ellie kept even with him, playing the light around. When her back was turned, I topped the rise and sprinted across. The land dipped down again on the other side, but not by much. There was no shelter, just dead grass, gravel, and snow that hadn't melted before the latest cold front blew in. A hundred yards ahead in the middle of a flat, exposed field was a sparse stand of trees. Would Susan have tried for it? I was acutely conscious of the wasted time if I guessed wrong.

My doubts dropped away when I spotted a footprint in a patch of snow. The toe of a woman's shoe pointed right at the trees.

While Ellie faced the beach, I hurried over the open ground, throwing glances over one shoulder along the way. The first sign of her swinging in my direction and I'd have to drop flat. At night she'd see a moving object more easily than a still one.

I made the trees, ducking gratefully into their cover. Evergreens, thank God, with dark, obscuring snow-trimmed branches between me and Ellie's flashlight. I blundered through them, looking for the girl.

She was curled up all right, just as I'd imagined, but not asleep yet. Her legs were drawn tight to her chest, and she shivered like a dozen earthquakes. When she heard me, her breath caught halfway between a sob and a moan.

"It's all right," I told her, just loud enough so she could hear my voice and know I wasn't Lloyd. "I'm here to help." I was afraid she might bolt again, but she looked too cold to move.

Her face was marred by sheer pain. I yanked off my hat tossed it at her. It landed by her feet and she stared, unable to understand.

"Put it on, honey," I said, unbuttoning my coat.

She stiffly obeyed. I shrugged the coat off and got it around her shoulders, threading her thin arms through the sleeves. She didn't say a thing when I rocked her back and swept it under her feet to put the cloth between herself and the ground. It was like hugging a block of ice. I had a wool neck scarf as well and wrapped it around her head to tie the hat down. She looked like a child playing dress up.

"Better," she whispered, the word coming out with difficulty, but laced with gratitude.

"You're Susan? I heard them talking."

A shivering nod.

"Lloyd's your husband?"

Another nod.

"Who's Ellie?"

"His sister."

Nice family. "They want to kill you?"

She moaned again, an affirmative as far as I could tell.

"You know why?"

"Money for me," she murmured cryptically. Then like a child added, "I want to go home."

"As soon as possible. I have to take care of Lloyd and Ellie before I can get to my car."

"I can walk."

"It's too far." I didn't feel good about walking, either. After that dash, my head was ready to float off and explode.

"Won't there be a house?"

"Nothing's close enough. You sit tight and I'll get us a ride. On second thought, move around. Can you do that?"

"Think so."

There was liquor on her breath. Whatever false warmth a drink might have given would have worn off by now. The alcohol would do more harm than good in this cold.

"They try and get you drunk?" I asked, helping her up. She was small; the hem of my coat dragged on the ground.

"Yeah. We went out. Said it was a party for me. Made me drink, but I didn't like it." She couldn't have been more than seventeen, if that much.

"They wanted you to conk out, huh?' I took a few steps with her to keep her steady.

"Guess so. I got sleepy. Didn't wanna drink no more. Kept telling Lloyd I wanted to go home. He wouldn't listen, just laughed."

"What about Elle?'

"She laughed too, but said we should leave. People were staring."

"Then they drove out here?"

"Don't remember. Ellie said I had to take my coat off to get ready for bed. But I was in the truck, not home. Woke up some. Knew something was wrong."

That's for damn sure. We paced and turned, paced and turned. Even when slowed by the trees and the advantages that toughened my body, the icy wind was at last getting to me. "Then you ran away?"

"Pretended to be worse than I was. Told 'em I was gonna be sick. They took me out of the truck. I asked Lloyd for my coat, but he said I'd just mess it up and to hurry. Didn't know where I was, just somewhere by the lake. Somewhere quiet. No lights. No people."

So convenient for Lloyd and Ellie. Get the girl drunk, let her pass out, and eventually she'd freeze to death. Tragic, but understandable in this weather. I could have thrown up again.

"I ran. Lost 'em in the dark. It was so cold."

"I saw you on the beach."

"Thought you were Lloyd, then he come up behind you."

"Yeah, I know all about that part."

"You hurt bad?"

"I'll get by. You said they'd get money for you?"

"Insurance. Lloyd has a thousand dollar policy on me."

"A thousand? He's trying to kill you for—" I bit the rest off. A thousand or a million, it didn't matter.

"Mister, that's all the money in the world," she told me with awed conviction.

To people like Lloyd and Ellie, that was true. Last summer Roosevelt had announced that the depression was over. Maybe for him, but the rest of us weren't seeing much evidence.

"Wish Lloyd hadn't done it," Susan continued, talking more to herself than to me. "Things were getting better. He hadn't hit me for a good week; I thought he'd changed. Even Ellie was being nice. They were going to buy a store, they said, set up a real business. I'd ask where they were going to get the money and they'd just laugh, funnin' me. Then Ellie'd say, 'We're laughing with you, not at you, Susie.' But I didn't know what the joke was. I do now. Wish he hadn't done it."

He was going to wish so too after I got through with him.

"Susan. . .has Lloyd been married before?" The question popped out of nowhere. Some part of my mind was turning things over, trying to draw sense from the brief, but intense, impressions gained from Lloyd and Ellie.

It surprised Susan enough to stop her pacing. "Yeah. He didn't talk about her. He only said. . .said. . .she drowned. A stupid accident when they went fishing."

Or another murder. Or a real accident that inspired him to try repeating it for profit. Had there been other wives?

Susan looked up at me. "How'd you know?"

Then she got it and the realization was the same as if I'd smacked her with a brick. Why hadn't I kicked myself, instead?

"Oh, God," she groaned. "Oh, God."

I pulled her tight. She shuddered, went still, and shuddered some more. No tears. Maybe later, but not now.

"You going to be all right waiting here for a while?" I asked.

"Can't we just walk back to town?" Her voice was dull, thick.

"Not in this weather. I'll go for my car and come for you."

"But he's got his gun."

That was a problem I would try to avoid. "Where's this truck of theirs?" I hadn't noticed it on the road.

"Off the beach. Don't know where. I kept goin' for I donno how long."

"Don't stop. Keep moving here. I'll come back as soon as I can." Real soon. The wind was chewing through my suit like a rabid animal.

She nodded numbly, and I slipped away, pausing at the edge of the trees to check ahead.

Ellie was no longer in sight. She could be with her brother helping his search or sitting in my car, taking advantage of its shelter. I hadn't locked it. Reflections off the windows obscured the interior. I was too much a pessimist to hope she and Lloyd had given up and left.

Damn the lack of cover. All I had were the trees, car, and a line of telephone poles marching grimly out from the city.

I tried to vanish, just as an experiment.

Bad idea. Though I felt an encouraging flutter within, it was overwhelmed by the slam of fresh pain in the back of my head. At some point the scales would shift, and I could relinquish solidity and heal, but not yet.

Susan didn't have time for my recovering body to catch up with the situation and even I was starting to feel the cold. Only one way to fix that.

I dashed straight for my Buick like a ball player for home base, moving faster than any normal man. The best thing for Susan was to get her out quietly then deal with the others some other time.

My car was empty of lurking killers, but I winced opening the door. The keys were still in my overcoat pocket.

Damnation.

A setback, but not a total disaster. I fumbled under the dashboard, intent on making this the fastest hotwiring job in history.

Motion and light in the corner of my eye—some kind of vehicle was coming up fast from the south, headlamps bobbing. They belonged to a battered, open-bed truck. Behind the wheel I recognized the sleek shape of Ellie's scarf-covered head.

Hell. I couldn't get the car started before she reached me. She'd have seen the door hanging open and think it was Susan.

I'd have to confront them sooner or later. Better it's sooner and one at a time. I got out.

Ellie didn't slow until the last second, bringing the truck to a long, sliding halt on its bald tires. The brakes squealed like dying pigs. Her front bumper stopped a foot short of my back fender. Leaving the lights on and the engine running, she hurtled out the door, her expression tense.

She honestly didn't know me at first. I was without my bulky overcoat and standing up, after all.

And I was alive.

It was a pleasure to watch the changes flowing over her face. First the suspicion reserved for any unexpected and unpleasant surprise, then puzzlement, swiftly replaced by sick shock. Finally she showed the dawning that comes when one realizes something has gone really, really wrong with one's world.

She backed a step in reflex, then held her ground, not quite ready to accept that final impossibility. I was—I had to be—a stranger come out of the darkness, maybe a tramp, someone inconvenient who needed to leave. Quickly.

She yelled Lloyd's name, her voice strange and high with imperfectly suppressed alarm. She yelled again. No answer. She gave a little jump when I slammed my half-open door, not once taking my gaze from her. None of this helped my tender head or stirred-up gut. I wanted to be someplace warm and quiet, away from crazy people with their ugly, greedy plans.

Ellie pulled a little revolver from her coat pocket. Her hand shook. She steadied it with her other hand. Wish I'd thought to bring a gun, but I'd not anticipated the need for one just for a walk on the damn beach.

"W-who are you?" she asked, the words dribbling out shaky and not sounding right.

I started grinning. Couldn't help myself, it was too good. "Hello, Ellie. Let's have another kiss."

Her jaw dropped, but nothing audible came out, and that made it much more awful.

I hoped she'd turn and run but instead the gun's muzzle flared and jumped. The explosion was almost too loud to hear. Astonishingly, I felt nothing. Ellie was so spooked that from ten feet away, she completely missed me.

She wouldn't get a second chance.

I ducked around the front of my car, keeping low. Ellie followed, but I moved too fast, preventing her from getting a clear shot. Damn, if I could just vanish.

Five more misses and I could end this. Lloyd would certainly have heard something and be on his way from whatever rock he'd crawled under. Susan didn't have time to spare while I played squirrel tag with her sick sister-in-law.

Ellie wasn't wasting bullets, though. She was smart enough to wait for a clear target.

Skulking around the rear bumper, I glanced across the field. Lloyd shambled toward us. In one hand was his rifle, the other had Susan by the scruff of the neck. She stumbled along, her feet tangling in the flapping hem of my coat. Whenever she fell, Lloyd dragged her up again, hardly slowing his pace, like an adult dealing with a balky child. Her cries sliced the air.

He'd gotten clever and investigated the trees, probably sneaking up while I'd been sidetracked by Susan.

Ellie yelled at him from her cover behind the front fender of the car, waving him closer. He spotted me in the wash of light from the truck's headlamps and sprinted forward. For the moment he'd only see a new threat to be neutralized, not the corpse he'd left on the beach.

Ellie screamed at him to shoot me.

That made him pause, but he must have been used to doing what she told him. He closed up the distance to only twenty feet, released Susan—who immediately scrambled off—and brought up the rifle. I looked straight down the gun barrel. His aim was steady.

I dropped back to put the car between us, remembering Ellie a fraction too late.

I dodged, but not quick enough.

Her shot slammed into my ribs like a train.

I staggered from the impact, dimly hearing Ellie's crow of victory. The gravel shoulder of the road rushed up, but it missed hitting me as gray fog swept over my sight.

Vanishing, finally—

A fiery wrenching turned me inside out—

It's never been painful before.

Too soon after the head injury. No screaming allowed.

Ellie's triumph abruptly departed. She went silent.

Lloyd came up, but could get no reply from her about what had happened.

The wind threatened to carry my otherwise incorporeal self off like a scrap of paper. I reached out with a pseudopod of something that should be my hand and wrapped it around the car's bumper. I craved solidity, but was afraid to re-form. The sharp memory hot nerve being ripped from muscle and bone had me writhing unseen in the air.

I held in place, fighting that memory.

Lloyd and Ellie began to argue, swearing at each other. She couldn't bully her way back to the comfortable world she was used to, the one where dead men don't return then disappear like switching off a light.

Better to deal with a more easily solved problem. Ellie ordered Lloyd to go after Susan. The girl had headed back to the trees and their false safety.

He was reluctant, but Ellie grasped that they could finish the job more easily in that spot. Somewhere quiet. No lights. No people to stop them. No one to take Susan's part.

"They won't find her right away," Ellie told him. "We tell people she got drunk and run off. This'll work better."

That was a world more to her liking, where it's perfectly okay to murder a young girl.

Like skinning a rabbit, they'd strip my coat from Susan's small body and begin the killing process once more. Pain or no pain, I had to help her.

I cautiously eased toward solidity only to find the barrier I expected to hit wasn't there after all.

The grayness resolved into the recognizable shapes of normal reality. Sky, earth, and water mixed with the hard lines of human artifacts. . .and the humans, too.

I paused in the process, holding to a semi-transparent state until I got my bearings.

Lying on the damp gravel, I sat up, my hand gripping the bumper. I was ghostlike, able to see through myself.

So could Ellie and Lloyd.

Their bloodless faces stared down like the world ending.

Ellie brought her gun up and fired, but I felt nothing, only the wind. Unlike a bullet, which drilled through one small spot, wind hit me all over like a sail on a ship.

Ellie fired again. I grinned back and winked. Her confidence visibly collapsed; she blundered against Lloyd trying to get away. Her touch struck him like an electric shock, and now they couldn't move fast enough. They piled into the truck.

I checked across the field for Susan, but the headlight glare blinded my view.

Lloyd tortuously shifted gears; the truck lurched forward. I vanished again, letting the wind take me for a single second. Slamming into the hard metal of the truck's sides, I slid up, over, and tumbled into the open bed behind the cab.

The gears growled as Lloyd abused them; we picked up speed. There was nothing to hold onto; I worked toward the cab, sensing the small rectangle of smooth glass of the back window. More permeable than the metal of the truck's body, I slipped through.

The opening was small, and I hate sieving through glass. It always seems about to break and then doesn't. I pressed beyond its bitter barrier, rolling around like an invisible ball in the jouncing cab, then settling into an upright posture on the creaking seat.

They were on either side of me: Lloyd driving, Ellie tense on my right. She urged him to go faster. Again, he obeyed, struggling with the sluggish gears. Neither noticed the increased chill in the cab, which is a side effect I have in this form.

"You told me he was dead." Lloyd was close to tears.

"He was dead. I *know* he was dead!"

"What was that? You *tell* me! Oh, God. Oh, goddamn it."

"Just shut up!"

"Shut up yourself. What about Susan? What'll we do about her?"

"Leave her."

"But she'll—"

"It don't matter. We don't go back. The hell with her."

"Oh, goddamn it. Oh. shit. What was that?"

A maniac's grin sprouted again on my invisible face. This wasn't the vampire in me wanting payback—this was wholly human. It was dark, and it felt just fine.

I was still grinning when I partially materialized between them. Their panicked yells filled the tight space, their fighting brutal but ineffective. Lloyd's grip on the wheel slipped as he tried to hit me with a poorly aimed fist. Ellie tried to use her gun. Lloyd shrieked at her not to, struggling with the steering. I labored to hold myself in place, their flailing arms passing right through me. The truck went into a long skid as Lloyd jammed the brakes.

Bald tires useless on the slick road, we careened into a sudden patch of deadly silence: a patch of road ice that slewed us like a circus ride. The slender black shape of a telephone pole charged out of the night.

Lloyd hauled the wheel around. The truck slid madly, swayed, bumped, and abruptly spun free. I saw the ground and sky swap places with surprising speed and violence.

Instinct took me away in time, there, but not there, as everything flipped wildly over and over. Their bodies were thrown around, making heavy, meaty thumps. Glass shattered, there was a scream of tearing, crimping steel, the cracking of wood and bones, and with hideous speed it came slamming to a abrupt stop when we struck the pole.

Distantly, I felt the impact. Lloyd's body slammed into mine. . .or where mine should have been had I been solid. I shot clear, wanting no part of this.

The truck motor grunted and died.

Silence.

The wind wailed in my ears like an echo from a seashell.

I was solid, staring at the wreckage from the outside. I wasn't sure how I'd gotten there. Sheer terror, probably.

It was cold. That was why I shivered so hard.

The truck had folded sideways around the stump of the broken pole. The pole's top half lay over the back of the flatbed, lines snapped and trailing on the ground. Shattered glass glinted like new ice.

I did not have to breathe much to get a whiff of it, the bloodsmell. It was everywhere, mixed with the stink of gasoline, which was also everywhere. I kept a prudent distance, in case there was a spark.

Through the twisted frame of the back window I saw the shape of a head. Or it could have been a shoulder. No need to check. I did not want to know.

It moved. Someone inside moaned and coughed. I did not want to, but walked around to the front, glass grinding and snapping into smaller pieces under my shoes.

I hated what I saw through the spider web cracks of the windshield.

Ellie was smashed against the passenger door, her scarf pushed back. I noticed for the first and last time that she had dark hair—or maybe that was the blood making it dark. One of her eyes looked normal, apparently alive and aware and staring at me. The other was lost in a pulpy mess that went through the window.

She shifted a little and the hair shot up on my neck until I realized the motion was not her own but another's. Lloyd was trying to pry free. He couldn't open the driver's door. Desperation gave him inspiration. He brought up a leg and kicked at the cracked windshield.

Shards flew, struck the hood, and skittered off. He made a big enough hole and hunched forward to creep through it. He was covered in blood and lost more as he crawled out. His breathing was harsh, and he favored his ribs. He wheezed and cried and clutched his left arm. The sleeve from his woolen hunting jacket was torn. Most of the blood came from there.

He wormed over the hood, lost balance, and rolled off, hitting the ground like a sandbag. When his breath returned, he started whimpering for help.

I could not bring myself to move toward him.

Footsteps. Another set of lungs. Susan came up, small in my coat. She brushed hair from her eyes.

"No need to see this," I said, stepping between her and the wreck.

She kept coming, not to her husband lying on the shoulder of the road, but to me. I put my arm around her, selfishly glad of her company.

"They dead?" she asked in a clear and quiet voice.

"Ellie's dead. Lloyd needs help. He's bleeding bad." The bloodsmell teased me. "I should make a tourniquet."

"No." she said hollowly.

The belt on my pants would do. I gently pulled from her and started to unbuckle it. Susan's hands fell strongly onto mine.

"I said no, mister."

"But—" Then I read the look on her face. I read her bitter and bright eyes, that crystalline awareness transmitting right into me. Taking a life does that to a person. Despite rules and conscience, there is a terrible primitive joy in payback. I recognized it. She might feel bad later, but for this moment it was right and justified.

Wholly human.

"No," she said. "We don't do nothin'." Her gaze darted from me to the weakly shivering figure of the husband who had betrayed her and no telling how many others.

I sighed. "You sure?'

"Ain't you?" She read my face in turn and looked okay with the answer.

She walked over to her husband, stopping just close enough so he could see her, know her. She seemed taller—or he'd shrunk. "Wish you hadn't done it, Lloyd," she told him. "I was good to you, more'n what you were to me."

Through the pain he looked genuinely puzzled. He could have been too far gone to know what was going on, but my thought was that he had a certain kind of stupidity, the sort that made him incapable of understanding he'd done anything wrong.

"Help me," he whispered.

"You go to hell. You an' her both."

Susan walked back, seeming to diminish with each step until she was normal again, a small young woman, barely past girlhood. She looked up. "Can I go home, now?"

In answer, I took her arm, leading her to my car. It seemed a long walk. My hands were numb. The wind keened harshly, drowning out any small cries Lloyd might have made.

Hell, the way he was bleeding, he wouldn't make it to a hospital. That's what I told myself. That's what I'd tell Susan if she had second thoughts on the drive back.

I got the Buick's door open and hustled her in. The air was cold, but blissfully still, and the interior smelled comfortably of stale tobacco smoke and damp leather, not blood and gasoline. Susan huddled deep in my coat, her thin face tired but peaceful.

"The keys are in the right pocket," I said, almost apologetically.

"Oh." She dug for them, gave them over.

I let the motor run, then got the heater going. Cool, warm, then hot air blew on us.

My hands tingled from it.

The wreck was out of range of the headlights, but I could see it. Lloyd's insignificant figure no longer moved.

Someone would come by, find and clear the mess, break the news to the widow. I'd done my part. Overdone it. I'd not meant to get them killed, just scare them, but things went out of control just that quick.

Cruelty, suffering, stupidity, and senseless death: there was always more where that came from. Push me and I push back ten times harder, and it won't bother me as much as it should. I wasn't sorry for those two and this time I'd salvaged something out of the horror.

I put my car into reverse, turning the wheel. We backed up, facing the lake now. Its shifting black surface went on forever, horizon merging seamlessly with the sky. There was an awful lot of it.

Susan's white lips compressed. "You know something?"

"Tell me."

"When Lloyd took out that insurance policy, he took one out on himself. I guess it was so it wouldn't look funny later on."

"Guess so." I agreed.

"You know something else? He told me that if one of us died in an accident, the insurance would be twice as much."

"Well," I said, hauling the wheel around to take us back to the city, "accidents happen."

IZZY'S SHOE–IN

Author's Note: *Another invitation from friend, author, and editor Carole Nelson Douglas resulted in this non-supernatural romp for* WHITE HOUSE PET DETECTIVES *for Cumberland House. This introduces Izzy DeLeon, fearless girl reporter, who later shares the action with vampires Jack Fleming and Jonathan Barrett in* THE DEVIL YOU KNOW *from Vampwriter Books. Some of the events in this story did occur; a female reporter invaded the Hoover White House disguised as a Girl Scout, and Allen Hoover, the very handsome first son, did keep such pets!*

Washington D.C. 1933

At five-foot nothing in her flats, Izzy DeLeon was the tallest of the troop of Girl Scouts milling around her. At twenty-one, she was the oldest by ten years, but trusted that her uniform would provide all the cover required for her invasion of the White House. There was safety in numbers, and she counted four full troops gathered by the iron gates awaiting admittance to the grounds. In a hundred girls the chances of her being spotted as the cuckoo in the nest were small so long as she kept moving.

It worked well; she circulated unobtrusively until the adults called for order and they smartly marched toward the sweeping curved steps to the South Portico. There they stood under the big awnings. Scant protection against the summer sun, Izzy felt the oppressive heat sucking the energy from her. The other girls were as lively as sparrows.

A gap-toothed waif of eleven gave Izzy a curious stare. For an instant she wondered if she'd missed a spot when scrubbing her face clean of makeup. Would a lingering hint of powder or lip rouge betray her?

The girl said, "That's a lot of badges."

Izzy glanced down at her shoulder sash, which was covered with a number of merit badges, all of which held little meaning to her. Where she'd grown up you didn't earn such things, you learned those skills to survive. "I guess so," she admitted, pitching her voice high.

"You got a cold?" the girl asked sharply. The troops were here to sing patriotic songs to the president and first lady. Any Scout with a cold would be unwelcome in the chorus.

Shaking her head vehemently, Izzy then shrugged. "I talk funny, but sing just fine. My mom told me."

The girl looked dubious and turned away. Good. The less contact the better. Izzy had flattened her chest with bandaging, thrust her size six feet into size five shoes, and bitten her nails down to look right for the part. The uniform offered perfect protection from the adults, but not kids. One observant little girl could raise the alarm and bring an arrest, and Izzy doubted her editor would be sympathetic enough to bail her out.

Stick to fashion stories, Isabelle. You're female, write female-stuff, he'd say, then send her off to cover a daffodil festival.

Teeth grinding, she dutifully cranked out copy since that was her job, but craved more exciting, germane, interesting things to write. She'd not fought her way out of the lazy swamps of Florida, earned a scholarship, and worked hand over fist for a journalism degree merely to make a living. Izzy planned to be more than a reporter; she would be a world-famous journalist, destined for honors, applause, and the respect of her peers. . .if she could just get away from daffodil festivals.

The only way to prove herself worthy of an assignment with real meat to it was to go hunting for one. But strangely, in the heart of Washington, D.C., in the swirl of politics and the passionate vituperations resulting from the clash of one party against another, that proved frustratingly difficult. Requests to interview a senator or congressman always landed her in a parlor with their wives, sipping tea. While she managed to make enough copy to please her editor, those encounters had no national importance. The few wives who would speak to her were concerned with matters like raising children in the public eye or promoting their favorite charity or sharing a special fudge recipe. Laudable, but not what Izzy wanted.

But when Herbert Hoover took office, she mounted a more active campaign on the White House itself. Even if she was fobbed off to Mrs. Hoover, Izzy would count that as a victory. Lou Henry Hoover was highly well-educated and had traveled around the world with her engineer husband. She spoke five languages fluently, had received medals from other countries for her charity work, survived the Boxer Rebellion—surely *she* would have tales with real weight to share with the American public.

But after five months of sending in requests, it became more clear with each polite refusal (carefully typed on White House stationery and personally signed by the first lady) that though a gracious hostess, Mrs. Hoover shunned the spotlight. She was inordinately modest about her many accomplishments—unless it had to do with the Girl Scouts.

Having served as their national president, raising membership from a ten thousand to over a million girls, she was always ready to talk about *them*—and entertain them. Thus Izzy hatched her idea to get inside the great sanctum. A routine interview with one of the Scout mistresses sparked things. The woman had proudly mentioned her troop's upcoming visit to the White House and the whole scheme burst upon Izzy's mind in a flash brilliant enough to impress even Edison.

She bought the largest-sized scout uniform available at a local department store, a tight fit but manageable. With the connivance of a slightly-misled janitor at the local Girl Scout Little House (she bitterly claimed her baby sister had forgotten *everything*), Izzy got the Scout's schedule, and managed to blend in with the crowd of girls. There had been a few hair-raising moments when she thought one or another of the Scout mistresses had spotted her, but nothing came of it. As she'd hoped, each must have thought her to be with a different troop. Now she was only yards from the great oval of the Blue Room. Even coming this far would make a story, but to finally get inside. . .there. . .she spotted movement beyond the sheer curtains of the French doors: people shifting about in the shaded interior.

The girls were restless with curiosity, some jumping up to better see. Izzy missed Mrs. Hoover's entrance; had she opened the doors for herself or did one of her four secretaries do the honors or was it a servant? Details like that made interesting color.

Wearing a cotton dress with a green tint similar to the uniforms, Mrs. Hoover greeted the Scout leaders and troops with a friendly smile. She had pronounced eyebrows and a firm mouth. The smile softened her looks, made her more homey. She proceeded them, leading the way through the Blue Room to a wide, pillar-lined hall, taking their giddy, shuffling parade to the right. They ended up in the vast East Room where their concert would take place. Everyone milled through. Though told to be quiet and respectful of the surroundings, the girls gave in to enthusiasm, squealing at the wide echoing indoor space and impressive decor, which included a grand piano. It was irresistible.

Izzy hung back as much as she dared, torn between the desire to hear everything Mrs. Hoover might utter and the need to look into forbidden areas. Her chance came when a dozen girls surged toward the piano. The room resonated with loud and inexpert renderings—no, make that random pounding upon the presidential keys, much to the delight of the rest. More squeals, screams, and laughter followed. Control was quickly restored, but by then Izzy had slipped unobtrusively through a door at the southern end while the servants and Secret Service man were distracted.

She was in the Green Room, and it was thankfully empty. She counted herself lucky to find it unlocked, but part of the Scouts' visit was to include a tour of the public areas. It must have been left open in anticipation of that. Faced with a choice of five doors, she picked the opposite left, which brought her back to the Blue Room. Some people were talking at the northernmost end of its oval, but no one paid attention as she hurried across and breached the entry to the Red Room.

It was empty, lighted by the hot summer sunshine pouring through the open windows. Izzy found herself breathless more from excitement than the muggy afternoon heat. She'd hardly hoped to make it this far. If nothing else she would have an excellent piece about the lack of security within the house. Wouldn't that bowl everyone over? The nation's president vulnerable in the most famous house in America. . .of course he wasn't in this part at the moment, but there was a principle at stake here, and under the byline of Isabelle DeLeon, Izzy would triumphantly shout it forth.

She wanted more to shout about, though, and to do that required gaining the private quarters in the floors above. What little she knew of the public areas led her to believe access could be made through first the State, then the Family dining rooms. Heart in throat, she set forth.

* * *

As with many situations in life, it is far easier to land oneself into a predicament than to make a successful extraction from its coils. Thus did Izzy find herself crouched down behind a bamboo chair surrounded by potted palm trees in a sunlit room that should have been an upstairs hall. This wasn't on the diagram Izzy had gotten from one of her contacts, a maid who had worked here during the Coolidge administration.

Mrs. Hoover had been inordinately busy redecorating the family's private quarters, and she possessed firm, if exotic ideas on how to go about it. The fan-shaped floor-to-ceiling window at the far end washed the room with light, mitigated only slightly by an enormous bird cage full of frantically chirping canaries. Palms, ferns, and other plants loomed everywhere, bamboo furniture rested comfortably on a rattan rug, oriental vases dotted tables and shelves. It would have been a most pleasant place to relax under any other circumstances, but Izzy in her overly tight shoes and constricting, hot uniform was anything but comfortable. She was supposed to be gathering news to report, not hiding like a fugitive.

She had just been sneaking into what she thought was the president's own bedroom when a bell abruptly sounded, making three sharp rings. Not knowing if it was a fire drill or a burglar alarm, Izzy let instinct take charge and ran quick as scat down the hall, diving for the nearest cover. For the last half hour she had to hold perfectly still, which was becoming more difficult with the cramps shooting up her legs from her outraged feet. She pushed the pain aside, though, for the president himself sat within spitting distance of her hiding place. He and another man were in deep conversation, and though close, Izzy had to strain to hear them. President Hoover was infamous for mumbling into his tie, and she only caught bits and pieces of their talk.

"You'll want to watch yourself, Allan," he said. "I've warned them time and again that buying on margin will lead to trouble. I hope you'll advise your school friends to not take any such risks on the market."

The reply was lost to her, the other man was busy with the canaries, and their noise and flapping swallowed his words. Izzy couldn't believe her luck. Not only was she overhearing the president, but a private chat between the president and his son, Allan. Wasn't he supposed to be at Harvard? He must have come home for a summer visit.

"—really can't say much about anything, or they'll think you're trying to influence the market through me," he replied over his shoulder. Izzy could barely make out his form through the palm fronds. He looked to be as tall as his father, nearly six feet, and would probably fill out into the same strong huskiness.

The president lighted a large cigar, releasing a cloud of blue smoke. "I know. We must never misuse this office, or even appear to misuse it. It only fuels those Democrat-controlled rags. The way they natter on, you'd think I was the Communist. The things I'm accused of is beyond tolerance. Lies, all of it rubbish and lies."

"Don't pay any mind to them," said Allan. "They're always going to be whipping up something out of nothing to sell more papers. Criticism is the best way to do it. You'd think those blasted hack reporters had better things to do with their time—like going after that bootlegging Kennedy clan."

Both men chuckled.

Izzy set her mouth, used to the endless fencing match that existed between politicians and the press. Each needed the other much the same as a rhinoceros needed a tick bird. Well, she was anything but some hack reporter. She was after a *real* story, and this was it: the Hoovers at home, a warm, caring family of true public servants with a disliking for Democrats, Communists. . .and a predilection for canaries.

And dogs. Uh-oh. Izzy froze even more, if that was possible, as a couple of completely gigantic police dogs bounded into the room, one dark, the other white. Allan and his father greeted them, but some kind of altercation broke out with the animals, requiring sharp commands from both men to restore order.

"They just don't mix," said Mr. Hoover. "Better get those two out of here."

"The dogs?"

"Yes, the dogs, at least they know how to obey a command. They work better with the help around here than your herd."

Allan laughed and set about removing the dogs, calling for King Tut and Snowboy to make a quick exit. They reluctantly complied. Izzy breathed soft relief; she'd been terrified the dogs would sense her presence.

"I don't know how you manage to keep those things from eating everything in sight," Hoover admonished.

"They're not so much trouble," said Allan. "You should be around when I toss them raw chicken. Mother would stop complaining about how fast you eat."

"Just mind that they don't scare the servants."

"If I ever see any. Every time a bell goes off around here they're popping into closets like jack-in-the boxes in reverse. I wish you'd get over your dislike of dealing with them. They're only just people after all."

His father mumbled something in which the word *privacy* figured, and Allan Hoover chuckled.

So that explained the ringing alarm and why she'd not seen anyone. Izzy had no need to take notes, this was too extraordinary to forget.

"How did your downstairs concert go?" Allan asked.

"Fine, fine. Cheered your mother up. She does enjoy seeing all those bright faces. I think she'd like to be president of them again, given the chance, but she knows she can do more from here than any other place. Oh, get off, you overgrown newt! Look at that. He's trying to eat my shoe!"

Allan laughed again—what a cheerful sort he was—and there was a dragging sound followed by a strange hissing. "You behave yourself. You want the Secret Service to shoot you?"

Izzy didn't think he was addressing his father, so there must have been someone or something else in the room, perhaps another dog. But what kind of a mutt hissed?

There was a knock. Mr. Hoover bade them enter, though there was no real door, just a gap in a series of partitions meant to create a space removed from the hall. Like the rest of the room there was a heavy Oriental influence to the panels, reflecting the family's travels in China.

A man came in, tall, dark suit, with a grim and hasty manner. "Mr. President, we think there may be an intruder in the house."

"What? Another one?" Mr. Hoover sounded more annoyed than disturbed at the prospect. Izzy held her breath.

"Yes, sir. We're doing a room-by-room search, but for your own safety it has been suggested that you remove to your office. We've checked and cleared it."

"I was going back to work regardless," said the president. "It never stops, unless Mrs. Hoover insists on a pause for me."

Allan murmured agreement. "I suppose those Scouts will be gone by now. Mother will want to tell one of us about it. Shall I volunteer?"

"By all means, but she'll have you stuffing envelopes with her secretaries if you're not nimble enough to escape."

"I don't mind. This way I can keep an eye on her."

His father said something to the effect that Mrs. Hoover was more than capable of keeping an eye on herself. Neither seemed concerned about the intruder, which Izzy took for a favorable sign. If by horrible chance she got caught they might laugh it off. Might. She didn't think so. Not really. One of the men must have hit a signal button, for a moment later three rings sounded and they all left.

And not a moment too soon. Izzy flopped flat on the floor, stretching her legs in agony, and unsuccessfully stifled a sneeze caused by the haze of presidential cigar smoke. It came out as a kind of truncated squeak that closed up her ears. She worked her jaw until her hearing popped back to normal, then rubbed her abused shank muscles until she felt the pins and needles of returning circulation. She was tempted to remove her painful shoes before they permanently crippled her toes, but didn't dare as she'd never force them back on again. Since quitting her backwoods home for the city her feet had grown soft, used to the protection of shiny leather and fashionable heels. Her days of running barefoot through grass and swamp were long over.

She noticed an odd slithery sound, like something dragging roughly over the rug. Peeking above the chair she looked accusingly at the canaries. They seemed agitated yet at the same time were oddly silent. What a mess they made, feathers and seed husks everywhere. But enough of them, Izzy had to figure a way out of this place. The Secret Service itself was on to her presence, though lord knew how they found it out. Perhaps one of the people in the Blue Room mentioned seeing a straying Girl Scout wandering around. How could they deem that to be a threat to the president? No matter. She had her story; it was past time to skedaddle.

Her legs mostly functional again, she slowly rose from behind the plants, heading toward the opening to look at the rest of the hall.

Drat. Now there were servants moving around, one of them anyway. How to sneak past him? The longer she waited, the worse it would get. Maybe her Scout cover would hold. If she worked herself into some tears and pretended she'd gotten lost from her troop. . .what was the troop leader's name? Monahan or Houlihan? Not important, the White House staff would hardly know the difference. Bluff, bluff, bluff until blue in the face, then run like crazy, that was the way to get a story.

The butler was out of sight. Good, she could slip downstairs and only have to haul out the lost little girl ruse as a last resort.

She eased from behind the partition—

—And came face-to-face with an extremely surprised-looking man wearing dark livery. He had been on the other side of the hall and somehow silently moved up on her. Izzy hadn't wanted to test herself so soon. She'd not even gotten her tears in place.

He never gave her the chance. Before she could move or speak he hauled one arm back and smartly slammed his fist against the side of her head.

Light lanced behind her eyes and she dropped straight down, face in the rug, utterly unable to move.

Izzy never quite lost consciousness, but lay quite breathless and stunned. Instead of raising a hue and cry at discovering the intruder, the servant bolted off. She managed to crack one eyelid enough to mark his retreating feet. Oh, God, now she was in for it. Was trespassing at the White House a federal crime? She should have researched that. Maybe she could write a series about women in prison. Was there a women's federal prison?

Think, Isabelle. They'd not clapped the irons on yet, nor had he sounded the alarm. She could hide in a closet until the ringing in her skull died down. Ow-ow-owwwww. What a bully, hitting a helpless little Girl Scout. If she laid eyes on him again she'd show him a thing or three. . .

Ring-ring.

That hadn't come from inside her head. The president must be on his way back. Being found sprawled over the hall rug was too ignominious to be endured. She'd go back to her hiding place. Maybe later she could duck into a bedroom, knot sheets together, and escape out a window after dark.

Footsteps. Coming her way.

She managed to get to her knees, and crept past the partitions to her spot behind the palms. She was dizzy, and her head hurt miserably.

Flat on the floor again. How had that happened? Oh, her feet hurt, her head, ouch-ouch; she'd better get a bonus for this one, if she ever got away. Quiet, she had to be very, very quiet.

She put her back to a wall, drawing her knees up, the easier to cradle her pounding head. The president's lingering cigar smoke made her sick to her stomach. Adding to the misery was another smell mingling with the smoke, a strangely familiar musk, redolent of the swamp. There must be some stagnant water in one of the vases, left forgotten after the removal of its flowers. Phew, what a stink.

Two more people seemed to be in the room. Allan Hoover and a woman in the midst of expressing her irritation. Izzy recognized the first lady's voice.

"It's ridiculous," she said. "How can we not be safe in our own home surrounded by guards?"

"They're just being cautious, Mother. Once they've combed the house you can get back to work."

"I've much too much to do to leave it for long. There's mail to answer, dinner invitations to send, and those calling cards will want a reply."

"You don't have to respond to all of them."

"Allan, that's not proper or polite. Those people took the trouble to come and leave their cards, the least we can do is show our appreciation. This is their house, too."

"I think many leave a card just to get your autograph on the house stationery."

"You have a poor opinion of the people of this country."

"The people are just fine, it's the politicians we want to watch out for."

"Oh, Allan." But there was affection in her tone. "Just let your father hear that."

"I'm certain he would agree."

Despite her nausea, Izzy still took mental notes, albeit with the suspicion that she could just possibly be dreaming. A bang on the head might do terrible things to one's brain, creating hallucinations. Had she imagined that butler? Where had he gotten himself?

"Have they cleared this floor yet?" Mrs. Hoover asked.

Allan went to the opening. "They're still looking around. It shouldn't be too long."

"Please tell them to hurry. There aren't that many places to search. Certainly no closets to speak of." That sounded like a pet grievance of hers. A house this huge with no closets? Unthinkable.

"Not yet, anyway. Any day now I expect you to start tearing into the walls."

"The place needs shaking up. Never did I see such a drab old barn in my life. I don't know how Mrs. Coolidge stood it, and she was always so ill here. Poor thing should have gotten more sunshine. That would have set her right. Always worked well for you two boys."

"Yes, Mother." Allan left, calling to someone in the distance, then went off.

He was gone for longer than the first lady had patience to wait. Izzy heard Mrs. Hoover give an audible sigh, then follow her son.

Izzy wondered if now would be the best time to show herself. After hearing a mother's affectionate talk with her son, Izzy began to realize how she might feel having an uninvited stranger eavesdropping in her house. This had gone too far. Time to stop no matter the consequences. They might go light on her. Surely if Mrs. Hoover heard a personal appeal to her well-known humanitarian instincts, along with a groveling apology. . .

But Izzy couldn't do that. The bash in the head had her going silly. Good heavens, she was tougher than this. She could stick it out a little longer. Besides, this was likely the safest place to hide. She'd wait, escape, and then apologize. Anonymously. From a distance. Chicago, maybe. She could do stories on Al Capone. Unless they fobbed her off to Mrs. Capone.

Izzy blinked herself alert to the present, not the future. Yes, she could stick it out, but this seemed to be a favorite gathering spot for the family; what else might she overhear? Personal talk was the bread and butter of the yellow press, but she had higher standards than that. Human interest was acceptable, but one had to draw a line. And what if the dogs were brought in again? They'd been distracted earlier, but sooner or later they'd sniff her out. Perhaps they wouldn't eat her—she'd been raised with coon hounds and knew how to stall excited canines until help arrived—but avoiding the circus would be best for all concerned.

Conscience wanted her to do otherwise, though. Common sense said that throwing herself on the first lady's mercy would be better than explaining things to the Secret Service. Those fellows were uncommonly serious. All right, well and good. Isabelle DeLeon, soon to be a former member of the Washington press would emerge, confess, and apologize. Besides, it would put everyone's mind at rest about the so-called intruder. No bomb-throwing Bolsheviks, no Communists, just one diminutive reporter with more enthusiasm than wisdom.

Decision made, Izzy unsteadily emerged from her bolt hole. At least now she could get rid of these awful shoes, though on second thought it might not be the right sort of behavior to display before this well-bred crowd. She didn't think Mrs. Hoover would approve of people walking about in socks.

Smothering a groan for her feet and head, Izzy started toward the opening. Mrs. Hoover was in conversation with others from the sound of things. Servants, perhaps? Though from that bell-ringing earlier the clear-the-halls signal applied to her as well as her husband.

Then Izzy saw that darn butler again. Where had he come from? What in heaven's name had he been doing waiting around in this room the whole time she'd wrestled with her conscience? Now he'd spoil everything by giving away her presence before she was ready. She had to get to Mrs. Hoover first.

Izzy shot forward, beating him to the hall, then halted cold in her tracks, frozen with absolute shock.

Just ahead of her, moving at a quick pace for its size, was an honest-to-God *alligator*.

It couldn't be a hallucination, not with that stagnant water smell. How in heaven's name had that monster gotten here?

The answer could wait. It was heading straight for the first lady, long mouth gaping wide, and she seemed quite unaware of its threat.

Without thinking, Izzy launched bodily toward the thing. It was nearly as long as she was tall, but she knew how to deal with the varmints. She and her brothers had pulled more than one of them out of the hen house. If you were strong enough you could grab the tail and haul backwards, and if quick enough, jump clear before the head whipped around to bite off anything important. Izzy was quick, but lacked the muscle power for heavy hauling.

Instead, she landed on the reptile in a flying tackle, pushing down hard with all of her ninety-nine pounds and clamping her small hands onto its snout. The beast had a fearsome bite, but first it had to get its jaws open. Preventing that took surprisingly little effort. However, the rest of its body was pure muscle, especially the tail. She wrapped her legs around the gator just as it bucked and rolled, twisting with outrage. Izzy knew she would tire before it did and unashamedly shouted for help, hoping the Secret Service would shoot only it and not her.

"Run, Mrs. Hoover!" she put in for good measure. "I've got it! *Run!*"

Mrs. Hoover did not run, and in fact looked remarkably calm about the whole business, calling for her son. "Allan, will you please remove this reptile from that poor girl?"

The gator had other ideas and twisted again, violently thrashing until it was on top. She tried to hold it firm, but its great head began to get away from her, which could be deadly. She felt the shape of the teeth under her fingers; one slash from those in the right place would cut to the bone and beyond.

Then a man stepped into her field of view, made a successful grab at the snout, and pulled the thing right from her. He danced backward with it, nearly blundering into a Secret Service agent brandishing a gun.

"Shoot it!" Izzy yelled.

"No!" the man yelled back. He was Allan Hoover and seemed much taller from Izzy's low vantage point. In very quick order he had the gator under control. He charged toward the partitioned end of the hall, and released the thing, skipping away in time to avoid getting whacked by the tail. Her brothers couldn't have done better. Young Hoover puffed, grinned, and shook his rumpled suit back into place.

"He's going to be mad for awhile," he said. "We better stay out of there until he settles down."

"Allan, I think it's time you put that beast in a zoo."

"Oh, Mother, he's not even half grown yet. He behaves so long as people don't surprise him." He glowered down at Izzy, but failed at truly intimidating her. After wrestling with an alligator she didn't think very much else would.

Goodness, but he was handsomer than his photos. His cleft chin was more pronounced than his father's, and he had his mother's forthright eyebrows. All in all, an impressive combination.

"Don't go scaring the chid," said Mrs. Hoover. "She's been through enough."

"I'm all right," Izzy ventured. She started to pick herself up—how many hours had she been on the floor today?—but the agent with the gun came forward.

"Don't move," he ordered, sighting down its short muzzle at her.

Izzy had no intention of arguing with him, but Mrs. Hoover did. "Do put that away, Mr. Borden. I'll take care of this."

"Sorry, ma'am. Orders."

"I said to put that away." She did not raise her voice, but there was a note in it that would brook no argument. She wasn't used to repeating herself, this was *her* house, and in domestic matters she was in full charge of it. All that in half a dozen words combined with a slight lifting of her chin. Light flickered off her eyeglass lenses, concealing some of her expression, but none of her dynamism. The agent wavered. "Use your head, Mr. Borden, this little girl thought she was saving me from being eaten alive. Isn't that right, dear?"

Izzy nodded. Could her disheveled Scout disguise be working? Probably not. Mrs. Hoover seemed the type not to miss much. Allan Hoover had begun to smile. Or was that a smirk? Going suddenly red, Izzy yanked her skirt down to a more socially acceptable level.

"But, ma'am—" agent Borden looked unhappy, reluctant to abandon his protective instincts.

"Report it to the appropriate party," said Mrs. Hoover. "In the meantime, I'll look into this. Allan, she seems in need of help."

Allan readily stepped forward and assisted Izzy to her feet. Ow, they were still in agony, and she was still sick; the aftermath of the fight left her shaking from unused adrenaline.

"Are you injured?" he asked, supporting her.

"The gator didn't hurt me, it was that butler who hit me in the head."

"What butler?"

"One of the butlers or footmen or someone socked me one in the noggin," she said. "Then he ran off."

Allan looked at the agent. "I think she's seen your intruder, Mr. Borden."

"Where?" Borden demanded.

Izzy waved toward the sun room. "He was in there a minute ago."

"The Palm Court?"

This time Mrs. Hoover did not demure. When Borden gestured decisively toward the other end of the hall and some stairs, she went without a word. Allan, also silent, followed, helping Izzy limp along. She was too slow for him, though, so he swept her up just like that and carried her down. She was too surprised to protest. Besides, it was very nice to be in the strong arms of a handsome young man, made her glad she wasn't really a Girl Scout.

Borden shouted, and a number of men in dark suits bounded upstairs. At the lower landing several more surrounded the Hoovers, leading them away. Someone had forgotten to ring the signal bells to warn of the first lady's approach. Two maids carrying linens were caught flatfooted by the quick-moving parade and hurriedly ducked around a corner. Izzy hoped they wouldn't get into trouble. That would hardly be fair.

They finally came to something resembling a sitting room, but without windows and only one door. Izzy wondered if it might have originally been a storage cupboard converted to a waiting area. Borden shut them in with one of his men and rushed outside to see to other duties.

Allan set Izzy down on one of the chairs. It must have been a leftover from Lincoln's day, it had the look, and she became conscious that she was not only disheveled, but smelled strongly of alligator. Ugh.

"Felling better?" he asked.

"Very much," she lied. "Thank you, and I owe you both a huge apology."

"Why don't you tell us your name first?" suggested Mrs. Hoover, taking a chair opposite. "Then you can explain the details behind your apology. Are you or have you ever been a Girl Scout?"

Izzy winced, having collected the instant impression that the first lady would be as rankled by the misuse of this uniform as any military man upon seeing an undeserving civilian masquerading in full officer's kit. Wrestling another alligator would be preferable to this particular accounting, that or getting shot by the Secret Service. She could make a run for it. The man by the door would cut her down point-blank. . .but no. Izzy had already resolved to bare all, but for that butler spoiling things.

Besides, these shoes made running quite impossible.

She offered a weak smile, squirmed, gave her name, and began talking, starting with her desire to get an interview to her impersonation idea, to her misinterpretation of the gator's intentions. It was explained to her that the beast had indeed been looking for food, but seeking out Allan to give it some, not to make a meal of the first lady.

"Father will be none too pleased," Allan said, referring to the business of the interview and the eavesdropping. Izzy had apologized frequently and sincerely.

"He won't be the only one," agreed Mrs. Hoover. "However, Miss DeLeon exhibited a remarkable turn of wit and nerve to get so far, and then to leap so boldly upon that great reptile. . ."

Allan's smile returned briefly. "That was smooth. Miss DeLeon, you're the only female I've ever met who wasn't terrified to shrieking at the very sight of my pets. That puts you ahead of a number of men, too."

"Pets?" she squeaked. While growing up Izzy had had to deal with occasional gator incursions. They were a sometimes dangerous nuisance and more often than not turned into the family's dinner depending on who had the gun that day, but certainly nothing you'd want to keep as a pet. A coon hound was much more practical. "You have more than one?"

"I've matched set. A Mr. Cornell Woolley gave them to me a few years ago when we lived on S Street. They were whizzer. I was the only boy in the whole town with my very own alligators."

From that perspective his enthusiasm for the distinction was understandable. Mrs. Hoover's expression was reserved, but it was clear she was holding back her private opinion concerning Mr. Woolley's questionable generosity. "Allan still keeps them in the bathtubs at night. It's a wonder we have any servants left."

Allan seemed used to this particular observation. "They're better than the Marines. In all that time on S Street, were we ever worried over burglars?"

"No, just finding ourselves short of a cook some morning, whether she departed in the night of her own accord or had been untimely consumed. But we are losing the point. What are we to do with you, Miss DeLeon?"

Izzy had a number of proposals, all of which ended with her being free to leave the grounds, never to return. She would gratefully totter home, tender her resignation to the paper, and hop the first train to New York or Chicago where things were safer. So far as she knew, no gators roamed free in the houses of the rich and refined there. And after this debacle, interviewing the likes of Al Capone would be far less fatiguing or perilous. But Izzy never got the chance to voice her ideas; Borden returned.

"Are we free to leave?" Mrs. Hoover asked him.

"Sorry, ma'am, no."

"You've still not found him?"

"We have and we haven't."

She raised her brows, inquiring.

"We made a search of the house and rounded up every man in servant clothing. Some are new to the general staff, but all are known to each other and the house usher. If this miss would make an identification of the culprit we can clear it up right away."

"I only got a glimpse," said Izzy.

"Miss, you are in very serious trouble. The best way to ameliorate things is to cooperate with us."

"At least give it a try," said Allan. "Shall I carry you again?"

If his mother had not been looking on with a shrewd eye Izzy might have taken him up on that. "I can manage now." Biting back the shoe discomfort she stood, but had a genuine need to lean on his arm.

They went to a wide hall, the equivalent of the one on the floor above, but with majestic pillars marching down its length. What a grand impression it must make on visiting heads of state. Izzy felt a swell of pride to have her country represented in such a beautiful manner. Between the pillars on one side nearly twenty men in servant livery were gathered, looking remarkably alike except for the dark faces of the Negroes. With a jar, Izzy noticed that to a man, they were all exactly the same height.

"The one who hit me was white," she whispered to Borden.

At a word from him the ranks were thinned. The men dismissed from the line-up—for that was what it looked like—were slow to leave, obviously curious to know what was going on. Mrs. Hoover took off her glasses and twirled them. They instantly departed.

"Which one?" asked Borden.

Izzy checked each remaining face, none were remotely familiar. In a fit of inspiration she examined their trouser knees for signs of crawling around. Last she inspected their shoes, and finally shook her head. "I'm sorry, but he's not here. The man I saw had old, worn-down heels. He'd polished his shoes, but there was too much scuffing to cover up the damage."

"Good eye for detail," said Allan. "Miss DeLeon should be working for you. Well, if he's not here, then he's still upstairs. Is my father is safe?"

"Yes, Mr. Hoover. I doubled the number of men around him. They're alert for trouble."

"The man may still be on the same floor," said Mrs. Hoover. "Just in a very good hiding place. I trust you looked under the beds in the family quarters?"

"Yes, Mrs. Hoover." Borden seemed unpiqued at having so basic a point raised. "We will check all over again."

"The windows are wide open with this heat. Perhaps he made an exit by that means."

"From so high up?" asked Izzy, then remembered she'd planned a similar escape using knotted sheets. "It could be possible that. . ."

"What?"

"Well, something Mr. Hoover said about not having burglars at your previous residence. I'd been hiding a very long time in that sunny room."

"The Palm Court?"

"Yes, and the alligators were there the whole while?"

Allan nodded. "They like to sun themselves. It scares the canaries, though."

"I think they scared more than the birds. If this man got up to the Palm Court, hid himself, then realized he was sharing his bushwhacking blind with a pair of gators—"

"He'd have been too terrified himself to move. Oh, this is smooth! I think you have it. Mr. Borden, let's go hunting."

"Sir, I can't allow you to—"

"Bother that, follow me!"

Allan charged up the stairs, Borden and his men hastened after, and sore feet or no, Izzy charged too, since no one told her to stay put. Mrs. Hoover called after her son, but to no avail. Perhaps he'd been so quick to go in order to prevent parental restraint.

Izzy had to hang onto the hand rail at the top; she wasn't quite up to her best yet, but wanted a prime location to watch.

Borden reclaimed enough of his authority to compel young Hoover to hang back a sensible distance. Two men were doing their best to stand in front of him while Borden and two others made their way cautiously toward the dividing panels.

"Don't shoot my alligators," said Allan in a very low voice, pitched to carry only a few feet.

Borden gave no sign of acknowledgement, his whole attention focused on listening. All Izzy heard were the birds, singing and flapping in their big cage. She inched forward. Just inside the Palm Court lay one of the gators. Its tail toward them, its head was partly turned. Evidently it was aware of Borden's presence. He hesitated. Though protecting the president required flinging himself between his charge and assailants, dealing with a testy alligator was likely not a normal part of his job duties.

Getting an idea, Izzy took off her shoes. Oh, dear lord, that felt good, but she couldn't pause to enjoy the exquisite relief. She said *psst*. Borden turned. She motioned for him to move to one side. He got her intent and stepped clear. Izzy had the eye and arm for throwing things, and the official Girl Scout footwear was a very sturdy, heavy item, built for tough use. Izzy made use of it by a hard and, as it turned out, accurate throw at the gator's head.

The gator snapped irritably at the object as it bounced off its flat skull.

Izzy threw the remained shoe, this time so it landed past the snout. The thing scrabbled after, snapping it up like a prize.

With the way clear, Borden and his men entered the court, guns ready. Izzy held her breath and could tell Allan did the same. No one moved for a moment, then Borden emerged, disappointment on his face.

"No one's there, sir," he said to Allan.

"My alligator." Allan moved past them. "If he swallows that shoe it could kill him."

Saving the gator was not Borden's concern, but Izzy felt a touch of responsibility. She followed Allan into the Palm Court. It was bright and hot compared to the dim hall, the light dazzling her. Allan was on his knees straddling his pet's back. As if from long practice, he grabbed the alligator's jaws and pulled them apart like a lion tamer.

"Would you retrieve your shoe, Miss DeLeon?" he asked.

Izzy didn't like to risk getting her arm bitten off if his grip slipped, but she couldn't flinch now. The shoe was hanging half way out, anyway. She snagged it up and backed away.

"Watch out, there's the other one," Allan advised.

Turning, Izzy saw the second gator approaching from the other side of the room, attracted by the activity. "Maybe you'd better feed them," she said.

"Yes, then they might forgive me for all the abuse they've been through." Allan released his hold and jumped back. "Perhaps we can—" He stopped, staring at something behind Izzy. She whirled. A man clambered through the open window. He had firm hold of a thick, knotted rope that extended upward. Apparently he'd just climbed down from the roof.

Without thinking, Izzy aimed and threw again. Her official Scout shoe smashed square into the side of his head. Allan yelled for help, then tackled the reeling man. Secret Service agents rushed in; there was a mad scuffle for about four seconds, then everything went quiet. The man was lying face to the floor and handcuffed. Allan Hoover, puffing a bit, stood.

"Whizzer!" he said, grinning at Izzy, then looked down at the captive. "Who are you?"

"I have an appointment with the President," the man stated. His voice was muffled, his mouth partly imbedded in the rattan rug.

"I think not. People with appointments don't lurk, and *you* were lurking."

"I was trying to get away from those monsters! Kept me from my duty half the day!"

"For that they will get extra chicken. Sounds like his pot is cracked, Mr. Borden."

"We'll find out for certain, sir." Borden, who had been part of the rescue mob, now supervised the man's removal. "This miss needs to come along, too." He put a hand on Izzy's arm.

Allan Hoover removed it. "I'll vouch for her, Mr. Borden."

"But, sir, she—"

"I know, but Mother and I will look into it. I'm satisfied she meant no harm. On the contrary, she and my alligators have endeavored to do your job."

"I'll have to make a report, sir."

"Looking forward to reading it, if Father allows it. Come, Miss DeLeon. Let's get your other shoe before my pets eat it."

In the hall, Izzy padded along, shoes in hand. Mrs. Hoover waited by lower landing, staring after the agents as they led the intruder away. He spoke rapidly about his missed appointment with the president.

"Dear me, if he'd just left a calling card he'd have gotten an invitation to one of our receptions," she said. She looked at Izzy. "Well, Miss DeLeon, what are we to do with you? As a staunch supporter of the Constitution I cannot curtail freedom of speech as represented by the press, but—"

Izzy raised a conciliatory hand. "Not to worry, Mrs. Hoover. This is a heck of a—I mean a great story, but I'd rather forget it ever happened. I promise to respect your privacy and that of your family for as long as I live. My word of honor as a not-quite-Girl Scout."

Mrs. Hoover blinked a few times, digesting this, and looked at Allan, who nodded. "Then your word is good enough for me, Miss DeLeon. I think you should leave now, but I will expect you back here this evening. We serve dinner at eight sharp."

Izzy felt a case of shock coming on.

"That is, if you're up to it?"

"I. . .yes! I'll be here!" No bump on the head would keep her away.

"Very good. Allan, see that she gets a ride. Good day, Miss DeLeon." Mrs. Hoover left them.

"Dinner," Izzy breathed. Had she heard right?

Allan shrugged. "My parents never eat alone unless it's their anniversary. This is Mother's way of thanking you for your help and providing you with a safe story to write. Wait 'til my father hears this."

Oh, this was wonderful. . .terrific. . .whizzer. "Dinner at the White House!" Saying it aloud made it more real.

"You'll enjoy it. Can't say that I always do." He took her arm, leading her gently off. "Don't quote me, but this big old barn has always given me the willies." So said a man who kept alligators for pets. He gestured back toward them. "Seems to agree with *those* two, though. . ."

THE QUICK WAY DOWN

Author's Note: *The original version of this 5,000- word Vampire Files story sold to DAW Books for their anthology MOB MAGIC. I tweaked and expanded things, so consider this 8,000-word version to be "the director's cut." Here we get to see a bit more of the working relationship between vampire Jack Fleming and gang boss "Northside Gordy."*

Chicago, May 1937

Gordy Weems trudged up to my table, his phlegmatic face showing a subdued combination of annoyance and disgust, which was as angry as I'd ever seen him. "I got a stiff in the men's john." he stated.

I refrained from making an obvious joke. He was too serious. The Nightcrawler Club, of which he was the owner and where I was presently seated, was a class operation; bodies in the washroom were not normal despite Gordy's reputation. Sure, he ran a very large hunk of Chicago's underworld territory, but he was too careful and smart to bump anyone off in his own yard—not so he'd get caught, anyway.

"Natural causes?" I knew the answer, but had to ask.

"A pill in the heart. I figure a .22. There's not much blood. When his tie's in place, it hides the hole."

I had no curiosity to ask how he'd determined that detail. "Who?"

"Alby Cornish."

"You're kidding."

But Gordy is no kidder.

"Damn."

Alby was—or had been—an up-and-coming boxer being groomed for more important fights. He'd been able to throw a right that could knock down a barn and known how to take a dive and make it look real. A number of big shots would be unhappy about his demise.

Gordy would get the blame.

He turned his head slightly, making sure no one was close enough to eavesdrop. He'd have done that before speaking in the first place. This told me how nervous he was. "Alby was here all evening with that singer, Ruthie Phillips. They were living it up pretty good until about an hour ago."

"What happened an hour ago?"

"Ruthie's boyfriend caught them."

No need to say more. Ruthie Phillips tight as a tick with Soldier Burton, a tougher-than-average mug who got the moniker for his uncanny ability to march from courtrooms free and clear of all charges, if not of all suspicion. He started out as an enforcer during Prohibition and now ran a string of bookie joints. I could guess that he'd taken Ruthie to the fights one time too many, and the sight of Alby's sweaty, well-muscled body had made an impression on her.

Gordy snorted. "The bouncers said everything looked okay. Nobody made a fuss. Ruthie took off, leaving Cornish and Burton at the table. They talked and had drinks, watched some of the show, then went to the lobby. I figure they stopped in the toilet for a leak, and Burton popped him during the drum finale."

The club's band had a hell of a drummer. Between his work and the blare of the horn section during that number Burton could have fired a cannon and no one would have noticed.

"I need help, Fleming," Gordy said.

Now I was surprised. He was a man more used to ordering up help, not asking for it. "You got it, but you have ten other guys who can move a body just as easy as me."

"Yeah, but they don't need to know about this and be talking to the wrong people. Soldier Burton's got big ideas. He's been trying to bite pieces off my territory for over a year now. It's no accident he left Cornish here. He wants to put me in Dutch with the New York bosses. Short odds are that he's already called the cops."

The drum finale had been about five minutes ago. "We better get the lead out, then."

He nodded once, and I boosted from my regular table on the third tier overlooking the stage and followed him to the plush lobby.

"Where was the wash room attendant?" I asked, pitching my voice low and casual.

"On break, getting a sandwich. When a show's playing, not many get up to use the john, so he takes a minute. Tonight he comes back, finds what he found, and tells me about it."

"Will he spill to anyone else?"

"He'll keep shut. Likes his job too much. He's taking another break. A long one."

The men's room was fancy: pale-veined black marble floors, gold-plated faucets. You expected the water flowing out of them to be perfumed. There was only one patron now, just drying his hands. We waited for him to leave, then Gordy went to the last stall and pushed the door wide. Alby Cornish was slumped on the toilet seat, legs splayed and arms dangling, looking asleep, but definitely not breathing. He'd had a fighter's beaten-up face, but was dressed sharp as a Broadway hoofer.

Gordy had been right about the tie hiding the bullet hole, but I caught the tang of fresh blood the instant we walked in. I don't breathe regularly, but drew in air to speak and got the scent. It teased at me, as it always did, the way the smell of baking bread used to before I'd been killed last summer. Unlike Alby, I got over being dead, trading it for being undead. It has its advantages, if you're not squeamish.

I'd fed earlier that night at the Union Stockyards, so my corner teeth stayed a normal length, but regardless of that the sight of Alby's pathetic remains would have dispelled any hunger. Damn, he looked young. I tried not to wonder if he had family somewhere, a mother with a heart to break when she got the news. I tried, but was not successful. That's why I would not do well as one of Gordy's employees: unlike the others I had empathy and too much imagination.

I caught Gordy looking at me and knew he was reading things in my face.

"Sorry, kid."

"I know." I owed Gordy favors; he owed me favors. Neither of us kept track, but this wasn't about paying what's owed. When a friend calls for help, you be stand-up and help him, even if it costs a piece of your soul.

"If there was any other way—"

"We pretend he's drunk?" I asked, because we shouldn't waste time.

"Yeah."

"Where do we take him? The lake?" Gordy had an efficient means of getting rid of inconvenient corpses, though I never asked for details. I could infer efficiency, since the mugs he disappeared never surfaced again.

"To Soldier Burton's place."

"Wha—?"

"He wanted to make trouble for me. It's gonna bounce right back on him."

No need to ask for an explanation, I'd find out soon enough, unless the cops interrupted us.

We lurched from the john with Alby between, his limp arms hauled chummily around our shoulders. God, he was still warm.

A few of the regulars in the lobby bar saw us dragging him past and hooted at his inability to hold his liquor. A couple of the bouncers looked our way, but Gordy waved them off, saying he'd handle things. We collected Alby's hat from the check desk and jammed it on his head. It made him look more like a foolish drunk than a dead man.

We got him out into the muggy heat of an early summer night. Even the breeze off the nearby lake was no help at clearing the close air. Bloodsmell rose thick from Alby's corpse, throwing me off stride as we took him down the steps.

"Cops," I said, spotting a radio car as it turned onto the far end of the street. "C'mon, my buggy's just over here."

Even as we shoved Alby into the backseat of my Buick, the prowl car pulled up and both uniforms got out, hands on their guns, skepticism on their faces. Apparently they'd been told what to expect.

Gordy straightened to his full height, which was considerable, and waited. He made no outward show, but I could tell he was dangerously tense. His heartbeat was loud to my sensitive ears. There was a chance he could simply buy these two off, but it would give them a hold on him.

"Lemme handle it," I said out the side of my mouth.

His gaze flicked sharply at me, and he made a very tiny grunting sound.

"Evening, officers." I moved to the left so I was under the full glare of a street lamp. What I planned required light enough for them to see me. "Is there a problem?"

Two minutes later they drove off, calling in to report a false alarm. I'd learned their dispatcher sent them to the Nightcrawler to check an anonymous tip about a body on the premises. Then it was just a matter of persuading them that a drunk with a grudge had wanted to make trouble. Gordy and I got in my car and took a another route to get clear.

"How do you do that?" he asked, sparing a glance out the back window for the cops' receding taillights.

"Native talent." It hurt my head, especially behind my eyes. I'd hypnotized the cops faster than a stage magician. "It comes with the condition."

"Along with the blood-drinking and vanishing act?" Gordy knew all about me being a vampire.

"Yeah."

"Jeeze." He'd seen me do my special evil-eye whammy on people before, but was still impressed. I asked for directions to Soldier Burton's place. He gave them, and then settled back in silence for the rest of the ride.

I knew he had a high regard for my other, less exotic qualities, like being able to keep my mouth shut. Since making it clear I had no interest involving myself in his business and possessing my own reasons to avoid official notice, he trusted me to a degree that was considered unwise by his peers.

We'd met last August, soon after my murder at the hands of another gangster. At one point while under orders from his boss, Gordy had tried to beat information out of me, but I didn't hold that against him. It's a tough world. Besides, after what I'd been put through—dying and coming back—a couple fists in the gut were a cakewalk. Over the course of a few rough jams we'd developed an odd sort of friendship and mutual respect. That's why I didn't think twice about helping him move a corpse halfway across Chicago. If he'd dispatched the man himself I'd not have done it, but in that case Gordy would never have asked me in the first place.

I parked in a dark spot by the service door to ten stories of swank apartment building and cut the motor. Gordy's plan was simple: Get what was left of Alby Cornish up to the penthouse where Burton lived, then call the cops.

"I know a homicide dick who's been itching to lock up Burton for years," Gordy said.

Good enough for me. I could now see another reason why I was along: He needed me to get in. I vanished and slipped through the crack between the threshold and the locked doors, which would only open from the inside.

Once in, I pushed on the bar and Gordy strolled past, carrying Alby's two hundred thirty pounds on one shoulder with apparent ease. We found the service elevator and took it to the top without encountering anyone.

"Wouldn't it be better if Alby were actually in the apartment?" I asked.

"It would, so long as you don't get caught."

"Fat chance."

I did my vanishing act again, this time slipping under the servant's entry to reappear in a dim kitchen, which was cleaned up for the night and empty. The place was quiet; Soldier Burton was probably off making an alibi for himself. I edged the door open and told Gordy I'd take it from there.

"You don't have to."

"It's being practical. If someone walks in I can get scarce, you can't. Go down to the car, find a phone, then call your tame cop to come over. I'll be gone by the time he arrives with the cavalry."

A reasonable man, he handed the body over, along with the hat. If it weren't so damned macabre, the whole thing would have struck me as being a fraternity house prank. Things were too serious, though. I could feel the dead man's weight right down to my core. Not an hour ago he'd been leading a crooked, but fairly harmless life, having a good time with a pretty girl. Now he was a piece of meat heading for the coroner's knife.

I kept in mind that the man who had so casually created that meat was somewhere close.

I'd hoped to find a bathroom and prop Alby on the toilet, but leaving him at the kitchen table would be good enough. Gingerly pulling a chair out, I seated him in it, and damned if he didn't lapse into the same sprawling posture as in the club's washroom stall. I placed the hat on his head at a jaunty angle, thinking he wouldn't mind.

His killer would pay—and I had no reason to doubt Gordy's line of reasoning or his word. Sure, he and Burton had a stew going between them over territory, but from what I knew of it, Burton was more annoyance than threat. This business had just upped the ante. Too bad for him that Gordy was a sharper player and had an ace like me in the hole.

Then the kitchen light flicked on. I jumped half a block, startled by a new player in the game.

Facing me was a blond angel: soft curves under a satin bathrobe, with a look on her kisser that declared her to be tougher than a keg of nails. Before I fully registered its presence, the revolver in her dainty pink hand spat viciously in my direction, and burning pain exploded above my left knee. My leg stopped working. I pitched over, clutching fire, bleeding, and cursing.

She didn't say anything that I noticed; I was too busy trying to stay solid. The lead had gone right though my thigh. The holes were knitting up. The process was fast, but damned painful. My usual reaction to a bad hurt is to vanish, which would instantly heal me, but it didn't seem a good idea to give in to it while angel-girl was watching. I was in no state to try hypnotizing her. When I was this mad I could snap minds like twigs.

"Ruthie? What the hell are you doing?" A man's startled voice called from farther inside the flat, accompanied by approaching footsteps.

"What do you think? I told you I heard something." Ruthie Phillips, for I recognized her now, rounded on someone behind her. "You jerk! You said you took care of Alby!"

"I *did* take care of him, honey. What's—" The man came within view and stopped short to gape at me wounded on his tiled floor and Alby at the table gradually going into rigor. Returning the favor, I took in a handsome, no-nonsense mug with about forty years' worth of strong-armed living behind it: Soldier Burton, in bathrobe and slippers, his hair combed and his razor thin mustache unblurred by stubble. If he and Ruthie had been in the sack, they'd been damned tidy about it. "Who the hell are you?"

I didn't feel like talking except for more profanity, which I determinedly stifled. What an interesting bit of useless information about myself: I wasn't in the habit of swearing in front of women, even when they shot me.

Ruthie broke the silence. "He's one of Gordy's. Hangs around the club like he owns it. Dates their headliner, Bobbi. She talks about him like he's the Second Coming or something."

Burton glared down. "Did Gordy put you up to this?"

I assumed he meant my dumping Alby on the premises. I didn't feel like answering that one either and continued to hold my leg, plowing inch by inch through the fiery pain. It slowly—far too slowly—receded.

"What do we do with him?' she asked.

"Lemme think." Burton frowned mightily.

I looked at the woman. "Why'd you want to bump poor Alby?"

Her sweet-looking bee-stung lips curled into a sour sneer. "We both did. The dumb lug didn't dive when he was supposed to and cost us plenty in the—"

"Can it," said Burton sharply. "He don't need to know anything."

"Does it matter? You're not letting him go, are you?'

"Of course not. What's your story, ace? Bring Alby here, then ring the cops?"

"A favor for a favor," I said as cheerfully as I could manage, given the state of my leg. "They should be here pretty soon, too."

"Dammit." But Burton didn't seem that upset. He must have finished thinking. "Okay, doll, cover this punk while I carry Alby."

"Carry him where?"

"The roof. You—" he snarled at me. "On your feet and walk."

My blood was everywhere; Ruthie's bullet had clipped me good; I'd lost plenty before putting pressure on with my fingers. Had I been a normal human I wouldn't have been up to moving. Instead, I peeled myself off the floor, taking my time because I was dizzy. Another stop at the Stockyards later tonight would be necessary—if these two allowed me to leave. I didn't think they would.

Now that I was calmer I speculated about hypnotizing them same as the cops, but there was a booze smell from them which would hamper any effort I made in that direction. Two at once with booze was always tricky. One or the other might pick up that something was off and object.

I limped out under Ruthie's eagle eye. She kept far enough back so I couldn't lunge for her. Not that I'd try; she looked more than ready to pop my other leg. My condition made me fast enough, but I was curious as to how they planned to get out of their mess. A body and a guy dripping red all over their floors would need a hell of an explanation.

Burton was powerfully built, but grunted under Alby's weight. He took small fast steps to the service hall and hit the elevator button. It was a long wait for the cage since Gordy had taken it to the ground floor. The doors finally parted, and we crowded in.

They hadn't noticed that my bleeding had stopped. I was healed up now, skin, bone, and muscle like new. Too bad I couldn't say the same for my ruined pants.

The doors parted to hot, humid air blowing strongly from the lake. It was no cooler up here than on the street far below. Ruthie urged me out, and I went, continuing with the limping gag. Burton dropped Alby, then got behind me and snaked his arm around my neck, pulling hard. I was taller, but he had the balance and dragged me backward toward the low wall that marked the edge of the roof. I let him get away with it for the moment. If my curiosity hadn't been up I'd have turned and folded him in two the wrong way.

"Don't do anything stupid and I won't snap your neck," he told me.

"Grrhg," I said agreeably.

We were the highest building for several surrounding blocks. Whatever he had planned would be untroubled by witnesses.

"Ruthie, get the bullets out of the gun."

"What?"

"Just do it."

She grumbled but did it. "Now what?"

"Put the gun in his hand. I want his prints all over it."

She grinned, liking the idea. I reluctantly cooperated but made a mess of it, smearing my bloodied fingers on the gun's surface. Even the FBI wouldn't pick up anything useful from it, but I planned not to let things go that far.

Ruthie, holding the gun by the satin sash of her bathrobe, was busy putting rounds back in their chambers. She clicked the barrel into place on the frame, and turned it so the two empty shells were in the right position for having just been fired. Smart, smart girl, but she'd forgotten about her own prints on the bullets. Interesting that Burton didn't remind her about them.

"What's this about?" I asked, when the pressure eased slightly on my windpipe.

"That's for the cops to figure."

"You want them to think I scragged Alby? Why would I do that?"

"As a favor to your boss, Gordy."

"The DA won't buy that as a motive," I said, hoping to hear more. "I'll walk free of this one."

Amusement was in his voice as he spoke into my ear. "I don't think so."

I wouldn't like whatever would come next. I'd sensed the tension in his body. He was braced for resistance. He had no idea just how much.

"Hey, big boy!" Ruthie called out, her voice a biting command to look her way.

I was just dumb enough to fall for it.

She'd opened the satin bathrobe wide, treating me to a full view of a luscious and beautifully naked body. Alive or undead, a man's going to pause in surprise and be off guard for an instant.

Which was all Burton needed.

With terrible speed and strength he wrenched my head around with his big, competent hands. A nasty, loud snap seemingly inside my ears surprised me, then all feeling died below my neck. My head lolled as my weight shifted, and the world spun, sickening, insane.

If I'd been breathing I'd have gagged and begun suffocating.

I could not move. It was like those last moments before I conked out for the day on my home earth. A heavy involuntary paralysis takes over, and until I learned not to fight it, the feeling was horribly unpleasant.

But the timing was wrong. Dawn was hours and hours away.

He broke my neck. The son of a bitch broke my neck!

I was released and dropped bonelessly to the rough surface of the roof. It should have hurt, but I couldn't feel anything.

Ruthie giggled, a bubbling, full-throated sound of absolute glee. Two dead men in front of her was funny.

"Hey. . .big boy. . ." She threw herself into Burton's arms. He caught her hard, and they indulged in some heavy breathing for a moment until he pushed her away.

"He said the cops were coming, doll."

"We can do it before they get here. Come on."

"Soon as I'm done."

"I'll die if I don't, come on!"

I heard a slap, followed by a surprised gasp—then she giggled again, ready for a second round.

"You won't die," he said. "Get to the kitchen. Clean up the blood. Cut up this belt thing and flush the pieces. Cut 'em small. I'll be down to help in a minute. Do the back hall, too. Got it?"

She grumbled, but went away, taking the service elevator.

Burton must have suspected I'd smeared the prints on the gun. As soon as Ruthie was gone, he dropped to one knee and wrapped my fingers around the grip and trigger, then aimed and fired anther bullet into Alby's body. I couldn't stop him. I was unresisting dead meat.

This was how he marched out of court. He paid attention to details. The cops were to think Alby and I had a beef going, I got shot, took the gun away and shot Alby in turn. But how to account for my broken neck? I didn't want to find out.

Why can't I vanish?

I tried, frantic, not caring if he saw, but nothing happened. The nerves thatransmitted my will to my body weren't working. I had no sense of up or down, no feeling for the position I lay in, no pain, no numbness; beyond the casing of my skull the world went on without my influence.

Burton grunted with effort as he moved me. My fixed gaze took in a scenery change I couldn't immediately understand—sheer, gibbering panic prevented it. A street, buildings. . .at the wrong angles, my arms flopping and swinging above my head. . .

Down, I'm looking down.

I understood too late. He let go, and my inert form tumbled over the low wall.

It takes only a few seconds for a man to drop a hundred feet.

Flashes of things impressed on my shrieking mind: rush of air, windows tearing past, sidewalk coming up. The appalling, helpless agony of falling.

I would hit headfirst.

* * *

Shreds of a consciousness flowed toward a centrality until enough pooled together to be marginally cognizant.

Outside of time, it dreamed, but without comprehension for the harsh emotions that churned and rolled over the remains of memory. The creatures engendering such terrors were alien things imprisoned in solid flesh, enslaved by the needs of that form. They hungered and lusted to feed and propagate, creating more of their kind.

Efficient predators, they killed threats to their kind.

I was a threat.

They'd killed me.

But awareness of a self began to reluctantly return.

After some struggle, it recalled that it had a name:

I had been Jack Fleming, once a reporter; I hung out in a gangster's club and did odd jobs for him and another friend. I had a girl who was too good for me, and survived a hell of a lot of nonsense since my murder last August. I used to enjoy beer; then I drank blood. It kept the machine running. It kept the machine running and able to do wholly impossible things. . .like. . .like. . .

* * *

I forgot, waking up fully.

Screaming.

Not much to it without air in my lungs, and when I got a breath I clamped my jaw tight. For all I knew something worse might happen. I needed to hear it coming.

There is the impossible, and then there is the unthinkable. I flinched from the latter, which is what I'd just been through.

At some point—which my mind had thankfully blotted out—my ability to vanish had taken over and saved me. Whether that had happened before or after my body impacted did not matter. It was sufficient to know it had worked, and I was sobbing inside with gratitude.

Some while later I tried to move. In this disjointed and shocky aftermath I got the impression my amorphous self was spread like a pancake over a large portion of flat surface, a portion larger than I had any right to cover. That was new.

I pushed off the worrisome thought that I might not be able to recover.

It took no small measure of concentration to persuade my invisible self to pull back into its normal shape—whatever that might be. I could not see in this form, only knew what felt right and what felt wrong.

When instinct told me I was ready for it, I cautiously resumed solidity.

I stood upright, unsteady, but on whole legs. No bullet holes, no shattered bones, everything in place. I didn't have so much as a bruise for a souvenir, no damage at all unless you counted the stark terror still shrieking through my rattled brain like a tornado.

Trembling uncontrollably, I sat down, leaning my back against a building to let the excess adrenaline run its course. There was no point rushing things. It would wear off, given time. A few decades should do it.

After a while, I bothered to get my bearings: the service alley, no one in sight at this hour, no sign of Gordy. He was probably waiting down the block wondering what was keeping me. I was glad to help a friend in need, but goddammit, there is a limit.

The shakes gradually passed.

I found my feet in time to step into a shadow, avoiding notice from a cruising prowl car. It was closely followed by another vehicle with a similar radio antenna. I thought I knew the driver. If he was who I thought he was, then Gordy did indeed have clout in the city, and Soldier Burton had been a fool to make a challenge.

Things would not run his planned course, though. Alby Cornish was out of sight on the roof. With my body gone from the alley there was no reason for people to look up to see where I'd fallen from. Alby could be there for weeks before anyone found him…unless Burton went back and dumped him in some other spot inconvenient to Gordy and started the mess all over again.

Burton's intended conclusion to explain the broken neck—that I'd shot Alby, then in a fit of remorse stepped off the roof for a hard landing—had been scotched. He'd would think up something else once he found out I wasn't where he'd dropped me, and he would march free.

To hell with that.

However much I wanted to go home and have a nervous collapse I'd have to put it off. The only way for Burton to get his proper payback required that I stick around and get some payback of my own.

Had Burton looked over the side to see how my body had landed? Of course he would, but the spot would be pitch black from his vantage. He might stroll out later to check, but not while the cops were watching.

The gun, with my prints, was still on the roof, too.

I had to get up there.

The fastest method was the way I'd come down, but just thinking about it made me sick. My ordeal with gravity aside, I hated heights even on my best night. After this incident I expected the condition to get worse.

Fear is a healthy emotion. It keeps you from doing stupid things like walking too near a fatal edge; something I would not choose to do, but Burton had taken that choice from me. With his history he'd taken choices from a lot of others. Alby and I were just the most recent.

Crap, I wasn't letting that bastard keep the upper hand. I had to get over that hurdle, so to speak, right now, before it got too high to jump.

At least by vanishing I didn't have to look down. I felt the press of the wind on what should have been my back as I floated up the side of the building. The brickwork seemed to go on forever. I didn't dare go semi-transparent to check my progress. Pushing things this far was all I could ask of myself. If I drifted to the side and rose at an angle, I still rose; the wall would end at some point.

With vast relief I bumbled over the lip of the low barrier and onto the tar and gravel surface to go solid again.

Burton and Ruthie were gone. Nothing else had changed.

Poor Alby—I was feeling quite sorry for him by now—was exactly where he'd been dropped, and so was the gun. I picked it up and wiped it clean on my already ruined clothes, then wrapped a handkerchief around it.

Gun in my pocket and hoisting Alby over one shoulder, I found the service stairs. The elevator would be too noisy to call up from the penthouse level. I went down one flight, put him next to the kitchen entry of Burton's flat, and listened at the door.

Voices. I'd been right: Gordy had influence. One of the cops was Lieutenant Nick Blair of homicide. He was good at his job. We'd had a few run-ins, and he didn't like me despite my evil-eye whammy suggestions to the contrary.

Hypnosis was quirky and sometimes unreliable. A suggestion that went along with a person's normal inclinations, such as I done with the cops outside the club, could last for weeks, even months. A suggestion directly opposed to one's inclinations did not last long at all.

Lieutenant Blair was one of those with a decidedly mistrustful attitude toward me; I never could make him a friend. There was no point trying to change him, so I did my best to keep out of his way. I didn't dare let him catch me here with Alby's body and the murder weapon. Even if I stuck around to persuade him that Burton was the killer I'd still get hauled in on general suspicion. I could not risk that; the city jail had no facilities for vampires.

The voices were muffled. I could make out the conversation, though.

Burton was a perfect impersonation of mystified resentment as he tried to determine what could have prompted such an invasion of his home by the cops. Blair wasn't sharing much, and from the shrill noises Ruthie made the other men must have been enjoying a quick, uninvited search of the penthouse looking for bodies. I could assume they'd already covered the kitchen since it was empty.

Alby was as well placed as I could hope for, giving the circumstances. If he'd been killed in Burton's flat, then the logical spot to leave him would be the service hall and its convenient elevator. If the cops found him they might conclude Burton had planned to carry him out of the building via that route.

There was a matter of fingerprints on the murder weapon, though. Ruthie's prints were on the bullets; I wanted Burton's on the gun.

But how to separate him from the herd? I couldn't think of anything. I'd have to bide my time and hope for an opening.

I was tired, though. I'd lost blood and had used up much of myself with all the vanishing. A trip to the Stockyards would cure things, but no time for that now.

The kitchen door was unlocked. I quietly let myself in. Everyone was in the living room. Blair's men hadn't found anything; he had no reason to stick around. Soldier Burton was about to phone his lawyer.

Right, no time to plan, just throw a monkey wrench in the works and hope something breaks.

With a silent apology to Alby, I dragged him inside the kitchen, shook rounds from the revolver onto his chest, slammed the door loudly, and vanished.

There must have been a cop just outside. I sensed him charging in to check the noise. He paused, probably staring, opened the hall door, and grunted disappointment that no one was there. In a wonderfully calm tone he invited Blair to come see something interesting.

The next few minutes were entertaining, better than listening to *Gangbusters* on the radio.

When confronted, Burton squawked his innocence, Ruthie just squawked, and Lieutenant Blair phoned for more cops to join the party. He now had a bona fide murder investigation. His first question to Burton was to ask about the accomplice who had brought the body in. Burton had no reply. In his world the less said to a cop the better.

While they were distracted I floated past, trying to figure the layout of the place. The living room was easy to guess simply by location and size. I couldn't tell how many were in it, and kept going. I bumped into walls, found furniture, and eventually made my way by touch through the maze toward what I hoped was a bedroom.

The commotion faded with distance, and I took a chance, going semi-transparent.

Bingo.

The big bed was still neat, covers turned down and waiting. A red silk scarf draped over one bedside lamp threw a rosy tint on the walls. Drinks were ready on a table, the ice melted. My initial intrusion must have interrupted a romantic celebration.

Good. They'd spoiled my evening and certainly Alby's.

No point in planting the gun until it had prints. The cops would find it in Burton's sock drawer easily enough, but proving he'd fired it was something else.

Then I saw his suit draped over a chair, and things suddenly got simple. His belt was still inside the loops of his pants; change and a wallet were in the pockets. I slipped the little revolver into the right-hand front pocket. The gun was a perceptible weight, but if he was distracted he might not catch on right away.

Voices. . .coming closer. . .Burton made threats about what his lawyer would do to them all. I retreated to a closet and left the door ajar to watch. It was dark inside, and I could vanish quick if anyone opened it.

Two uniforms were with Burton, both grinning. He let drop that he'd make it worth their while if they treated him with some respect. He was told to get dressed so they could respect him downtown.

He stepped into his pants, one leg at a time, same as anyone. I looked for some hint of reaction when he became aware of the gun, but he gave nothing away, not even puzzlement for its presence. It was impossible for him not to be aware of it, especially when he sat to pull on his socks and shoes. That done, he reached for his suit coat, but one of the cops was faster and grabbed it. He checked the pockets.

Damn. I'd considered putting the gun in his suit coat and changed my mind. A man might leave home without his coat, but never his pants, hence my choice. I'd been smart and not realized it.

When he was ready I expected them to put the cuffs on, but Blair must have been wary of going too fast. You have to know when to set the hook before reeling in.

They walked out, and Ruthie came in, accompanied by a matron who'd arrived with Blair's reinforcements. Ruthie snarled at the other woman, but unselfconsciously dropped her robe and began to dress. I had a fine view, but it was nothing I'd not seen before, and the goods were tainted past the point of all appeal. She'd participated in two murders, my own included, and had tried to seduce Burton right in front of my dead body. That was one cold, cold dame.

She finished and was about to leave when I dragged a suitcase from a closet shelf and slammed it through the closet door, and I mean *through.* Big noise, lots of splinters.

Then I vanished.

It made a terrific crashing racket. Both women yelped, and the men charged in to investigate. I slipped past to the front room, found a corner as far from everyone as possible, and went semi-transparent.

There's an art to it; I had to concentrate to not go too solid, but if I held still I'd get to watch without being spotted.

Everyone looked toward the bedroom. Blair was out of sight, probably checking things for himself. A couple plainclothesmen, one with a big camera, called questions. The same two uniforms flanked Soldier Burton, and the matron had a guiding hand firmly on Ruthie's elbow, keeping her in place.

I needed another monkey wrench.

An armchair would do, something heavy, noisy, and impressive.

Getting behind it, I went solid long enough to lift and throw it across the room, vanishing immediately after.

That livened up the party. Maybe too much. I heard shouts and scrambling, and then things suddenly went dead quiet.

I was itching to peek.

The flat had a broad bank of windows, very modern. The windows had long curtains. I retreated behind them.

Solid again, I felt like I'd been running for hours. I had to grab a wall to hold steady against a wave of dizziness.

Later, I'll collapse later. I forced myself to stand and peered around the edge of the curtain.

My stunt with the chair had been thoroughly upstaged by Burton. He'd taken advantage of the opportunity better than I'd hoped. He had the small gun in his big fist, covering the cops while he backed out through the kitchen. Ruthie was right with him, holding the door wide, a crazy smirk on her face. She was having the time of her life.

Blair was in front now, his hands palm down, telling his men to take it easy, and advising Burton to do the same. None of them knew the gun was empty, but no one was taking chances. Burton was in charge, though, and made predictable threats.

He backed into the kitchen. Ruthie would get the service door for him, and then what, the service elevator or the stairs? The latter would be less confining.

Figuring out what to do, I stopped being solid. I rushed past and got to the stairs first, materializing on the other side of the access door. Sure enough, a few seconds later Ruthie tried to push it open. I had my full weight against it. She'd have better luck shifting the Rock of Gibraltar.

She yelled at Burton, who put a shoulder into it with no effect.

They'd have to take the elevator.

It was ready for them, since he'd left it on the penthouse floor after his business on the roof.

I had just enough left for one more vanishing and then I'd have to rest for longer than half a minute. I quit the stairs and slipped in with the escapees just as they began to descend.

"They'll be waiting for us at the bottom," Ruthie fretted.

"We can do this. None of 'em wants to get drilled. Move over, lemme operate it."

Ruthie protested. I found myself abruptly bumping against the ceiling. Burton was taking us down at top speed.

"You'll kill us!" she screeched.

He laughed. "We'll beat 'em, doll."

I started to re-form. Not wise of me, but I'd had enough.

It was a big elevator, tall and deep. You could haul some sizeable things in it. Still, Burton and Ruthie must have found it to be much too small when they noticed me hovering a yard off the floor like. . .well, a ghost.

They didn't react right away, just stared open-mouthed.

I started laughing. Couldn't help myself. It was silent. Not enough of my lungs and larynx were there to make noise.

Ruthie spoke first, her voice down to a hoarse whisper. "You said you took care of him!"

"I *did* take care of him!"

Now that was funny. They'd said almost exactly the same thing in the kitchen. I shook my head, grinning, which caused Ruthie to shrink against Burton.

I pointed at him, index finger straight, thumb up. . .used by kids everywhere when playing cops and robbers and mimed shooting him.

Bang-bang, you're dead.

He couldn't take it and pulled the trigger on his empty gun. He kept pulling it, one empty chamber after another trying to kill a man he knew was dead.

When he worked out its uselessness I expected him to throw it at me, but he didn't get that far.

The elevator had safety measures, which was just as well for these two. Burton had forgotten to keep track of things, like how fast we were dropping. A buzzer went off, and some kind of emergency brake kicked in. While I continued to hover, my companions on the ride were thrown off their feet by the jolt and abrupt stop.

Good enough.

I went solid all the way, and knocked Burton out completely.

Ruthie fled to the back of the car. I was between her and the exit. She looked to be just this side of screaming, but held her own.

I wanted to knock her out, too, but something in me—another useless bit of self-knowledge—rebelled at smacking a woman around, however much she deserved it.

Instead, I bent and removed Burton's necktie. It was a nice one, real silk. Strong.

Ruthie ended up screaming bloody murder and fighting like mad, but she had a right. It's not every night that a man comes back from the dead to hogtie and leave you on the floor of an elevator.

She was still screaming as I opened the doors, but there was a different tone to it. Maybe she'd decided that Burton hadn't snapped my neck after all. Fury replaced her fear and her curses followed me as I made my way across a dark basement to some stairs and let myself out.

The alley again. Crap, was I ever tired if it.

At one end was a police car with a couple of uniforms hanging around.

I yelled at them, sounding urgent.

One had a flashlight, but I put a hand up to obscure my face and crouched to hide my height. I waved them closer.

"They're in here! It's the killers! Hurry!"

They came running. I kept up the act until they were past, then sprinted down the alley. Too tired for more disappearing games I could still run like hell. I slowed after a block and turned for a look back.

Nothing to see, all the fun would be inside. Those guys would be busy for the rest of the night trying to figure it out.

My Buick rolled up, Gordy at the wheel, looking concerned.

"What happened to you?" he wanted to know.

"Be glad to tell you, but first I need a drink."

"No problem."

"You owe me a new suit, too."

"No problem." he said in the same tone and drove me to the Stockyards without another word.

I like that about Gordy. Anyone else would be eaten alive with curiosity and give in to questions, but he held his peace. A patient and remarkable man, he held it even after I emerged from the Yards, eyes still flushed blood red from feeding and feeling two hundred percent better.

"Back to the Nightcrawler?" I asked.

He nodded. At this late hour the streets were fairly clear. I filled him in on the details.

His head bobbed back and forth. That was his version of a belly laugh. It took him a while to get control of himself. I laughed a little as well, but it didn't feel right. I was tough, but needed some internal healing, the kind that I couldn't get simply from a fresh dose of blood.

I'd downplayed the part where my neck had been broken, and the part about being dropped off the building. Gordy was a friend, but there are some things about myself I don't talk about to anyone.

That knot of fear was still there, slightly looser than before. It would ease with time, given how I'd made myself go up the side of the building.

"How do you think they'll explain the suitcase and that chair you threw?" Gordy asked.

I shrugged. "If they're smart, they'll ignore it."

A few nights later we got an answer, of sorts.

I was back at my favorite table at the Nightcrawler, wearing my new suit and watching the show when Gordy came up again, this time sitting with me.

The band was once more in the midst of the big horn and drum number. The players got through it flawlessly, crash-bang-boom, followed by applause.

"Poor Alby," I said.

"He's covered." By that Gordy meant that he was paying for the funeral. It turned out that Alby didn't have any family at all, but he wouldn't wind up in Potter's field.

"That's square of you."

"I owed him. Between the two of you Burton's off my back for good."

"Give Alby the credit. He's the one who lost the most."

"He's getting the credit."

"Oh, yeah?"

The band swung into a new song. Couples quit their tables to dance to it.

Gordy pulled out a newspaper folded to an inside page and slid it over to me.

We'd been keeping up with the headlines about Soldier Burton and his arrest for the murder of Alby Cornish. Burton wouldn't be marching away from this one; the DA—in possession of the murder weapon, prints, and with half a dozen of Chicago's finest to testify to Burton's violent resisting of arrest and escape attempt—was a happy man.

In all those stories no mention was made of flying suitcases or furniture. . .until tonight.

The paper was one of the lesser tabloids, not worthy of sharing newsstand space with the *Tribune*, but the headline was bold: *Did the Ghost of Alby Cornish Nab His Killer?*

The story was long on conjecture and short on facts, such as the reporter's source. She disclosed only that an anonymous member of the police force confided details to her about Burton's arrest. Those details had not made it into the official report. There was a mystery about a thrown suitcase destroying a door, and some violent poltergeist activity centered on an otherwise ordinary looking armchair. Soldier Burton had used the distractions to attempt his escape, threatening the police the same weapon that had killed Alby Cornish.

Who or what force was behind the ghostly activity was a great mystery, but the reporter speculated that Alby himself might have returned from the grave to help get his (alleged) killer behind bars.

Gordy's head wobbled again from laughter, and we sat there not saying anything, just watching the dancers. I thought about Alby missing out on it all, but maybe somewhere he was laughing, too.

THE SCOTTISH PLOY

Author's Note: *Editor Denise Little asked me to write something a bit outside my box for her collection* MURDER MOST ROMANTIC *for Cumberland House. I'd been watching a lot of* Xena: Warrior Princess *reruns, so the hero in this bit of lighthearted dash bears a strong resemblance to New Zealand's Kevin Tod Smith, who played Ares, the god of war. This delightful actor was taken from us far too soon. I hope his other fans enjoy this one.*

Cassie Sullivan slammed her clipboard onto the props table, causing the sword collection that lay there to jump. One fell to the floor with a solid clank. The abrupt noise startled everyone, giving her the undivided attention of the whole cast and crew. "If just one thing goes wrong, I'm calling an exorcist!"

Nell Russell left off wiring together tree branches that were to be part of Burnam Wood. "What's happened now?"

"Trevor Hopewell backed out."

"*What?*" Similar expressions of dismay and shock flowed from the others, who stopped work on the set to come closer, faces tense.

Cassie looked at them all before speaking, but this new disaster was no one's fault. The company's poltergeist could not be responsible for this flavor of random bad luck. "Hopewell got a starring role in a straight-to-video horror movie they're shooting in Canada and grabbed it."

Nell's mouth twisted. "He chose that over the lead in *Macbeth*?"

Some of the more nervy members of the cast winced and groaned.

Nell rounded on them. "Oh, get over it! You can say the name of the play out front, just not backstage. "Cassie, he can't do that. Why would he want to?"

"Money. They can pay him more. The option's in his contract." Everyone nodded, understanding perfectly. The Sullivan Theater Company, for all its members' sincere enthusiasm, was small change to an actor like Trevor Hopewell. Apparently his commitment to keeping theater alive wasn't deep enough to survive the lure of film dollars. Cassie herself could side with Hopewell to a degree, but there was such a thing as fair warning.

Opening night was only a week away.

"What'll we do for a new Macbeth?" asked Willis Wright, the stage manager. No one groaned, since he referred to the character, not the play.

"Hopewell's agency is sending over someone named Quentin Douglas as a replacement."

"Who?"

Cassie shrugged. "He's done some commercials."

A general groan. Nell joined in. "What kind of commercials?"

"Who knows? Foot powder, shaving cream, talking sandwiches—I don't care so long as he can project the lines. They said he played Macbeth in college—"

Another groan.

"—so he knows the part. If Isabel likes him, he's in."

"Great. Did he save his old costume?"

Cassie glowered. "Don't get me started. At this point I may do a nude production."

"That would sell more tickets. Think of all the sword jokes."

"Argh!" Cassie looked around for something else to slam or throw, but nothing non-breakable presented itself. The company watched her, somewhat wall-eyed. Her tempers were infrequent and short lived, but infamous for their intensity. Everyone knew to get out of the line of fire for the brief duration, but this time no one seemed to know which way to jump.

She put her hands palm-out in a peace gesture. "It's okay, boys and girls. I just hate surprises. Chalk this up to the production poltergeist and get back to work. Let's keep it to one life-and-death crisis every ten minutes instead of every five. Okay?"

A rumble of agreement. They resumed their tasks. Nell hung close, though. "This sucks."

"I know, and I shouldn't blame the poltergeist."

"Please, let's do."

"You're not into superstition," said Cassie.

"I wasn't, but this show could make me a believer. Much more of this and I'll be tossing salt over my shoulder. When's the foot-powder wonder boy due?"

"Sometime today. I just got the call from—"

"Miss Sullivan?" Baritone voice. Rich. Chocolate-smooth delivery. Built-in projection. No need for a body microphone.

Cassie turned to take in the owner of the voice. *Oh, my gawd.* Hair like jet, soap opera hero's face, body of a personal trainer, thin line of beard edging his jaw—perfectly in keeping with a Shakespearean character—straight white teeth in a friendly, open smile.

"I'm Quentin Douglas—the Gilbert Agency sent me?" Hand outstretched. Expecting her to respond.

"Yes, they certainly did," she murmured, still goggling. She put her own hand out and connected with his firm grip.

The vision spoke again. "I hope I can work out for you."

His "hope" momentarily sparked a variety of emotions in Cassie, which she quickly smothered. You're off actors, Cassie-girl, you are immune no matter how gorgeous they are. Anyone that good-looking is going to be attached or gay. "I'm sure you will, Mr. Douglas." She was still holding his hand. Belatedly, she released it.

"Please, call me Quentin."

Before she could call him Quentin, she felt an urgent tug on her shirttail; Nell obviously wanted to be included in the first-names fan club.

"Quentin, this is Nell Russell, she's playing Lady MacDuff, Hecate, and Young Siward."

"I'm very versatile," Nell purred, oozing forward to shake his hand, too. She had no misgivings about fraternizing with actors, usually bestowing one broken—or at least bruised heart—per production.

Quentin tendered another easy smile, his royal blue eyes twinkling. "Glad to meet you. Is there much doubling up for roles in this one?"

"A few," Cassie answered, since Nell seemed to have forgotten her next line, basking as she was in his presence. "None of the principals, of course. Go through there to my office, the red door. I'll be right along."

Quentin Douglas departed, walking smooth as a panther on ball bearings. Nell made a low moan of appreciation deep in her throat, ogling at the snug fit of his jeans on his perfect backside—not to mention the muscular set of those sculpted shoulders. . . .

The view wasn't lost on Cassie, but she made herself look elsewhere, gritting her teeth.

"I didn't think they made them like that anymore," Nell sighed.

"Down, girl."

"I thought they were all CGI effects, costume padding, and makeup."

"Just don't go breaking him before we even start."

"But *he's* the one."

"What? Your own true love? Nell, you've said that on every—"

"No, I mean I know who he is! He's the sports drink shower guy."

Cassie blanked. "O—kay."

"You know, that commercial where the guy takes the shower and they pour sports drink all over his sweaty body. Relief from your killer thirst in sloooow-mooootion."

"I'm surprised you even noticed his face." Not much of a TV watcher, Cassie had no recollection of the ad. She quelled a sudden feeling of deprivation.

"I've seen him in *As the Day Passes*, too. He can act."

"On TV. I've gotta find out if he's any good for stage work."

"Cassie, he looks like he'd be good for all kinds of things!"

"Yeah, but can he cook?"

"You've got to get over your allergy toward dating actors. They can be lots of fun."

"Like a root canal." Cassie hurried to her office before she caught Nell's terminal case of carbonated hormones. Yes, Quentin Douglas was a prime physical specimen; yes, he could probably act, but having once fallen far too hard for that type, Cassie had sworn them off forever. Of course, that was difficult to remember when face-to-face with Quentin across her cluttered desk. He had an energy that beat against her like a sunbeam. She refused to be burned by it, but quietly rejoiced; that sort of dynamism was priceless. He just might be able to make a whole theater feel it.

"Here's my résumé," he said, handing over a sheet of paper stapled to a head shot.

She compared the photo to the reality. Usually publicity pictures were an idealized improvement of the subject. Not this guy, though. Would his looks detract from the production? Possibly, considering Nell's reaction. On the other hand, it wouldn't hurt to have a drop-dead handsome, virile Macbeth leaping around the stage waving his sword. "Know how to play with your weapon?" she asked. "I mean—do you know stage combat?"

"It's a passion of mine." He flashed those perfect teeth. "I don't get much call for it in commercials."

"This job doesn't pay as well as TV work."

"It's experience. I'm always looking to hone my skills." He kept up with the eye contact.

Is he flirting with me? she wondered, conscious she was in her second-best work shirt, her third-best jeans, with her red hair piled every which way from its hasty morning pinning. But Quentin had live theater in his background; he'd know how grungy things could get. *No matter. I'm immune to his type now. Stick to business.* She found a copy of *Macbeth* and handed it over. "Let's have a reading, then."

"Sure. What would you like to hear?" Quentin was remarkably self-possessed. Most of the actors she'd dealt with had panic attacks at the prospect of a cold reading. Not this wavy-haired and cool cucumber.

Cucumbers? Why did I have to think about them? Cassie cleared her throat. "How about Act Three, Scene Four? Macbeth's talking with the First Murderer at the banquet." There, a highly charged scene to work with; would he know the right level to hit?

Quentin found the spot in the book right away, indication that he knew the play well. She fed him the lines of the First Murderer. After a glance at the pages, he delivered flawlessly and in such a manner as to make the arcane language easily understandable to a modern audience. He also got the emotions across without snacking on the scenery.

Cassie tried not to look too enthusiastic. "Okay I'm happy, but the decision rests with the show's angel, Miss Isabel Graham. I'm directing, but she's the producer and star and has final say." She expected a response from him on the name. Millions of people knew of her. Even Cassie had seen an episode or three of Isabel's hit comedy series, *I Love Isabel.*

"Shouldn't be a problem," said Quentin, not batting an eye. "I've worked with Bel before."

"Really?" Cassie did not miss the affectionate diminutive of Isabel's name. Only a select few had the privilege of calling her that.

"She and I were in college together," he explained. "In fact, we were in *Macbeth* one semester. The same roles."

"How. . .convenient." Cassie spotted the confirmation of this on the resume.

"Bel's career took off faster than mine. I did a stint in the navy to pay for college, which delayed things for a couple of years. I'm catching up."

"That's great." I think. "So Isabel already knows you're here."

"She's the one who recommended me to the casting agency. But I wanted to get the part on my own, not just because she told you to put me in."

"That's very considerate of you both. What if I'd turned you down?"

"Then it's back to the agency to nag my agent for other jobs. No point being in a show if the director doesn't like me for the part."

He respect for him went up a few notches. "Just as well it worked out, then. Let's introduce you to the others. Rehearsal starts in an hour. We'll go over the blocking for Act One."

"All right. How's the curse going for this production?"

At this out-of-nowhere shot, Cassie paused in mid-boost from her desk, and sat down again. Rather abruptly. "Curse? Who told you?" she blurted before thinking.

"This is the bad-luck play," he said, eyes twinkling again. "So what troubles have you had?"

"I don't believe in the curse," she answered dismissively.

"The Weird Sisters' spells are supposed to be real, and it's always been bad luck to quote from the Scottish play while backstage."

"Only because in the old days it meant the current production was about to close early. Companies could throw *Macbeth* together quickly to fill up the schedule gap. If an actor heard anyone rehearsing lines from it backstage, it meant his show's run was doomed."

"I've not heard that one." He fixed her with a more intense look. "But you've not answered my question, Miss Sullivan."

"Cassie," she said automatically, and let it hang between them for a very long moment. Or did time just telescope when he looked at her like that? *But he does have such riveting eyes.* She broke out of their spell and came up with a reluctant response. "We've had a few glitches that we blame on the production poltergeist."

"Your theater's haunted?"

She smiled. "Strangely, it is not. It's old, but the only deaths here have been the fake kind on stage. Mishaps happen in theater, it's the nature of the craft. My stage manager started calling things like that the work of the production poltergeist. He's fond of alliteration. We're having no more problems now than for any other show."

"Forgive me, but that's not what I've heard."

Cassie could fix people with a formidable look herself, and did so now with Quentin, her green eyes stiletto-sharp. "And just what have you heard?"

Unlike others she'd ever used it on, he didn't seem to recognize the danger signal and leaned forward, not remotely intimidated. "When I found out I was going to be sent to replace Trevor Hopewell, I phoned Bel to thank her for the boost. She gave me an earful. I know about the missing costumes, props breaking, sets falling down, electrical shorts, flooded bathrooms—the works."

"We found the costumes in the trash and put that down to cleaning staff error, the rest is just accident and coincidence. It's an old building. It would be odd if things didn't go wrong with. . .things."

"What about the rash Bel got from her makeup?"

"Allergic reaction to a new brand. We changed it."

"And Trevor Hopewell finding that dead rat in his codpiece?"

"It crawled in there to die. We made him a new one and set out traps."

"And the needle that turned up in Bel's corset? She got a bad scratch from that."

Good grief, he knew everything. Cassie fought down her anger. "The costume crew was careless. They apologized. The rest is coincidence. What are you getting at with all this, Mr. Douglas? Do you think someone is after Isabel?"

"I think Isabel thinks someone is out to kill the production."

"That's ridiculous. I've been with the people here for years, there's no way—"

"Bel worked herself into a good upset once she started talking. She's willing to lay the blame on the play's traditional curse, but she's also willing to consider non-supernatural alternatives. You may know and trust everyone here, but she's an outsider."

"Mr. Douglas, I can tell you right now that all the people in this company are two hundred percent behind this production. We're working to make it a success because we need the money. Isabel's agent approached me with her offer to foot the bill for the whole thing so long as she gets to play Lady Macbeth, and I gratefully accepted. The publicity this playhouse will get from her name will give us the financial help we've always needed. There is no way anyone here is going to jeopardize that."

"But maybe talk about a curse might embarrass her in some way? The tabloids love this kind of thing."

Ouch. He knew how to hit low. "Miss Graham wants to prove to the world she can play high drama as well as middle-America comedy, and a little bad publicity is not going to stop her. She's a total professional and knows that the show must go on."

Quentin, his gaze still steady, nodded slowly, as though he'd found something he'd been looking for and liked it. "You're aware of how important this is to her."

"If she blows it the critics will be merciless. She's put a lot of trust in me, an unknown backwater director—"

"Whose parents were the darlings of Broadway once upon a time."

It was no secret, but she was surprised he knew that. "Yes, they were, and they taught me everything they knew when they invested in this theater. I want to do proud by their memory, and I will give Isabel my best effort."

"Then we're all in accord." He suddenly relaxed and smiled.

She couldn't help but smile back. "Yes, I suppose we are, but—"

Someone banged urgently on her red door. "Cassie! Emergency!"

It was Willis Wright, stage-managing in overdrive from the sound of him.

Heart thumping, she shot from her chair, on full alert. In any given production there were a hundred emergencies, but his tone of voice made this one serious. She hauled the door open and nearly collided with him.

"What is it?"

"We've found a body up on the gridwalk."

"What?" She pushed past, tearing toward the stage. There she saw the whole company staring upward to the dark heights of the grid, the steel construction that held the lights and backdrops. She stared herself, trying to pierce the shadows. "Flashlight!"

Willis slapped one into her hand. Its beam was pale from use and didn't reach far, but she saw a man-sized shape dangling ominously over stage center.

"Oh, my God. Is that for real? Someone get up there and find out."

Willis himself saw to it, scrambling up the metal ladder affixed to the backstage wall. He reached the grid and gingerly stepped onto it. The hanging figure swung heavily. Several of the people around her gasped.

"Everyone back out of the way!" she snapped. Still staring up, they reluctantly moved clear. And only just in time. Willis yelled, "Look out!"

The thing high above suddenly plummeted. The body smacked into the stage with a resounding thud, inspiring screams. Cassie jumped in reaction, but held her place. She became aware of someone looming behind her. Quentin. Generating a lot of heat. He stared over her shoulder at the body.

It was only a dummy from props—for which Cassie heaved a great sigh of relief—but its appearance sent a chill up her spine. With a hangman's noose around the neck, it was dressed in her own distinctive working uniform of jeans, cowboy boots, and her best blue work shirt, which had gone missing yesterday. Topping all was a red wig, the color matching her own mane. Most disturbing was a huge prop butcher knife, smeared with dark red paint, sticking out of the thing's chest.

She felt Quentin's warm hand on her shoulder, gripping tight.

"Good God. . .that's supposed to be you."

She recoiled at the suggestion. "I hope not."

"That's *sick!*" Nell all but shrieked. "Absolutely sick! Who did this?"

No one stepped forward; no one looked the least bit guilty or smug, but then, most of them were actors.

No. I'm not going to go there, Cassie thought. These are my friends, they're family!

An unfamiliar hollowness invaded her guts. Fear. Real fear. That fake knife had been buried right to the hilt in her effigy's chest. Like it or not, she had to deal with it. She steeled herself, went over, and pulled it out. All eyes were on her as she held it up like a trophy.

She fully milked the moment, making a slow turn to take them all in, keeping her voice rock-steady. "All right. Listen up. I am *not* amused. Somebody could have been killed if this thing had fallen at the wrong time. There's no harm done, but no more tricks. I'm talking zero tolerance, folks.

I find anyone, absolutely anyone, screwing around and I will personally bury them. Is that clear?"

Nods of comprehension and sober looks. She tried to read their expressions and body language for any clue as to who might be the guilty party, but it was impossible, so she concentrated on not trembling from the adrenaline rush. Rule One for any good dramatic scene: never let them see you sweat.

"Cassie? What's going on here?"

She turned to face Isabel Graham, the show's patron, producer, and leading lady. Though known as a brilliant comedic star by means of her hit TV series, at the moment Isabel truly resembled Lady Macbeth. Her blue eyes were wide with shock, her mouth set in a grim downward turn. She looked at the bloody knife, then at the dummy.

"Just a sick joke, Isabel," Cassie wearily explained, wishing she could lose the knife.

"Another one?" This came from Isabel's manager, James Keating, also her most recent fiancé. Like Nell, Isabel fell in love a lot, but had been careful not to follow through to marriage just yet. According to the tabloids, though, Keating just might be the one to break the rule. He was movie-star handsome, had a shark's attitude when it came to business, and was totally devoted to Isabel. He was shocked enough to put away his ever-present cell phone to stare at the dummy sprawled over center stage. Quentin was on one knee, his back to them, examining the "remains."

"That's supposed to be *you*?" asked Isabel, horrified.

"It's a rotten likeness. I have a much better figure."

Isabel puffed out a short, mirthless laugh. "Not funny."

"Absolutely not," agreed James. "This is a deliberate and cold-blooded. Bel you—"

"Quentin!" Isabel squealed, suddenly noticing her new co-star. Cassie dodged clear just as Isabel launched herself at him. He rose with a grin and obligingly grabbed her up in a full body hug and spun her slender form around.

Short attention span, thought Cassie. Isabel had loads of talent, but when she wasn't performing she was as easily distracted as a kitten was by a new piece of string.

"You've grown!" crowed Isabel when Quentin set her down.

"Nope, you just got shorter."

"Did not! You get those big muscles in the navy?"

"They're rented, but if they work out, I might buy them."

James Keating watched the exchange between the two old friends with thin-lipped tolerance. Cassie knew how he felt. Her last—completely last—actor-boyfriend had thrown her over for someone else. He'd been just as public about it, too. Was James worried about a rival?

Willis came up then, or rather down, having just quit the metal ladder. He also inspected the "body," especially the noose rope. His focus served to draw Isabel back to the immediate problem.

"What is it, Will?" Cassie asked.

He shook his head. "This was set like a booby trap. I found fishing line leading from the dummy's noose to the ladder and down the rungs on the inside. The noose was just barely snagged on a hook up there with a loose loop knot; one good pull on the line and it's off and dropping. I accidentally tripped the gag when I got to the top. Whoever set it wanted to pull it down from a distance. It would have worked, but the setup was clumsy. If there'd been a good draft it might have come tumbling down beforetime and killed someone."

She went cold. All over.

"Cassie, you should call the cops on this. James is right, this isn't a joke anymore. Maybe the rest of the stuff you can fob off on the poltergeist, but somebody put work into this thing—and it had to be somebody with free access to the building. This came from the basement props and costume storage."

"Not the clothes," she said.

"Those are yours, aren't they?" asked Isabel.

"Don't hold it against me. I'll buy something nice for opening night."

"Stop with the joking already," said Nell. "This a deliberate act of terrorism!"

"I agree," said Quentin. "You need to report it."

Keating echoed him, putting a protective arm around Isabel.

"And have the tabloids eat us for lunch? I don't think so." Cassie had already dealt with several overly-friendly reporters looking for the inside scoop on a perfectly—well, almost—ordinary production of *Macbeth.* They'd been interested in getting dirt on Isabel, of course.

Isabel shook her head. "Never mind the so-called press. I can take a little heat so long as they spell my name right. This could be a life-threatening situation. You have to call the police!"

Cassie raised her hands in a placating gesture. Unfortunately, the prop knife was still in one clenched fist, causing everyone to back away a step. "Okay! I'll phone them, but I am not terrorized, I'm mad as hell. Everyone here should get mad, too."

Nell visibly thought that one over. "What? Like an acting exercise?"

"No! I mean if you put all the poltergeist stuff together, most of it doesn't mean squat, but this is different. Someone wants to kill this show, for reason or reasons unknown."

"Over my dead body," said Isabel, her eyes flashing blue fire. "I'll call in a security firm and lock this place up like Fort Knox before I let that happen."

"Right," said Cassie. "That's what I'm looking for—I want you and everyone else mad and on red alert. If we all play watchdog, look out for each other, anticipate problems before they happen, then they can't happen. Am I brilliant, or what?"

"Or what," Nell deadpanned. "You want us up here twenty-four/seven to revoke Murphy's Law?"

"Whatever it takes," said Cassie.

"Lemme tell you, girl, when it comes to theater, Murphy was an optimist."

* * *

Cassie filed a report with the police, but knew they couldn't do anything. It was not a crime to dress up a dummy and hang it from anything; no harm was done. The officer was sympathetic, but even the promise of free tickets for opening night wasn't enough to lure him into staying until then. He did ask if she could have Isabel's autograph, which Cassie got for him, since he was kind of cute.

Her pep-talk galvanized the company. For the rest of rehearsals Cassie concentrated on directing, which almost made her forget about the poltergeist—for whole minutes at a time.

It helped to have amazing actors to work with, though. Quentin Douglas's romantic, hot-blooded—if slightly psychotic—Macbeth quite overwhelmed the brooding, anger-driven version Trevor Hopewell had attempted. Even without the drawing power of Isabel Graham's star name, this production was shaping into something special. Cassie was thrilled. She wanted the audience to see the characters, not the actors playing them.

Complications still arose. Mostly in the form of Quentin finding all kinds of ways to stick close to her when he wasn't busy killing people on stage. She pretended not to notice his attentions and focused on business, which drove Nell up the wall.

"He *likes* you, Cassie! Are you nuts? Total studs like him are thin on the ground."

"He's an actor. Actors are off my menu."

"Unbend a little, girl. At least have coffee with him sometime so he doesn't think you hate him."

"I don't hate him! I'm being professional. Go for him yourself."

"I tried—but all he did was get me to talk about you. The least you can do is date him so I can have a vicarious thrill when you tell me about it."

"I've no time. The play opens soon, and in two weeks it closes; he'll be history. End of problem."

"You wish."

* * *

Despite everyone looking out for each other, Murphy's Law continued with a vengeance. Opening-night jitters became the norm days too early, with more missing or damaged costumes, broken props, and damaged scenery flats. Frustration rose, tempers shortened, and arguments were frequent. Isabel's presence helped; she could stop a fight with her smile alone. At her own expense she had the locks changed and hired off-duty policemen to keep an eye on things. To no avail, with so many crew and actors milling hurriedly about to bring the production together it was impossible for the security types to watch everything. The incidents continued.

After the effigy business, Cassie started sleeping in the theater. She'd often done so when work had gone too late to drive home. With spare clothing, a comfy couch in her office, and showers in the dressing rooms, it was no hardship. She rather liked it.

She was well over her fit of denial, facing the ugly fact that someone in the group was out to kill the show. Cassie absolutely hated the idea, but found herself looking at familiar faces with new eyes. She began to come up with motives for each and had to bite her tongue to keep from blurting out an accusatory question that could destroy a lifetime of friendship.

So she kept quiet about her after-hours guardian duty, hoping that if she did discover the culprit they could settle things privately. As for the possibility that an anti-Shakespearean ghost had taken up residence in the theater. . .well, Cassie had yet to meet a poltergeist who was any match for a furious redhead armed with a baseball bat.

The nights were uneventful, giving her much time to think back on the various pranks—especially the deadliest. The guilty party behind the effigy had to have access, time, and privacy to set it up. The knots made her think of sailors, but Quentin Douglas was newly come to the show, unfamiliar with the layout of the theater, and had no motive. Besides, most of the company knew how to do special knots; it was part of normal stagecraft training.

That clue shoved to the side, she thought seriously about motivation. Why would anyone want to kill the production? Not one of her people would benefit if it died—quite the contrary.

What about Isabel? She believed in this show, but was that just a cover? Her grand plan to prove herself to be a powerful dramatic actress as well as a comedy star was backfiring in the tabloids. Derisive articles were surfacing without any of the writers having seen her work. Unfair, but bad news sold. If Isabel stopped the production in the face of the mishaps, then the critical feeding frenzy would never happen. Of course, she'd lose the chance to dispel the mockers by delivering a solid performance.

Perhaps James Keating? He'd more than once voiced the thought that they should quit and close down the show before anyone got hurt, but always deferred to Isabel's wishes. Could he be tired of playing second banana?

By the third night at watch, Cassie was exhausted. She had to keep up a strong front to inspire confidence, but that and the hard work of rehearsals drained her. At eleven she said good-night to the last of the crew, locked the door, and made a round of the dark and silent theater. While others might find the cavernous quiet and deep shadows ominous, she was in her home element. Each creak was as familiar as her own breath. When no boogeyman obligingly leaped out so she could whack him with her bat and solve her problems, she retired to the dressing room area to get a much wanted shower.

Having seen the Hitchcock movie enough times to be sensible about the vulnerability of bathing females, she not only locked the dressing room door, but propped a chair under the knob. Any would-be Norman Bates would have a tough time sneaking up on her, especially if the toolbox she'd balanced on the chair fell off.

Which it did, just as she finished her final rinse and cut the water.

The terrific crash nearly made her leap out of her freshly scrubbed skin. Dripping, she struggled frantically into a terry robe and grabbed her bat. Her heart hammered so loud she could barely hear anything else as she approached the dressing room door—

Which was being forced open.

Swallowing her fear and outrage, she nipped quick as a cat behind the door, ready to deliver a Babe Ruth-style homer to the intruder.

The chair abruptly tumbled over, and a black figure cautiously edged inside. She gulped again. He was awfully *big* for a poltergeist.

No matter. He was a trespasser and she was within her rights. She swung the bat hard, giving a banshee yell for good measure.

He whirled barely in time to duck and deflect the blow to the side. He yanked the bat from her grasp and drove bodily toward her. She buried her fist into his belly, using plenty of knuckle. The man doubled over. Cassie dodged, rolled, and grabbed up the bat again, coming to her feet with it ready in hand as he recovered enough to turn on her.

"*You?!*" she screamed, caught between disbelief and rage.

"*Grrg!*" said Quentin Douglas, holding his gut.

"What the hell are you doing here?"

He waved one hand, palm out, backing away from her threat. "Uh-a-ha-ooo?"

"I'm watching the place," she answered, understanding the question even if articulation was lacking. "Why are you here? *You're* the poltergeist?"

He violently shook his head, then found a chair and dropped into it, breathing heavily. He didn't look like a poltergeist. *But then he's an actor*, she reminded herself.

"I'm here to watch out for trouble," he wheezed out a few moments later. "With the stuff that's going on. . .it seemed the right thing to do. I was worried about you."

Wow. Her last guy would never have done *that* for her. "I can take care of myself."

"I noticed," he said, rubbing his stomach.

"How long have you been here?"

"Since the first night I arrived."

"What? You've been creeping around every night without me knowing?!"

"I happen to be very good at it. That's why Isabel recommended me when Hopewell gave notice. She knew about my training. She thought it might be an asset to theater security."

Cassie relaxed. Marginally. She still held her bat ready. "Are you all right?"

"Just bruised pride. If my service buddies ever found out I was decked by a half-pint like you—"

She growled and tightened her grip on the bat.

"Take it easy! That was a compliment. You've got a killer arm. If red hair is mentioned they won't hassle me."

Mollified, she eased off. "Why'd you come in here? Trying to cop a peek?" She tightened the tie on her robe, suddenly aware of drafts.

"That would be wonderful, but I saw someone lurking in the hall outside. I chased him, then lost him. When I returned I found the door's lock jimmied, so I thought I'd better check to make sure you weren't hanging from a coat rack with a knife in you."

"Oh. Well. Thanks. Shouldn't we go looking for the lurker, then?"

"We—sure, when you've dressed for the part, but don't go to any trouble on my account. In the meantime, I'll start looking around."

"Oh, no you don't. You stay right here and watch my back."

He grinned, his wicked eyes lighting up.

"Figuratively!"

Growling, she retreated to the shower and threw on clothes, then returned, still damp, but ready for anything.

Apparently recovered from the blow to his gut and pride, he reported that all was quiet. "He's probably gone by now. I didn't get a good look at him. It was too dark. It might have been a woman."

"I'm still turning on all the lights and going through this place room by room." She headed for the master switches backstage.

"Wait a second. . .do you smell gas?"

She sniffed. He was right.

"Basement," she said decisively, pivoting and running for the stairs. "We have butane tanks to fuel stage-fire effects, but they're locked up in a cage. I don't see how—"

Quentin followed, using the flashlight he carried to guide them down the stairs. "Who has the keys to the cage?"

"There's no key, just a trick padlock, it's a joke around here—" She stopped cold. On the bottom step was a single candle burning in a holder. She scrambled the rest of the way down and slapped the flame out. The gas smell was worse; she felt a headache coming on.

Quentin surged past her. Some of the cage wire had been cut through. He thrust his hand into the hole and shut off the valves on the hissing tanks.

"Out!" he ordered, and she did not argue with him.

* * *

Three hours before curtain Cassie called a meeting. She was mad as hell, but not showing it. In fact, she looked cheerful and rested. That was enough to alert her people that something was up.

"We're going to have the best show we've ever put on," she said as an opening.

Nell, who knew her very well, showed alarm.

"We can also relax, our troubles are over. The poltergeist blew it. I know who's been trying to kill this production."

"Who?" demanded Keating, holding tight to Isabel's hand.

Cassie grinned. "Someone who didn't know the ins and outs of this old place. One of the jokes here is the huge padlock on the butane cage." She quickly explained about what she and Quentin had discovered the night before. "This theater was supposed to blow up, burn down, or at least be so damaged as to make the show impossible. The culprit, not knowing that a trick catch on the padlock would open it, didn't have time to cut through the hasp, and smashing it might have been too noisy, so he cut the cage wires instead—and that was the giveaway."

"How so?" asked Isabel.

"A woman or a small man could have got a hand through the cage wires and wouldn't have needed to cut the wires to turn the tank valves on. Anyone inside the Sullivan company would have known to just pop the trick padlock. Only an outsider, a man unable to get his big hand through, would have thought it necessary to cut the wire to get to the tanks."

People exchanged looks and Nell's eyes narrowed. She would be the one to point out the flaw in Cassie's logic—that a member of the company would be smart enough to cut the wires as a cover.

Cassie pressed forward before Nell could speak and spoil the build. "So why the hell were you trying to kill this production—Mr. Keating?"

Keating, no actor, went a sickly gray. "That's slander!" he snarled. He stood, squaring his shoulders, recovering his cool. "My lawyers will strip you to the bone."

Isabel shot to her feet. "James?"

"Bel," he said patiently, "this is what happens when you deal with amateurs."

She looked at Cassie.

Who looked right back and asked, "Did he happen to go missing between eleven and twelve last night? As in turn off his cell phone?"

Everyone knew he *never* did that. The annoying thing was always going off during rehearsals, and even Isabel couldn't get him to silence it.

She went pale as she rounded on him. "Where were you?"

"I had a business call and took it in the hotel lobby. I didn't want to disturb you."

"That would be a first. You're always on that thing. You don't care who's around."

"Oh, Bel, really. We've had talks about your ego before—"

"*My* ego?"

"Sweetie-pie, you need a reality check. This project of yours is too expensive, even as a tax write-off."

"You self-absorbed, penny-pinching bastard! It's *my* damned money!"

"And the critics are eating you alive even before opening night. Face it, you're a *star*, not an actress!"

Cassie calmly fitted her baseball bat into Isabel's hand. "Here, honey, have a party."

* * *

The Graham-Keating engagement, along with James Keating's right arm, which he'd raised to ward off the blow, was officially broken, so screamed a tabloid headline a few days later.

Despite Keating's threats of legal reprisal for slander and assault, everyone in the company stuck to the story that he'd fallen off the stage into the old orchestra pit. The police investigation stalled, while the show went on.

Isabel Graham, drawing from that afternoon's inspiration, gave a riveting performance as one of the most vicious, bloody-minded Lady Macbeths the critics had ever had the pleasure to cower from; they also enthused about newcomer Quentin Douglas, sparking talk of a Broadway revival of the play.

"Two weeks and he's history," chided Nell to Cassie at the opening night celebration party. "Yeah, sure. You change your mind about dating actors yet?"

"Maybe," Cassie admitted, returning Quentin's look from across the stage. He started toward her, eyes twinkling again. "He didn't seem to care that I clobbered him, so there's hope. . . ."

"Then you go, girl!" Nell pushed her forward. "And give him one for me!"

GRAVE–ROBBED

Author's Note: *I always wanted to do a story where vampire Jack Fleming crashes a séance and the invitation to trib to* MANY BLOODY RETURNS, *edited by Toni L.P. Kelner and Charlaine Harris was not to be missed. But this vampires and birthdays-themed story did not come easy. Originally Jack's partner Escott was going to be in on the action, but after 17 hours of tearing my hair, trying to write him in, I gave up and reluctantly kicked poor Charles to the curb. After that the story just about wrote itself. A writer's sub-conscious always knows best!*

Chicago, February 1937

When the girl draped in black stepped into the office to ask if I could help her with a séance, Hal Kemp's version of "Gloomy Sunday" began to murmur sadly from the office radio.

Coincidences annoy me. A mournful song for a dead sweetheart put together with a ceremony that's supposed to help the living speak with the dead made me uneasy—and I was annoyed it made me uneasy.

I should know better, being dead myself.

"You sure you're in the right place?" I asked, taking in her outfit. Black overcoat, pocketbook, gloves, heels, and stockings—she was a walking funeral. Along with the mourning weeds, she wore a brimmed hat with a chin-brushing veil even I couldn't see past.

"The Escott Agency—that's what's on the door," she said, sitting on the client chair in front of the desk without an invitation. "You're Mr. Escott?"

"I'm Mr. Fleming. I fill in for Mr. Escott when he's elsewhere." He was off visiting his girlfriend. I'd come to his office to work on the books since I was better at accounting. Littering the desk were stacks of paper scraps covered with dates and numbers—his usual method of recording business expenses on the fly. After a couple hours of dealing with the monotony, I was ready for a break.

"It was Mr. Escott who was recommended to me." Her tone indicated she wanted the boss, not the part-time hired help.

"By who?"

"A friend."

I waited, but she left it at that. Nothing unusual in it, much of Escott's business as a private agent came by word of mouth. Call him a private-eye and you'd get a pained look and perhaps an acerbic declaration that he did not undertake divorce cases. His specialty was carrying out unpleasant errands for the unable or unwilling, not peeking through keyholes. Did a séance qualify? He was interested in that kind of thing, but mostly from a skeptic's point of view. I had to say mostly since he couldn't be a complete skeptic what with his partner—me—being a vampire.

And nice to meet you, too.

Hal Kemp played on in the little office until the girl stood, went to the radio, and shut it off.

"I hate that song," she stated, turning around, the veil swirling lightly. Faceless women irritate me, but she had good legs.

"Me, too. You got any particular reason?"

"My sister plays it all the time. It gets on my nerves."

"Does it have to do with this séance?"

"Can't you call Mr. Escott?"

"I could, but you didn't make an appointment for this late or he'd be here."

"My appointment is for tomorrow, but something's happened since I made it, and I need to speak with him tonight. I came by just in case he worked late. The light was on and a car was out front. . ."

I checked his book. In his precise hand he'd written 10am, Abigail Saeger. "Spell that name again?"

She did so, correct for both.

"What's the big emergency?" I asked. "If this is something I can't handle I'll let him know, but otherwise you'll find I'm ready, able, and willing."

"I don't mean to offend, but you look rather young for such work. Over the phone I thought Mr. Escott to be. . .more mature."

Escott and I were the same age but I did look younger by over a decade. On the other hand if she thought a man in his mid-thirties was old, then she'd be something of a kid herself. Her light voice told me as much, though you couldn't tell by her manner and speech, which bore a finishing school's not so subtle polish.

"Miss Saeger, would you mind raising your blinds? I like to see who's hiring before I take a job."

She went still a moment, then lifted her veil. As I thought, a fresh-faced kid who should be home studying, but her eyes were red-rimmed, her expression serious.

"That's better. What can I do for you?"

"My older sister, Flora, is holding a séance tonight. She's crazy to talk with her dead husband, and there's a medium taking advantage of her. He wants her money, and more."

"A fake medium?"

"Is there any other kind?"

I smiled, liking her. "Give me the whole story, same as you'd have told to Mr. Escott."

"You'll help me?"

"I need to know more first." I said it in a tone to indicate I was interested.

She plunged in, talking fast, but I had good shorthand and scribbled notes.

Miss Saeger and her older sister Flora were alone, their parents long dead. But Flora had money in trust and married into more money after getting hitched to James Weisinger Jr., who inherited a tidy fortune some years ago. The Depression had little effect on them. Flora became a widow last August when her still-young husband died in a sailing accident on Lake Michigan.

I'd been killed on that lake. "Sure it was an accident?"

"A wind shift caused the boom to swing around. It caught him on the side of the head and over he went. I still have nightmares about the awful thud when it hit him and the splash, but it's worse for Flora—she was at the wheel at the time. She blames herself. No one else does. There were half a dozen people aboard who knew sailing. That kind of thing can happen out of the blue. You can't anticipate it."

I vaguely remembered reading about it in the paper. Nothing like some rich guy getting killed while doing rich-guy stuff to generate copy.

"Poor James never knew what hit him, it was just that fast. Flora was in hysterics and had to be drugged for a week. Then she kept to her bed nearly a month, then she read some stupid article in a magazine about using Ouija boards to talk to spirits and got it into her head that she had to contact James, to apologize to him."

"That opened the door to the medium?"

"James is dead, and if he did things right he's in heaven and should stay there—in peace." Miss Saeger growled in disgust. "I've gotten Flora's pastor to talk to her, but she won't listen to him. I've talked to her until we both end up screaming and crying, and she won't see sense. I'm just her little sister and don't know anything, you see."

"What's so objectionable?"

"Her obsession. It's not healthy. I thought after all this time she'd lose interest, but she's gotten worse. Every week she has a gaggle of those creeps from the Society over, they set up the board, light candles, and ask questions while looking at James' picture. It's pointless and sad and unnatural and-and—just plain *disrespectful*."

I was really liking her now. "Society?"

"The Psychical Society of Chicago."

Though briefly tempted to ask her to say it three times fast, I kept my yap shut. The group investigated haunted houses and held sittings—their word for séances—writing their experiences up for their archives. Escott was a member. For a buck a year to cover mailing costs he'd get a pamphlet every month and read the more oddball pieces out to me.

"The odious thing is," said Miss Saeger, "they're absolutely *sincere*. When one has that kind of belief going, then of course it's going to produce results."

"What kind of results?"

"They've spelled out the names of all the people who ever died in the house, which is stupid because the house isn't that old. The man who supervises these sittings says that's because the house was built over the site of another, so the dead people are connected to it, you see. There's no way to prove or disprove any of it. He's got an answer for everything and always sounds perfectly reasonable."

"Is he the medium?"

"No, but he brought him in. Alistair Bradford." She put plenty of venom in that name. "He looks like something out of a movie."

"What? Wears a turban like Chandu the Magician?"

Her big dark eyes flashed, then she choked, stifling a sudden laugh. She got things under control after a moment. "Thank you. It's good to talk with someone who sees things the way I do."

"Tell me about him."

"No turban, but he has piercing eyes, and when he walks into a room everyone turns around. He's handsome. . .for an old guy."

"How old?"

"At least forty."

"That's ancient."

"Please don't make fun of me. I get that all the time from him, from all of them."

"I'm sorry, Miss Saeger. Are you the only one left in the house with any common sense?"

"Yes." She breathed that out, and it almost turned into a sob, but she headed it off. The poor kid looked to be only barely keeping control of a truckload of high emotion. I heard her heart pounding fast, then gradually slow. "Even some of the servants are under his spell. I have friends, but I can't talk to them about this. It's just too embarrassing."

"You've been by yourself on this since August?"

She nodded. "Except for our pastor, but he can't be there every day. He tells me to keep praying for Flora, and I do, and still this goes on and just gets worse. I miss James, too. He was a nice man, a good man. He deserves better than this—this—"

"What broke the camel's back to bring you here?"

"Before Alistair Bradford came all they did was play with that stupid Ouija board. I'd burn it but they'd just buy another from the five and dime toy aisle. After *he* was introduced they began holding séances. I don't like any of that stuff and don't believe in it, but he made it scary. It's as though he gets taller and broader and his voice changes. With the room almost totally dark it's easy to believe his nonsense."

"They let you sit in?"

"Just the once—on sufferance so long as I kept quiet. When I turned the lights on in the middle of things Flora banished me. She said my negative thoughts were preventing the spirits from coming through, and that I was endangering Bradford's life. You're not supposed to startle a medium out of a trance or it could kill him. I wouldn't mind seeing that, but he was faking. While they were all yelling I had my eye on him, and the look he gave me was pure spite. . .and he was *smiling*. He wanted to scare me and it worked. I've kept my door locked ever since and haven't slept much."

"I don't blame you. No one believes you?"

"Of course not. I'm not in their little club and I'm just a kid. What do I know?"

"Kids have instinct, a good thing to follow. Is he living in the house?"

"He mentioned it, but Flora—for once—didn't think that was proper."

"Is he romancing her?"

Miss Saeger's eyes went hard. "Slowly. He's too smart to rush things, but I see the way he struts around, looking at everything. If he lays a finger on Flora I'll—"

I raised one hand. "I get it. You want Flora protected and him discredited."

"Or his legs broken and his big smirking face smashed in."

That was something I could have arranged. I know those kind of people. "It's better if Flora gets rid of him by her own choice."

"I don't see how, I think it's too late. I called here on Saturday to make the appointment, but—" She went red in the face. "I could just *kill* him!"

"What'd he do?"

"The last seance—they have one every Sunday and that's just wrong having it on a Sunday—something horrible happened. They all gathered in the larger parlor at the table as usual, lighted candles, and put out the lights. Soon as it went dark I slipped in while they were getting settled. There's an old Chinese screen in one corner, and I hide behind it during their séances. Negative feelings, my foot, no one's noticed me yet, not even Bradford, so I saw the whole thing."

"Which was?"

"He put himself in a trance right on time. It usually takes five minutes, and by then everyone's expecting something to happen, you can feel it. He starts out with a low groan and breathing loudly, and in the dark it's spooky, and that's when his spirit guide takes over. His voice gets deeper and he puts on a French accent. Calls himself *Frere* Leon. He's supposed to have been a monk who traveled with Joan of Arc."

"Who speaks English?"

"Of course. No one's ever thought of talking to him in French. I doubt Bradford knows much more than *mon Dieu* and *sang sacre*."

She'd attended a good finishing school, speaking with the right kind of pronunciation. I'd heard it when I'd been a doughboy in France during the last year of the war, and had picked up enough to get by. Much of that was too rough for Miss Saeger's tender ears, though.

"And the horrible thing that happened?"

"It was at the end. He pretends to have *Frere* Leon pass on messages from James. He can't have James talk directly to Flora or he'd trip himself up. He doesn't pass too many messages, either, just general stuff about how beautiful it is on the other side. She tries to talk to him and ask him things and she's so desperate and afterwards she always cries and then she goes back for *more*. It's cruel. But this time he said he was giving her a sign of what she should do."

"Do?"

"I didn't know what that meant, until. . .well, Bradford finished just then and pretended to be waking from his trance. That's when they found what he'd snuck on the table. It was James' wedding ring, the one he was buried with."

I gave that the pause it deserved. "Not a duplicate?"

She shook her head, a fast, jerky movement. Her voice went thick. "Inside it's engraved with *To J. from F. - Forever Love*. He never took it off and it had some wear: two distinct parallel scratches, and it wasn't a perfect circle. Flora showed it to me as proof that Alistair Bradford was genuine. She didn't want to hear my idea that. . .that he'd dug up and robbed James' grave. But I said it. I thought she'd slap me. She's gone crazy, Mr.—"

"Fleming. Call me Jack."

"Jack. Flora's never raised a hand to me, even when we were kids and I was being bratty, but this has her all turned around. I thought Mr. Escott could find something out about Bradford that would prove him a fake or come to a séance and do something to break it up, but I don't think she'd listen now. The last thing Bradford said before his trance ended was 'you have his blessing.' Put that with the ring and I know it means if he asks Flora to marry him she'll say yes because she'll think that's what James would want."

"Come on, she can't be that—"

"Stupid? Foolish? Under a spell? She *is!* That's what's driving *me* crazy. She should be *smarter* than this."

"Grief can make you go right over the edge. Guilt can make it worse, and I bet she's lonely, too. She should have gone to a head-doctor, but picked up a Ouija board instead. Does this Bradford ask for money?"

"*He* calls it a donation. She's given him fifty dollars every time. He gets that much for all his sittings—and he does thirty to forty a month. My sister's not the only dope in town."

My mouth went dry. Fifty a week was a princely income, but that much times forty? I was in the wrong business. I'd gotten twenty-five a week back in New York as a reporter and counted myself lucky. "Well. That makes robbing banks seem respectable. Your sister can give him more by marriage?"

"Yes, her trust money and the estate from James. Bradford would have it, the house, everything. Please, can you help me stop him?"

I thought of the people I knew who broke bones for a sawbuck and could make a man disappear for twice that. "I need to check this. I only have your side of things."

"And I'm just a kid."

"Miss Saeger, I'd say the same thing to Eleanor Roosevelt if she was in that chair. Lemme make a phone call. Anyone going to be worried you're gone?"

"I snuck out and got a taxi. Flora and I had a fight and she thinks I'm sulking in my room. She's busy, anyway—the new séance tonight."

"Uh-huh." I dialed Gordy at the Nightcrawler Club and asked if he had any dirt on an Alistair Bradford, professional medium.

"Medium what?" asked Gordy in his sleepy-sounding voice.

"A swami, you know, seances, fortune-telling. It's for a case. I'm filling in for Charles."

He grunted, and he sounded amused. "You at his office? Ten minutes." He hung up. As the Nightcrawler was a longer than ten-minute drive away

I took him to mean he'd phone back, not drop by.

"Ten minutes," I repeated to Miss Saeger. "What's with the black get-up?" You still in mourning for your brother-in-law?"

"It was the only way I could think of to cover my face. I'm full grown, but soon as anyone looks at me they think I'm fifteen or something."

"And you're really. . . ?"

"Sixteen."

"Miss Saeger, you are one brave and brainy sixteen-year-old, but I'm sure you're aware that this is a school night."

"My sister is more important than that, but thank you for the reminder." There was a dryness in her tone that would have done credit to Escott. A couple years from now and she'd be one formidable young woman.

"What time is this seance?"

"Nine o'clock. Always."

"Not at midnight?"

"Some of the older Society members get too sleepy if things go much past ten."

"Why tonight instead of next Sunday?"

"It's James' birthday. Bradford said that holding a sitting on the loved one's birthday always means something special."

"Like what?"

"He won't say, he just *smiles*. It makes my skin crawl. I swear, if he's not stopped I'll get one of James' golf clubs and—" She went red in the face again, stood up, and paced. I did that when the pent up energy got to be too much.

I tried to get more from her on tonight's event, but she didn't have anything else to add, though she had plenty of comment about Bradford's antics. Guys like him I'd met before, they're always the first to look you square in the eye and assure you they're honest long before you begin to wonder.

The phone rang in seven minutes. Abigail Saeger halted in mid-word and stride and sat, leaning forward as I put the receiver to my ear. Gordy was like a walking library for all that was crooked in the great city of Chicago, with good reason: if he wasn't behind it himself, he knew who was and where to find them. He gave me slim pickings about Bradford, but it was enough to confirm that the guy was trouble. He'd done some stage work as a magician, Alistair the Great, until discovering there was more cash to be had conjuring dead relatives from thin air instead of rabbits. He preferred to collect as much money in the shortest time, then make an exit. The wealthy widow Weisinger was too good a temptation to a man looking for an easy way to retire.

"You need help with this bo'?" Gordy asked.

"I'll let you know. Thanks."

"No problem."

"Well?" asked Miss Saeger.

I hung up. "Count me in, ma'am."

"That sounds so old. My name's Abby."

"Fine, you can sign it here." I pulled out one of Escott's standard contracts. It was short and vague, mostly a statement that the Escott Agency was retained for services by, with a blank after that and room for the date.

"How much will this be?"

"Two bucks should do it."

"It has to be more than that. I read detective stories."

"Special sale, tonight only. Anyone walking in here named Abby pays two bucks, no more, no less."

For a second I thought she'd kiss me, and I was prepared to duck out of range. If my girlfriend found out I'd canoodled, however innocently or briefly, with a mere pippin of sixteen I would find myself dead for real and for ever after.

Abby signed, fished two dollars from her pocketbook, and took a receipt in exchange. I put the money and the contract in Escott's top drawer along with my shorthand notes. He'd have a fine time trying figure things out when he came in tomorrow morning. I harvested my overcoat and fedora from the coat tree in the corner, and ushered my newest client out, locking up. She made it to the bottom of the stairs, then pulled the veil back over her face.

"Afraid someone will recognize you?" I asked. The street was empty.

"No sense in taking chances."

Now I really liked her. I opened my new Studebaker up and handed her in, checking the sky. It had been threatening to sleet since before I got up tonight; I hoped it would hold off.

"Nice car," she said.

The nicest I'd ever owned. My faithful '34 Buick had come to a bad end but this sporty replacement helped ease the loss. I got the motor purring, remembered to turn the headlights on, and put it in gear, pulling slowly from the curb. "Where's your brother-in-law buried?" Abby's chin was just visible; I could see her jaw drop.

"Why do you need to know that?"

"I want to pay my respects."

"The cemetery will be closed."

"Which one? And where?"

She told me, finally, and I made a U-turn and got us on our way. Chicago traffic was no worse than usual as we headed toward Lincolnwood.

Following Abby's directions we ended up driving slowly along Ravenswood Avenue. A railroad track on our left obscured the cemetery grounds. When a cross street opened, I took the turn under the tracks. A pale stone building with crenellations, Gothic windows, and a square, two-storied tower with a number of slender, round towers at the corners and along the front wall looked back at us. It had too much dignity to be embarrassed. The gates that blocked its arched central opening were, indeed, closed.

"Told you," said Abby.

"Is Mr. Weisinger anywhere near the front?" This place looked huge. They only put fancy stone buildings like that in front of the really large cemeteries.

"Go back south and turn on Bryn Mawr. I'll tell you when to stop."

What the lady said. It took awhile to find a sufficiently secluded place to park, then Abby provided very specific directions to the grave, which was not too far from the boundary wall.

"What are you going to do?" she asked.

I was about to say she didn't want to know, but decided that would get me an observation about not treating her like an adult. "I'm going to check to see if the grave has been disturbed enough to bring in the law."

"But the police, the papers—"

"A necessary evil. If they show up asking Bradford how he got that wedding ring, how long do you think he'll stick around?"

"Would they put him in jail?" She looked hopeful.

"We'll see. You gonna be warm enough? Good. I'll be quick."

"Don't you want me along?"

"I'll bet you're good at it, but you're not exactly dressed for getting around fences."

She looked relieved.

I slammed the door, opened the trunk, and drew out a crowbar from the toolbox I kept there. Since Abby didn't need to see and try to guess why I'd want one, I held it out of sight while approaching the cemetery's boundary. It was made of iron bars with points on top, an easy climb if you were nimble.

I had the agility, but slipped between the bars instead. Literally. One of my happier talents acquired after my death was being able to vanish and float just about anywhere I liked, invisible as air. Since it was dark and there was some distance between me and the car, I figured Abby wouldn't see much if I partially vanished, eased through, and went solid again. Blink of an eye and it was done.

The cemetery grounds were covered with a thick layer of mostly undisturbed snow. Trees, bushes, and monuments of all shapes showed black against it. I made my way to one of the wide paths that had been shoveled clear, looking out for the landmark of an especially ornate mausoleum with marble columns in front. Weisinger's grave marker was just behind it. The dates on the substantial granite block told me he'd been born this day and was only a few years younger than I, the poor bastard. Another, identical block sprouted right next to it with his widow's name and date of birth already in place.

The snow lay differently over his plot, clumped and broken, dirtier than the stuff in the surrounding area. Footprints were all over, but not being an Indian tracker I couldn't make much from them, only that someone had recently been busy here and worn galoshes.

I poked the long end of the crowbar into the soil, and it went in far too easily. Ground that had had seven months to settle and freeze in the winter weather would have put up more resistance. Bradford or someone working for him had dug down, opened the coffin, grabbed the wedding ring, and put the earth back. Then he'd taken the trouble to dump shovelfuls of snow on top so a casual eye wouldn't notice. He was probably hoping there'd be another fall soon to cover the rest of the evidence.

The ghoulishness of the robbery appalled me; the level of greed behind it disgusted me. I knew some tough customers who worked for Gordy, and even they would have balked at this level of low.

The moment Abigail Saeger told me about Weisinger's death on the lake, I'd signed myself onto the job. Something twinged inside me then, connecting that death to my own and to that damned "Gloomy Sunday" song playing on the radio. I didn't want to believe in coincidences of the weird kind; signs and portents were strictly for the fortune-teller's booth at the midway.

But still. . .I got a twinge.

It was different from the gooseflesh creep that means someone's walking over your grave. When it came down to it, I didn't have a grave, just that lake. The people who'd murdered me had also robbed me of a proper burial. Weisinger had gotten one but Bradford had violated it.

That was just *wrong*.

And just as that thought crossed my mind the wind abruptly kicked up, rattling the bare branches as though the trees were waking up around me. They scratched and clacked and I tried to not imagine bones making a similar noise, but it was too late.

"All right, keep your shirt on," I said to no one in particular, stepping away from the grave. It sure as hell felt like someone was listening.

I was dead (or undead), surrounded by acres of the truly dead. The wind sent snow dust skittering along the black path. My imagination gave it form and purpose as it swept by. A sizable icicle from high up broke away and dropped like a spear, making a pop as loud as a gunshot when it hit a stone marker and shattered not two yards away. If my heart had been beating, it would have stopped then and there.

It's easy to be calm about weird coincidence when one is *not* in a cemetery at night. I decided it was time to leave. That I winked out quick and sped invisibly over the ground toward the fence faster than a scalded cat was my own business. Anyway, I went solid again as soon as I was on the other side.

Abby and I needed to get to her house before nine.

That's what I told myself while quick-marching to the car, consciously not looking over my shoulder.

* * *

Rich people live in some damned oddball houses. The Weisinger place started out with Frank Lloyd Wright on the ground floor, lots of glass and native stone, then the rest looked like a Tudor mansion straight from *The Private Life of Henry VIII*. I could almost see Charles Laughton waving cheerily from an upper window, framed by dark wood crosspieces set into the plaster.

"It's awful, but roomy," said Abby as I parked across the street to indulge in a good long stare.

"You okay for going back in without getting caught?"

"Yes, but aren't you coming?"

"This is the part where I do some sneaking around."

"They'll catch you; they'll think you're a burglar!"

"You hired an expert. Look, we can't go through the front so you can introduce me to everyone. It'll put Bradford on his guard, and your sister will be within her rights to kick me out."

"What will you do?"

"Exactly what's needed to get rid of him—and for that *you* need an alibi so they'll know you aren't involved. This means you can't hide behind that screen as usual. You said there're servants? Do they eavesdrop? Perfect. Think you can eavesdrop with them?"

"It wouldn't be the first time."

"Good for you. Whatever happens I want them to truthfully vouch that you were with them the whole time. This keeps you off the hook with Flora. I'm going to do my best to make Bradford look bad, so you have to be completely clear. Can you look innocent? Never mind, you're a natural." I checked my watch: twenty to nine. "I need a sketch of the floor plan."

I pulled a shorthand pad from the glove compartment and gave her a pencil. A streetlamp on the corner bled just enough light to work by as she plotted out an irregular shape, dividing it into squares and rectangles, putting a big X in to mark the parlor.

"That's the ground floor." She handed the pad over. "Kitchen, dining room, card room, music room, small parlor, large parlor: that's where they have the séances. How will you—"

"Trade secret. You'll get your money's worth and then some. Now beat it. Shuck those weeds and keep some witnesses around you. Don't be alone for a minute." She got out of the car quickly, coming around the driver's side. I rolled the window down. "One more thing. . ."

She bent to be at eye level. "Yes?"

"When the dust settles, don't give your sister any 'I told you so's,' okay?"

Abby got a funny look, and I thought she'd ask one more time about what I'd be doing, and I'd have to put her off, not being sure myself. Instead, she pecked me a solid one right on the mouth, and honest to God, I did *not* see it coming.

"Good luck!" she whispered, then scampered off.

No point in wiping away the lip color; she wasn't wearing any. Dangerous girl. I felt old.

I took the car around the block once and found a likely place to leave it, close behind another that had just parked along the curb. A line of vehicles of various makes and vintages led to the Weisinger house. Partygoers, I thought. A well-bundled couple emerged and stalked carefully along the damp sidewalk toward the lights. Slouching down, I waited until five to nine, then got out and followed.

Not as many lights showed around the curtains now, but I could hear the noise of a sizable gathering within the walls. The possibility sneaking in to blend with the crowd occurred, but I decided against. Groups like the Psychical Society tended to be close-knit and notice outsiders. With his membership card Escott could get away with bluffing himself in (his English accent didn't hurt, either), but I was a readymade sore thumb. Better that they never see my face at all.

I took the long way around the house to compare it to Abby's sketch. She'd not marked the windows, not that I needed to open any to get in. Picking a likely one above the larger parlor, I vanished, floated up the wall, and seeped through by way of the cracks.

Bumbling around in the space on the other side, I regretted not getting a sketch of the second story as well. The room was big and I sensed furniture shapes filling it. Though my hearing was muffled, I determined no one else was there and cautiously re-formed, taking it slow. An empty, dark bedroom, and laid out on the bed was a man's dressing gown. Neatly together on the floor were his slippers. The rest of the room was in perfect order, personal items set out on a bureau, no dust anywhere, and yet it didn't feel lived in. No one is ever this tidy when they're actually using such things.

The hair went up on the back of my neck.

This stuff was too high quality to belong to the butler. The *J. W.* engraved into the back of a heavy silver hairbrush confirmed it—the room was a shrine. I concluded that Flora Weisinger was in sore need of real help to deal with her grief and guilt, not well-meaning morons with Ouija boards.

The upstairs seemed to be deserted, but I crept softly along the hall, ready to vanish again if company came. The downstairs noise was loud from several conversations going at once, the same as for any party, but no music, no laughter.

Nosy, I opened doors. The one nearest Weisinger's room led to Flora's, to judge by the furnishings and metaphysical reading matter. I never understood why it was that rich couples sometimes went in for separate bedrooms, even when they really liked each other.

Her closet was stuffed with dark clothing, all the cheerful print dresses and light colors shoved far to either side. Women wore dark things in the winter, but this was too much. There was an out of place-looking portable record player on a table by the bed. The only record on the spindle was Kemp's "Gloomy Sunday."

Enough already. I got out before I had another damn twinge.

One of the hall doors opened to a sizable linen cupboard. I stepped in and put on the light. With my vision the night is like day to me if there's any kind of illumination, but not so much in interior rooms with no windows. This place reminded me of the hidden room under Escott's kitchen where I slept while the sun was up. I took off my overcoat and hat, putting them out of sight in the back on an upper shelf. I wanted to be able to move around quick if required.

Sheets and towels filled other shelves, along with some white, filmy material that I figured out were spare curtains. When I was a kid my mom drafted me twice a year to help change the winter curtains to summer and back again. No matter that it was women's work, I was the youngest and available.

I held the fabric up and it was just like what Mom used. In a lighted room you could see through it, but in a dark place with only a candle burning and imaginations at a fever pitch—yeah, I could make good use of it. The widest, longest piece folded up small, and I easily pushed it into the gap between my belt and shirt in the back.

But I wanted something more spectacular than a fun house spook. The items in Weisinger's room would do it.

From his bureau I pocketed the hairbrush, a pipe, a comb, and some keys, and checked out a bottle of aftershave cologne. Aqua Velva was good enough for me, but rich guys had to be different. I shook some into my hands and gave myself a thorough slapping down, face, neck, hands, and lapels. Fortunately, it smelled pretty nice.

Downstairs, things suddenly went quiet. The séance must be starting.

No time for further refinements, I vanished and sank straight through the floor until I'd cleared its barrier and was sure it was now a ceiling. I hovered high, listening.

They sang "Happy Birthday."

I could have done without that.

The mostly in-key singing ended, then a man gently urged, "Blow them out and make a wish for him, Flora."

The soft applause that followed indicated success, then there was a general shuffling and scraping as they took seats. No one spoke, which was odd. People talked at parties.

Silence now, a long stretch of silence. I took the pause as an opportunity to explore the edges of the room. Certainly I bumped and brushed into people, and they'd shiver in reaction, because in this form I'd feel like a cold draft to them, but the silence held. Without much trouble I found a corner and determined this was where Abby hid herself. She was absent, so I gradually re-formed.

The Chinese screen—and I didn't have much experience with them—was seven feet tall and wide enough to conceal a sizable serving area. When holding formal receptions, you didn't have to see the servants messing with the dishes. There were spaces between the painted panels that I could peer through, though. Each sliver of space provided a different angle on things.

The large parlor was much bigger than. I expected. A long table was set up in the middle and seated eight to a side. Each chair had an occupant, and they were a motley group: some wore formal clothes, others were artistically Bohemian.

An older, more polished, more somber version of Abby sat at one end on the side opposite me: Flora Weisinger. Behind her was a framed portrait of a young man in his prime: her late husband. In front of her was a large birthday cake, its candles dead. She clutched a wadded handkerchief in one hand; in the other, pinched between thumb and forefinger and held up like an offering, was a gold ring. I could guess whose. Her posture was tense, expectant, her big dark gaze fixed on the tall man next to her.

At the head of the table, clearly in charge, stood Alistair Bradford, Having seen a few mediums in the course of my checkered life, I knew they ran to all types, from self-effacing, lace-clad ladies, to suave young lounge lizards with Vaseline-slicked hair. Bradford was lofty and distinguished, his own too-long hair swept back like that of an orchestra maestro. It suited his serious features. He was handsome, if you liked that brand of it, and his slate blue eyes did look piercing as they took in the disciples at the table.

"Now, dear friends," he said in a startlingly soft, clear, beautiful voice, "please let us bow our heads in sincere prayer for a safe and enlightening spiritual journey on this very, *very* special night."

Such was the influence of that surprising voice that I actually followed through with the rest of them. I had to shake myself and remember he'd violated a grave to get to that ring in Flora Weisinger's fingers. The wave of disgust snapped me out of it. The next time he spoke, saying *amen*, I had my guard up.

Down the whole length of that big, bare table there were only two candles burning, leaving the rest of the room—to their eyes—dark. It was as good as daylight to me.

"And now I ask that everyone remain utterly quiet, and I will attempt to make contact," he said, smiling warmly.

I expected them to hold hands, touch fingers, or something like that. So much for how things were done in the movies.

Bradford sat, composed himself with his palms flat on the table, and shut his eyes. He drew in a deep breath, audibly releasing it. In contrast, no one else seemed able to move or breathe. Flora looked at him with an intense and heartbreaking hope that was terrible to see.

His stertorous breathing gradually got louder. The man knew how to play things to raise the suspense.

And I knew how to bust it.

His noises got thicker with more throat behind them, so I could guess he was ready to turn it into a good long groan so *Frere* Leon could make his entrance.

I went invisible, floated until I was exactly behind his chair, went solid while crouched down, and drew a big breath of my own. During the brief silence between his puffings I cut loose with loudest, juiciest Bronx cheer I could manage, then vanished.

In a tense, emotion-charged room it had a predictable effect. I slipped behind the screen to watch.

His rhythm abruptly shattered, Bradford looked around in confusion, as did the others. Some seemed scandalized, a couple were amused, and one guy suggested that perhaps there was a playful spirit in the room already. A more practical man got up to check my corner, which was the only hiding place, and announced it to be empty.

A few of them noticed the cologne and mentioned it. Much to their delight, Flora finally confirmed that it was James's scent hanging in the air. She sounded awful. Bradford made no comment.

After some excited discussion that didn't go anywhere, they settled down, and Bradford started his routine again. I watched and waited.

Frere Leon eventually began to speak through Bradford, and to give him credit, it was a damned well-done French accent. His voice was rougher, deeper in pitch, very effective in the dark.

I ventured forth again, keeping low while he gave them a weather report for the other side, and went solid just long enough to call out a handy bit of French I'd learned while on leave in Paris. The loose translation was *How much for an hour of love, my little cabbage?*

Or something like that; it had usually been enough to get my face slapped.

Then I clocked him sharp on the back of the noggin with the hairbrush, dropped it, and vanished.

I was back to the screen, going solid in time to see things fall apart. A few in the room had understood what I'd said and were either flabbergasted or trying not to laugh. Bradford's trance was thoroughly broken; he launched from his chair to look behind it, startled as the rest. He remembered himself, though, and flopped down again, apparently in a state of collapse. They fussed over him, and switched on the electric chandelier.

Somewhere in the middle of it Flora spotted the hairbrush. She screamed and sat down fast, sheet white and pointing to where it lay on the floor.

It took attention away from Bradford, and I was betting he was none too pleased. The knock he'd taken bothered him—his hand kept rubbing the spot—but I'd hit to hurt, not cause permanent damage. He'd earned it.

I kept myself out of sight for the duration, going solid in the empty room next to it. Vanishing took it out of me. I'd have to stop at the Stockyards before dawn for some blood or I'd feel like hell tomorrow night.

Some guy who seemed to be the one in charge of the Psychical Society was for canceling the sitting, but Bradford assured everyone that he was fine. Sometimes mischievous spirits delighted in disrupting things unless, of course, there was a more earthly explanation. With Flora's permission the ground floor was searched for uninvited guests. I had to not be there for a few minutes but didn't mind.

Elsewhere in the house, probably the distant kitchen, I heard strident voices denying any part of the business. Abby's was in that chorus, her outrage genuine. Good girl.

This time it took longer for everyone to settle. Though the hour inched toward ten, none showed signs of being sleepy enough to leave. The entertainment was too interesting.

The hour struck and they assembled in the parlor again. On the long table fresh candles were substituted for the ones that had expired. The chandelier was switched off.

From my vantage point at the screen I tried to get a sense of Flora's reaction to things. She had the silver-backed hairbrush square in front of her and kept looking at it. She had to be the gracious hostess, but her nerves were showing in the way she played with that handkerchief. She'd rip it apart before too long. As she took her seat again close to Bradford, she held the wedding ring out as before, but her fingers shook.

Third time's the charm, I thought, and waited.

Bradford did his routine without a hitch, and before too long good old *Frere* Leon was back and in a thick accent offered them greetings and a warning against paying mind to dark spirits who could lead them astray from the True Path.

That's what *he* called it. I just shook my head, assembling my borrowed weapons on the serving table, a napkin scrounged from a stack at one end to nix the noise.

Flora gave *Frere* Leon a formal greeting and asked if her husband was present.

"He is, *ma petit.* 'E shines like the sun and speaks of 'is love for you."

She released a shaky sigh of relief and it sounded too much like a sob. "What else does he say? James? Are you sure? Tell me what to do!"

Bradford's old monk tortured her a little longer, not answering. He said he could not hear well for the dark spirits trying to come between, then: "Ah! 'E is clear at last. 'E says 'is love is deep, and 'e wants you to be a'ppy on this plane. You are to open your 'eart to new love. Ah—the 'appiness that awaits you is great. 'E smiles! Such joy for you, sweet child, such joy!"

Flora shook her head a little. Some part of her must have known this was all wrong.

Time to confirm it.

I'd pulled out the curtain material and draped it over my head, tying one of the napkins kerchief-like around my neck to keep the stuff from slipping off. It looked phony as hell, I was sure, but in the darkness with this crowd it would lay 'em in the aisles.

Picking up Weisinger's things, I eased from behind the screen. Everyone was looking at Bradford. He might have seen me in the shadows beyond the candle glow, but his eyes were shut.

Made to order, I thought, and accurately bounced the keys off his skull. It was a damned good throw, and I followed quickly with the other things. The comb landed square in the cake, the pipe skidded along the table and slid into Flora's lap. She shrieked and jumped up.

If *Frere* Leon had a good entrance, that was nothing to compare to that of Jack Fleming, fake ghost-for-hire.

I vanished and reappeared but only just, holding to a mostly transparent state—standing smack-dab in the middle of the table. The top half of my body was visible, beautifully obscured by the pale curtain. The bottom half went right into the wood.

It didn't feel good but was pretty spectacular. Their screaming helped.

With some effort I pressed forward, moving right through the table, candles and all, down its remaining length, working steadily toward Bradford. His eyes were now wide open, and it was a treat to see him shed the trance to see some real supernatural trouble. When I raised a pale, curtain-swathed hand to point at him, I thought he'd swallow his tongue.

Then I willed myself higher, rising until I was clear of the table and floating free. I made one swimming circuit of the room, then dove toward Bradford, letting myself go solid as I dropped.

I took in enough breath to fill the room with a wordless and hopefully terrifying bellow and hit him like bowling ball taking out one last stubborn pin. It was a nasty impact for us both, but I had the advantage of being able to vanish again. So far as I could tell he was sprawled flat and screaming with the rest.

Remaining invisible was uphill work for me now, but necessary. I clung close to Bradford so he could enjoy my unique kind of cold. I'd been told it was like death's own breath from the Arctic. Through chattering teeth he babbled nonsense about dark spirits being gathered against him and that he had to leave before they manifested again. He got some argument and a suggestion they all pray to dispel the negative influences, but he was already barreling out the door.

I stuck with him until he got in his car, then slipped into the backseat and went solid. He screeched like a woman when I snaked one arm around his neck in a half-nelson. I'm damned strong. He couldn't break free. When he stopped making noise, I noticed him staring at the rearview mirror. It was empty, of course.

Leaning in, my mouth close to his ear, in my best imitation of the Shadow, I whispered, "Game's over, Svengali. Digging up that grave pissed off the wrong kind of *things*. We're on to you and we're *hungry*. You want to see another dawn?"

He whimpered, and the sound of his racing heart filled the car. I took that as a yes.

"Get out of town. Get out of the racket. Go back to the stage. Better a live magician than a dead medium. Got that? *Got that?*"

Not waiting for a reply, I vanished, exiting fast. He gunned the motor to life and shot away like Barney Oldfield looking to make a new speed record.

* * *

As the wrecked evening played itself out to the survivors in the parlor, I made it back to the linen closet, killed the light, and parked my duff on an overturned bucket to wait in the dark. I needed the rest.

The house grew quiet. The last guests departed with enough copy from tonight to fill their monthly pamphlets for years to come. Escort would have some interesting reading to share. I got the impression Flora was not planning another sitting, though a few people assured her that tonight's events should be continued.

The residents finished and came upstairs one by one. Flora Weisinger went into James's room and stayed there for a long time, crying. Abby found her, they talked in low voices for a time, and Flora cried some more. I wasn't sorry. Better now than later, married to a leech. Apparently things worked out. The sisters emerged, each going to her own room. Some servant made a last round, checking the windows, then things fell silent.

I'd taken off the spook coverings, folding the curtain and napkin, slipping them in with similar ones on a shelf. Retrieving my coat and hat I was ready to make a quiet exit until catching the faint sound of "Gloomy Sunday" seeping through the walls.

Damn.

This night had been a flying rout for Bradford, but Flora was still stuck in her pit. She might dig it even deeper until it was a match for her husband's grave.

Someone needed to talk sense into her. I felt the least qualified for the job, but soon as I recognized the music I got that twinge again.

I did my vanishing act and went across to Flora's room.

The music grew louder as I floated toward it, just solid enough to check the lay of the land. The lights were out, only a little glow from around her heavy curtains, enough to navigate and not be seen.

Quick as I could I re-formed, flicked the phonograph's needle arm clear, and pulled out the record. It made a hell of a crunch when I broke it to pieces.

There was a feminine gasp from the bed, and she fumbled the light on. By then I was gone, but sensed her coming over. Another gasp, then—

"James?" Her voice quavered with that heartbreaking hope, now tinged with anguish. "James? Oh, please, darling, talk to me. I know you're here."

She'd picked up on the cologne.

"James? *Please . . .*"

This would be tough. I drifted over to a wall and gradually took shape, keeping it slow so she had time to stare, and if not get used to me, then at least not scream.

Hands to her mouth, eyes big, and her skin dead white, she looked ready to faint. This was cruel. A different kind from Bradford's type of torture, but still cruel.

"James sent me," I said, keeping my voice soft. "Please don't be afraid." She'd frozen in place and I wasn't sure she understood. I repeated myself and she finally nodded.

"Where is he?" she demanded, matching my soft tone.

"He's with God." It seemed best to keep things as simple as possible. "Everything that man told you was a lie. You know that now, don't you?"

She nodded again, the jerky movement very similar to Abby's mannerism. "Please, let me speak to James. I must tell him—"

"He knows already. He said to tell you it wasn't your fault. There's nothing to forgive. It was his time to go, that's all. Not your fault."

"But it *was*."

"Nope." I raised my right hand. "Swear to God. And I should know."

That had her nonplussed. "What. . .who are you?"

"Just a friend."

"That cologne, it's *his*."

"So you'd know he sent me. Flora, he loves you and knows you love him. But this is not the way to honor his memory. He wants you to give it up before it destroys you. He's dead and you're alive. There's a reason you're here."

"What? Tell me!"

"Doesn't work like that, you have to find out for yourself. You won't find answers in a Ouija board, though."

Flora had tentatively moved closer to me. "You look real."

"Thanks, I try my best. I can't stay long. Not allowed. I have to make sure you're clear-headed on this. No more guilt—it wasn't your fault—get rid of this psychic junk and live your life. James wants you to be happy again. If not now, then someday."

"That's all?"

"Flora. . .that's a lifetime. A good one if you choose it."

"I'll ... all right. Would you tell James—"

"He *knows*. Now get some sleep. New day in the morning. Enjoy it." I was set to gradually vanish again, then remembered— "One last thing, Flora. James's wedding band." I held my hand out.

She shrank away. "Oh, no, I couldn't."

"Yes, you can. It belongs with him and you know it. Come on."

Fresh tears ran down her face, but maybe this time there would be healing for her. She had his ring on a gold chain around her neck and reluctantly took it off. She read the inscription one more time, kissed the ring, and gave it over.

"Everything will be fine," I said. "This is from James." I didn't think he'd mind. I leaned over and kissed her on the forehead, very lightly, and vanished before she could open her eyes.

* * *

For the next few hours I drove around Chicago, feeling like a prize idiot and hoping I'd not done even worse damage to Flora than Alistair Bradford. I didn't think so, but the worry stuck.

Eventually I found my way back to that big cemetery and got myself inside, walking quickly along the path to the fancy mausoleum and the grave behind it.

I was damned tired, but had one last job to do to earn Abby Saeger's two bucks.

Pinching the ring in my fingers as Flora had done at the séance, I extended my arm and disappeared once more, this time sinking into the earth. It was the most unpleasant sensation, pushing down through the broken soil, pushing until what had been my hand found a greater resistance.

That would be James Weisinger's coffin.

I'd never attempted anything like this before but was reasonably sure it was possible. This was a hell of a way to find out for certain.

Pushing just a little more against the resistance, it suddenly ceased to be there. Carefully not thinking what that meant, I focused my concentration on getting just my hand to go solid.

It must have worked, because it hurt like a Fury, felt like my hand was being sawed away at the wrist. Just before the pain got to be too much I felt the gold ring slip from my grasp.

One instant I was six feet under with my hand in a coffin and the next stumbling in the snow, clutching my wrist and trying not to yell too much.

My hand was still attached. I worked the fingers until they stopped looking so clawlike, then sagged against a tree. What a night.

I got back in my car just as the sleet began ticking against the windows, trying to get in. It was creepy. I wanted some sound to mask it but hesitated turning on the radio, apprehensive that "Gloomy Sunday" might be playing again.

What the hell. Music was company, proof that there were other people awake somewhere. I could always change the station.

When it warmed up, Bing Crosby sang "Pennies from Heaven." Someone at the radio station had noticed the weather, perhaps, and was having his little joke.

I felt that twinge again, but now it raised a smile.

THE COMPANY YOU KEEP

Author's Note: *In the Vampire Files series I introduced a new bloodsucker to the cast, the unpredictable—and often unstable—Whitey Kroun. This story sold to Moonstone Books in 2009 for their DRACULA AND THE LEGIONS OF THE UNDEAD anthology. In case you wondered, there is such a cave in St. Paul and gangsters did hang out there.*

St. Paul, February 1938

Gabriel "Whitey" Kroun drove to St. Paul because it wasn't Chicago.

In a new town chances were good no one would know his face and thus his reputation. The reputation belonged to the part of him nicknamed Whitey, but he was gone and Gabe was now in charge. He was still getting used to it.

Gabe had few memories of being Whitey Kroun, but counted it to be a good thing. Whitey had been bad company, a real bastard. Gabriel, however, was a nearly blank slate, thanks to the bullet still lodged in his head. He needed to figure out what to do about himself, so he drove to St. Paul, found a hotel, and paid for a week's worth of thinking time.

But one full evening of staring at the walls gave him cabin fever, not insight.

On the second night he asked the desk clerk about local distractions, preferably noisy ones that closed late. He'd noticed a bowling alley farther up the street. He didn't know if he could bowl, but the option to find out was there. He might like it. Instead, the clerk recommended a nightclub close to the hotel called the Royal Arms—which turned out to be in a cave.

Well, that sounded interesting.

Local lore had that the place was originally used to grow mushrooms until the owner found more money was to be had in the booze business. A later entrepreneur fancied up the entry to look like a castle, complete with crenellations and fake drawbridge, which was nuts, but the gimmick worked. Business boomed even through Prohibition, and had attracted dubious types like Dillinger and Baby Face Nelson.

Gabe thought he'd fit in unnoticed.

Inside, away from the snow-laced wind, he decided the place would appeal to anyone looking for something different. The natural cave had been improved on, carved more deeply into the side of a massive hill. The barrel-vaulted stone ceiling about ten feet overhead flowed seamlessly down into rounded walls. Except for tables, chairs, and the bar, there wasn't a corner or sharp angle in sight. It looked like a giant worm had burrowed out a huge cavity for itself, then unaccountably left.

He decided not to check his hat and coat, unsure of how long he'd stay. His shoulders kept trying to crowd his ears, as though reacting to the press of surrounding stone. The room was huge and a heartening number of electric lights made up for the lack of windows, but what if the power failed? However excellent his night vision had become, he didn't like the dark, which was ironic, but there it was.

For all the Royal Arms being under the insulating ground, it was gratifyingly loud. The stone walls threw the band music back, forth, and inside out if you counted the echoes. People trying to talk over it added another layer to the din. He liked the distraction.

He pointed toward a table where he could sit with his back to the wall. A cheerful waitress who didn't see anything odd about that led him over. He ordered coffee.

"What do you want in it?" she asked.

"Sugar," he said with a smile and wink, giving her fifty cents. "Keep the change, cutey."

She flashed a bigger smile back and bounced away. He liked the view. Maybe he just needed company, female company. That was a possibility—if this was the kind of place where one could arrange such a transaction. He checked things over, appraising the crowd.

The band was small: a piano player, drummer, and a guy who switched between a horn and a clarinet, depending on the tune. The three played as though it was the first time they'd ever worked together. It'd be embarrassing but no one paid them attention. The few couples in the room weren't dancing, absorbed by their own concerns. Other drinkers had the bored air of long-time regulars with nowhere else to go. Most glanced his way when he came in, but that's how it always was when a newcomer shows up.

He spotted some familiar-looking mugs, but only because their type was to be found in every town. The odds were that he didn't know them personally, but Gabe kept an eye open for the subtle and not-so-subtle signs of recognition.

Like the ones coming from the guy over there in the corner with his back to the wall. He was in shadow, which would otherwise have made him invisible to anyone else. Gabriel let him keep his illusion and pretended not to notice how the man's face tightened, making his eyes go hard and narrow.

Two things would happen: the guy would leave him alone or he'd come over. If he came over he'd either pay his respects or cautiously ask if there was a problem. Gabe would assure him there was no problem and not be believed.

Cripes, I should have gone bowling.

The waitress brought him a cup of coffee and a sugar bowl.

"Can you take a load off for a few minutes?" he asked. "I don't like drinking alone."

In his solitude of the hotel room he found the acid from his newly-formed and inexperienced conscience had an easier time of etching holes in his brain, which was annoying. The bad stuff had been Whitey's doing, after all. He wanted some practice being Gabriel, whoever the hell he might turn out to be. Getting out and about with strangers would help.

She glanced around and slipped onto the chair across from him. "I guess so, it's slow tonight."

"One of these guys your boss?"

"He's keeps to his office, doesn't like the band we got in this week."

"I've heard better." Gabe pushed the coffee toward her. "Here, I don't want it after all."

He knew he must have drunk coffee in the life he'd had before waking up dead and craving something entirely different, but now it smelled like cigar ashes. She said she couldn't, but he mentioned it'd be a shame to let it go to waste.

"If you're sure. . ." She spooned in three sugars, sipped, and apparently liked the result. He wondered if that much sugar would sweeten her own taste, should he get the opportunity to taste her.

He could easily make that happen. All it took was a little hypnosis, one of the advantages of being a vampire. Fix her with a focused look, whisper a few words, and she'd do anything for him. He could lead her outside into dark and freezing shadows and drain her dry. She wouldn't be aware of it. When he was done, he'd leave the body in a drift to let the flying snow blanket her from view. They wouldn't find her for weeks. That'd be funny.

Gabe's muscles twitched as though from electric shock, and he had to fight to keep the revulsion from showing. Such sickening ideas were nightmare remnants of the dead and unmourned Whitey. As a human he'd been monster enough, God help the world if he'd survived as a vampire.

That's not me. I'm not like him.

Gabe was better than that.

He wanted to be, anyway.

Gabe got the young woman's name—Inga—how long she'd worked at the Royal Arms, and when she expected to go home tonight. She shared a flat with another, she added.

"That's lucky," he said, noting that she left out whether her flat mate was friend or lover. "No chance to get lonely. You've got someone to talk to."

"I guess I do," she agreed. "But maybe I'd like talking with someone else for a change."

She didn't get huffy when he mentioned his hotel room might be a good place to have a conversation. He took it as being only fair when she mentioned she'd like more than a forty-cent tip. They settled on a sum and a time to meet so he could walk her over, then she asked if he wanted another cup of coffee. Inga had finished his.

"A glass of water is fine." He gave her dollar tip for that one, and she seemed to glow a little brighter. If things went well, they'd both have a fine evening ahead.

He smiled fondly after, enjoying the view all over again as she went back to the bar. Inga had dark hair, which was a contrast to her name. He thought she must have some Swede in her, but weren't they all blond? Were they different from dark-haired girls once the lights were out? He'd not had opportunity to look into it. That had to do with his future, one of the things he'd come here to think over, though he now had a chance to talk it out instead.

He hoped—afterwards, of course—that Inga would be a good listener. He could always pay her extra. Didn't crazy people give head-doctors lots of money to talk about their troubles? Gabe didn't want a doctor who would take notes and give advice, he wanted a pretty girl who would lend a sympathetic ear for an hour or two. What she heard wouldn't matter; he'd make sure she forgot everything before she left. Using hypnosis gave him a headache, but he needed only a few seconds, well worth the risk. She wouldn't even wonder about the marks on her throat.

His improved mood was spoiled when the man from the shadows came over. He looked down at Gabe for a moment, then sat as though invited. He seemed not to notice when Inga came up with the glass of water. She shot Gabe a nervous look, which told him just what kind of man was across from him. Gabe gave her a brief smile and another quick, subtle wink. He had everything—whatever it was—well in hand.

"Yeah?" he said, just to get things rolling.

"I know who you are. Whitey Kroun."

Gabe no longer thought of himself by that name. The bastard was dead and good riddance.

"I'm Harry Ziemer," the stranger announced. He seemed to expect some kind of reaction to that fact. He was solidly built, just starting to go bald. His mud-brown eyes had that soulless cast some guys get when they've killed one man too many or hadn't killed nearly enough. Not a face one would forget, but still unfamiliar.

Gabe had learned early on that the best way to compensate for a memory that didn't exist was to not respond and let the other guy do the explaining. "Oh, yeah?" A useful phrase, he'd picked it up in Chicago.

"Things are gonna stay friendly and quiet here, no need for you to trouble yourself."

"Uh-huh."

"My friends and I are gonna do our deal."

"Uh-huh."

"We got an understanding?"

"Whatever you say, Harry Ziemer."

"Thanks. Whitey."

Gabe felt a shifting inside him, like the throwing a switch.

He'd just found out something new about his reborn self: he hated that name, but it was still his and he'd not given this bozo permission to use it. He didn't like the accompanying smirk. He didn't like the man throwing his weight around as though he owned the world. If he'd shown even an illusion of respect Gabe would have let it go, but he hadn't.

And, since to some people he was still Whitey Kroun, he could not ignore it.

Ziemer left the table, returning to his friends. It was no surprise that they were the mugs Gabe had spotted earlier. Of course they'd be armed like their boss. Ziemer's shoulder rig was blatantly visible through his suit.

Gabriel was also armed, having a revolver in his overcoat pocket. Six shots. If it came to it he could miss twice or—more likely—have two bullets left over.

He had to only look at a target to hit it square; you couldn't learn that particular talent. You were born with it. Whitey Kroun had been born with it; when he died and Gabriel Kroun emerged, the talent had carried over.

This is nuts. I was imagining it. He wasn't. . .

Ziemer looked right at him, smirk firmly in place. He murmured to the mugs. They chuckled and looked as well, smiling as though they'd put something over on Gabe so slick that he hadn't yet caught on.

His long fingers went around the base of his water glass to pick it up. He let it slip, and water slopped over the table. He grimaced and waved to Inga, pointing at the mess. She hurried up with a towel.

"I'll get you more," she said.

"Never mind that, cutey. Who's Harry Ziemer and why is he here? No, don't look at him, just do what you're doing and smile at me."

"He wants to be a big shot. He's been moving in on things, takes 'em over. Garages, taverns. He's been loafing here for a week. There's rumors we're next."

"How's he operate?"

"He talks the owner into signing over the deed."

"At gun point?"

"I wouldn't know about that. The owners always get out of town right after. Leastways no one sees 'em again. If Harry Ziemer's got a beef against you, you should maybe leave, too."

"You'd think so. Relax, cutey, we've got a date." He smiled, but her walk wasn't as bouncy when she returned to the bar. Couldn't blame her. Any time now she could have a new boss or be out of a job or worse. With guys like Ziemer there was always a worse.

Ziemer and his cronies were gone from their table. The last of them was just walking into some kind of cave passage off the main room. Maybe it was the call of nature. One way to find out.

The hall was wide and low, the ceiling and walls rounded. A wire with bare bulbs every ten feet hung from hooks in the ceiling. Their glow, all fifteen watts of it, wasn't much help against the darkness, not that Gabe was worried. It was plenty bright to his eyes.

Maybe this was where they raised the mushrooms once upon a time. The size of the place surprised him. Wasn't it easier to build walls than carve out a hole? Had to be. People were nuts.

I should know.

He sniffed the air, for the first time picking up the kind of dank scent associated with caves. . .and tombs.

Now why the hell did I think that?

If only that smirking idiot had called him "Mr. Kroun" and not overstepped with the too-familiar "Whitey."

I should be out in the main room charming the socks off Inga, not doing this.

The racket from the inept band faded with distance and a turn.

A few yards along, he came to a branching. One way was absolutely black, even to him, and the source of the dank air. It must have led to the outside; he picked up the scent of snow, dead leaves, and moldy earth. Something dead and rotting was down there as well, but the stink of decay was so faint that a human would not have noticed.

The other branch had light, a weak glow far down where the hall turned again. Gabe could see it, but only because of his supernatural edge.

The bare bulbs on their wire had been shattered in this whole section, making a powerful discouragement to anyone without a flashlight.

He went that way, drawn by voices echoing off the stone. Glass was underfoot. He kept to the one side, wincing when he couldn't avoid stepping on the shards. The crunching sounded very loud to him.

No one can hear me, they're too busy talking.

The hall had shrunk in width and was more like a tunnel. His shoulders hunched up again. He forced them down.

He reached the turn, took it, and came even with what seemed to be the boss's lair. It wasn't a room in the sense of having a door and a chamber beyond, but an especially deep alcove cut into the side of the tunnel. It had a big desk, chairs, file cabinets, and plenty of light, which was cheering.

On the floor almost at his feet was a wide scatter of desk clutter, pencils and other junk, including a stone paperweight the same pale color as the walls. The name *Lars Pargreave* had been carved into one side. It was too small to be a cemetery marker, but the image crossed Gabe's mind regardless. He could picture Ziemer swaggering in and knocking things from the desk as a way of getting the owner's attention.

A blond man—most likely Pargreave—sat behind the desk that faced toward the tunnel. His doughy face was sheeted with flop sweat. Even at ten feet Gabe picked up on air made thick and sour by the man's fear.

He had a right to it. Harry Ziemer, smiling, leaned over him with a gun muzzle pressed hard against his head. The smile had reached Ziemer's dead eyes, animating them. He clearly liked his work.

The other three were ranged loosely around the desk with their backs to Gabe. Like Ziemer, they were too focused on their prey, hyenas who'd not yet noticed the lion walking up.

There was a long piece of paper on the desk that had the look of a legal document. The blond man was trying to hold a fountain pen in his shaking hand. It had to be hard to concentrate while four guys with their guns hanging out stared at you like that.

Gabe came fully around the corner. "Harry!" he cheerfully called. "How you doing?"

All five men jumped. Gratifying.

Ziemer snapped around. He lost his smile. "We had a deal."

"Of course we did. I came to watch." Gabe bent and picked up the paperweight, hefting it idly.

"Watch?"

"Yeah, it was this or bowling." He swung the stone experimentally like a bowling ball to demonstrate, then put it on the desk. The men were looking at it and not noticing his other hand, which was in his coat pocket holding the revolver. "Doing a little taking-over?"

"Whitey. . ." but Ziemer didn't seem to know how to finish. Must have been a new kind of situation for him.

Gabe drummed his fingers on the stone, gauging distances. He could bean the guy at the end, grab Ziemer and toss him over the desk at the other two, but one of them could still get a shot off. "The band out there stinks. I hope you'll be hiring better talent."

"I'll make money, don't worry," Ziemer said. "Whitey. . ."

"Hm? Oh, don't let me stop you. Go on with what you were doing. Act like I'm not here."

That had to be impossible, but Ziemer finally gathered himself and turned his attention back to the sweating man. "Sign it, Pargreave. Now."

The hapless Pargreave somehow managed to hold the pen long enough to scratch his signature on the paper. He shrank, visibly shrank, inside his ample skin. He was nothing to Gabe. For all he knew the man might be worse than Ziemer, but Gabe wasn't here to defend any side but his own.

I should just leave. These guys aren't worth the trouble.

Ziemer had the smile back. His eyes were bright and alive as he put a couple steps between himself and the moaning Pargreave, sighting down one extended arm.

Gabe recognized that look, and thought he knew what it felt like. Some black ghost of a memory scuttled out from a corner of his mind, grinned, then darted from sight again.

Whitey Kroun used to look like Ziemer—or so Gabe imagined. Whitey put himself forward to do jobs like this so he could feel the kind of thing Ziemer was now feeling.

That's wrong.

Gabe had a conscience, just not much of one yet. It still managed to give him a twinge. It wanted him to do. . .something.

"Harry?" Gabe spoke loud enough to disrupt the headlong rush to bring death in.

Ziemer flinched, irritated. "What?"

"There's witnesses out front."

"They won't know. This far in you can fire a cannon and they'd never hear it."

"Really?" That was interesting. "What about the cops? Won't they wonder about this guy turning up dead?"

"Cops here won't do squat. We keep our business under the table, don't bother them, and they leave us alone."

Gabe had heard about St. Paul's infamous deal with the gangsters. The pact between law and disorder was an uneasy one, but mostly worked so long as the town got its share of the take. "Glad that's covered, but come on, Harry—think about the mess. You'll get blood and brains all over your nice bill of sale or whatever that is."

Ziemer was sufficiently distracted now. He looked fully at Gabe, not Pargreave. "What?"

"Scrag him if you have to, but not here. Take it from one who knows. Blood soaks right into stone like this, you'll never get it out."

"What do you want?"

"Nothing. I'm just saying you can do this better someplace else. You'll have this guy's leavings all over what's going to be your desk. Instead, you ought to be sitting behind it from the first minute, laying down the rules like a big shot should."

One of the mugs who had the wit to move clear of Ziemer's line of fire nodded. "He's got a point, boss."

"You don't want to get that stuff on your suit," Gabe added. "Any of you guys in a mood for carrying a body around and cleaning up afterwards?"

A silent exchange of looks between the three of them resulted in a unanimous shaking of heads and murmurs against such lowly labor.

"I'm getting rid of him," stated Ziemer, teeth on edge.

"Well, of course you have to, just not here is all I'm saying." Gabe stared indifferently down at the terrified Pargreave and thought of that branching into blackness and its stink of decay. "I bet *you've* got a place where you do that kind of business. Somewhere here in these caves? Yeah, I thought so."

Pargreave, shivering now, hadn't given an answer. Ziemer and his pals saw what they wanted to see in the man's gray face.

"What do you think, Harry? Let's make him take us to where he buries his bodies."

"Why do you wanna know? What do you care?"

Gabe gave a shrug. "I help you out and maybe down the road you do me a small favor. It's how the business runs, you know that. Think about it: what'll it do for your reputation when it gets out that you got backing from Whitey Kroun himself?"

"How small a favor?"

"I was thinking free drinks from your new bar."

They gave a short laugh. Pargreave didn't, but they talked over him.

"You don't want a cut of the take?" Ziemer was reasonably suspicious.

"The take from a joint like this is peanuts to me. I'm just here 'cause I'm bored. Like I said: it was this or bowling."

They laughed again, and he could see his death in their eyes.

I could be wrong. But killing an interloper is what I'd have done a few months back.

He wasn't that man anymore, but some piece of him lurked within.

Gabe couldn't recall Whitey, not exactly, but could judge him by the company he'd kept. Much of it had been scum like these.

That's why I understand them so well.

Ziemer got an idea. "You've heard of me. That's why you came to St. Paul. You heard what I'm doing."

Gabe sobered and slowly nodded, approving. "Good. . .you figured it out. Word gets around."

"So what's your real angle?"

"Harry, I'm here to size you up for the big boys, see if you're someone we can work with. How you handle this—" he indicated Pargreave, "—with kid gloves or a wrecking ball, tells us what we need to know. I'll give you a hint: use the kid gloves, and we'll cut you in on bigger and better things."

Ziemer looked as though he had the number on what they were talking about. Hell if Gabe knew. He was making it up as he went.

Ziemer's smirk was back, and he relaxed by a whole inch. "You're all right, Whitey. I heard stories about you, but they—"

With unnatural speed Gabe pulled his revolver free and shot four times. The noise was deafening in the confining space.

He braced for return fire, but none came.

He blinked against the smoke and ascertained there were four bodies on the floor, none of them getting up again. They had that look.

Under the tang of gunpowder, the heavy perfume of their blood suddenly bloomed in the alcove. It seemed to fill his head. He made his normally dormant lungs take in a full measure of the scent, but not for a moment did he consider feeding. Those mugs were garbage, and you got rid of garbage.

Gabe glanced at Pargreave, who looked like he'd swallowed his own tongue.

"You gonna be a problem and remember any of this?" Gabe asked.

Pargreave struggled past his shock, shaking his head. "No, sir," he finally whispered.

"Can you make them disappear?"

"Y-yes, sir."

Gabe didn't trust him, though, and put him under anyway to make him forget. He washed himself from Pargreave's memory, put the revolver in his hand, and told him it was self-defense, then walked quickly back down the tunnel before the man woke up.

Gabriel returned to his table in the club's main room, noticing that nothing had changed. The music from the amateurish band continued uninterrupted. His nerves settled, and the tightness inside his skull abruptly eased and vanished.

Inga came over, face solemn. "You okay? Something wrong?"

He found himself smiling warmly at her. "Nah. It's copasetic."

"What's going on with Ziemer?"

"Just wanted a card game is all. I'd have joined in, but you and I have a date."

"I should get them drinks."

"Leave 'em. They'll come out when they're thirsty."

Inga was doubtful, looking at the hallway opening.

"Hey." He reached out, gently taking one of her hands. "Lemme ask you something."

Her attention shifted to him.

"Do you think if I slipped the bartender a couple of bucks that he'd let you off early tonight?"

She brightened again. "I'm pretty sure he would."

"Go find out for me, would you?"

Inga bounced away, and Gabriel's gaze swept the room again. Nothing. Absolutely nothing. Not one hint of what had happened and just as well.

But four men dead. Just like that.

For the two seconds it took for him to draw and fire and put them down Gabe had been a machine. He'd had no thoughts, no feelings; he'd functioned well with cold efficiency.

Gabe didn't like being a machine. He suspected that if he allowed it run one time too many it might open a door in his mind that would allow Whitey to return. That would be bad.

Gabe was aware he possessed faults and flaws like other men, and on the really tough nights only a tenuous hold on sanity. He thought insanity had to do with loss of control. But back there he'd been in complete control, of himself, of the situation. He'd gone in, eyes open, knowing—

Four men dead.

He couldn't feel sorry for them, though.

But shouldn't I feel something?

He looked for, but didn't find anything more than a sense of letdown.

Then it occurred to him that he'd not felt the unholy joy he'd seen in Ziemer. Whitey had been like him once upon a time, but not the reborn Gabriel.

That had to make a difference. Maybe that's what it was about.

Or not.

Inga returned, pulling a coat on, her face bright with a big smile.

Nuts. He'd think about that crap later.

She was much better company.

DEATH IN DOVER

Author's Note*: Imagine being asked twice to do a story for an Anne Perry collection! This one sold to* DEATH BY DICKENS. *It had a short deadline, so there was no time for me to actually read a whole Dickens novel for research, but I did get in enough chapters from* A Tale of Two Cities *to write this story. Jonathan Barrett—not yet a vampire—returns with Cousin Oliver to share an adventure with a future celebrity.*

Dover, England, November 1775

I ventured to pull back the flap of the coach window for a glimpse of what lay ahead and was disappointed by the near-unrelieved darkness. The only glimmer of light emanated from the distant gray sea, which stirred restlessly under a wind out of the bitter north. Some of that cruel zephyr cut its sharp way round the stuffy interior of our swaying conveyance, causing a large, red-haired, red-faced woman to make a most indignant remonstrance against my curiosity.

"Faith, Mr. Barrett, if you've pity in your heart, spare us from your gawping lest we all perish of cold. You'll be seeing the town soon enough. It's been there for hundreds of years an' not like to run off now, is it?"

As a gentleman it was my lot to meet harsh speech—at least when it flowed from female lips—with humble apology. I tied the flap back into place. "I do beg your pardon, Miss Pross, and yours as well, Miss Manette."

By this I acknowledged the smaller, younger lady who seemed to be her mistress. Miss Manette had caught the attention of all the gentlemen since she first came aboard with her forceful companion. The coach's confines were such as to kindle interest in any member of the fair sex who happened to be there, but her delicate blond beauty would command attention even in a great throng. In Miss Pross, though, she had so fierce and wild a protector that none had been able to draw her into polite conversation.

The passing of pleasantries was difficult anyway. The most innocuous of exchanges had to be conducted at the top of one's lungs because of the rumbling of our wheels. The violent rocking as we tumbled over broken and muddy roads kept most of us occupied hanging on to leather straps to avoid a degree of intimacy not generally shared by the average English subject with his fellow countrymen.

There were seven of us crammed in rather tight: the two ladies, my good cousin Oliver, myself, and three other gentlemen. The fellow next to Oliver was Sir Algernon. . . something. I'd missed his whole name. He was a tall, handsome specimen, but dolorous of aspect and dressed in the deepest mourning. Traveling with him was his child—a boy of no more than eleven years—also impeccably dressed for sorrow. Because of this outward declaration of a private tragedy we left them to themselves. The man was disinclined to speak, and the boy miraculously slept, leaning against the third gentleman. This was M. Deveau, a Frenchman who was the boy's dancing and sword master, the male equivalent of a governess.

He and the boy, Master Percy, had the misfortune to share the opposite bench with the females. I say misfortune, for the lady next to Percy was the redoubtable Miss Pross, who acted as a bastion of protection for her delicate charge, who was on her other side. Though it was clear by manner and dress that none of us—for we were one and all clearly gentlemen—would presume to make unwelcome overtures to the young lady, Miss Pross seemed to have decided we were rascally adventurers of the worst sort. I was certain she had a pistol, or at least a leaded cudgel, concealed in the large traveling bag she clutched to her person, and was equally certain she would find a use for it if she determined any of us to be the least importune in our behavior.

"Are there no lights in the town at all?" I asked. Even the most squalid parts of London had lamps here and there.

Oliver barked a short laugh, which roused Master Percy from his slumber. "Oh, lots, but they don't get much use. It's a rare lamplighter who makes aught but a poor living in our coastal hamlets on certain evenings. Haven't you something like it on your Long Island?"

"Smugglers, is it?" They preferred a pitch-dark night for landing goods on shore. Any fellow with a lamp would be looked upon unkindly by such free-traders, often to the point of violence. Indeed, it was said that the lamplighters, unable to make a wage, were themselves in on the smuggling. "I'm positive we do, but the family estate is set well inland, so I've not had the opportunity to make a firsthand observation. Of course, one hears tales, and the place has a dark history. It was a haven for Captain Kidd, you know. They say his treasure is buried somewhere along one of the beaches, but none have found it.

As I'd hoped, the mention of that name caught the interest of Miss Manette (and the boy). She peeped shyly at me, her blue eyes bright in the dimness of the coach. "Do you speak of the infamous pirate, Mr. Barrett?"

Had there been space to do so, I would have made her a proper bow of courtesy. A partial one from my seat had to serve, its sincerity marred by the movement of the coach. "Indeed I do, Miss Manette. Long Island, where I am from, was a favorite hiding place for his stolen booty."

"Where is this island?"

"It is part of the colony of New York in the Americas," I replied.

"And you are then an American?"

"A loyal American subject of our good King George, God save him."

A murmur of "amens" went 'round the interior.

Since coming to England to complete my education at Cambridge, I'd learned to answer similar questions with that phrase and thus avoid unpleasant social complications. Things were unsettled enough between Mother England and some few of her wayward children in the New World, and I did what I could to assure my countrymen that I was not one of those troublemakers.

"Why are you come to England, sir? Miss Manette asked. "And Dover in particular?"

"Hush, my ladybird," admonished her companion. "Vex not the gentleman" —Miss Pross emphasized that word slightly—"with idle questions. I'm sure he has other things to think about."

Her incivility put the devil in me, so I smiled and bowed as well as I could to her, and in such a way that she couldn't possibly object without looking wholly boorish. "Not at all, dear lady. I am here to read law at Cambridge. My cousin, Mr. Marling, who is to be a doctor, and I are come to Dover to conduct a bit of private business."

Young Percy stifled an unexpected guffaw. I took that to mean he well understood our errand, which made him perceptive beyond his age. The noise of the wheels grinding upon the road served to cover his sudden expression of amusement, so the ladies quite missed his reaction. Not so for M. Deveau, who, from the glint in his eye, also guessed the truth of the matter.

"Will you be proceeding to the Continent?" asked Miss Manette.

"I think not. Is that your destination?"

"I believe so, sir."

Under the hard glare of Miss Pross, I knew an inquiry over why the ladies would hazard the Channel in this unsettled season would be too direct. "Then I wish you a very easy and uneventful journey."

"You are most kind, sir, but 'uneventful'?"

"Indeed, miss. It is a gracious fate who allows us to be free of cares when traveling. I was half bored to death when making my crossing to England, but it was a blessing. All travelers should be afflicted with acute boredom, for that means a safe passage."

I was rewarded with a smile for this and might have pursued the topic further, but for being interrupted by a change in our pace and a shout from the coach driver. Our arrival was at hand. I burned to have another look as we rolled into town, but Miss Pross wore a glower sufficient to discourage a saint from praying, so I forced myself to have patience until we came to a stop.

The head drawer for our hotel—which happened to be the Royal George—pulled open the door, welcoming us to Dover. The ladies gathered themselves and were the first out. Sir Algernon was next, then followed my cousin with me straight behind. The boy had politely indicated I should proceed him, and M. Deveau was last. I think Master Percy wished to avoid a continuation of his proximity to Miss Pross. She was shouting in a most challenging manner for people to make-way-make-way for her "ladybird," though the only ones about were the driver and the drawer, who showed no concern for this display and went about their business of unloading the coach.

The night air was the chill and deadly damp as only England can make and rife with the slimy stink of dead fish. Still, it was better than the stuffy coach. Thunder grumbled angrily in the distance, and I was thankful we'd arrived ahead of what promised to be a wonderfully malicious storm. I stretched my cramped cold body, feeling the strange shakiness that inevitably follows the abrupt cessation of a long, uncomfortable ride. Oliver seemed to be in the same sate of shock from the change.

"I say, Coz," he said, distracting me from looking about. "Let's have something hot to restore the flow of blood, then I'd dearly like to put myself around a joint of beef if they have one."

At this reminder I realized I was quite hollow. As Miss Pross pointed out, Dover would not be running off. It struck me that wandering about after dark in a strange town populated with smugglers would be as unhealthy as the dank air.

Oliver had stayed at the hotel on previous journeys, and after sending up our travel cases, led us to the coffee room, which was quite large, the long, low ceiling stretching far away into shadows. It smelled divinely of that hot, black brew, and we availed ourselves of a curative dish each, well-laced with good French brandy. With it, we threw off the rigors of the road, along with our cloaks and hats, and took up a post before a sizable fireplace. The ladies and their baggage were conducted upstairs to more private quarters for their refreshment. Sir Algernon and Percy took themselves to a dim corner, giving their order to a waiter, content with their own company. M. Deveau was elsewhere, probably securing rooms for his master and young charge. The only other occupant was an orderly-looking man of sixty or so, dressed in drab brown, which made a sharp contrast to his shining, flax-colored wig. Another waiter approached him respectfully.

"Miss Manette has arrived, sir," he said. "She says she would be happy to see the gentleman from Tellson's, if it suits your pleasure and convenience."

"So soon?" asked the man in brown.

The waiter's response escaped my hearing, for I noticed the father and son both looked up at the mention of Tellson's, a name I did not recognize. The brown-clad fellow left, unaware that they marked his departure.

"What's Tellson's?" I asked Oliver, who also noticed the exchange.

"Bankers. Very old and so fearfully respectable even my mother has nothing to say against them."

"They must be truly formidable. Wonder what's afoot to bring one of their people out to meet with the fair Miss Manette?"

"No business of ours or so that Pross creature will inform you. You've not a hope with the young one, dear Coz. Besides, what would the beauteous Miss Jones say if she knew your attention had wandered from her?"

I pretended to unconcerned by that prospect. "Wandered? I was only making conversation to pass the time. You had plenty of chance to have a try, but you didn't, so I stepped in."

"Oh, bother, I never know what to say to proper young ladies, especially when they are so closely chaperoned. It's dangerous, too."

"How so?"

"One stray remark about the weather, a cordial smile, and before you know it you're engaged. I've seen it happen countless times. Those London girls are the most frightful predators you'll find this side of any wilderness. They can't abide the sight of an unmarried man, and from birth are set up and schooled for the sole purpose of getting an otherwise happy fellow under wedlock-and-key."

"What's this? Has your mother found another prospect for you?"

He shuddered. "I shall have to engage myself in some sort of revolting tomfoolery so she won't speak to me for the next few months. By then the wretched girl will have moved on to stalking another victim."

"Take care what you wish for." I thought about the delightful Miss Manette and our too-brief exchange. "I don't think she's English-born, though. Did you not mark her accent? Very slight, but charming."

"French, I'll warrant, considering the name. She's probably off to Calais to meet with relatives, and the banker's here to provide her with a bit of spending money and perhaps protection for it. Though God help any thieves trying to get past the Pross."

"Indeed."

The waiter came to us in our turn, inquiring what we would like in the way of food.

Some short while later, replete with half the contents of the kitchen inside our bellies, we were in a wonderfully lethargic mood. The *cafe noir* made us wakeful, though. Instead of going up to the room prepared for us, we idled before the fire, content to slowly roast, smoking our pipes.

"When?" I asked Oliver.

He looked at a clock on the mantel. "Not too much longer. Word will be about. We can expect someone at any time."

"And you'll be able to trust him?"

"Certainly not, but that's what makes it so amusing."

M. Deveau had returned to break bread with his master, and that party lingered at their table for a time until Sir Algernon retired upstairs. Young Percy had schooling to do, though. He and Deveau produced books and papers and went to work. I caught enough to hear a French lesson in progress. Percy had an excellent accent, speaking as rapidly as a native. Mine was quite rusty by comparison, and though I had a good and careful tutor at his age and after, I wasn't up to his rapidity of speech.

Our digestion was abruptly cut short by some sort of disturbance upstairs.

"What's that?" Oliver asked, stirring from his near-doze. "The Pross is raising the devil."

"Or fighting him," I put in. "What a row."

A moment later the owner of the George came quickly into the coffee room, and upon spying us, approached. "Mr. Marling?"

Oliver sat up straight. "Yes?"

"There is a—that is—the young lady—has been taken suddenly ill, and Miss Pross says that you are a doctor. . . ."

"Well, not quite yet I'm not, but I can have a look at her if you like."

The man seemed supremely relieved. Oliver, perhaps anxious to prove himself already worthy of practicing the physician's art, took himself off with a cheery wave to me.

The disturbances temporarily halted the French lesson. M. Deveau closed the book they studied. "Ah, M. Percy, this is of little interest to you when some real adventure takes place only a room away, is that not so?" His English was as superb as the boy's French.

"Indeed, sir," responded Percy, his gaze fixed on the door through which Oliver had gone. In the distance one could hear the outraged Miss Pross carrying on with much gusto.

"Then go satisfy your curiosity while I have a pipe."

For all his obvious eagerness to leave, the boy bowed to each of us before departing, as grave as any gentleman thrice his age. Then he clattered upstairs, a child again.

"May I join you by the fire, Mr. Barrett?" asked Deveau.

"Please."

He rose and came over, prepared his pipe and lighted it, and stood silhouetted before the flames, warming his back. The storm had arrived in force by now, and some of the rain made its way down the chimney to strike hissing on the burning wood. It made one humbly grateful for the pleasures of being under a solid roof with good food and ready warmth at hand.

"You English have an excellent idea of how to build a proper fire," he remarked affably. "There are homes in France where such a space would be used as a receiving room."

I enjoyed his exaggeration and offered to share from the bottle of wine Oliver and I had been working through. Deveau accepted with thanks and asked when I expected to place an order for more. He had rightly deduced the nature of our errand to Dover.

"Soon," I said. "We're to look for anyone coming our way wearing a red flower in his hat."

"That is the game of it. A certain color flower for some, a handkerchief for another. You have dealt with the gentleman before?"

That must have been his term for those who made a living on the free trade of wine and spirits. "My cousin has done this many times and will see to the details."

"That is good. Many of the fellows who avoid the king's excise men are rough by nature and bear watching."

"You know something about it?"

He gave an expressive non-English shrug. "It was a family concern once upon a time. My father was a French Captain, so I grew up with it. My English mother was not fond of the dangers of the sea and encouraged me to less perilous pursuits, and so I am here."

Deveau seemed to think this to be a sufficient explanation of himself, and, for two travelers sharing a pipe and a sip of wine, it was exactly right.

Master Percy returned just then full of news, yet so self-possessed that he did not forget his position as a young gentleman and offered a proper greeting to me. This required that I stand and return his bow and invite him to partake of some of the wine. He was a bit young, yet, for smoking a pipe. He declined, though, and reported that there was considerable excitement upstairs, most of it caused by Miss Pross.

"Miss Manette was speaking with the Tellson's banker, a Mr. Lorry," said the child. "He must have had bad news for her, for she fainted dead away. Miss Pross discovered what happened and is in herself a state, running about blaming everyone, especially Mr. Lorry. She's carrying on most fiercely. The maids and waiters are hiding lest she fall on them like the storm outside."

"An interesting picture, young sir," I said. "How fares my cousin Oliver under the assault?"

"Oh, he's ignoring her and looking after the lady. Most calm he is."

Oliver had had much practice at ignoring loud, fit-throwing females, what with his mother being an exceptional example of that ilk. He would make a fine doctor. "Did the banker say what caused her to faint?"

"Not a word, sir, but then bankers are like that and bankers from Tellson's more so than most. By coincidence, my father's estate is in their charge. When we heard that the man was from them, we thought he might have some business with us, but we were wrong."

I was framing a polite query on just who his father was, but an interruption—three of them in fact—barged into the coffee room, dripping wet and complaining about the foul weather. Deveau gave one and all a narrow, careful look. A rough lot they appeared to be, too. Though their clothes were acceptable, they brought to mind a gathering of ungroomed plow-mules dressed up in polished harness. Each wore a red flower of one kind or another in his hat.

"Is your cousin acquainted with any of these fellows?" Deveau murmured from the side of his mouth as they scrutinized us in turn.

"No," I replied. "He was going to speak to whomever came tonight and pick the best bargain of the lot."

"As Mr. Marling is elsewhere, may I put myself forward in his place?"

This from a man who grew up in the trade. I gratefully accepted his generous offer. Percy took Oliver's chair and watched the exchange with sharp interest.

The three tradesmen, not gentlemen, came over, and each presented himself to us: Captain Shellhorse, Captain Keech, and Captain Talmadge.

Keech was the largest, most pugnacious of them and put himself to take the lead. His hat's red flower was made of paper. It being late in the season for fresh blooms, that struck me as a clever substitute. He and

Deveau stepped off to the side and spoke quickly in low tones for several moments, then Shellhorse, who wore a much-faded rose, had his turn, then Talmadge, whose scarlet blossom was so small as to be easily overlooked. They each retired to separate tables as Deveau returned to confer with me.

"How much brandy were you planning to buy?" he asked.

I told him. Brandy, wine, and a long list of other items.

His eyes went wide. "So much? Are you buying for a whole town?"

"Er, no, just for my house at the university. With Christmas and the new year coming up we'll want a good stock in place for the celebrations of the season."

"How many are in your house?"

My answer astonished him.

"So few? For so much drink?"

"That's university men for you. We require ten times more than other chaps."

He found that amusing, as did Percy. "I shall see what I can do."

Deveau returned to his task of interviewing each of the captains. Not one of them blinked at the quantity of my order, but a disagreement broke out between Shellhorse and Talmadge over who could deliver the quickest. It threatened to come to blows until the owner of the hotel made an appearance and commanded silence. Clearly he held their respect, for the argument instantly subsided. I got the impression that he turned a blind eye to their trade, allowing them to conduct business under his roof—providing no trouble came of it. Certainly it was to everyone's mutual advantage to behave.

But when our host left, Keech put himself forward, declaring that he had better quality stock for a better price. Deveau expressed interest, but Shellhorse and Talmadge instantly made lower bids. Keech waiting until they'd exhausted themselves, in their auction in reverse, then underbid them both. He collected a murderous reaction, but they eventually backed down.

"Ye'll leave yersel' penniless an' starving at tha' price." said Shellhorse with satisfaction. "Me an Talmadge'll be selling for double that to the next man down the road. You see if we don't!"

Talmadge spat on the floor in a show of agreement.

Keech seemed unconcerned. "Aye, but what I 'ave now is mor'n what I started with this dawn. I'm pleased with my lot."

As was I, for I instinctively knew that Oliver would not have gotten a better price for the goods. At this point I was able to take over and sort the details of delivery and payment. We determined that money would be exchanged once the kegs and bottles safely arrived at our house in Cambridge. Keech had a man who could be trusted with the task, but I was not as confident.

"Worry yersel' not over 'im, sir," he said by way of assurance. " 'E does his job 'onest or 'e gets to wear 'is smile down low." To illustrate, he tilted his head back and drew his finger slowly across his throat. The show was obviously for Percy's entertainment. The boy shuddered appreciatively, eyes bright.

Shellhorse bellowed a laugh. "If that be yer usual man, then ye best ride on the cart with 'im an' not shut eyes the whole trip."

"Tha's my brother yer talkin' idle about. You don't know nuffin' on 'im!" said Keech, going red in the face.

"Oh, so you can talk of cuttin' 'is throat, but no one else is 'lowed a word ag'in 'im?"

"Tha's right, Bob Shellhorse, so you keep yer dirty mouth shut!"

" 'Ere now, stifle that," put in Talmadge, coming between them. "We don't want the drawer to be throwin' us out."

But a scuffle followed, with much grunting and cursing, but strangely quiet, as each tried to assert himself but not in a way that would bring down the wrath of the hotel's owner. Deveau, alert to trouble, plucked Percy easily from harm's way as the trio staggered into the lad's chair, knocking it over. Shellhorse fell, dragging the others with him. There followed a spiritedly distracting show as the small mob rolled around the floor of the coffee room.

It was at that moment when Oliver chose to return. His long face went longer with astonishment, and he nimbly avoided getting caught up by the juggernaut with a quick, wide leap.

"I say!" he crowed, delighted. "What's all this about?"

I spread my hands wide, shaking my head and laughing.

"Perhaps we should stop them," Deveau suggested. "This is a respectable hotel, not a bear-baiting pit. If Captain Keech is in gaol. . ."

That was enough to induce me to enter the fray. I grabbed a coat collar at random and hauled back, Deveau and Oliver stepped forward, each making a successful catch. The combatants were winded, but we still had our hands full keeping them apart.

"Git yer dirty 'ands off me, ye damned Frenchy!" cried Keech, trying to shake off Deveau's grip, which was apparently very strong. "If you were a gennelman, I'd call you out!"

Deveau released his man in the direction of the door, somewhat forcefully. Keech, who wore a cutlass like his fellows and now drew it, waving it at Deveau. That man, in turn, darted smoothly to one side of the door where a line of pegs held a collection of coats, cloaks, and hats belonging to guests. In a tall container next to them were a number of walking sticks. He seized one as though it was a sword, rounded on the captain, and, in a move so fast that I could scarce follow, sent the cutlass flying across the room. It struck a wall with a startling pot-metal sound.

Keech was in a red-faced fury, eyes blazing, then suddenly seemed to realize his hand was empty. He had been neatly disarmed, not by a sword but with a simple length of wood wielded by an obvious expert.

Deveau smiled gently, "Sir, if you have a quarrel about my ancestry, I shall be pleased to offer you satisfaction at any time of your choosing."

With a remarkable effort of will, Keech collected himself. "Tha' is to say. . . I mean . . ."

Deveau was generous. "Perhaps the captain was caught up in the heat of battle. It is my understanding that the English are born warriors and how difficult it must be to curb so great a predisposition."

The speech might have been delivered in an insulting manner, but Deveau was at once conciliatory and showing admiration. I was unsure if Keech grasped the words so much as the tone of voice. It worked, though. Perhaps he comprehended that it was poor business to quarrel with customers.

"Come, sir," said Deveau. "Let us toast this excellent trait with some fine English ale. You would honor me greatly if you allowed me to stand you a pint."

While the rest of us—including the other captains—fairly gaped, Deveau and Keech left to seek out the hotel's tavern, arm-in-arm like the best of friends.

"That was smooth as goose grease," declared Oliver in a hushed voice.

"Aye," said Shellhorse, also impressed by the performance.

Captain Talmadge shrugged free of my grip and nodded. "That be old Deveau's get an' no doubt of it."

"You know his father?" I asked.

"Father an' son both, the lad's the dead spit of 'is sire. I ain't clapped eyes on either of 'em in years, but there's some men as ye cants ferget. What's the boy doin' playing fancy to the gentry, I wonders?"

Master Percy stepped forward. "Captain, sir, M. Deveau is my tutor in French, Latin, dancing, and the sword, among other things."

Talmadge nodded. "Well. Young sir, you pay mind to 'is sword work an' no one'll 'ave the better of you in a duel when the time comes. If 'e's that dab with naught but a stick, what might 'e do with a real blade? I'd pay good money to see!"

* * *

The remainder of the evening was less exciting. The storm lashed the town with more rain than was rightly necessary, and thunder boomed like siege cannons. The three captains took rooms and departed each to his own, and by the devil's own luck the hotel owner remained ignorant of their altercation. We later learned that Miss Pross kept him fully engaged upstairs with complaints and suggestions of how to better run his trade. The only evidence of the occurrence was a red flower left on the coffee-room floor, fallen from one of the captains' hats. Percy took it as a memento of the grand occasion. M. Deveau wisely cautioned him that mentioning the incident to his father might add to his existing distress, thus obtaining a poignantly solemn promise of silence.

Oliver and I retired to our room, each pleased with the success of our trip. He was in particular happy with the bargain that Deveau struck in his stead. "What a square fellow he is. I daresay he must be more English than French. Let's invite him to our Christmas celebration. Think you that Sir Algernon can spare him?"

"I've no idea, Coz." I left my coat and waistcoat over a chair, removed my traveling boots, and dropped into bed. "Ask him in the morning."

"Ask who—Deveau or Sir Algernon?"

"Both, Either. Sir Algernon, I suppose."

"One hates to bother the poor fellow. I heard stories about his sad plight. Married a beauty and two years later she slipped into hopeless madness. Not raving, mind you, but the quiet kind. The family's been living on the Continent all that time. He's looked after her, best doctors and all that. She's recently died, as you might have guessed."

I grunted, staring at the bed canopy. The story was eerily similar to my own father's plight. He'd married a beauty as well, and she had also slipped into a kind of madness, but not the sort for which one is locked away. Hers was a willfully cruel and controlling agitation that she was careful to reveal only to her immediate family. We few, we unhappy few.

"For all that," Oliver continued, "it's left Sir Algernon quite brokenhearted, for he loved her dearly, I hear. Saw him in the hall during that business with Miss Manette. Looked half-distracted himself over her distress. Good thing he's got a solid sort like Deveau looking after the boy."

"Is the lady all right?"

"Oh, she'll be fine, an ordinary fainting spell. I don't know what brought it on, but gathered that the Pross won't allow it to happen again."

"Excellent. I want no more rows, only a good night's rest."

"We'll get that here, my lad. You won't be kept awake by bedbugs in these sheets, I'll warrant."

"Good. My God, look at the hour, half-past nine if it's a minute. No wonder I'm tired."

Oliver dropped down onto his side, and we had a small contest for the lion's share of the covers before finally settling with equal halves. To my annoyance he closed his eyes and almost at once began snoring. I preferred to be the first to fall asleep, for then his nasal dissonance would go unmarked. I prodded him to turn over, hoping to curtail the noise, then turned myself, seeking sweet slumber.

It was not to be. A most dreadful shriek jolted me wide awake, and it seemed to come from beneath our very window. What terrible mischief was that?

Staggering from bed, I rushed over and pushed the shutters wide, staring into the blackest of nights, rain and wind cutting my face. With an awful thrill I saw that devilry was indeed afoot. Exactly below me two men—shadows thrashing about among thicker shadows—were engaged in desperate struggle. One had already come the worst of it, for he was seemed the weaker and no match for the other. He hung on to his foe to prevent the man's escape, but once more there came from him a second unearthly cry of pain that turned my bones to jelly.

I roared out something, I'm not sure what, and that had an instant effect on the attacker, who wrested violently away. His lesser opponent clutched at him, but was brutally struck down. I heard the sickening crack of wood striking bone. One shadow collapsed to the ground; the other stumbled, regained his balance, and hurtled away as though caught by the wind.

I became aware of Oliver dragging me clear for a look himself. "Dear God, but it's murder!" he shouted.

We were not the only ones aware of the row. The screams without had roused this wing of the hotel, and we found the passage full of people in various stages of dress, clutching blankets and shawls to their bodies, their white faces full of fear and questions. I pulled my boots on, grabbed my smallsword, and pelted downstairs. Oliver was ahead of me, bringing his doctor's bag along with his own blade.

A crowd was knotted by the front doors, but the landlord refused to open them. Oliver and I were not to be thwarted, though.

"There's a man dying outside, sir!" Oliver cried, indignant.

"Aye, an' he might have more company," came the chill response.

"Bother that!" Oliver pushed past, turned the key, and in a moment we were out and blinking in the storm. "This way!"

We raced 'round the corner. Several more men were at our heels, grooms, waiters, guests and the like, one of them thought to bring a lantern. We quickly found the victim of the attack. He was sprawled on his face in the mud, and when the light shone on him, there was a collective gasp at the dreadful wounding on his head. Blood was everywhere, and the poor man's skull looked to be caved in. Oliver felt for a pulse, but there was no doubt that this patient was quite dead. With a grimace we turned over the body. The far-seeing, yet empty eyes of Captain Keech stared past us as though searching for his swiftly-fled soul.

* * *

The storm grew more violent, matching the foul and unsettled mood of everyone sheltering under the Royal George's roof. One and all, guests, host, and servants, gathered in the great coffee-room. The body of Captain Keech, shrouded by a tablecloth, lay in improvised state in one of the small parlors, and his brutal demise was much discussed.

Several times I was subjected to close questioning to ascertain who I had seen below my window. To their unanimous chagrin, I refused to divulge a single word of what I'd seen and heard. Not that there was much I could say, but I insisted it was best to wait until the authorities were sent for and then give my rather thin witness to them.

For all I knew anyone in this hotel—saving myself, Oliver, and Percy, who was too small—could have murdered the man. I could not discount the females, for Miss Pross was a tall woman whose temper was belligerent to the task of doing violence if provoked. It was easy to imagine her attacking anyone who gave insult to her friend, Miss Manette.

I was thankful for Oliver's presence, not only for his support, but his good sense, for he brought me a large brandy that helped steady my thoroughly shaken disposition. It is not every day that one sees—and hears—murder. No matter whether you know the victim or not, a fellow creature has fallen before his natural time, and the sheer horror of the act inflicts a profound devastation upon the spirit. I stood close to the huge fire, yet felt no warmth.

The owner of the hotel was also in something of a state, doubtless fearing the crime would either drive away custom or attract the wrong sort of guest. He many times stated that such a thing had never before happened in his house, and when it came to the truth of the matter, the violence occurred outside the hotel, and therefore had nothing to do with his establishment.

The banker from Tellson's, Mr. Lorry, quietly reminded him that Captain Keech was a guest, and therefore. . .but he was not allowed to finish. Miss Pross cut in and confidently asserted we would be murdered in our beds if the miscreant was not immediately caught and gaoled. Lorry looked fearful, but of Miss Pross, not the prospect of being bludgeoned in the night by some deranged assailant.

At this point Captain Talmadge revealed that a duel had almost taken place between Keech and Deveau, and that the latter had used a walking stick as a weapon. Such a stick was found only yards from the body. Instant silence followed this disclosure, and all eyes turned to Deveau, who was still fully dressed, unlike the majority of the company.

"What of it?" he asked. "We did not actually fight, and afterward I shared an ale with the man to mend things. The innkeeper will bear witness for me that we were amiable the whole time, and when the captain left I came here to enjoy the fire and a pipe."

"Alone?" asked Mr. Lorry.

"Yes." Deveau was obviously aware this admission was not in his favor.

"Then you mayn't be telling us ever'think.' said Talmadge. "We don't knows if that be the truth. Easy enough to get Keech drunk as a tinker, for all Dover knows 'ow fond he were of 'is own wares. Then you takes 'im outside an' whack! 'E's done in like a bullock at the butchers."

Deveau went red in the face at this, not from guilt, but rather suppressed fury. "Captain" —he spoke quietly despite his ire— "I will draw your attention to the fact that I not only had no reason to inflict harm upon Captain Keech, who was otherwise a stranger to me, but also that I am quite dry from top to toe, a state I would not be in had I been out in this Noah's deluge. You, however, are quite soaked."

"As are a dozen other men who went outside," said Mr. Lorry. "Based on that, I am cautiously inclined to believe M. Deveau, but we require the authorities here to sort this in a proper and legal process."

"There's no need fer sortin'!" put in Shellhorse. "It were the dirty Frenchie what dun fer 'im! 'E changed 'is clothes, is all!"

As a man raised with a wide ocean between himself and ancestral grudges, I was unprepared for the vehemence of ill feeling between the English and the French in this otherwise civilized setting. It was as though their ancient quarrels down through the centuries had take place only that afternoon, so strong was the wave of animosity that rushed through the room to break squarely upon M. Deveau. I called for reason, but was unable to make myself heard above the others. Catching Oliver's attention, he hurried to my side, and we took up posts next to Deveau, prepared to defend him from what promised to turn into a mob.

Then, unexpectedly, Sir Algernon took charge. He had been somber and silent through the arguments and accusations, but now he stood—an imposing figure he was with his great height. In his black mourning he reminded me of a hangman.

He possessed a most piercing gaze, and it touched on everyone present. "Good folk, I agree with Mr. Lorry that this matter must be looked into by the proper authorities. Someone will guide the way for me, and I will fetch them myself. Until then, I require that everyone retire to their several rooms and compose themselves to cooperation, not vituperation. I would also most strongly suggest that prayers be said for the departed soul of the poor man. As to the guilty who committed this violence, his sins may find him out, you may be sure of it."

Sir Algernon did not look at any one man for long, perhaps wary that it might inspire riot, but I did notice who he paid special attention to: the remaining captains, M. Deveau, Oliver, and myself. I felt a flush creep into my cheeks at this scrutiny, along with the fear that I might also be unfairly and unreasonably accused. Sir Algernon then took the arm of the hotel owner and moved him purposefully toward the door.

Master Percy, who stood on a chair to view the madness of the adults, dropped down and rushed to his father, drawing him to one side for a whispered conference. The boy looked agitated and earnest, but Sir Algernon clearly had other matters on his mind. He patted his son's shoulder in an absent way and departed on his errand. Percy stared after him, then went next to M. Deveau.

"Sir! I must show you something important!" he cried.

"What might that be?" Deveau bent slightly to see.

Then Percy launched into very rapid French, which was possibly the worst thing he could have done in that restive crowd.

"Frenchie spy!" shouted Talmadge. " 'E's leadin' even the lad astray!"

A few others took up this chorus, rounding on Deveau. Had he been the devil himself they could not have been more outraged.

"He's no spy!" I roared. This time I was loud enough to make an impression, halting them. They were still on the edge, though; I had but a moment to turn them back to common sense again. "and I know he is *not* the murderer!"

This was met with derision from the two captains, their opinions backed up by a few other men demanding proof of my declaration. For the first time I noticed that a number of rough-looking fellows had gathered close to them. Shipmates, I thought. A chill of unease ran up my spine that had naught to do with my wet clothes. The men were likewise soaked from the rain for having been outside not a quarter hour ago. Might one of them have been out longer than the rest of us to do his evil work, then join our party as we rushed to aid his victim? I tried not to shiver.

"Who did it, then?" demanded Miss Pross, her voice cutting across the length of the room.

I felt a tug on my shirt and glanced down. Master Percy's bright gaze fairly burned through me. He held one hand to his chest, closed into a fist. He moved his hand, opening it so only I could see. I stared at what lay there, not comprehending its import.

Deveau murmured, "Not now, sir. They'll tear us to ribbons. Trust me on this, I know them well."

"Who is the Cain here?" shouted the Pross, looking around. "Who has so wickedly slain his brother?"

I was at a loss for an answer, but happily fate intruded. The delicate Miss Manette, who stood next to her, suddenly fainted. This set the Pross off again. She vented a loud scream of distress for her charge and swooped to aid her, calling for water, and a cold cloth and a dozen other remedies that are necessary when a lady collapses. Oliver started forward, but I grabbed his arm and signed for him to wait.

"Why?"

"A moment, you'll see."

Pross took charge like Caesar, sending servants hither and yon, and commanding that several of the maids lift her companion and bear her up to their room instantly. She bellowed fit to captain a whole fleet of ships herself, ordering the roughest of the sailors aside.

"Make-way-make-way for my poor ladybird!" she shouted, pushing men twice her size from her path. Bless me if they did not move quick as spit.

"Now!" I said, and urged Oliver forward.

He caught my intent. "I am a doctor! Let me through!"

Next I nudged Deveau, who allowed himself to be swept along in the general exodus. I trusted that Percy could look after himself, as bright lads have an instinct to place themselves where that want to be no matter what obstacles may stand between.

As I hoped, the confusion of the moment served to protect us, and in a short time we were up the stairs and in Miss Manette's room, along with a dozen others caught up in our parade. The Pross spied Oliver and dragged him over to see to the young lady, then shooed the excess gapers out the door. That would have included myself, Deveau, and Percy, but her charge abruptly wakened from her swoon and gently requested a cessation of further row.

The Pross was decidedly full of opposing feelings about this turn, but was finally persuaded to back down. She regarded us with suspicion, but when asked by the girl, who swore it would fully restore her, left the room to fetch a pot of tea. Oliver was told—ordered, rather—to act as chaperon, the Pross trusting that as a prospective doctor, he was a sober, responsible sort. How little did she know.

Once the door was shut, Miss Manette favored us with a small smile. "Please forgive her. Her heart is in the right place.

"Of course, mademoiselle," said Deveau, with a bow. "Are you unharmed by your misadventure?"

"I am very well, *monsieur*. But you should know that it was a sham."

"Indeed?"

We regarded her with increased interest.

She continued: "It is true that I did faint earlier this evening, but not again in the coffee-room just now. My earlier event gave me the idea for it, though. Mr. Barrett seemed in need of help, and it was the only thing I could think of to do. I knew my dear friend would make a great fuss, and that it might change the situation, but it grieves me to have troubled her so."

"Mademoiselle's conclusion was correct," I said. "I am most deeply in your debt for the timely rescue." Now was I able to execute a proper bow, including a little flourish with my smallsword, which was still in hand. "And please do not trouble yourself about Miss Pross's feelings. It's quite obvious that she enjoys making a fuss. You have provided her with considerable happiness."

"Before she returns, please, sir, will you tell us what you know? If there is a murderer under this roof, then it is our duty to catch him."

"I would be glad to tell all, but I know little. The darkness and weather hid his face from me as perfectly as any mask."

"But I thought—"

"I know, but I was trying to distract that crowd from doing harm to M. Deveau. His innocence was certainly plain to me, since he was the only dry-shod man in the room, but they weren't of a mind to hear sense."

"I believe," said Deveau, "That one of them was of a mind to falsely blame me for the crime and thus escape. I also believe that Master Percy holds the proof of it in his palm, do you not, young sir?"

Percy, who had slipped in unnoticed, now stepped forth. Again he opened his hand. I stared at the small red flower there, as did the rest.

"That's proof?" asked Oliver. "Bless me, but I don't see it."

"The hats," I said, with sudden inspiration. "This flower fell from one of the captains' hats in their scuffle tonight. I remember Percy saved it."

We then had to explain to Miss Manette the business about red flowers being used as a sign by certain ship captains wishing to conduct private business. We did not specify what that business might be.

"Still don't see it," Oliver repeated.

"The hats," I repeated in turn. "Talmadge and Shellhorse were still open for trade. They had red flowers in their hats."

"So?"

Percy said, " Captain Talmadge lost his flower in the fight. I have it here. But he found another. Made from red paper. I saw it when we were in the coffee-room."

The significance was unknown to Oliver, for he had not noticed what sort of flower was worn by each captain. He'd not dealt with them, after all. "So Talmadge murdered Keech over a paper flower?"

"I haven't a clue as to why he murdered," I said, "only that he took Keech's paper bloom."

"Or his hat," suggested Deveau. "Much more likely."

"Ah." That did make more sense. "They each lost their hats in the fight outside, and then he grabbed the wrong one. I remember the man who fled seemed to stumble. He might have been picking it up instead, and I mistook his movement."

"Indeed, but a man cannot be charged on anything so feeble as that. There must be stronger proof."

"Well-a-day, then we shall just have to find some."

Miss Pross returned, armed with tea, bread, and jam, and decided that our presence was no longer required. Even Oliver was summarily turned out, though he raised no objection. The only disappointed face belonged to Miss Manette, who would not hear what I had in mind to resolve matters.

Since Oliver had lodged here before, I asked what he knew of the servant's stairs in the building.

"I suppose there must be some, there always are, but bless me if I know where to find 'em."

"Come, sir," said Deveau, "I learned to navigate most of the harbors on both sides of the channel by the age of twelve; I'm sure together we can find the back stairs here. What then, Mr. Barrett?"

"We find the servant's entry to the parlor where poor Keech is and slip in there."

"For what purpose?"

"To find his hat."

I explained—after the four of us, with young Percy eagerly in the lead, found the stairs—that it wasn't enough to point out the detail of the flowers to the authorities, but we had to be certain that Talmadge didn't find a paper bloom elsewhere. In a few moments we quietly entered the dim parlor where the dead captain lay stretched upon a long table. We lighted more candles to better see. His muddied shoes were visible beyond the hem of the tablecloth shroud, but the rest of his large form was carefully covered. Most important, someone had placed his hat on his chest. Sad relic it was, battered, damp, and also muddy.

Picking it up, I examined it for a maker's mark, but found none.

"Now what?" asked Oliver.

"Nothing pleasant. We see if it fits his head."

He wanted none of that, but saw the sense. With somber respect he drew back the table cloth enough to expose as little as necessary. Master Percy stood a little closer to M. Deveau, but maintained a man's stout bearing through the course. While Oliver lifted Keech's head, I attempted to fit the hat to it. The article kept falling off.

"That settles it," said Oliver, wiping his bloodied fingers on one end of the cloth. "Not his bonnet, to be sure."

"But it may be argued that the damage to his skull altered the shape of it," Deveau pointed out.

"Not unless it had been thoroughly crushed—like a boiled egg that's been stepped on. I'll take an oath that that's not what happened here. 'Tis true he has a fearful and fatal wounding, but the greater portion of the bony structure is intact, and so his own hat would still fit. Unless he preferred a loosely fitted one."

"A ship's captain with a loose hat?" questioned Deveau. "Never. He would have it snug to his head or lose it in the wind. Look at his forehead. The line is still there that marks where I was accustomed to wearing it. I saw Mr. Barrett bring the other hat well over that line, therefore it does not belong to Keech. But we still have a problem of proof. Talmadge could claim that in the confusion of carrying the body inside that he got his hat mixed with Keech's. Forgive me, but in light of the strong feelings running between my shared countries, it is more likely his word will be believed over mine. I am but half-English, and he is an Englishman bred and born."

"As am I," said Oliver. "And I'm ashamed to call him countryman, but you are not without allies. Cousin Jonathan and I will vouch for you, and certainly Sir Algernon will have a great influence in the matter."

"That will certainly serve to keep me from the hangman, but how to bring the guilty to justice?"

"We find out why Talmadge would want to do for the fellow."

Deveau made a throwing-away gesture. "Many of these captains are honorable men, but there are some who resent the success of others and are always ready to remove the competition. I would hazard to say that Talmadge took exception to Keech's winning this night and acted upon it. I would think with Keech out of the way, he would approach you later on with an offer to sell you spirits."

"Grim way to conduct a trade," I put in. "He said that he remembered you from when you were a lad."

"I do not recall. I think he was not a captain, for I knew all their names. One had to, but back then he could have been a first mate, perhaps."

"Sir!" cried Percy, who had been examining the hat close by the light of the candles. "See what I have found!"

We gathered near. There was a much weathered ribbon on the outside running between the brim and the crown, and Percy had peeled it back. Within was a store of small reddish flowers.

"I sometimes hide things in my hat this way," said the lad. "I wondered if it might be the same for him, and so it is."

Oliver thumped a hand on the boy's shoulder. "So it is. That's brilliant of you, young sir. As soon as your father returns—"

" 'E'll 'ave other things on 'is mind, I'm thinkin'."

As one, we turned to behold the depressing visage of Captain Talmadge, who, with a muddy hat in hand, stood blocking the doorway that opened to the main hall. Crowded behind him were several of his men. They were grinning—a singularly alarming sight. Deveau quietly put Percy behind him, and I sensed him marshaling for immediate action against this threat. However, Talmadge drew a pistol from his coat and aimed it at him.

"There'll be no mischief from you, Frenchie. "Ever-un keep shut and quiet as little mice an' we'll finish up 'ere an' be gone an' no 'arm done, eh?"

"What do you want?" asked Deveau.

"I'll thank ye to return me 'at, then we'll be off. You fine gennelmen'll keep shut or it'll go 'ard on the lad."

Percy had slipped a little off to better see, and his young eyes went wide as Talmadge swung the pistol in his direction.

Deveau kept his voice steady. "You harm that boy and there will be no safe port for you anywhere."

"The world's a wide place. Come now an' show sense. Ol' Keech 'n me 'ad a quarrel, an' I won the day. None of it's yer concern, so we'll just be off after I gets me rightful property. An' to make sure you behaves while we leaves, the lad's coming along 'til we're clear. 'Less 'e'd perfers ter see the world. We're short a ship's boy and this 'un looks a likely sort. . ." His gaze shifted suddenly to me. "You be droppin' that blade, Mr. Barrett, or you'll 'ave innercent blood on your soul."

I froze. I'd been easing to one side, hoping to lunge with my sword and disarm him. Deveau shifted ever so slightly, and I feared he would charge the lot of them, collecting a pistol ball for his effort. Perhaps if I offered them a substantial bribe and got their attention on me. . .

Percy made a strong snapping motion with his wrist, sending the hat spinning right into Talmadge's face. It was a fine distraction, but the man pulled the trigger on his pistol. There was a flat crack, strangely muffled.

Providence had smiled on us; the damned thing had misfired. Talmadge's threat was without force, and before he could react to his change of fortune, Deveau leaped upon him like a tiger. I thrust my blade at the nearest of the henchmen, wounding his arm. He yelled and fled along with two others, which was most gratifying.

Oliver's blood was also up, for he roared like a savage and charged one of the men who topped him in size by a good half foot. Nonetheless, he won his contest, for Percy dropped low and curled himself tight behind the man's legs. When Oliver slammed into him, the wretch went tumbling over this unexpected obstacle. By the time he caught his wind, his captain was also on the floor, knocked insensible by Deveau's good right fist.

The row brought a crowd, of course, and it was some while before everything was properly sorted out, even when Sir Algernon returned with the authorities. It was nigh on to midnight before the house was settled and the guilty and wounded marched away to be locked up.

The landlord was guardedly pleased to have the trouble resolved, and stood us a round of brandies. It served to remind me that Oliver and I would now have to deal with Captain Shellhorse to complete our errand in Dover. I was not unduly put out by the prospect. Indeed, Oliver and I faced the likelihood of having many more brandies and invitations to tell the tale of this night's events once we were back in Cambridge. If not for the ghastly demise of poor Captain Keech, we might have counted this as an excellent adventure to share with our friends.

"That was dangerous business with the hat, though," I said to Percy. We were again gathered before the fire in the coffee-room, along with most of the hotel. "He could have killed you but for the devil's own luck that his pistol failed to fire."

Standing on a chair, young Percy flushed under the admiring scrutiny of the adults. It must have been a heady experience to him, for we had pledged that he was the hero of the hour for his actions, perilous though they were. "It was not luck, Mr. Barrett, only logical reasoning," he said with much dignity.

"Indeed? How so?"

"It's a shocking wet night out, sir. Captain Talmadge was soaked coming here, and more so when he was outside quarreling with Captain Keech, and again when he helped bring in the body. It struck me that the rain would have made his pistol very safe, so I—"

"Brilliant," said Oliver, and he called for a toast to Master Percy Blakeney's—only now did I collect the family's full name—very good health and wits, and suggested additional celebration was in order.

The boy's somber father even looked pleased, but gently reminded us that the hour was late and the morning would be early as it always must be for travelers. Deveau agreed with this, and Sir Algernon preceded them toward the door; Deveau and his charge close behind.

Their progress was slowed by the number of well-wishers who patted the boy on the head or, in the case of ladies, bent to kiss his cheek. He squirmed a bit under that particular reward except when it came to Miss Manette. He seemed to rather like her and lingered long enough to collect a kiss on each side of his face and another on his forehead from her. He bowed low as any gentleman and professed himself to be at her service.

Then Percy gave a little cry and tore back to the chair he and been standing upon, and from it retrieved a by now much crushed specimen of the flower that had been Talmadge's downfall. The boy hurried to Deveau with his trophy of the hunt.

"What the devil sort of weed is that, anyway?" Oliver called after him.

Percy paused, at a momentary loss until Deveau stooped and whispered discreetly in his ear. "It is a scarlet pimpernel, sir!"

"Deuced peculiar name for a plant," muttered my cousin as they left. "Who'd have thought so little a thing could make such a thundering great mischief?"

I clapped him on the shoulder. "Well, never again will that happen if we live to be a hundred. Come, good Coz, another brandy. Let us celebrate and be thankful for small favors."

DRAWING DEAD

Author's Note: *In 2008 I decided to self-publish an all new Jack Fleming story and offer it, along with some reprinted stories, as a signed, limited-edition from my website. But the intended 10,000-word story,* THE DEVIL YOU KNOW *bloomed into a full length novel! In the original version of TDYK I had a long scene where Jack takes on some card sharps on the train ride to New York, but concluded that it just didn't fit into the rest of the book. I yanked it out, did some tweaks to make it more of a stand-alone, and here is the shiny new result.*

Chicago, March 1938

Long journeys are as complicated for vampires—or at least this vampire—as they are for regular people. You have to figure out food, shelter, and hope your luggage arrives on time and in the right place. In my case I would be *in* the luggage, another complication. Since my change from normal human to blood-swilling creature of darkness I tended to avoid travel.

Vampire. Yes. That's how I spell it. Look it up in the dictionary, but don't believe everything you read.

I'm a bloodsucker, but I am polite about it. No leaping out of alleys or seducing damsels for me, not while the Union Stockyards has cattle pens. Before leaving town to see to my errand in New York, I'd stopped there and drink my fill, which would cover my needs for the next few nights.

There were no direct lines running from Chicago's LaSalle Street Station to Long Island, necessitating a changeover at Grand Central

Terminal. I'd be in the baggage car of the *Twentieth Century Limited* for most of the trip, specifically inside a large trunk, only it wasn't so roomy once I was stuffed in along with clothes and a bag of my home earth. Uncomfortable and boring, but you can't beat the privacy. I could afford a sleeping compartment, but didn't want to wind up being a problem for a day porter. Post-sunrise, I'm literally dead to the world, which alarms people should they find my body. Of course, they get even more agitated when I unexpectedly wake up, so it's best to just keep out of the way.

A porter charged in with a trolley and swept my trunk away, shoving it in next to a mountain of similar items being efficiently loaded into the baggage car. I slipped off, glanced around to make sure no one was paying attention, took a bead on the trunk, and vanished.

Hurtling forward in a straight line, I blundered into something that was the same size and shape and tried to sieve in. Whatever I'd found was packed solid with no room to materialize. I slipped out, fighting claustrophobia, and felt around, but it was hopeless. Those porters were *fast*. I gave up and clung to the top of something else, riding it into what I hoped was the right car. A man bawled directions on where it was to go. I drifted free, my weightless, formless self bumping gently against the ceiling, and went semi-transparent to get my bearings.

Just enough sight returned to allow me a faint glimpse of my target below. Anticipating problems, I'd slopped a big X on my trunk's sides and top in white paint the night before, and the precaution paid off. I went invisible and dove in before the next load buried my refuge.

Re-formed again and safe, my rump on a flat bag of home earth and knees crowding my ears, I half-listened to the rowdy racket outside. Strangely, I didn't feel closed in; it must have been the presence of my home soil. During the day I needed it next to me so I could truly rest, but I'd never considered that it might have a general calming effect at night. Don't ask for explanations for the why of it, because I don't know. So long as it worked I had no complaints.

For something to do in the pitch darkness I fished out a quarter and practiced rolling it across my knuckles. That was possible to do by touch alone, though I dropped the coin more often than not. The magician who'd played at my club and taught me how had made it look easy.

I had a flashlight and plenty of magazines, but it was too cramped for reading. After a weary wait I heard rumbling followed by a solid slam and clank, signaling the car's wide door was shut. Not long afterward the train began lurching eastward, taking it slow until we cleared the city.

When the click-*click*, click-*click* of the wheels on the rails and the car's rocking steadied, I vanished and eased out of the trunk. It took a few minutes to feel my way to a clear spot to materialize.

More pitch blackness, I used the flashlight. The place was as I'd expected, noisy, cold, and loaded with crates, bags, and trunks. I couldn't see mine from here, but I'd find it again. If nothing else the soil itself would draw me in the right direction.

Thinking about it, *that* was a little creepy.

I made my way toward the passenger area of the train. To avoid trouble I'd bought a regular ticket. It was easier than dodging the conductor all night.

The lounge was crowded, but I found a chair, pulled two magazines from my coat pocket, and settled in for adventurous distraction courtesy of Street and Smith's *The Shadow*. I couldn't always catch the radio show, but two new stories every month almost made up for it. I had both January issues, bought but unread. Which to read first? *The Crystal Buddha* was the earlier story, but *The Hills of Death* had a more interesting cover with a motorcycle cop bursting through a map covered by the Shadow's red silhouette. I opted to be chronological and took on the Buddha tale to find out why The Shadow found it necessary wave one of his .45s at a startled man in a green turban.

A waiter or porter or whatever you call them when on a train asked if I wanted a drink. I ordered water and tipped a quarter just to show I wasn't cheap. Having a glass at hand might keep him from bothering me again. Water was best, no one minds if you don't drink it. Order coffee and you have to keep turning down a fresh hot cup every ten minutes.

"Traveling far?" a man in the next chair asked.

People hate a reader. They can't stand when someone's not also bored. They interrupt, want to know what you're reading, if it's interesting, and then discuss what they like to read. At some point in the encounter they've ceased being bored and suddenly you are, thoroughly.

I gave discouraging grunt, not looking up. Hell, we were all headed toward New York, wasn't that enough information?

My neighbor moved off to find someone more sociable. The bar did a brisk business and enough conversations were going on elsewhere in the car to allow me and Lamont Cranston—only he seemed to be Kent Allard in this one—to get on with the plot.

It didn't last. Just as The Shadow was about to make his first appearance, someone tapped my shoulder. I looked up, annoyed, into the cheerful open face of a natural-born grifter.

Over the years I'd developed an instinct about certain types of people. Some you warm up to instantly and know you'll be best friends for life; for others you just as instantly comprehend they're planning to nail your hide to the barn wall and scrape it clean.

He'd come to invite me into a card game. Maybe I look like someone who plays cards on trains. I try not to, but after two years of hanging out with gang bosses and gamblers some of it must have rubbed off.

But more likely it was because I appear to be in my young twenties wearing an expensive new suit and overcoat. He must have taken me for a well-heeled college kid, ripe for plucking. I checked the two players already at the table, who waved and smiled. They looked okay. Then I spotted the first man's partner buying a new deck of cards and matchboxes at the bar. He nodded absently at me, cracking open the cellophane wrap from the cards.

They looked exactly like a couple of regular guys wanting another player for a friendly game of poker. The man said they'd play for matchsticks, not money, a harmless way to pass the time.

How could I say no? Besides, if not me, then they'd just pluck some other bird.

In the interest of the public good, I folded my magazine back into a pocket and joined them, shaking hands, exchanging casual introductions. The grifter calling himself Sawyer shuffled, clumsily, chuckling when a couple cards went flying out. He gave the deck to me and watched as I also demonstrated bad shuffling. I apologized and said when I was at school I did more reading than anything else, and passed the deck to the guy on my right. He muttered, showing better dexterity at the art. He said he and the wife played a lot of bridge. I'd never been able to figure that game out, so he had my instant respect.

The second grifter, calling himself Fogelson, gave each player a box of matches. We spilled them onto the table and started the first hand.

Just to be clear, I don't like poker. It's not as interesting as a faster game of blackjack, so it goes without saying that I'm a terrible player. Sawyer and Fogelson made me feel like a champ, though. An hour later I won the pot, breaking the matchstick bank. I would have felt proud if I'd had anything to do with it. My improbable lucky streak gave me to understand I was to be their mark.

We divided the matches up to start over. The two other men were better players, dealing straight when it was their turn; I only won when Sawyer or Fogelson had charge of the deck. As the game stretched on this interesting point went unnoticed. They had to work at it since I had a bad habit of throwing away good cards. Must have been frustrating for them, but entertaining for yours truly.

Around eleven the other two potential marks said they had to get their beauty sleep and left. In the course of the game we'd gotten to know each other. One sold insurance, had five kids, a wife, and in-laws to support; the other was going to Altoona to repair and sell used furniture with his brother. The grifters spoke of similar bland backgrounds; I didn't bother to memorize them.

I topped them all, going to the trouble of cleaning up my usual slang and letting drop that my name was William (call me Bill!) Wollmuth. My doting pater was on the board of several banks, and I'd be expected to step into his shoes some day (not too soon!). College was the pip, and I'd even met a sweet little gal I was sure I could take home to mater. Once I got that elusive degree there was a bright future ahead.

I thought I was laying it on too thick, but Sawyer and Fogelson couldn't get enough of my autobiography.

Wish I could have taken the credit for it, but I'd lifted the story from a dime magazine I'd read the other week. In that one, young Bill had been kidnapped, but won the heart of a kidnapper's sister. They eventually escaped the bad guys to commit first-degree matrimony.

Not the writer's best effort, but it worked wonders on the grifters.

I used to be a terrible liar. I still am with friends. But a couple of card sharps hoping to skin me blind brought out the worst in me. I enjoyed every minute, guilt-free.

The lounge's population dwindled to a couple holdouts dozing in chairs and the three of us. I turned down offers of drinks, assuring my new friends I was a confirmed teetotaler due to an unfortunate allergy to alcohol, which was perfectly true.

"I want to be alert, anyway," I added. It was about time for me to start my own con game. I hoped this first cast would land right.

"For another hand?" asked Sawyer, casually shuffling the deck. His fingers were clumsy-looking, but during the course of play I'd noticed him using the mechanic's grip. It gave him a lot of control over what cards to deal and hold back. Plenty of honest dealers use it, but he wasn't one of them. Knowing what to look for helped me spot him at work, but he was a fast bastard.

"I should like that, but I wouldn't want to miss seeing the ghost."

As a conversation stopper, it did the trick. Up to that point I'd been successful at passing myself off as a naïve collegian with more money than experience. Now I was moving into more-money-than-sense territory. This angle needed to be examined before they took me to the next stage of the plucking process.

"Ghost?" asked Fogelson, nibbling the bait.

"You never heard of the *Twentieth Century Limited* ghost?"

They were an excellent team, not even exchanging a glance. They'd do whatever it took to keep me playing. "Uh, well, I always thought it was just one of those stories."

True enough, since I was making things up as I went, this time with no dime magazine inspiration.

Sawyer seamlessly took the cue and allowed that he thought he'd once heard a rumor of a ghost on a train but not on the Limited.

I obliged them with a sad tale of a friendly card game gone wrong. One of the players had been shot right through the heart when he caught out the others, who were cheating. They'd thrown him off the back of the train just as it crossed a river. His body was never found.

Now my new friends traded glances. I caught only a suggestion of it in my peripheral vision since I was studying my new hand. They'd be wondering if I was on to them.

"Apparently his spirit got trapped on the train, unable to rise to heaven or drop into hell," I went on, oblivious. "And to this day he haunts the line. The train company hushed the murder up, of course, but people talk, and the stories get passed around."

"Stories?" prompted Sawyer.

"When people see him. First everything gets cold. That's how you know he's around, the air gets like ice. He's supposed to be a solid as you or I, but look close a second time and he's gone. Houdini could have learned a thing or three from him about disappearing. Don't bother asking the conductor or the porters, it's as much as their job's worth to talk about him."

"Hell of a yarn, Wollmuth," said Fogelson.

Any second he might telegraph a signal to his partner to write off their evening of setup as a lost cause, but I cast out one more line.

"That's why I decided to play in the first place. It's said the gambler's ghost looks in on card games. There's stories about him scaring the bejeezus out of unsuspecting bridge players. I thought a poker game, even with just matchsticks in the pot, might lure him out."

"Huh, maybe that's what's put him off." He lighted a cigar and leaned back in his chair, wearing a thoughtful face.

"Oh, yeah?"

"Matchsticks wouldn't interest a real gambler. Bridge players will go in for a penny a point. That's what drew him out. The money."

"You think if we played for cash something might happen?" I asked.

He shrugged. "Never know. Pennies in the pot might not impress him."

"You're probably right. I tell you, I'd be willing to lay out some real dollars for a chance to see him, but I wouldn't think of imposing on either of you."

No imposition, they assured me, none at all. It would make the game even more interesting. They had to be pleased that I'd been the one to suggest playing for cash, saving them the trouble of persuading me.

"Have to be careful, though," Fogelson cautioned. "There's rules against gambling."

"So I've heard, but the porter will turn a blind eye if we slip him a decent tip." I found my wallet and brought forth a handful of ones and fives, making sure Sawyer glimpsed the healthy supply of tens and twenties bending a money clip out of shape. "Will this do for a start?"

Hell yes, it would.

They'd snapped, and I'd just set the hook.

* * *

This time I played as well as I could, which was still lousy. They had to do some energetic card culling to throw good hands at me. The idea behind it was to get me warmed up and thinking I was in the throes of a lucky streak. Otherwise I'd have lost everything in the first hour.

The pot was just over twenty bucks. A week's good wage for most, but these two had an eye for the rest of my cash and plenty of patience. I had a long stretch of time before dawn and an ace in the hole they could not possibly imagine.

With three of us the play went faster, but I kept looking restlessly around for the ghost. The grifters were too professional to show annoyance, but it began to get to them. Fogelson slapped the cards down harder than usual to get me back into the play. Sawyer would clear his throat now and then. I wondered if it was his nerves or part of some private signal code between them.

"It's chilly in here," I said putting some hope into my tone.

There was nothing wrong with the heat, but the power of suggestion can go a long way when the circumstances are right. We were alone in the car; the bar was closed, even the night porter had gone off to do something else. The lights were low, and shadows had crept into the corners.

"Don't think so," said Fogelson. He also used the mechanic's grip, and was good at keeping the top and bottom cards exactly where he wanted them. He dealt me an eight, three sixes, and one of the jokers, which were wild cards, temping me with a four of a kind hand.

"You've had a drink or two to keep warm, maybe you don't feel it yet. What about you, Mr. Sawyer? Don't you think it's gotten a little colder in the last few minutes?"

Sawyer was quiet, shooting an uneasy glance over his shoulder.

"Maybe," he said with some reluctance.

Fogelson spared him a narrow look, just a flicker, enough to warn his partner to stay focused. During this tiny break I let the joker fall into my lap, and slipped in an ace that I'd palmed during the last hand. A wild card would be much more useful to me later.

The magician at my nightclub had given me a few pointers about card tricks. I'd not practiced that much and amazed I was getting away with it, but the grifters had no reason to think I'd be cheating.

Good entertainment's hard to find.

A few months ago I might have hypnotized them and had other kinds of fun, but they wouldn't be turning themselves in to the cops at the next stop. The ability to influence bad guys with my evil-eye whammy was forever lost. The temptation to use it was there, but so was the certainty of something inside my skull exploding and killing me. I was tough and had survived a lot, but why take chances?

Even thinking about it sent a warning twinge through my brain and made me wince. I shook it off and checked my cards, finding a suspiciously good hand: three aces, a four and a ten. I had a potential full house depending which of the latter cards I threw away; Fogelson, who was dealing, would have one or the other ready to deliver to me.

So I threw both away.

He hid his exasperation extremely well.

He had a pair waiting in the wings and dealt me a couple of fives from the bottom.

Being an inexperienced player and this game was on the friendly side—for the moment—I let myself smile and bet the rest of my cash.

When the cards were on the table, Sawyer had a straight flush, all hearts.

That was disappointing. They were going to settle for a lousy twenty bucks? No…not likely. Sawyer generously invited me to another hand to win it back, which I accepted.

Then I gave a sudden start, whipping around. It was convincing enough to make Sawyer jump and stop Fogelson in mid-deal.

"I felt something tap my shoulder," I whispered, sounding excited. "Did you see anything behind me?"

"Nope," said the more laconic Fogelson. He shot a look at Sawyer, who was checking the rest of the car. "Must have been a draft."

"I felt fingers," I insisted. "Two fingers." I tapped the table twice with my own. "Just like that." I got up and went around the car, checking the corners and shutting off lights until only the one over the table was on. "Maybe he'll come closer if it's not so bright in here."

Sawyer must not have liked that and cleared his throat. It sounded natural, but was probably a signal to his partner. He wanted to leave.

"Another hand," said Fogelson, decisively. "You want a chance to win that pot back, don't you, Wollmuth?"

"Oh, yes, I guess I do. My luck's been pretty good tonight. You know, I think using money over matchsticks has done the trick. Let's give that old card player something to see."

"If you're sure..."

I returned, fired up and ready to go, and put a few tens on the table. "Absolutely!"

It took some doing, but they built the pot up. I won more than lost, and the wins got smaller while the less frequent losses got larger. Apparently unaware of this, I worked at keeping Sawyer distracted by observations about the temperature and strange movement of shadows. Fogelson held things together, seeing to it I got the right cards at the right time for the right stakes. I hardly needed to play at all but made an effort.

At some point I got hold of the second joker without them noticing and held it safe in my palm next to its brother.

Around two in the morning they'd gotten set up for the kill. The pot was over a thousand dollars, half of it had begun the evening safe in my pocket. The rest was their investment in the game.

I checked my hand, and it was a damned good one. Fogelson had dealt me another full house: three queens and two jacks. They looked very cozy together. Sawyer probably had another straight flush, but four of a kind would do just as well to clean me out.

As expected, I bet everything I had. Sawyer matched it; Fogelson had folded his hand with regret, but didn't look nervous.

When it came time to show our cards I'd swapped the jacks for the wild cards and presented five of a kind, my queens beating Sawyer's straight flush of spades.

The grifters froze. I took the opportunity to shuffle the cash together. "My gosh—that was some game. I'm glad you explained wild cards to me. I was temped to throw them back." I did my best to sound like a cheerful fool.

Sawyer cut a murderous look at Fogelson, who gave the smallest head shake. He'd not been careless with the deal; something was wrong. By the time their attention swung back to me I had the cash in a neat, easy-to-grab stack.

"Wollmuth. . .I think you've been less than square with us," Fogelson sounded dangerous.

I pretended shock. "Really? In what way?"

They stood at the same time, looming over me. "You know why."

"Gentlemen, I have played this game just as square with you as you have with me." I managed to deliver that one absolutely deadpan.

The grifters were not appreciative of my acting ability. Two to one, they'd be dirty fighters, and hadn't I given them the idea of throwing another gambler off the train?

"One more game," said Fogelson. "Cut for high card. Give us a chance to recoup a little."

"Tomorrow," I said firmly. "This has been the pip, but I'm awful tired now—"

He slammed the table with the side of his fist. "Cut for high card."

I grinned, closing my fingers tight around the wad of cash, and raised the bait up to eye level. They tensed, ready to pounce as soon as I tried something stupid.

Instead, I vanished. Like switching off a light.

Dead silence.

"The hell. . . ?" said Fogelson.

I wrapped my non-corporeal self around the more vulnerable Sawyer. In this state I'm a cold portent of the grave, and have been told that it's remarkably unpleasant. He yelped, twitched, and backed away, cursing in a high, strained voice.

"What's the matter?" Fogelson demanded.

"It's him. *He's* the ghost. He's on me!" There was a fine panic to Sawyer's tone.

Fogelson didn't have a comment for that. As he might be feeling left out, I floated over to wrap around him. He didn't move. "This is shit," he concluded. "This is shit!"

"He's a ghost, dammit!"

"He tricked us. There's no ghost. It's a trick."

If he didn't believe in ghosts, then it was a good bet he'd not think of other night-walking creatures like vampires. Reassuring.

I slipped away and went solid, crouching out of sight behind the bar, money still in hand. I shoved it safely into a pocket and looked around for something noisy to throw. Nearly everything was breakable glass, then I found a bunch of steel cocktail shakers.

Good enough.

I sent three hurtling in the grifters' general direction and at least one connected. Sawyer squawked and broke for the door leading to the next car.

Getting there ahead of him, I went solid.

He rocked back on his heels just a hair short of collision, registering shock, then anger. He swung hard, but I shifted to semi-transparent, and his fist went right through.

Solid again, I shoved him, sending him stumbling into Fogelson.

By the time they recovered, I'd vanished and got behind them. Solid, another shove sent Fogelson to the floor along with a few chairs.

To give the man credit, he knew how to keep his head, whatever the circumstance. He hauled a gun from his pocket, a little twenty-two revolver. Nothing much, but I didn't want shooting.

I darted in, unnaturally fast, and snagged it.

He rolled and tried to tackle me, but I faded to near-transparency and rose toward the ceiling.

Sawyer didn't seem to be armed, but then he was too busy gaping to move.

Twisting in the air, I floated feet first toward the door, glaring down at them. It had to look impressive; when I righted myself and touched down solid they were frozen.

"No call for violence when you play a square game—I should know," I said, holding the revolver up. "It was a couple of sharps just like you who killed me in the first place."

"Killed you?" Sawyer's whisper was almost too soft to hear.

"You know who I am. I told you about my untimely death." I opened the revolver and let the bullets tumble from the cylinder.

The last gun on which I'd tried this party trick had been larger; this model was no effort at all. I grabbed the cylinder and frame and twisted until they snapped apart.

Fogelson went green.

"You boys stay off my train from now on," I said. "Got that?"

Sawyer nodded.

I lowered my tone to a sinister whisper. "Or the next time we play cards it will be for your *souls!*"

Corny, but the shadowy darkness made it work. Maybe I'd never been on stage, but knew a good exit line. I dropped the broken revolver pieces and rushed toward the grifters, vanishing just before impact. They got another chance to experience of my special kind of cold.

Sawyer and Fogelson's departure was hasty. Too bad I couldn't see it; it sounded hilarious with the stumbling, jostling, crashing furniture, and curses.

The door slammed shut.

Counting to thirty, I re-formed and looked around. Nobody here but one amused vampire.

I cleaned up the mess, including the bullets, set chairs right again, and sank into one. Between the concentration required for the card play and the invisible acrobatics I wanted a rest.

What a great way to waste an evening.

Okay, not waste. Counting the money, I was five hundred and ten bucks richer. I'd earned it.

I got my magazine out. Dawn was still hours off, and I wanted to see how The Shadow handled crime in *his* neck of the woods.

.

KING OF SHREDS AND PATCHES

Author's Note: *I was asked to write something for Martin Greenberg's* ROTTEN RELATIONS *for DAW and immediately thought of Shakespeare's* Hamlet *as prime material to use. That family had everything: murder, incest, madness, and at least one ghost roaming the castle. Talk about putting the "fun" in dysfunctional! But what if Young Hamlet had it wrong and his Uncle Claudius was NOT the one who bumped off King Hamlet. . . ?*

Elsinor Castle, Denmark

Here do I set down for posterity, a true and exact record of the misfortunes that have lately besieged the court of Denmark. Whoever finds this, I ask and pray that you hold all knowledge of it from my beloved Queen Gertrude should I predecease her.

-- Claudius Rex --

The death of my brother, King Hamlet, could not have come at a worse time for Denmark.

I was in my chambers, setting to paper a detailed recounting of all that I saw and heard in Norway while acting as his ambassador there when the news of the calamity was brought to me.

Rather than a soft knock from one of Elsinore's countless pages, I was startled from my task by heavy pounding from a hasty fist. It occurred to me that my fears of an invasion from Norway were about to be fulfilled. I threw down my quill and, being alone, unlatched the door myself and pulled it wide, interrupting a second assault. Old Polonius stood without.

"What is amiss, sir?" I demanded, for obviously something of great import was wrong. His face was as white as his beard except for two red spots high on his cheeks from recent exertion. His breath came hoarse and hard. I'd ever known him as a man well able to keep control of his emotions, now he was positively tottering from inner turmoil. I took his trembling hand and led him inside. "Is it war?"

"W-war, your lordship?" He gave me so blank a look that he might have been struck by one of those strange convulsions that takes a man's mind away. "There is no war."

"Then speak, what is amiss?"

His lips quivered and overcome by whatever troubled him, he bowed his head and groaned. I glanced at the open doorway, but none were with him who might inform me of the nature of this trouble. That was odd. He usually had no less than two pages in tow the whole of the day to run his errands. I looked down both ends of the hall, but all was quiet in this part of the castle. From one of my windows I ascertained the courtyard below was also peaceful. It was the end of the hot part of the afternoon, and those who had no duties would take rest while they could.

In a firm tone I charged Polonius to explain himself. That seemed to break through, and he slowly raised his head. His eyes streamed tears, and without knowing the matter, I felt a kindred ill-omened leadening of my heart.

"Speak, sir," I whispered.

"Oh, good lord Claudius, your royal brother is dead."

Let God Himself be my witness, I almost laughed, for it was clear the dear old man had lost his wits and was ranting. "Impossible. I saw him take his walk upon the upper platform this morning as always. He waved greeting to me and I to him."

But Polonius shook his head again, as though to dislodge a stubborn fly. "Would that I were a liar, your lordship, but he is dead and gone and nothing can change that or bring him back to us."

I still could not take it in. "How comes this? Was it a fall?" Elsinore was full of stairs, many very steep.

"A fall? No, he was asleep in his orchard. He lies there still."

"What? Have you sent for a priest?" He blanched even more, and I knew that he had not. If there was the least breath of life remaining, then my brother must give his last confession lest his soul needlessly suffer. Perhaps Polonius was wrong. His sight was dim now with age, and though wise in statecraft, he was often wrong in more mundane matters—not that the death of a king could be considered as such.

"Lord Claudius, King Hamlet is *dead*. For hours, perhaps."

"And no one sent for help or told me until now?"

"As soon as I saw for myself, I came straight from there to you—wait, sir! There is more!"

But I was striding swiftly away. I loved Polonius like a second father—he had taught me much of the wisdom of his craft that I could better serve my brother and thus Denmark as ambassador—but could not wait upon him. Impatience and fear engulfed me. Grief, too, though I pushed that roughly from my heart. I could not and would not believe it; Hamlet could not, *must* not be dead.

Those inhabitants of Elsinore I passed to reach my brother's apartments continued their normal business with the peace of ignorance. Apparently Polonius spoke the truth about seeing me first, and word had not yet spread. Only when I descended several flights and entered the arched hall leading to Hamlet's private orchard did I perceive signs of trouble. Six guardsmen stood clustered before the orchard door. As a man, they had their swords ready in hand, tardily prepared to defend their royal master, but against what? Death? When his bony hand falls upon your shoulder, what mortal army can turn his purpose?

"Let me pass," I said.

The tallest, Francisco, planted himself in my way. "I beg forgiveness, Lord Claudius, but Lord Polonius ordered that we arm and keep all from the enclosure until his return."

My flare of anger was reflected in their frightened faces. "Even the king's brother?"

"Even so, lord." He looked to be highly unhappy with his lot. "I will send a man to fetch him here, though."

I could have bullied my way in, but chose to hold back. If it was true, if my dear brother was dead, then it would be best to follow the forms of custom and wait. "Do that. And quickly. He was last in my chambers."

Francisco nodded shortly to the youngest in his charge, who sheathed his weapon and hurried off.

"Do you know aught of what has happened?" I asked.

"Only that at the telling of the last hour Lord Polonius went to rouse his majesty from his sleep as usual. I was on watch. His lordship came out, seeming most stricken. He told me to bring more men, and when I did he then instructed us to stand firm and let none inside."

That made sense. The unexpected death of a much-loved king was bad enough, but letting the news fly forth without consideration for its effect on the common people could cause disorder. Polonius was well aware of the impending threat from Norway; the last thing Denmark needed was to be thrown into chaos and thus be seen as vulnerable by the rapacious Fortinbras.

"You did well," I said. "We'll wait for the lord chamberlain's return."

"Lord? Do you know what is wrong?" Behind him, his men cast uneasy glances at the closed door to the orchard, ominous in shadows. They would be guessing the worst, of course. In light of Polonius's odd actions and orders, of me here at this time of day, of the king not showing himself, they would guess rightly. If the worst were true, then this would have to be handled with great care.

"Be at peace, all will be revealed soon."

That did little to bolster them, quite the opposite. I curbed my impatience as best I could until Polonius arrived, short-winded and troubled. He must have known his orders would have gone ill with me, but I put a reassuring hand on his arm to let him know I was not offended. He had done the right thing.

"Stand down," he puffed at Francisco, "and let Lord Claudius pass."

One of them thrust open the door and the yellow light of late afternoon flooded the dim hall. I blinked against the glare and stepped into it, looking around. There was a strong scent of apple blossoms on the sea-washed air. This was my brother's sanctuary from the cares of his crown. Few were allowed here: myself, his queen, their son, Polonius, and a gardener whose only job was to tend this great garden. He worked alone and was always gone when Hamlet desired its peace. Ever busy with other concerns, I'd not been here in decades, not since Hamlet and I played within its high walls as children and certainly not since he was crowned king all those years past.

I recalled childhood memories of this place, but they were of no use now. Whatever paths we played on then were changed. Trees had grown, died, been uprooted, and replaced with other growth. This space covered no more than an acre, but the plantings were high and dense, and one could easily become lost.

Polonius was at my side. "This way, lord."

"Have you sent for a priest? For a physician?"

"Both, lord. They will be here anon."

He took me on a twisting path that seemed to lead toward the center. It was a cunning design, giving the illusion of a goodly walk, and within a turn or two it felt like we were in a shady orchard miles away. The branches above laced together in some spots concealing even the looming bulk of Elsinore castle.

I recognized a landmark. Ahead, overlooked by an old apple tree, was a vast stone bench. It was part of the very base of the massive sea cliff that Elsinore rested upon. The thrust of stone was larger than two beds pushed together and much longer. A master hand had, in ancient times, carved it with fantastical shapes and patterns on the sides. The top was smoothed to within a foot of the ground, and polished. It had served as throne, fort, feasting table, ship, riding steed, and other imaginings in our childhood play until we outgrew it. Now it was covered with thick robes to lend ease to the hard stone and there would my brother find respite from his cares.

And there he lay in his last rest.

I'd seen battle, and knew death's countenance. At a dozen paces I recognized the stillness peculiar to its presence. That it had come for my brother was true after all, and I was no longer master of my progress. Halting, I leaned on Polonius as the certainty swept over me. With no mind to the words, a prayer fled from my lips, and I crossed myself.

"This is trouble enough, but a harsher, more evil woe awaits," he told me.

"What mean you?"

For once Polonius was unable to summon words for explanation and again would only shake his head. My curiosity became stronger than my anguish. Hanging on each other like two old women, we slowly approached my brother's final couch of rest, my heart filled with dread.

The cushioning robes were in disarray, tossed about as though Hamlet had fought desperately against a relentless foe. His arms were flung wide over his head, hands turned into grasping claws, his whole body twisted and frozen in a posture of extreme agony. As we came closer, more details revealed themselves to the eye, but the mind denies such awfulness as being too impossible to exist, and so we stare and stare and stare into overwhelming horror.

My poor brother's skin was crusted and splotched with some loathsome excretion, as though he sweated the puss of vile infection through each and every pore. Crusted also was his very blood, which had burst from his eyes, nose, and gaping mouth. A stench like that of a man dead for a week, not mere hours, rose from him to merge with the sweetness of the apple flowers. Flies buzzed in legions around him.

Grabbing up one corner of a robe, I drew it over his bloated face. Had he not been in garb familiar to me I should never have recognized him.

I had seen men die from paroxysmal fits when their hearts stop, and I'd seen what the ravages of contagion could do to a body, but this. . .a bitterly cold hand closed hard around my spirit. What had taken my brother away was neither fit nor sickness.

The fear I'd felt before was a pale thing compared to what seized me now, for now I was round full with terror.

And I dared not show it.

"Lord Claudius?"

I looked at Polonius. . .and wondered. Could *he*. . . ?

Thus did he return my look. I saw my own thoughts running panicked behind his blue eyes.

"You remember?" I asked.

He nodded, his lips thin with the effort to compress them together, lest he speak anything aloud.

"And think you it was I who did this?"

"I think nothing, your lordship," he said most carefully.

I was too stunned to be angered. "I understand your suspicion, but. . .see me, good friend."

"Lord Claudius, I—"

"*See* me!"

He looked from me to Hamlet's shrouded form and back. Polonius seemed balanced on the very edge of a cliff.

I had to pull him from it. "Recall you the service of my *whole life* as I recall yours. You above all others know my heart and the honest love I bear my brother—a match to your own, is it not?"

He teetered for a long moment, then cast his gaze downward. "I am most desperately shamed, lord. 'Tis a wicked devil who placed doubt in my mind."

"And mine, too."

I took up his trembling hand, seeing truth and trust restored in his withered features and with each fresh tear that started from his eyes. "So, despite our knowledge of such dark matters we are guiltless of this deed. That leaves us to find who is responsible. Who and how."

"And why," he added, wiping his cheek with his sleeve.

"Then avenge ourselves and Denmark for this treason."

The physician and the priest, one for Hamlet's body, the other for his soul, both arriving far too late, came up the path. I withdrew as they each tended to their spheres of influence, notwithstanding their appalled reactions to the condition of the king's body.

While the priest continued with prayers, the physician approached us and bowed. He seemed shaken, but who would not be?

"Your lordship," he said to me. "If it please you, I am most heartily sorry that—"

"What caused my royal brother's death, sir?" I said abruptly. "Speak plainly and quick."

"Sir, I believe it was poison that left him in so lamentable a state."

My heart fell. If word got out that the majesty of Denmark had been murdered. . .

"What poison?" asked Polonius, assuming an air of reservation.

"Most likely from an adder slipped over the wall."

What? My surprise was genuine. Was the man a fool? But perhaps his experience was insufficient to the task. He was very young, having taken over most of the duties of his father, who had taught him his skills. Not well enough, it appeared.

Polonius and I exchanged a look. A shared memory was the cause of our moment of shared distrust. We both knew no serpent's sting would bring about such a putrid sweating as to leave a body bloated and stinking in the space of a few hours. Only a powerful poison could do that—one crafted and distilled by an expert hand.

Twenty years and more ago, as a young courtier dispatched to Italy, it had been my lot to learn of a death by identical means of dispatch. A cuckolded gentleman, unable to give challenge because of his advanced years, chose to kill his wife's lover by poison. The artificial infection (it was found) was poured into the unfortunate's ear as he slept and shortly he succumbed to convulsions, the sweat, and the bleeding, passing in terrible pain from this life to the next. The husband was judged to be within his rights and acquitted, and his wife took herself away to a nunnery, which, considering the nature of her marriage, was a much safer place to be than home.

I'd brought the tale back to Denmark, telling it to Polonius, among others, but only he knew the particular signs of that concoction, which was called juice of hebenon, though it was made of many other things as well. Some might know the name, but not its nature or how to make it. And like myself, my old friend could not tell a henbane plant from rosemary.

Yet still we stared at one another, for he had memory of the story the same as I. But by that we each knew the other would have instantly known, therefore, neither could have done it. Only someone else. . .

"An adder?" Polonius questioned sharply. "Are you sure? What sort?"

"There are many," said the doctor. "I know of none whose bite would ordinarily cause such a reaction. However, just as one man may suffer the sting of a bee and move on while another falls and dies from it, I believe his majesty may have had the same susceptibility as the latter wretch. If he was overly sensitive to the venom, then would he quickly succumb with great violence to it. Perhaps, bitten while he slept, he awoke too late to call for help and thus passed from life."

Polonius nodded and looked to me. The explanation was reasonable, and though we knew it the wrong one, we had no choice but to make it serve for the moment.

"Then the orchard must be searched from top to bottom," I said. "If such a serpent is loose here, none are safe. Perhaps it pleased God to take our king from us in such a hasty and terrible manner, but I am not pleased and would have the instrument of His use destroyed."

"Presently, your lordship," said Polonius. "That shall be seen to presently, but there are other necessities pressing. We must organize. The other lords must be informed, and dear God, but the poor queen must be told."

This would destroy her, I thought. Gentle Gertrude hung on my brother's every word as though her life came from him and not Heaven. "I will do that. And it must be done softly. She cannot see her husband while he is in so abhorrent a state. Her ladies should be at hand, and you as well, doctor. You will also be needed to see to the cleansing of my poor brother's body and to stop rumors of plague or pox so none may take alarm. See to it."

"I am at your service, my lord."

Polonius threw him a sharp look at the error. I was not king, and therefore not his or anyone else's lord, but the old man couldn't say so to him while I was in hearing.

I shook my head at Polonius, so he saw it was of small matter to me, which it was; we had larger matters to discuss.

But not now. I could hold my grief back no longer. I turned quickly from them and walked a few paces into the trees to escape their sight, and there gave in to it. They would doubtless hear my sobs, but allow me the necessary privacy for as long as it took until the first wave subsided. It was my lot to set things in motion. In the days to come my public duties would intrude upon my private mourning. But for this hour I ached bitterly at this unexpected sundering from my onetime playmate, lifelong friend, and finally king. My beloved brother was dead, and I felt his loss like a mortal wounding from a dull blade.

* * *

When my parents died, it had fallen to others to see to the forms and processions of grief. I was able to mourn for as long and as deeply as my soul needed. Now the heavy responsibilities were on me, and I had few friends to help with the burdens. But that dear old man, Polonius, proved to be my greatest ally, advisor, and most trusted support through the worst of it.

My position in Denmark's court had never been an enthusiastic one, for there were many lords who vied to be my late brother's favorite and thus was I mistakenly perceived as an interloper ready to subvert their ambitions. They were fools to think their links to him could prove stronger than my own constant link of blood. Certainly Hamlet found grim amusement in their antics. However, their ever-shifting games of vanity and power were nothing to me; I did not play. It was far better to watch than participate in such politic comedies.

There was also a most important detail that these strivers continually overlooked: I had *no* desire to increase my power nor possessed designs on the throne. That sovereign seat was destined to go to my nephew, young Hamlet, and he was welcome to it. In the course of years, if I was spared, I fully expected to serve the Danish cause as his loyal ambassador in his turn.

But his father's sudden death at this, the worst possible time, usurped his anticipated succession. Within a week Fortinbras—who was clearly preparing to take back the lands his father lost to us—would hear of King Hamlet's passing; within a week after that the young firebrand's armies would be ravaging those border lands he wished to reclaim, shattering our long peace and prosperity beyond mending for years to come.

Fortinbras would not—with *his* aspirations to glory—stop at the disputed borders, though, but continue from Elsinore to Esbjerg, taking everything between in bloody conquest. The Danish nobles would defend each their several lands, but not unite to effectively defend Denmark as a whole unless they had a king to lead them. Separately they would fall, only together could we triumph.

But Prince Hamlet was in Wittenberg, a full month's journey away for the fastest messenger. He couldn't hope to return in less than two months, and by then he would have no kingdom to return to; it would be too late.

Polonius and I discussed this thoroughly and with much pain and care as well as consideration for young Hamlet's position. Had we some way to acquaint him with the crisis, he would have approved the necessity of instant action to preserve the state. Above all, Denmark must have a sound king, but particularly now.

The solution, Polonius said, was for me to assume the crown and do so without delay.

I confess the prospect was not a desirable one; I preferred my lesser position. "Let another be elected from the nobles of the land."

"Who?" he asked. "Who of that self-serving lot would you trust? This such-a-one is more ambitious than Fortinbras, that such-a-one too rabbit-like in manner to defend us in need or another is so grand in his vanity that he would bankrupt the whole of the treasury for a single suit of raiment. No, Lord Claudius, none of them have your understanding of what it truly means to rule wisely and well. You stood at your brother's side through many years and before that witnessed and learned from your father's long term. Young Hamlet does not possess such experience, and he's not here to be advised by either of us. Anyone else will bring eventual ruin to Denmark."

"But the nobles like me not. They will never elect me to be their lord."

"A majority of them will, at a word from me. The rest will fall in with the vote to prevent rivals from rising above their station."

" 'T'would be better were their confidence be wholehearted and freely given, not forced."

"There will be no force, only persuasion. Once I set the facts plain before them, they'll be willing enough to have you stave off the invasion. Your report on what is afoot there—"

"They'll say I'm creating a threat from Norway to further myself."

"That they cannot do. Think you that yours were the only eyes and ears for Denmark in that court? I know of a dozen nobles with spies in place there, and to a man they will confirm the ill tidings you brought. They all want Fortinbras stopped. If you present them with a plan for that—"

"I had a recommendation prepared for—for my brother's approval. . ."

"Too late now for him to hear it, but in life he heeded your counsel more often than not, and your advice was ever sound—another fact to put before the nobles. Your lordship, you *must* walk this path for the state to live on preserved from strife, and it must be an immediate starting."

I had other objections, but in my heart knew he was right. If we waited two months for Hamlet's return it would be too late, and Fortinbras would have swept in.

Thus did Polonius persuade me to my duty.

But I nearly ran craven from it when he broached the subject of the queen.

"She is loved by the rabble," he said. "Win her to your side, and you win their hearts as well."

I did not take his full meaning, thinking he meant her support for my cause was all that was needed. "She will prefer her son over me for the throne, which is to be expected. But once she knows the seriousness of this difficulty, she will come around."

"Do not count on that, for she has a blind eye when it comes to the lad. However, if played gently and well, she will prefer her *husband* over her son."

This was a day of thick sight for me. "But my brother is gone."

"I refer to you, sir. Become her husband."

To that I responded with a staring eye, unsure if I heard him aright.

He pressed on. "The advantage is obvious. The queen remains the queen—which to her is far better than being the queen mother. She retains her honors and respect and position in the court, you have gained her approval and with that the support of the rabble, which counts for much, and young Hamlet is *still the heir*. Denmark is made secure by keeping the crown within the stability of a long-established royal family, its care in the hands of an honorable and well-schooled lord who will hold and protect it most diligently."

A wily old fellow was Polonius, but he seemed to have overstepped himself with this outrageous suggestion. A marriage was quite absurd, though it was sound politics and nothing new to me.

Many years ago in my youth I'd been betrothed to a number of young ladies. My father's political maneuverings demanded such matrimonial alliances, and I took none of them seriously. Sometimes the girl died, in others the contract was cancelled as her father in turn arranged a better match. On one occasion negotiations went so far that I was able to meet the girl, which was a bit of an advancement. She seemed a comely quiet sort, but things never progressed beyond that first meeting. The alliance ceased to be of import and the marriage postponed indefinitely. So far as I knew I might still be engaged to her, but had long since forgotten her name.

Of course I'd availed myself of fleshly pleasures, cheerfully leaving abstinence to those priests who chose to give attention to that vow. I'd had mistresses here and there where my duties carried me, for I found foreign women to be wonderfully captivating. But for good or ill I had never been the sort to lose my heart to any one woman for any length of time. I had no desire to father children, and if I had done so, then their mothers kept the glad tidings to themselves. The expectation of marriage had ceased to be of import to me for whole decades, so Polonius had much work convincing me to even listen.

But for the sake of the state, I did give ear to his argument, and after much thought concluded that he was right. This would not be the first time a ruler made a bride of the previous king's wife, but I was uncomfortable that this was my brother's wife. For most, such an alliance would stink of foul incest. However, Polonius had arguments against that, supported by Holy Scripture no less.

With a sigh, and an unaccustomed palpitation in my heart inspired by terror, not love-sickness, I gave him leave to speak to Gertrude on the matter. He must make clear the fact that this marriage was strictly for the good of the state, and that I'd never presume to make overtures to her for any other reason. I had too much respect for my brother's memory for that. She was still in the deepest mourning for him, and on several occasions we sat together in the company of her ladies and grieved together, which had provided much comfort to me. We'd known each other for over thirty years, and I thought of her as a friend, nothing more.

To Polonius I said I would consent to offer suit to my former sister-in-law *only* if she was willing, and the arrangement of the marriage bed—or beds in their separate chambers—was entirely up to her. There was no need for us to beget an heir, after all, so a consummation was not necessary.

Polonius, choosing his moment most carefully, broached the subject with Gertrude. I know not what he said to her, but with his soft persuasions and influence he added royal matchmaker to his list of accomplishments.

What another shock it was to learn that Gertrude *desired* to be my bride—in the traditional sense.

Whether she wanted me for myself as a man or as some remnant of her late husband, as her protector or a means to continue as queen, perhaps all and more, I did not inquire. Let it suffice that I spent some hours talking with her with this new aspect included in the conversation and began to see her in a wholly different light. She had happily retained a great portion of her youthful beauty and charm and used it to good effect. Combined with her artless sincerity of warmth toward me I stood no chance and suffered the supreme loss of composure that occurs when a man of middle years falls in love for the first time.

After that, events set their own course. The nobles supported me to take the crown, which I did, and within a month of leading the procession for my poor brother's internment I was leading the wedding party in to feast. Though the crowning and especially the marriage were scandalously quick, the results were as Polonius predicted. Fortinbras held back to see what direction I would take. Certainly the quick activity in the Danish court had served him an unexpected turn. I made certain his spies had every chance to observe how busy the shipyards and armorers were—the first orders I issued as king were to give them custom. With no other hint of my intent, Fortinbras was free to draw his own conclusions, and so he hesitated. All to our advantage.

There was some grumbling in my court about the expense of arming, particularly for a battle that might not happen, but I knew it was cheaper to build for war than to have war itself, and with the building, stave off conflict. By spending a hundred on weapons that might never come to use, I saved the land ten times ten thousand and more in bloody conflict—an excellent bargain.

Of course it did not hurt to write in secret to the old uncle of Fortinbras, a long-time friend of mine, and let him know what his nephew was about. Though ancient in years, he still held influence over the boy, and with a stern lecture, a bribe, and a suggestion to direct his wrath and energy against our common enemy, the Polack, disaster for us both was turned aside.

All seemed well—except for the dark shadow of my brother's most strange and unnatural death hanging over my heart. Polonius and I devoted many hours to discussion of this man or that, trying to discover who could have been responsible. One by one we proposed and ultimately discarded them all. None in the court had anything to gain by Hamlet's death and much to lose. They knew the crown would have gone to young Hamlet, and if anything happened to him, then an election would be held to decide the next king. No one of them held so much power or the esteem of his fellows to guarantee to influence the vote to himself. There likely would have been factions and perhaps even civil war as a result.

My next progression, which I kept very much to myself, was to consider Laertes, Polonius's son. Laertes was a fit young fellow and skilled to action—but in Paris at the time. He might have set some agent of his to do the actual murder, but what reason could he have to kill our liege? He was a virtuous man, almost monk-like and full of love for others, and like the rest of us expected young Hamlet to inherit the crown. He had nothing to gain.

Who was left? Not gentle Gertrude, who had loved her husband as land loves the rain, and I did not for an instant think she had the savageness nor the knowledge to do it.

We questioned Francisco most closely, the poor man. I daresay he thought we were preparing to accuse him of treason, but even as he stood watch at the orchard door, other guards stood their watch within his sight. Between them their movements were accounted for and it was clear that no one had entered the orchard.

Of course, that meant nothing if the murderer had concealed himself there earlier in the day. He could easily elude the patrols of the one gardener until the afternoon, and then escape later in the confusion after the body was found.

Ultimately we concluded that some agent for Fortinbras had carried out the assassination, for he could be the only one advantaged by the crime. It must have been a sore disappointment his ploy did not work as he'd planned.

How it rankled that we could not make a fair and open accusation against him, but for the sake of Denmark's continued peace we remained silent, and publicly gave sad credence to the physician's conclusion that a serpent's sting was to blame for so strange a death. A search was made and many snakes were found, but all were the benign sort that, lacking venom, cleanse the land of rats and mice. Though innocent of regicide, they were slaughtered by an army of gardeners.

So the days and weeks passed, our griefs were gradually softened by our joys, for Gertrude was an absolute delight to me, and peaceful order replaced the disruption in our lives.

Until Hamlet returned home.

Of course he was considerably upset, not only by his father's death, but in finding that I had—in his eyes—stolen the succession from him. He objected also to the marriage, making clear our *haste* was what infuriated him the most. Had his mother delayed and ruled as queen, then might he have made his claim. We had considered that as a possibility, but discarded it. Gertrude was no soldier, and though popular with the people, to the gathered nobles she was merely a weak woman, and they would not follow a woman's orders.

Polonius and I both tried to reason with Hamlet on the dire nature of the threat from Norway, but a disaster that never happens is easily disregarded, and he did so, loudly and often.

That was when we became aware of an odd change in him. As well as being versed in the rougher arts of a high-born gentleman he had ever been a pleasant, studious sort, most charming in his manner, a trait he'd inherited from his mother. Now was he darker in his moods and raiment, surly, and given to fits of passionate rage with no cause. We seemed to be dealing with a rebellious, uncontrolled youth of fifteen, not a grown man of thirty.

He'd returned to us from Wittenberg gaunt of face, his eyes wild, and often his speech wandered in ways comparable to Polonius's convoluted, but canny method. But there was no plan in Hamlet's ramblings, unless it was to give pain to those closest to him. I was his chief target for insult, but for Gertrude's sake I endured it. She and I set some of Hamlet's old friends to watching him in an attempt to discover the source of his rash behavior, but he was as guarded with them as I was years ago while acting as ambassador to the Polish court. He could not or would not divulge the reason for those periods of turbulence that bordered on the dangerous, though he had confessed to them that he was aware of his behavior. It occurred to me that this might be some childish means to gain attention. If so, then a bout of healthy sea-voyaging might set him right again.

But before I could act upon the idea it was with great hesitation Polonius put into words that which I feared, that young Hamlet was indeed truly losing his wits. Certainly his doting mother noticed, though she vainly hoped it to be a temporary thing brought on by his unrelenting grief for his father's death. She prayed nightly he would find a cure and be restored. She later fixed on the idea—put forth by Polonius as a straw to comfort her—that her son was mad with love for the old man's daughter, Ophelia.

"It is not for love of *my* daughter, though," he said to me in private after we'd witnessed a harrowing encounter between Hamlet and Ophelia that reduced the poor girl to tears. " 'Twas love for another's daughter that's the root of this."

"Whose?" I asked.

"A nameless trull in the brothels of Wittenberg has obviously passed the French pox to him."

Oh, dear God, no. I objected greatly to this. I did not want it to be.

"My lord, I have seen its like before. He shows the signs, and his mind grows more bewildered each day."

"I know the signs, too, and it takes years, even decades for the madness to establish itself. 'Tis a slow process or so I've always been told."

"Who is to say it has not? When he was yet beardless the first cravings of manhood might have taken him to a whore tainted with the rot. It could well have happened fifteen or more years ago and *now* the pox begins to briskly manifest. That which pollutes his blood is proceeding with its foul work far faster than normal, or so it appears to us who have not seen him in over a year. His friends are perhaps unaware of it for they've grown used to its gradual rise. He has his lucid moments, but they decrease in duration, while his ravings increase. You've yourself marked his deterioration. He is sinking into madness as surely as a ship stranded on sharp rocks, battered by the waves, is taken apart piece by piece. At this pace within a few months he will be wholly lost to us."

I loved my nephew, so the sight of the change in him was most painful to me. For those with eyes to see—myself and Polonius, among others of the court—young Hamlet's doom was upon him like a black cloud over his head.

Poor Gertrude. Poor Denmark. "We must do something."

"I know of no cure, lord."

"Nor I." I gave some quick thought to the matter, recalling what others in my position had done to deal with such difficulties. There were few choices open, and now I had to also freshly consider the succession since he would likely die before me.

The contagion gnawing at his brain would consume him to full madness in too short a season. Even if in that time I arranged a marriage and he bred an heir, the child would likely also suffer enfeeblement. My duties in other courts had been depressingly instructive. I'd seen at first hand how the indiscretions of one generation were passed to the next, resulting in malformed or simple-minded progeny who died young. Yet often would they come to the rule of their land regardless of their competency, which ever and always led to disaster.

I discarded that possibility and put off for the moment the succession issue. Now was I a stepfather as well as an uncle and had to think how to deal with this coming tragedy.

Had Hamlet been suffering from any other kind of pox, plague, or cancer, there would be no question of our providing him the best of care here in his home for as long as needed. It would have been highly painful to his mother and myself, but in that pain we might find a kind of comfort in knowing that one is trying one's best to give succor to a much-loved child.

But madness such as this would be too terrible to endure. His outbursts, so unlike his normal self, were an agony to Gertrude and promised to become worse in time. Should her last memory of her son be of him tied to a bed raving and spitting vile words at her blameless self? I would not put her gentle soul through that hell.

"He cannot remain here," I finally said. "We will spare him the humiliation of having his family and friends watch his decline. He can go to England and live out what time remains there. We'll tell him he's to collect their tardy tribute to give purpose to the journey so it doesn't appear to be banishment."

"Might he not raise a force against you, lord?" Polonius was ever worried about upstarts disrupting the peace of the land.

"Hardly there. Their king has no stomach for foreign wars. We will also send a letter for his eyes only, requiring him to keep Hamlet under watch and out of mischief. When the boy is no longer capable, he's to be placed under care in some gentle hospice monastery. A portion of the tribute money will pay for it. We trust our ambassador there; he will see to it our prince is looked after according to his station."

This news was hard received by little Ophelia, despite her a distressing encounter with Hamlet, who had shown a side of himself that none should see. But the hearts of young girls can become fast fixed, even when it means their own destruction. She was a sweet child and quite unspoiled, but for this love fantasy of hers. Sadly, it had once been fueled by Hamlet himself. During one of his summer visits he'd spent some time with her, and she had taken his casual attentions too seriously. Indeed there was a time when the girl expected to be Hamlet's bride, and put it forth among her ladies as though it was inevitable. The rumor was enough for my brother and Gertrude to see her privately. Apparently Gertrude was in favor of such a joining, but a royal prince is not free to marry as an ordinary man might. This was most clearly explained to Ophelia. Gertrude said the child fled the room in tears, but such is the way of things, and in time she recovered.

When Hamlet returned, though, Ophelia's feelings for him were stirred up again, and Polonius and even her brother Laertes had to step in to curb her spirited affections. Hamlet inadvertently helped with his brutal rejection of her. Polonius had ordered her to return some small gifts as the prince had given during lighter days, and he took it badly, venting his temper on her. Polonius and I watched the sorry show from hiding, ready to emerge to protect her should Hamlet turn violent. Thankfully, he did not, but the encounter was a traumatic one for all, and I was very relieved when Hamlet finally stormed out.

Ophelia, in that moment, must have finally realized he was mad, but still she pined for him. Certainly there could be no match between them now. I would have no objection were he robust and back to his former gentle self, but to inflict a diseased lunatic upon that fragile girl would be cruel folly. Her father made an end of the suit, and though it was hard for his daughter, better that than a ruinous marriage.

So might we have peacefully proceeded in the plan to send him packing had I but known Hamlet was hatching a plot of his own to bring me into disrepute. Its culmination took place the night a troupe of traveling players came to Elsinore. What a dreadful outcome did they, unknowing, bring about.

Things began well, for Gertrude took Hamlet's interest in holding a play for the court as a good sign. He had been in a high humor that day, more like his old self, but to me there still seemed to be a sharpness to his manner that was not quite right. Many times I caught him throwing looks my way that might as well been daggers. It made my heart ache, but I'd grown used to the fact that he would likely never forgive me for my expedient actions to save the throne. It was also in my heart that he was aware of his deterioration, and knew he would never live to inherit that seat. Of course, he could never admit it to himself. It was far easier to blame me for all offenses.

Members of the court took their places in the audience, and Gertrude and I came in and settled ourselves. Hamlet made a bit of a scene with Ophelia, which caused a general discomfort to those who heard. Gertrude tried to distract him over to herself, but he continued to walk on the brink of provocation with the girl. Though sweet of temper, she wasn't particularly clever, and he still possessed enough of his wits to sting her with jibes and near-insults. She understood that he was bullying her, but wasn't quick enough to hold her own against attack, retreating into red-faced silence until the play began. I thought I should have words with him afterward, but Gertrude shot me a glance that said she would deal with him. Clearly he still had some control over himself and harrying an innocent like Ophelia was not gentlemanly behavior. He'd been raised better than that.

The players went through their traditional prologues and miming to which I paid scant attention, focused as I was on Hamlet. If he continued to be a nuisance to Ophelia I would step in and halt things.

Would that he had done so, but he seemed aware of my attention and behaved himself, more or less. He shifted to making comments about the presentation, which was irritating but tolerable. The player king and queen stumbled through their lines as though they'd but learned them in that same hour, and the whole time Hamlet's old school friend from Wittenberg, Horatio, held his gaze on me like a hawk. I knew some devilry must be afoot, but could not imagine what it might be. The man was too far distant to make a physical attack on my person, which was what I most dreaded. My guards would cut him down quick enough, so I felt safe, but hated the idea of more tales of scandal being heaped upon my court.

There, too, was the possibility that Hamlet might, while others were distracted by the show, attack me. He was armed with sword and dagger as was the fashion and necessity of the time. However, I had instructed my guard to be particularly alert to any threatening move on his part. After that awful business with Ophelia I concluded that he might eventually give in to a violent impulse and direct it at me. They were well aware of Prince Hamlet's growing madness and prepared, I hoped, to deal briskly with it should he lose control.

But he had no need. I was the one who fell into a fit, maneuvered there by a cunning made vicious by his disease.

Rumor has it I stopped the play out of guilt, for the players enacted a performance of a man's murder in a garden, his assassin, who was his own nephew, marrying the shallow and betraying widow in order to inherit everything.

At first I could not comprehend what I was seeing. I thought I must be interpreting it the wrong way, but as each ill-memorized line pressed upon my ears the more my disbelief gave way to rage.

The offensive parallels to my brother's demise were too great to be ignored, nor could I possibly contain my fury at so brazen an insult. I'd *loved* my brother, and to be accused of killing him by a boy I loved as much as a son was vile beyond imagining, yet Hamlet had imagined it, and it was at his instigation that the show was carried out. Only true madness could have created and birthed such a twisted thought from his innermost mind.

I rose and roared for lights, bringing to an end to the mockery. The players stood rooted in place, horror on their painted faces. They knew they had committed a supreme offense, but were obviously ignorant of what it might be. My gaze next fell upon Hamlet. On his face was a look of such vicious, lunatic exultation that I actually felt sickened at the sight. I'd not had such a reaction since the day I'd fought at his father's side in my first battle. The fighting itself inspired a perilous euphoria, but afterwards, when one sees the bloody bodies strewn helpless and twitching in their death throes on the field. . .I was not impervious to pity or revulsion and had staggered to one side to spew my guts on the red-stained grass. It took all my self-control now to keep from repeating that youthful weakness in front of all. I gulped back the impulse, breathed deep of the thick, smoky air from the lamps and torches, and inwardly vowed that young Hamlet would pay dear for this indecent cruelty.

This was not the time or place to confront him. It must be done in private—after I'd mastered myself. Until now his tragic disease had been a family matter; by this display he'd made it devastatingly public.

The disaster of the play alone was more than enough woe, but on this terrible night an army of troubles began ravening within Elsinore's walls.

After leaving the great hall in considerable disorder and disarray I took myself in haste to the chapel. It was one place where I thought I'd be left in peace by the constant press of courtiers, but two of them turned up to disturb my attempt at calming devotions. As there was no ignoring them, I ordered them to prepare for their instant dispatch to England with my wayward nephew. They fled, quickly to be replaced by Polonius who informed me that Gertrude had summoned Hamlet to her closet. My old friend promised to listen in on that exchange and acquaint me of the details soon after, and took himself away.

Alone for the moment, I bent both knees and spent time in sincere prayer in an attempt to soothe myself to coherence, but it availed me not. I was not a man used to being angry, and containing it did not sit well with me, nor was I in a position to express it as before my rise in rank. There were many times when I saw my father and brother bound by the same circumstance. How it rankled them that they could not be forthright, but had to bury their feelings deep for the sake of the state. I had little to no practice at this bitter portion of royalty, and certainly those waiting without quickly backed down when at last I emerged from the chapel, still thunderous of aspect. None offered useless words of kindness or comfort, but maintained a wise silence.

I shortly called a small gathering to my council room to formally deal with the crisis. This very night Hamlet would depart for England, in fetters if need be. The timing was wretched, for it would indeed appear that I'd been stung with guilt inspired by the mummery of the play. In truth, I had put off sending him to sea, for his presence was a dear thing to Gertrude. She seemed to take her very breath from his glance, and I was loath to bring her pain. But I measured the brief sharp hurt of his leaving against the ongoing agony of months of his out-of-control rants and accusations. If he turned his wrath upon her. . .better to cut the festering limb off now before the poison spread to the rest of the body.

While I made more detailed arrangements to carry the wretch to foreign shores where his ravings would be ignored, Gertrude attempted to impart some measure of parental authority to Hamlet in her chambers. At the least she would keep him busy while I set things in motion for his removal. I judged she of all would be safe, especially while Polonius played both watchdog and witness as he'd done so many other times before under a variety of circumstances.

But young Hamlet, deranged and worked into a frenzy, did, in the violence of his madness, discover and murder loyal Polonius right in front of poor Gertrude, running him bloodily through with his sword.

Oh, God, what a foul and fell deed it was, and when I learned of it I was torn between boundless grief and a matching fury at the senseless death of a harmless old man. In my heart I called Polonius my second father; if depth of grief could be measured by depth of love, then never would I struggle free of the darkness that enveloped my heart.

But. . .the demands and duties of office forced me to rouse, put off my feelings, and deal with the calamity. There would be no trial, sparing Gertrude that agony. There could be none, since lunatics are not responsible for their wildness. Hamlet would depart for England that night, and so he did, under the close guard of two watchful courtiers.

Then all that remained was this second anguish to live through, and I felt it even more keenly than the loss of my brother, for I might have prevented this death by arresting Hamlet immediately after the disrupted play. Again and again I berated myself for not sending a guard along with Polonius, or instructing him to have a trusted man within close call.

Alas, Gertrude withdrew from me. The ordeal of seeing gentle Polonius murdered had been too much. She'd witnessed a side of her son she never knew existed, not only his mindless ferocity, but his staring awe when he conversed with empty air as though his father stood before them. This reminder of her first husband must have plucked a deep chord of guilt in her heart. I wanted to give her comfort, and perhaps in the giving receive some crumb of it for myself, but from that night on, she held herself aloof from my solitary company, even if only to talk as one friend to another. Without her, without Polonius, I was utterly and wretchedly alone.

Time might have eventually closed even these bleeding wounds to our family, but it was not to be. Young Ophelia was unable to accept her father's death at the hands of the very man she loved to distraction. Ever excessive in her affections, now did she also slip into madness. Hers was not violent though, and her wandering speech soft, if disturbing. I conjectured then if Hamlet had not at some time pressed his attentions to the point of bedding her, and thus passed on his affliction. I consulted several physicians about the progress of such a disease and was again assured its onset toward madness was slow. It was her mind and spirit that were shot through with lunacy, not her body.

But I had other concerns to keep me engaged.

The news of Polonius's murder ran fast to the general rabble, causing much unrest, for the old man was popular with them. We gave him an obscure burial, which turned out to be a mistake on my part. As a lifelong servant of the court he deserved better, his bier heaped high with honors and ceremonial ostentation, with proclamations about his virtues made to the people, but at the time I thought it might better to keep things quiet and private. Instead, the scandal of his death was only magnified by this seeming suppression of his passing.

Rumors flew about like scattered birds, the worst being that I had killed him or commanded his death be carried out by a man masquerading as the virtuous Hamlet, then spiriting the assassin away to safety. It was folly, of course, but if a lie is repeated often enough it becomes truth, and there were those in the court who would be glad to see me toppled. There would be no surprise in me to learn Hamlet, in the forefront of that gathering, turned out to be the source of the falsehood.

A garbled version of events traveled swiftly to Paris and thus to Laertes. He sped light along the roads with few companions, changing mounts and pausing to sleep only when he actually fell from the saddle. By the time he reached the borders of Denmark there were crowds waiting to greet him and declare him to be the next king. He used them to expedite his safe passage to Elsinore and to break through my own guards, storming into my chambers threatening hot revenge.

However much the mob hailed him, though, he persuaded them to stand down and wait without, and that was how I knew him to be uninterested in the crown itself. He was a hurting son wanting his father, nothing more.

Gertrude's presence also brought him up short, made him more willing to listen. She was like a second mother to him and bravely seized upon his sword arm lest he raise it to strike me. I had no fear of him, though. After so many batterings from other quarters I could deal with one angry young man, but it did take all my skill of reasoning to turn him around. Once he saw my own ravaged face an understanding came to him that our hearts were as one in our mourning for a lost parent.

Then did Ophelia come wandering barefoot through the chamber, festooned like a bride in blossoms and weeds alike, singing ribald songs a maiden should not know. Gertrude collapsed into tears from this, and Laertes was frozen by such a shock as to be struck dumb. Ophelia recognized him not, but happily insisted on decking us with some of her garlands as if in celebration of a wedding. For each she had a story or saying that herbalists use to memorize the qualities of each plant.

That is when the awful truth came to me, painful as a knife in the vitals. I felt my legs go weak in reaction, as sick at heart as I'd ever been. I had to sit lest I drop into a womanish faint.

Gentle Ophelia—who knew the name and nature of every flower in the land, who distilled their petals into sweet perfumes and their leaves into cures for small ills—could she not just as well concoct a deadly brew of henbane and other poisonous plants and roots? She knew the story of the gentleman's revenge that I'd brought from Italy as well as any; might she also have learned the ingredients for making juice of hebenon from some forgotten volume in Elsinore's book room?

She had right of entry to the orchard when the king was not there. If she hid herself within its twisting paths well before my brother's arrival—then all she had to do was wait until he slept, then steal soft upon him and. . .

And let herself out later. Or, if there was sufficient confusion attending the discovery, add herself to the gathering and thus make her egress. I'd not noticed her presence that day, like all others, my attention was elsewhere.

But *why*?

For her thwarted love of Hamlet?

It seemed a foolish, petty motive to me, but to an inexperienced girl caught in the excessive throes of first love. . .I recalled the heat and anguish of my own youth. In those hasty days there is no restraint to the extremes of emotions, and one chafes bitterly against the unfair limits set by others.

And—most telling of all—it was less than a week before my brother's murder that he'd forbade Ophelia's marriage to his son.

With this in mind it was like a book opened to a telling page that revealed all. No man would benefit by the king's death, only this otherwise innocent young girl. In the course of time Hamlet would assume the throne and claim her as his bride, sweeping her off to be his queen as in some old tale told in the nursery. How she must have repeated it to herself in the dreaming dark of her virgin's bed. How must she have resented and despised my brother for trampling upon her perfect musings.

The fates can be kind in their way, for it was just as well that Polonius was dead, never to know this terrible truth. Would that they had granted me a similar ignorance.

Never could I speak to Gertrude about this, for she might well reproach herself for indirectly causing her first husband's death. If she'd argued just a little harder for the marriage. . .that was where her mind would take her.

Nor could I speak to Laertes. He had enough misery.

Dear God, but I wanted someone to talk to, but a king's lot must needs be lonely, his burdens heavy beyond bearing, and only death can bring him to lay them aside.

Laertes and I did come to an accord on one matter, and that was our blaming Hamlet for Polonius's murder. Yes, it is wicked to hold a lunatic responsible for his rash acts, but a man's nature can only endure so much and no more, and we had reached our limit. When I received notice that Hamlet had somehow slipped his watchers' leash and was returned to Denmark it was too great for either of us to continue without taking action. Laertes was all for waylaying him on the road or cutting his throat as he prayed in church, but I with a cooler head and more experience had a better plan. Ironically, it was with Ophelia's unknowing help.

While visiting Polonius's chambers, ostensibly to sort out state papers, I also made a sortie to the maid's own room. It was in considerable disorder as might be expected given her deranged state, but there did I find all the evidence needed to confirm that it was she who murdered my brother. Upon a long bench did she store and refine her perfumes and potions, and in certain bottles hidden behind more innocent distillations she kept the deadly results of her shadowy delvings. There was no mistaking them. Though the bottles were sardonically labeled with names like *Heart's Desire* and *Maiden's Wish* they stank foul of the grave. I took them away, confident she would not miss them now and in secret tested each on vermin supplied to me by the castle rat catcher.

It was frightening to see the effect of her dire inventions, more so to realize that she'd gone unsuspected all these months. At any time she might have taken it into her head to deliver a cruel finish to all of us had she chosen.

But I mentioned none of this to Laertes and only produced one of the poisons, along with a design to remove Hamlet's destructive presence from us altogether. All Laertes had to do was meet his father's murderer and make a public reconciliation with him. Then they would conduct an apparently friendly passage of arms as a means to settle a wager. During the course of their demonstration I would see to it Hamlet drank from my own cup of wine. Within the hour he would be dead, seemingly from overexertion, and that would be the end of the matter. It is not unknown for an otherwise fit and hearty man to fall if pressed to his limits. His mother would be sore grieved, but hold none to blame and accept it as God's will.

Some might think this a cold and malicious action on my part, but along with the burdens of rule it is also a king's grim lot to order the execution of those who threaten the stability of the state. I would have been entirely within my royal duty and powers to have him arrested and beheaded the same night of the old man's murder. Only my love for Gertrude held me back from meting out justice.

Laertes then surprised me by also producing a poisonous unction. The smallest scratch would finish Hamlet off, he said. I knew he'd bought it to commit royal murder on my nephew and perhaps even myself, but held back from comment. I, the king, was about to sanction that nephew's death, changing it from murder to a lawful execution by my word alone. Besides, Hamlet was dying already, we were but speeding the process. Such was my power, and Heaven knows I took no pride in it.

For all that sorrow, the thought came to me of who to declare as my heir once Hamlet was gone. With the troubles that issue from bearing the weight of a heavy crown, it was not a responsibility I would willingly lay upon anyone. I had discussed several possibilities with dear Polonius, one of whom was Laertes himself. He was a good and studious man, perhaps too good of heart to be a ruler, for one is often required to do unpleasant acts for the health of the state. But his fiery resolution to avenge his father, tempered by his willingness to hear my side before taking rash action decided me to name him my heir after the duel.

He has my pity, but I can think of none better suited. I've learned to my grief what a terrible burden it is to be king. The state lives on, hopefully in good health, but in the effort to preserve that health for others my own life has been ripped to shreds and patches. May it please God to spare me from further miseries.

Here Gertrude comes, and there is a look on her weeping face that augurs more sorrows for us. In my heart I fear some evil has befallen Ophelia and her sins have found her out. . .

* * *

Last night I dreamed of my dead brother walking the upper platform of Elsinore as was his habit in life, but clothed in warlike raiment. This bodes ill for my beloved Denmark.

Dear God, whatever transpires in the days ahead, I pray You send me wisdom enough to do right for all.

Now and in the times to come,
angels and ministers of grace defend us.

--Claudius Rex--

FUGITIVE

Author's Note: *I became a gushing fan of Lois McMaster Bujold in the 90s, reading and re-reading her Miles Vorkosigan series not only to gleefully relish in the characters and their stories, but to improve my own writing from her example. I had to be peeled off the ceiling when she invited me to contribute to her science fiction collection with Roland Green, WOMEN AT WAR. The following story in my files was tweaked to fit the theme. Changing the original protagonist from male to female brought a new level to things, and made the main character even more paranoid and ruthless.*

Have I mentioned that writers never stop tinkering? Some 16 years after publication, the length of this story doubled as I gave it a tune up for this collection and its "voice" took on a decidedly British accent!

Cold wind cut Kella's eyes as she crept to the crest of the hillock to look for hunting parties in her wake. Nothing on two legs was in sight, just dusty gray and brown vegetation covering thousands of identical hillocks in every direction. The western horizon was still blurred by smoke, which surprised her. Things must be bad if they'd not gotten the fires under control by now. Maybe the prison authorities decided to let the place burn.

The sky was empty of movement. The attack that had enabled her escape would have knocked out any fliers or, at minimum, their control systems. One good pulse would fry anything left unshielded. Of course, if the orbiting scanners were working then this was for nothing and she and her companion would soon be picked up and—

She cut that thought off and scrambled down to where Farron lay curled on the lee side in an attempt to escape the wind. His head rested on one crooked arm, and he was sound asleep. Kella envied his easy surrender to the physical. Her own body craved rest, but her mind wouldn't settle enough to allow it; she had to focus to keep it from racing in useless speculation about the future. Useless, since it was unlikely she had one. Options for escapees from Riganth were limited to a return to their cells or death. Freedom was a fool's hope.

Kella gave an inward shrug. Fool or not, she would die before going back to her cage.

She was tempted to leave Farron where he lay, but the man's skills were her only insurance against an unknown future. He was not wanted, but necessary. If they were lucky they had a few hours left to reach their goal—her goal; Farron was too doped to think straight. If they hurried, a few hours might be enough. After that, what was left of the authorities at the prison would have reorganized and begun tracking down strays.

Farron protested the hard shake and subsequent pull to his feet, but followed as she threaded between the higher bits of drab landscape. Except for the cough he'd picked up in prison, the only sounds in this primal world were their footsteps and the endless susurrating wind bearing them away to infinity. It stank of burning plastic, chemicals, and organics.

She took Farron's hand when he stumbled, leading him around the less obvious obstacles. Touching another human felt strange to her after so many days of isolation. In those stretches when she'd been aware enough to mark the time, she kept count of at least three hundred of them, though that had to be an underestimation.

Farron paused, his grip tightened, stopping her. He blinked, puzzled. "Are we outside?"

"Yes, we're outside."

"It's cold."

"Yes, it is."

Was he waking up or had he gone simple like so many others? The drugs given to the general population induced docility and suppressed the libido, but a percentage of prisoners reacted badly, their brains shutting down by degrees. The worst were taken away. She heard what happened to them. If Farron was too far gone it would be a mercy if she broke his neck now than—

He struggled to get out words. "But. . .we shouldn't be here. Should we?"

She felt a wash of relief. Cognition was intact somewhere inside his skull if he could form that complex a question. "It'll be all right. Come with me."

"My feet hurt."

He wore prison scuffs, which were not intended for walks in the wilderness. Her feet were encased in regulation boots, taken from a guard she'd particularly enjoyed killing. The boots were too large, but she preferred their chafing over bruises and cuts. "So do mine."

"I'm tired."

"We'll rest soon."

He accepted her word and came along. They put a few more clicks between themselves and hell.

The wind rose, roaring, thick with the smell of destruction. She checked the sky, cursed, and quickly dragged Farron to the steep base of a hillock, pulling him down next to her. Not the best shelter, but it would have to serve. The wind moaned like a living thing, whipping the low growing plants.

The orbit of Riganth's moon was such that it eclipsed the sun once a day. Its apparent disc was much larger, blocking light and warmth for a long, cold hour, sometimes more, depending on the planet's own orbit. It made the planet's weather system. . .interesting.

"What's wrong?" Farron asked.

"Take a nap, we're fine."

Farron lay down and kept himself to himself as she spooned her back against his front. She felt awkward, unused to such contact. The need for shared warmth was more important than her need for body space; she stifled the urge to move away. The wind wailed around them; sharp gusts eddied in, plucking at her. Oblivious, Farron coughed twice, fretting in his dreams. She tried not to breathe his breath.

The delay was impossible, but she resented it. They might stumble forward in this dry storm, and in the twists and turns needed to negotiate the rough terrain, they'd soon lose their way. It was just too dark.

She filled the time scanning the black sky for the telltale lights of a flier among the shredded clouds, unlikely as that might be. No pilot in her right mind would choose to go prowling under these conditions. That left remote scanners, their operators safe indoors, but those would be grounded as well. The little machines were tough, but had their limits.

If any operators were left. Kella became aware of an orange glow against the flying cloud cover.

Riganth *still* burned?

The moon's transit crawled to a conclusion; the day's second dawn asserted itself. Shivering, Kella stood and stretched warmth into her stiffened limbs.

"It's time, Farron."

He mumbled, coughed, and tried to roll away into the peace of his folded arms.

"Come on." She nudged him with her foot.

He shoved it away.

"Get up, unless you want to die."

He struggled briefly with his eyelids and lost. "There's no difference between catching it here or anywhere else," he mumbled. "One way or another we're dead. Yours is more work. I'd rather save myself the trouble."

His speech was reassuringly lucid. Some parts of his brain had slept off more of the drugs during the respite; the rest of him just hadn't realized it yet. All he needed was a little push to get moving. "Would you really? If you're that tired of living I can fix things for you."

"Don't do me any favors."

She stooped and closed both hands around Farron's throat and squeezed. She did it slowly. His petulance changed to panic and he struggled, then actively fought. He broke her hold and twisted away, gasping and coughing. She kept her distance, hiding her own sudden fatigue.

Farron was fully awake, on his feet, and glaring. "You rotten—you were really going to do it!"

She showed her teeth. "Who says I've stopped?"

"I do, I was just joking."

"Your humor could be the death of you."

"Only with you in the audience. All right, you got me up." He gestured for her to assume the lead, obviously reluctant to have her or her hands out of his sight.

Kella took a bearing from the sun and struck off.

"Where are we going, anyway?" he asked.

She tried to answer, but the words didn't so much as form in her mind, much less turn to speech. She had a mental picture of their destination, but her ability to tell him about it was . . .temporarily offline. "You'll see. We're close."

She hoped.

But their pace remained slow over the uneven ground. She was tired to the bone, hollow with hunger, and terribly thirsty. She speculated on the edibility of the plants, but knew better than to risk it.

Farron called for a stop; Kella ignored him and plowed on, right into a low solid object that cracked her shins as she fell onto it.

"Hey, didn't you see that? I tried to tell you."

It was a mound of metal and plas-crete, less than a meter across, sprouting from the earth like an exotic strain of edible fungus. It was colored to blend with the surrounding land. Kella stared, trying to recall what it was and why it was important.

"What's the matter with you?" Farron demanded.

"Nothing," she snapped. She ran her hands over the smooth metal top.

"Well, are we going in?"

Her memory flickered and she stood back, favoring her bruises. "You first."

He made a face. "Of course, always me." He examined a plastic housing. "Locked," he pronounced, "and probably for a good reason. This is part of the prison, isn't it?"

"No, of course not."

She'd fallen over a. . .the correct word escaped her. A door then, she impatiently provided. The one she'd been looking for, though not the one she'd visualized. Her expectations conjured something more vertical. With a building attached.

All right, so the building was underground, shelter was shelter, and this was the way in. "Open it."

He grimaced. "With what? I need specialized tools."

"What kind of tools?"

"A cutter and circuit probe would be helpful, and maybe a bypass with a program override."

"Improvise."

"With what, leaves and dirt? Without the right tools you'd need a battering ram to open that."

"I might just try one, providing the impact element is your head."

The look on her face was evidently inspiring. He found a rock and after several tries, cracked the housing, peering at the exposed works.

"This is more along your line," he stepped back. "Have a go."

Her fingers began trembling as she probed the mess. Her heart raced, and sweat suddenly popped out on her forehead. She broke off before Farron noticed.

"Anything wrong?"

"No, and this is hardly my line. You're the specialist, you do it."

Farron swallowed his puzzlement and had another turn. "I'm not sure what you mean. I'm expert enough with the right tools, but these multi-binary probability codes are a bit over my head—I could spend the rest of my life doing this."

"That is entirely possible," she said, with meaning.

"Still, I could try a more direct approach. This tech is just old enough for us get away with. . .there, press that down and hold it."

Kella had to struggle to keep from throwing up as he touched a bare wire against a contact. Sparks flew and her hand jerked back.

"Wants to bite," he remarked, sucking his own stinging fingers. He looked around. "What the hell is that pong? Something burning?"

She'd been too distracted to notice the worsening smell. The sky held more smoke than clouds. No point climbing a hill to look. She could hear the approaching fire. A vanguard of cinders tumbled toward them on the wind.

"Get it open, Farron. *Now.*"

He tore a ragged hem from his shirt for insulation. "Use this and hold it down hard."

There were more fireworks and slow smoke from melted plastic.

"I heard something give." He grasped a crank set into the door and gave it a turn. Kella had taken it for a decorative sculpture. It was stiff, but worked; deep within, metal grated against metal.

The lid came up with a rush of warm, stale air.

"Smells all right," he said hopefully.

She peered down a narrow circular shaft. A metal ladder clung to one section of the wall and disappeared into blackness. "Get in."

He hesitated. "I don't like the look of that. Isn't there an easier way?"

"If you want to go looking for it."

He glanced once at the landscape: endless hillocks, stinking haze, no food or water. To a man used to the finished walls and readily available comforts of an automated culture, running about unprotected on an open planet was the closest thing to hell.

That and. . .

"Hey. . .that—that's a fire," he said.

"They usually come with smoke. Get in."

"But it's a *fire*. Shouldn't someone put it out?"

She knew he wasn't stupid. He'd been raised in a superbly controlled environment where flame suppression systems kept people safe. A wildfire stretching from one horizon to the next was simply outside his experience. He couldn't imagine it. She didn't have to, feeling the baking heat on her back. She gave him a shove. "In, dammit!"

Objections forgotten, Farron swung his legs down, his slippered feet tapping against and finding the rungs. He shifted his weight and descended. Kella copied him, pausing as her head came level with the ground.

Flying ash, a roaring, the wind spiraled flames into reaching tentacles; the fire would soon roll over and past. They were safe enough, but the angle was wrong for her to pull the cover shut. It was designed as an exit. She couldn't reach the crank. There had to be a way to close it from inside.

Ducking, she spotted the control and a blinking red telltale. Its message that there was a breach in the base would be echoed somewhere, giving away their position. The control had a simple diagram. Even the most illiterate work drone would be able to figure out that pressing a button would move the cover in some way. Kella understood it, but could not bring herself to act upon it. Even the idea of trying made her hands go slick with sweat. Bad move, when she needed them to grip the ladder.

When her sight blurred, she looked away, and that eased things.

The hell with it. The Riganth authorities would come here first, regardless. Shutting one door wouldn't make a difference; there wasn't anything she could do. But that was the fool in her, the bleating, terrified creature that made excuses and distracted her from her goal of survival and escape despite the odds.

It was a stranger in her head. She'd not been born with that miserable whining voice. Sometime during those three hundred days it had moved in and learned how to paralyze her to inaction.

Before the burgeoning fear could take over, she raised a mental image of slamming a lead shield in its face. There. It could claw and bleat all it liked. She would keep it contained, leaving herself free to concentrate on the task at hand: getting down this damned ladder without falling.

Two rungs below the top she found the manual crank that would close the cover.

Her face went hot with embarrassment. *I should have known this would be here*. She worked it off, awkwardly turning the thing until her arm ached. Tech was her bane, but she could still operate mechanical backups. Perhaps they thought that such limits would make her harmless.

Bloody fools.

Slowly the lid lowered into place, taking away the fire and the sky, sealing her into the silent darkness.

Blind, but feeling safer, she felt her way carefully, one rung at a time. No need to hurry. There was enough shielding above to foil the most sophisticated scanners. Any searchers would gather only negative information; they'd eventually come back for a closer look and find the broken lock, but by then it might be too late.

If things worked out. *If* her fool's luck held.

Of course, searchers could skip a topside hunt, enter by the main door, and activate the systems. A little work with the internal sensors would—

But they might be delayed by the wildfire. The prison was still burning hours after the initial assault. She didn't see how that was possible; the place was fire-proofed and shielded as well as any military facility. There were weapons to get around such safety measures, though. She'd even used them once upon a time. They were expensive and hard to acquire. If the attackers had those in their arsenal, then the inmates could not have been of concern to them.

Farron puffed out that he'd touched ground. He was too winded to do more than stagger out of her way.

Coughing.

It was worse, a deeper, uglier in sound than before. After water and food, she'd have to find a med-unit for him.

Her boots hit bottom. She kept hold of a rung, breathing hard. Behind the ladder a faint light at eyelevel seemed bright in the blackness. She orientated to a round tunnel with enough clearance to walk upright. They were at a T-shaped intersection; small lights at long intervals emphasized the darkness and distance. More eye level lights indicated other ladders along the flat top of the T, part of an emergency escape system. Farron muttered something not meant to be intelligible but managing to express his unease.

"Better than nothing," she responded.

"Not by much. These are service tunnels? To where?"

She gave no reply, not sure herself.

The tunnels had been carved into the raw earth with flash-dry crete-foam sprayed to keep the walls from caving in, cheaper and faster than laying pipe. She couldn't smell sewage, which was a plus.

"Which branch do you fancy?"

"The center." She had no idea where it led, but she had to sound decisive.

"Think anything's living down here? And hungry?"

"You'll be the first to know." She gestured ahead with an open hand.

"Thanks very much. I suppose it hardly matters, I'm so starved now I wouldn't make a good meal anyway."

The pace was faster on a level floor. Kella counted steps; at fifty they reached a locked door in the right-hand wall.

"I suppose you want me to open it?" he asked without enthusiasm.

It could be a storage closet or a cavernous service bay for ships, no way to tell. She pressed a palm flat to the surface. "This might lead to the power plant, feel the warmth and vibration?"

He nodded. "How old is this place?"

"Why do you ask?"

"Radiation. Sometimes older complexes were thrifty on protection, especially down in the cellar."

It was a legitimate worry, but then Farron *liked* to worry. "This is the top," she reminded him.

"Oh, wonderful, that has to make a difference."

She continued along the main tunnel. "Come on."

"To where? Is there an end to all this?"

"When we find it. The maintenance crew had to live somewhere when they weren't working."

"Are they gone? I mean, *is* this place empty?"

"Yes."

"Seems odd to build something this big then move out. Was it System?"

"Who else would have the resources?"

"That means this is System military?"

"Yes. One of their groundside bases."

"But the soldiers—" His eyebrows climbed well up into his high forehead.

"They're gone," she told him in a firm tone. She'd overheard quite a lot from the prison guards on the subject.

"If it's empty, why is the reactor still online?"

"It has to be ready when they come back."

"When is that?"

She shrugged. "Everyone was pulled out and deployed elsewhere during the war. Losses were too high to make manning this base practical immediately afterward, but they meant to return and left the automatics running."

"I just hope no one stayed behind. Why are we here?"

"To look for a way out."

"That makes sense, since we just got in."

They approached another heavy door, this one with a thick transparent panel and garish warning notices attached. The lighting was better, and more pale light bled out from the panel.

Farron halted, crossing his arms. "That's the reactor section and I'm telling you flat out, I'm not going in."

Kella peered inside. There wasn't much to see, just an entry room and another door in the opposite wall bearing even more warnings. It was ajar.

She stopped breathing.

"You think the soldiers might come back?" he asked, shifting unhappily from foot to foot.

This was indication that they'd already returned. She had, in fact, been counting on it, but it seemed wise not to burden Farron with the knowledge. Kella tried the lever, but it was solidly locked, as it should be.

All that she could see through the second door was a slice of innocuous corridor. The lighting was dim, though. If the System had begun a reactivation of the base, the techs would have started here first to bring the power fully online, including plenty of light to work by.

Its lack reassured her. Only now did a wave of fatigue wash over her, and she realized how fast her heart had been beating.

"There's another opening ahead," Farron announced.

The lighting improved as they approached.

She tried the lever. It gave easily. One open door, especially in the reactor section was suspicious enough, but two. . . "I don't like this, it's not right."

"Someone just forgot to secure it."

At times the man could be as dense as a neutron star. "Or someone else was recently here instead."

That put a new face on it for him. "We can go back."

"Not a chance."

They cautiously entered a wide gray passage lined with more doors. The lights were closely placed and brighter, the walls finished and vertical.

Farron looked inside one of the empty rooms.

"Living quarters for drones. Nothing but bare wall cots. There has to be a mess hall close by. Drones have to eat."

Kella passed him, having spotted something useful. "Map."

It covered a large portion of the wall and might have been mistaken for decoration with its patchwork of colored blocks showing hundreds of sections. The code key and other labeling were dark, along with the info-screen. Kella rested a tentative finger on one spot.

"We're here, it's the only intersection of this type off the reactor area."

"If that red part is the reactor and not just a big lavatory."

"It's the reactor." There was an unnecessary edge to her tone. Farron had only been joking, she told herself. *Get a grip. Don't let him see you sweat.*

But Farron was too distracted to notice, busy tracing pathways on the map. "All right, then light blue is barracks, yellow is for halls, the access and service ducts are green, and dark blue is. . .?"

"Let's find out."

Ignoring side passages, they went straight to the dark blue sector, finding themselves in a large, dim room. It was furnished with chairs, gaming tables, entertainment screens, and other comforts.

"It must be the officer's lounge," she said.

"Decadence at last," Farron sighed and made straight for a long wall of food dispensers. He punched hopefully at their buttons, but nothing happened. He punched again; the panels remained dark, the servers empty. Slamming a hand against the unit in frustration, he dropped into a chair, finally overcome with dejection and fatigue. Even his cough sounded disappointed and depressed.

Kella smothered her own black feelings.

She needed to catch her breath, look around, and think what to do next. Perhaps a trip back to the reactor section—the map would provide another way in. If others were around, they'd be there, but she was in no shape to deal with them. She needed water, food, and . . . a year's rest in a revive unit.

She unfastened her now painful boots, easing them off. Despite the padding of the dead guard's socks she had blisters. She spied a basic aid box clamped to a wall and limped over, pulling it down.

As she hoped, the supplies inside offered a temporary fix. She passed over the tech items, found antiseptic spray and made use of it. The stuff was cold, but numbed things nicely.

She looked at Farron and felt an unfamiliar twinge. What the hell was that? Oh. Sympathy. For him. He was in worse condition, his prison scuffs worn through and bloodied. He'd not complained about it, though.

She went to him, setting the aid box on his table. He looked at it with no comprehension.

"Off," she said, pointing at the remains of his scuffs.

He obeyed, staring. She sprayed his damage.

Farron wiggled his toes, sighing. He had damned ugly feet, pale, with long, knobby toes, tufts of hair sprouting on the big ones. For some reason that amused her.

"Thank you," he said.

She nodded back, experiencing another twinge. Connective emotions like sympathy and gratitude could get you killed. They were to be exploited in others, but one should never get caught in their trap.

Farron pawed through the box. "No protein packs, no water. You'd think they'd put those in."

Given this venue, there was no need for either. Plenty of food and drink were available, when the power was on.

He tore open a cleansing pack and ran the wipe over his face and hands. "Some useful stuff here, though," he added.

She walked away to end the exchange.

I was not being kind. I did that to keep him functioning.

She abruptly forgot Farron at the sight of a control node on the other side of the room. She padded to it, the floor warm under her bare feet. Had minimal heating been left on when they closed this place or did it mean others had activated things? If the latter, how long before they noticed two intruders? She'd have to keep moving.

But the prospect of obtaining food outweighed the risk.

The labels on the node were intact; she had only to enter a basic security crack to turn on the power for the dispensers and eat. She knew dozens of them—

Cold sweat ran down her flanks, and her hands shook as they hovered over the buttons. Her too-busy mind stalled.

What did they do to me?

She had to turn away or be sick.

Damn them. Damn them for this.

She quit the node, found a chair, and sat. Weariness replaced the panic. Sleep might help, but she didn't dare. The aid box had stim patches. One of those would sort her out.

Farron stood over her with some kind of med device in hand. She'd been so far gone as to not notice. That was dangerous. She had to pay attention, dammit. He knelt in front of her, cupping one of her heels. She jerked, resisting the reflex to kick.

"Easy now, sorry for the cold hands. Just trying to help."

She stared, forcing herself to hold still as he lifted her foot. He had an auto-healer and waved it close over her blisters.

"Feel anything?"

"No, rack up the power."

He smiled and made a smaller adjustment. "That's a beginner's mistake, putting these things on full. "Have to work your way up or cause even worse damage."

The healer put out a barely audible hum, and he tried again. First it tickled, then burned.

"Ow."

He yanked the device away. "Too much. Let's try this level. . .how's that?"

"Itchy."

"Just right, then. Hang on. . ."

Her damage itched madly as the thing stimulated the nanites in her blood to focus on specific spots. Evidently enough were still left to respond.

He worked quietly, gently. It struck her that this was somehow a far more intimate contact than when she'd huddled against him during the eclipse. Of course, he'd been dozy from tranqs then.

"You're a good woman, Kella," he murmured.

"No, I'm not." Too late, she hadn't meant to say that aloud.

"Bother that. I know you're doing your best. I'm grateful you saved me. Maybe I can pay you back somehow."

"Count on it."

"We should rest here a bit."

"Sleep's for the dead."

He snorted, working on her other foot. "That's what I like about you, always such cheery company."

You can't like me. I will use that against you. This time she refrained from vocalizing.

But why even think a warning? That was not normal for her.

He'd formed an attachment to the outward shell she projected. It's what humans did automatically, a survival mechanism so groups could function and work together.

She balled both hands into fists.

Farron paused. "Did that hurt?"

"It's fine. Keep going."

She wanted him finished so she could put space between them. This level of physical proximity might encourage him to ask questions she couldn't answer, and, by not answering, undermine the illusion of command she'd taken onto herself. If he once realized just how dependent she was upon him, that it wasn't the other way around, then he might not be so cooperative. She needed his cooperation, his—she regarded the word with distaste—trust.

That's a good one for you, Kella. Needing trust when you can't give it. She had never before been troubled by that particular facet of human behavior. Its lack had helped her to survive this long, but until now she'd been supremely self-sufficient.

Was *still* self-sufficient. They may have jumbled some of her neurons, but the rest of her could get around it.

"Done," he said. "Looks like new. How's it feel?"

"Better." She remembered to add: "Thank you."

She got up before he could pass the auto-healer to her.

"There's some useful stuff here," he repeated as she walked away.

"Then use it."

Glad to be clear of the contact, she resumed exploration, checking a corridor that led to a series of private quarters. It was definitely officer country. Though stripped of personal effects, basic furnishings remained. If they had to starve to death at least it would be in comfortable surroundings.

Kella located a washroom and found the water running, which was something to celebrate. She gulped greedily from the tap, then cautiously shifted the lever, hardly daring to hope. . .yes, it grew warm, then hot. She splashed her face and neck, ducking her head in and scrubbing her scalp, reveling in the luxury of abundance and time. In the name of water conservation, Riganth allowed each prisoner a fifteen second spray in the icy showers for daily cleaning. The doped population never complained about the wet-animal smell, but some of the more sensitive guards wore filter masks.

She stopped the water and regarded the gaunt and wary face looking out from the mirror. It was less of a shock than anticipated, since she'd roughly gauged her own appearance from Farron's. Neither had had the benefit of grooming supplies. Prisoners were rotated every twenty days to have their heads shaved and beards (if any) removed. Her dark hair was shorter than she preferred, with a few premature gray strands at her temples and along her brow; there were new lines and deep circles under her eyes and a harder set to her expression—nothing unexpected after what she'd been through.

Farron called to her, fairly bellowed.

She rushed back, thinking that they'd been found, but his tone was excited, happy.

He'd gotten a panel open on one of the food dispensers. His face was coated with transparent goo.

"Come on," he urged. He dipped a hand into the guts of the machine. "There's plenty." He sucked the stuff down with gusto.

"Raw nutrient gel?"

"There's no taste to it, but it's food."

She'd wash the mess off later. There was a primitive joy to dipping both hands into the stuff and eating all she wanted. It had a chemical bite, faint, not enough to put her off. Perhaps they could get a prep machine going. It would turn the taste-neutral gel into something palatable, injecting flavor, form, and texture, heating or chilling to order.

Farron abruptly turned away. Coughing. He took longer to recover, and did not resume feasting. She tried to make out his coloring, but the light was too low. No matter. He did not look well.

She paused. "We should go easy on this stuff. We could deplete the tanks in one go."

"Not a bit of it, I checked. They're full up or nearly so, there's enough to last us for years."

"Dismal prospect."

"You're right, what we need now is some friendly company. The next lady that comes in will have her golden opportunity with me, providing she's pretty. On second thought, I don't care what she looks like."

"Let's hope she feels the same about you."

Yes, the suppression drugs were losing their influence if he was thinking that way again, unless it was force of habit. Farron loved his physical pleasures, she recalled. It amused Kella to know that he still regarded her as a work companion and nothing more. Not, she sensed, that either of them wanted more. Neither appealed to the other in that way and both were content with the arrangement.

He'd been a civilian tech on board at the wrong time when a System dreadnaught caught up with their ship and turned half the crew into freeze-dried corpses on the first attack. With the bridge fragged and internal communications gone, no organized defense had been possible. The survivors had been easily mopped up by a boarding party. Kella tried to escape; she'd modified all the shuttle pods with special coding for just such an emergency. If activated, any one of them would have enough shielding to sneak her safely past the dreadnaught's sensors, but she never got a chance to run. She'd taken a knock on the head that had flattened her for hours, waking up in the infirmary with the other wounded long after the fuss was over.

There'd been initial questioning and her current cover had not been good enough. The ship's computer picked up something on her ident chip and tagged her for special interrogation, which meant immediate transport to Riganth Prison. Farron, too, along with half a dozen others that the computer hadn't liked.

And what had happened to them? Dead or drugged to the eyeballs and past caring, she thought. It didn't matter now. Whatever information they'd possessed had been scraped from their heads long ago. The only relief she had about her own unwilling betrayal was that much of her data had been obsolete. Had the attack come a week later when she'd been scheduled by her cell for a new assignment. . .

Kella finished off another handful of gel and felt full. The stuff was concentrated in this form; it didn't take much.

"Why didn't you activate it?" Farron asked. Recovered from his bout, he settled in across from her for a second helping.

"Activate what?"

"You found the power node; what was so important to keep you from faking your way in and starting things up?" He seemed to take for granted she'd know how, but then anyone above drone level knew a few hacking tricks.

Aside from the fact that she no longer knew how and had panic attacks if she tried? "Nothing, I was too tired to think."

"That must have been a first for you. I'd about given up. Good thing I took a direct route."

"Yes, I'm delirious with joy."

"How'd you get so damp?"

"The water's running. It's even hot."

"Brilliant. I'll have a drink and you can figure out how to get us some real food."

"I'm bathing."

"Right, s'wonderful thought, I'll join you."

She gave him a look.

He choked on his latest swallow. "Uh—I mean—just leave some for my turn."

"Gladly."

He eventually hobbled toward the washroom. Kella remained, and found herself glaring at the control node.

The System interrogators at Riganth had ended the more obvious and painful forms of questioning months ago. When she'd physically recovered, they switched to subtler experiments that robbed her of sleep and left blank patches in her memory. On the last occasion it had taken her a full morning of concentrated and miserable effort before she remembered how to pull on her clothes. At the time it seemed unimportant, but when the drug-induced chaos in her head cleared, the implications of the lapse frightened her as few other things could. For all that she was more or less intact, meaning that the System had a use for her, favoring that over a clean execution. It might have been better to have been killed instead of captured.

But whatever they'd planned had been cut short by the prison break. As she dodged through the confusion and fighting, searching for an exit leading to sky, she'd abruptly recognized Farron among the drug-dazed inmates. His usefulness balanced his liabilities; she grabbed his arm and led him unresisting through the melee and into the wastes.

Providing he was still willing to be led, it had been a good decision; she needed his hands and undamaged mind to manage the technical problems that certainly lay ahead.

But how to manipulate him into doing things without giving away her own deficiency?

Kella became aware of the massive unnerving emptiness around her. The place was utterly silent. The walls were too far away for comfort. She quit the lounge, following the sound of Farron's cough. He'd claimed a room for himself and fallen asleep on a bare bed.

The smaller space made it easier to breathe. She explored a little more, found a washroom, and stripped.

The shower was hedonistic.

It was an illusion only, but she felt as though the abuses of the last few months were being scoured from her body by the almost painfully hot spray. She emerged, pink, puckered, and unsteady from the glorious heat.

No towel for drying, only an airflow mechanism activated by buttons that she had to ignore. Leaving wet footprints, she quit the room to look for something to wear. Her prison clothes were disgusting. No amount of cleaning would remove the stink of the place from them. She left the old coverings like a discarded skin.

She checked again on Farron, who was sprawled on his face now, oblivious to cares for an indefinite period. He coughed in his sleep, and his hands twitched from some deep dream. He'd be out for hours.

Naked, but not feeling vulnerable, she returned to the lounge and a line of dispensers along another wall. They appeared to be stocked with the usual packets of generic wearables and other supplies. The stuff was cheap, stored small, and was easy to recycle when it wore out or got too dirty for normal cleaning: a quartermaster's dream.

The only thing between her and the satisfaction of new garb was a damned power switch.

Her mouth went dry. The labels blurred and vibrated, mocking her hesitation. She licked her lips, shut her eyes, and stabbed at it with an inner scream.

She opened her eyes, shaking. But . . . nothing terrible had happened.

Gulping air, she slumped a little, enormously relieved. Maybe she'd be able to beat this, after all.

The control board lit, the info-screen came alive. It was like the one for the mess, but without security protocols. Food sources had to be protected from contamination, clothing did not.

Words appeared on the screen: *Welcome, Citizen. Please stand on the scanner pad for sizing.*

She did so without any symptoms surfacing. Evidently the conditioning was to suppress the ability to initiate action, not interfere with obedience to orders.

The machine scanned her in silence. The screen refreshed: *Thank you, Citizen. Please make your choice!*

Pictures of various items appeared. Anything she picked would fit.

But she could not raise her hand to tap the screen. She spoke her choice aloud, but nothing happened. Her voice wouldn't be in the system or the option was not active.

What harm would befall her if she touched the screen?

Absolutely none.

But she hesitated, fearing. . .something. This was self-preservation fear, the sort that kept you from stepping off a cliff. Staying put, not moving was safe. Taking action would kill her.

Intellectually, she understood that she would not die, but not emotionally, which was ironic. She'd trained to be free of such impediments, learning to use emotions as camouflage, to manipulate others, but not be their victim. The System techs had somehow bypassed that, conditioned her with chemicals and possibly aversion therapy to render her helpless.

What was done could be undone. They'd not completed things. Cracks were there. She just had to act and not think about it.

Right. She fixed on a garment: generic tunic and pants, the kind worn by millions of others. Color didn't matter, though here it would likely be military gray or black.

Walk it off.

She took a turn around the room, making herself remember something from her life that pre-dated Riganth. She'd been aboard a courier vessel, sharing a meal with others in a cramped mess room, pretending to get a joke. Farron was one of her shipmates. He always had a joke; people liked him on sight. Kella had studied him, trying to figure out how he achieved that without effort. It was a useful quality.

Passing the display screen, she blindly slapped at it.

The wall unit whirred and out popped a packet. Tearing it open, she found it was not what she'd expected.

Sleepwear—only it was much too short for warmth, semi-transparent, and edged with ruffles. She gaped at it, baffled, then the first genuine laugh she'd had in years escaped to assault the air.

* * *

Morning came when she woke. Kella hadn't meant to drop off, intending to explore, but her body simply shut down. She was on the floor, her back to the wall of machines, and jerked awake, disoriented. It was strange to be in a warm, silent place, dressed in clean clothes with fresh, filtered air to breathe.

She sat up, noted a number of new aches, muscles stiff from the previous day's forced march. Stretching helped.

The laughter brought on by the absurd results of her blind selection had had a relaxing effect, and she was able to slap the screen in a quick and random way. As long as she didn't think about it, it wasn't so bad. Of the many things that popped out she donned a System officer's black combat fatigues, which afforded durable freedom of movement. No need for underclothes. She was almost as flat-chested as Farron, having lost weight and muscle tone at Riganth.

Footwear was less complicated, with fewer choices: scuffs or combat boots. With her blisters gone she sealed on the boots and felt ready for anything—within reason.

She had another look at the control node for the food dispensers, but gave it up as too complicated. Raw nutrient was good enough for now. If Farron got hungry he could cheat his way in to get a properly flavored meal.

Kella fed in solitude if not complete silence. Farron's coughing was harder and more frequent. He moaned between bouts, which informed her he was awake and not enjoying it.

He looked far more miserable than when they'd slept in the open. His cough was thick with congestion.

"Hello," she said.

He looked up dully, his eyes flashed wide then relaxed. "Give a man warning. I thought you were one of them. Where'd you get the clothes?"

"Uniform," she corrected.

"I can see that, but have you noticed it's not for our side?"

"Are you hungry?"

"Donno, let me wake up first."

She had to help him sit. On top of the chronic prison stink she caught a strange sour taint. His hands trembled. His face had a slick yellow tinge, the kind one got from serious illness and not confinement. "What's wrong with you?"

"Nothing, I'm just tired, a little rest and I'll—"

"Fever?"

"What?"

"Don't lie, Farron, you're not good at it. Have you a fever?"

"I think so, everything hurts."

"Do you know what it is?"

He shrugged. "Something making the rounds in our section."

"What's the treatment?"

"Nothing. You got better or didn't."

"*Was* there a treatment?"

"Immuno boosters and anti-virals for the guards; the rest of us got more pacifying drugs, so no one cared what happened. Three of my cellmates died; I suppose it's my turn now." He said it in a matter-of-fact tone, expecting no sympathy or reassurances and getting none.

Kella was not a happy woman. "I suppose there's a better-than-even chance that I've got it, too."

"Probably. Does the back of your throat tickle?"

She felt her expression go more grim than usual.

"I'll take that as a yes."

"I'm having a look 'round. Rest and drink as much water as you can."

"When you coming back?"

"Stay in this area."

"Kella—!" He broke off, doubled over by his cough.

She walked out.

* * *

Damn, damn, damn, damn, damn.

The sound of her footfalls seemed to fill the empty, silent corridor. She stopped at critical intersections to check maps and kept the pace quick, finding a lot of locked doors. A few looked worth investigating, but could wait. Basic aid boxes were on the walls at strategic points next to fire extinguishing equipment, but their contents were for emergency trauma, not sickness. They had bandages, painkillers, stims, and respirators; the latter two might be useful to help Farron, but the anti-virals they needed were elsewhere. A complex of this size had to have a med-unit; it was only a matter of time before she found it.

She cross-sectioned the wing she was in, then took a connecting hall into the next area, which was central to the complex.

A single turn and she was abruptly facing the med-unit entry, its double-doors invitingly wide. She'd have gone right in if not for the bloodstain covering a substantial portion of the floor.

The red had dried to a rusty brown, but time had not mitigated its disturbing nature.

Her heart thundered loud enough to echo off the walls, or so it seemed for the first few seconds. Kella backed up, listening, hyper-alert, but whatever had happened here was long over.

She picked out footprints that had tracked through the stuff. Two sets, with drag marks between, led into the unit. One person injured, with friends to haul the body in for help. But the loss of that much blood. . .the injury had to have occurred on the spot.

Those open doors in the reactor section and drone quarters—she should have paid more attention to them, to what they signified. She should have been doing anything but lazing around stuffing her face and—

Never mind that.

She forced her scrambled thoughts into order.

All right, the System techs were *here*. She'd expected that from the gossip among the Riganth guards. It had been just another bit of useless information to her until a Resister assault group had dropped on the prison and blown everything wide open. Too far from the break to make contact with them, she'd seized a less likely route out by coming to the base. A risky move, but official attention would be focused on the fleeing Resisters, not on an incoming tech crew.

The techs would have a proper ship—not just a small, short-range shuttle—one with the kind of automatics that would allow even Farron to navigate them clean away.

Its accompanying techs would be no problem for Kella; she still retained her unarmed-combat abilities. The ease and speed with which she'd killed one of the Riganth guards was proof enough of that. Her plan had been to stay low and take out the crew one by one.

But the bloodstain was a complication.

Were the techs feuding amongst themselves? That hardly seemed likely. Had another prisoner gotten inside the base? For all she knew Riganth was full of bright specialists like herself, each one with access to the same gossip and also hell-bent on escape. Perhaps someone less crippled than herself was running loose here.

Competition was the last thing she wanted. The techs were now on the alert, blasters charged and ready, clogging the comm channels with calls for help.

Which should be here already.

The stain was at least two days old. Riganth would have sent a small guard party to look things over. She and Farron hadn't exactly been cautious. A quick check of the base computer would reveal their power consumption and thus their location. What had delayed their ignominious recapture?

This flashed through her mind as she checked the walls, ceiling, and floor. All sported the near-invisible thready scarring of blaster fire. The stuff was hell on human tissue, but caused little damage to non-organics, which made it a good choice for space travelers. Internal ship combat was tricky enough without causing undue damage to the systems.

Behind her, she found a ragged line marking missed shots that extended as far as the corner she'd come around. Someone had waited just out of sight there, ambushed three people, hitting at least one. They'd returned fire, dragging their companion to cover. The attacker had retreated . . . and could be anywhere in the complex.

She briefly thought of running back to warn Farron, but dismissed it as a waste of time. That was sentiment or friendship or whatever they called it, and would only delay her. He was fine where he was.

Kella went through the entry, following the blood trail to a trauma station. Here it pooled, indicating that the victim had bled out. The trail eventually she led her to the body, sealed in a stasis-bag, in cold storage. No need to open it, she wasn't curious. All that mattered was that she had one less target to remove.

The last marks of blood went to a sterilization alcove. The dead one's companions would have cleaned up, perhaps acquiring fresh clothing from the dispenser unit. It was active, left on standby.

Where had the three come from? How many remained? The last wall map indicated a large gray area ahead. Though the labeling remained dark, she was certain—having eliminated other options in the color coding—that meant hangars and the ship she wanted, the ship she absolutely had to take.

Much as it grated her to leave her back vulnerable to the mystery shooter, it was better to keep moving forward.

* * *

Shivering, Farron tried to find a comfortable position for rest and failed. His limbs twitched, his joints ached, and coughing was a painful bore. His chest and stomach felt like he'd been in a sparing match with a couple of stones and lost.

And dammit, he was *cold.*

He gave up trying to sleep and tottered into the lounge. He puzzled over a number of packets scattered around a dispenser, then remembered Kella's fresh black uniform. What was it with women and clothes? So long as he was there he punched an order for a bed blanket. It popped out, looking small until he opened the package and contact with the air expanded it.

That's comfort, he thought, pulling it around his shoulders. Real fabric, what a luxury. Riganth used plastic sheeting. Easy to clean, but always too hot or too cold, with a danger of suffocation by accident or design if your cell mates didn't like you. Now that the tranqs were out of his blood, he wondered how he'd ever lived through it.

I owe you, Kella.

He held no illusion that she'd rescued him for any other reason than that she had some use for him. She was one of those types that didn't have or try to make friends. He didn't understand them, but knew how to work with them. So be it. Whatever her motive, he was glad it got him free of that pit.

Ah, but for how long?

He owed her, but she was still an Elitist bitch. Always doing what's best for herself and the hell with everyone else. It was just like her to run off and leave him to die, same as on the ship when the System dreadnaught had surprised them. She'd been doing her damnedest to get into one of the shuttle pods and escape. Fat lot of good it would have done had she made it. The other ship would have either yanked her back in with its tractors or blown her up. Good thing he'd been around to tap her behind the ear just hard enough to save her from herself.

Of course, after her time in Riganth, she might not thank him for the favor.

That had been a surprise, seeing her tagged for interrogation. It only happened when you were not what you seemed and the computers found you out. For all he knew she could be Spec-Ops or something even more secret and nasty. He'd been taken away because he hadn't been military and they wanted to know why. Probably disappointed to find he wasn't a spy, only hired help; they'd simply shuffled him away with the other mundane prisoners. To be forgotten.

Until the break . . . when Kella plucked him from the milling herd.

Why? She'd have a use for him, but Ops agents were supposed to be the best, trained to specialize in everything. That was their legend: inhumanly self-sufficient, ready for any emergency. Maybe she'd figured out who had tapped her and had dragged him away for the satisfaction of watching him die. If so, then she was missing the best part of the show.

He coughed his way to the main control node and, after a try or two, cheated into the system. Any 4K-day-old tech knew a few basic shortcuts. Most outgrew the phase, but Farron had kept up, learned the more difficult code cracks. It's what made him good at his work, back when he'd had work. He brought up the power and looked over the food choices. He wasn't hungry, but a hot drink would help. Some kind of soup or tea or—

Adjust things and have a real *drink, old lad.*

There was an idea. Alcohol killed germs, and disinfecting things from the inside out held a certain logical appeal to him. He didn't want to think about dying; it was too damned depressing.

He fiddled with the base codes, introduced alcohol into a formula. The experiment took his mind off the wretched state of his body. While he waited for the request to cycle through, he used the auto-healer—gently—on the bruising she'd left on his poor throat. He dialed the intensity on the device down to minimum and went slow. Folk were always in a hurry with the things. Push the nanites too fast and they got in each other's way, adding to an injury. Can't have that.

A chime and blinking telltale called his attention to a liquid dispenser unit. Perfect timing. He pocketed the healer and tried the sample. It suited him: hot, thick, vaguely sweet, with a warming kick after it went down. He ordered a triple measure, then returned to bed to settle in for serious therapy. The stuff did seem to ease the aches. Blanket tucked around him, he drifted into a light doze. He couldn't go fully out because of the damned coughing.

It was a shock—a thoroughly unpleasant one—when a man walked into his room. Farron looked at the blue stuff in his cup and wondered at the ingredients. He was mildly drunk, but nowhere near the hallucination stage yet.

The stranger was average in height, and walked with the alert, controlled movements of a trained fighter. He wore a System uniform and carried what looked like a full-auto blaster. Unhappily, it was pointed at Farron. He squinted to get a clear look at the man through his swimming vision.

"Who're you?" he asked groggily.

"Stay where you are."

"Be glad to, I'm harmless, but don't come too close."

"Why not?"

"Just don't, I'm sick with something dangerous and you wouldn't want to catch it. I donno what it is, but it makes you feel so rotten that dying would be an improvement. Are you a med-tech, by any chance?"

The man shook his head.

"Never hurts to ask. How did you get here?"

"Walked." The intruder checked the room's attached lavatory, then focused on Farron. "Where did you come from?"

"The outside, up there." Farron pointed vaguely at the ceiling.

"From the prison."

"No, just a misplaced traveler—"

"Wearing prison fatigues and a beard?"

"It's the latest style off-world."

The man almost smiled, which was encouraging, but the gun didn't waver, which was not.

Farron shrugged. "Well, I had to try, didn't I?"

"Where's your friend gone?"

"What friend?"

"The one who doesn't pick up his clothes." His head jerked toward the lounge.

"Look, it's a bit awkward like this, why not have a seat and introduce yourself? My name's Farron, what's yours?"

"Alard," he snapped, ignoring a convenient chair.

"How do you do?"

"Where's your friend?" He adjusted the weapon's angle. "Answer straight or I'll blow your foot off."

Farron's toes curled in response to the threat. "She's gone away, I don't know where, I really don't."

"Why did she leave?"

"Well, I'm sick aren't I? She went to look for medicine. Not for me, mind, but because she might get sick herself. She's like that."

"Why did you come to this complex?"

"To hide, I suppose." His throat dried up, and he gave in to a coughing fit that left him too exhausted to move.

Alard put more distance between them. "Hide? On a military base?"

"Thought it was deserted," Farron whispered, out of breath.

"What else are you two after?"

"I just want to get better. I don't know what she's looking for."

"But you have an idea."

Farron managed a swallow of his drink. "I've lots of ideas, but no one's inclined to appreciate them. What're you doing here?"

"This base is being reactivated, I'm with a crew sent to prep the systems."

Farron finished the connection. If Kella had learned about a group of technicians working here she'd be after their ship. "Must be very interesting," he commented aloud.

"How did you escape the prison?"

"I didn't really, she did, and took me along."

"You're old friends?"

"She'd never admit it. . .for that matter, neither would I."

"Then why take you?"

"I have my uses. I'm very good at opening doors, for one thing. You know, you should have something done about the security systems here. They're terrible."

"How long has she been gone? What direction did she take?"

"Is there a med-unit in this place?"

The man gave a curt nod and headed for the door.

Farron had meant to stall, keep him distracted with innocuous questions. "Hey! Come back here! I need help, dammit!"

"Stay where you are," Alard repeated.

Bloody hell. I shouldn't have reminded him of the med-unit. As with Kella, Farron watched helplessly as the man strode out, protests ignored.

The bastard probably won't return either.

Something odd about him, though. Alard wore the black uniform with the proper equipment and trimmings, but his behavior was atypical for a System soldier. His first duty should have been to arrest Farron, then report. He'd had a comm-unit on his wrist, after all. Why hadn't he used it?

Unless he also wasn't what he'd appeared to be.

That particular idea gave Farron a shiver that had nothing to do with his illness.

"You're feverish, old lad," he said, his voice thin and small against the stark walls of the room.

It was quite likely that Alard had taken off to do bodily harm or worse to Kella if he found her. But if so, then why hadn't he shot Farron?

"Not that I'm complaining," he mumbled. "But it is untidy."

Farron went over his limited alternatives and decided that lying around drunk and waiting to die was the least attractive of the lot. With a groan he got up. Blanket wrapped tight around him, he stumbled forward.

Things were happening out there, somewhere, and if he didn't shift himself he might get left behind for good.

* * *

Pressed flat against the wall, Kella edged sideways, taking her time. She'd heard at least two people talking, their distorted voices bouncing off hard surfaces. A large chamber was close ahead that had to be one of the hangar bays. She could almost smell the ship. She crept another step closer. . .

And set off a motion sensor alarm.

It was a standard security item stuck to the wall less than thirty meters away and anything but subtle in appearance. She'd simply not recognized it. She tore back down the hall, but a stocky man in a System uniform was now in the middle of it, his blaster at ready. He burned a warning shot into the floor just short of her feet and swung the muzzle up to chest level.

Kella stopped short, her hands out. Behind him, a tall woman with fair hair trotted up, her weapon also held ready to fire. She shut the alarm off with a remote and stared. Kella was evidently not what they'd anticipated.

"On the floor," the woman ordered. "Spread your arms."

There was no room for choice. She lay flat and a heavy boot came down on the back of her neck.

"Search her, Darden."

He slapped and prodded. "She's clean."

Well, Kella had found them: the System techs she'd planned on killing in order to take their ship.

"Roll on your back and stay there."

With considerable disgust, Kella turned over, propping herself on her elbows.

"Who the hell are you?" The fair-haired one was a lieutenant and apparently in charge. Was it just the two of them? If there were others in the crew, they'd have come for a look by now.

"Ven Mavic," Kella answered in an Elitist drawl. "*Captain* Mavic from Riganth Prison. Your zeal is commendable, but not necessary. You can let me up."

"You're a convict?" Her tone was disdainful.

Kella looked pained. "Obviously not. I'm attached to the maximum security section. There was an escape and I've been hunting prisoners."

"Alone?"

"The rest of my unit is searching the base. We split up to cover more area."

"Without weapons?"

"They're not allowed. Drop your guard for half a second and even a drugged prisoner could steal it from you. Anyway, the man I'm after is unarmed and sick. Thought I'd found him in this maze until you two jumped out. Scared the hell out of me, I'll hand you that."

"Where'd you get the uniform?"

"The supply dispensers worked, so I helped myself. Mine was wrecked after chasing him all over topside. Is that damned fire out yet?"

"Where's your identification?"

Kella wearily raised her left arm to show the small bump on the inside above the wrist where all citizens were chipped at birth. "It's no good, though. A Resister attack pulsed the whole prison and mine got cooked. Have to put in for a new one. What are you doing here, anyway? I heard the System was going to reactivate the base. Is this it?"

"You don't really need to know, do you?"

She smiled. "I suppose not. May I get up? I need to report in—if they've got the comms working by now."

The lieutenant smiled back unpleasantly. "No, I don't think so."

"Then you contact Warden Sena. I'm Captain Ven Mavic. You can tell her one of the escapees is somewhere in this complex and—"

The lieutenant smashed her boot into Kella's side, not holding back. Kella grunted and lay flat, breath gone for the moment.

Darden jumped. "Eily, what are you doing?"

"Shut up and look at her, do you think that's a regulation haircut?"

"But what she said?"

"Don't trust a glib attitude, it means she's too smart for our own good. Get her back to the hangar while I reset the alarm, or did you forget that Alard's still out there?"

* * *

Farron paused and tried to force air into his starved lungs. Breathing was more and more of a conscious effort as he walked, and it frightened him. He'd seen too many others drown in their own congestion and now it was happening to him.

Good thing that other fellow had turned up, even if he was System. At least he seemed to know his way around. Farron would have lost himself several times over had he struck out on his own. He'd only just managed to keep up with the man, though, and if he didn't keep moving, that would change. It'd be stupid to wear himself out coming this far only to lose Alard and any chance for help. Even if they were System and returned him to prison, they'd have to give him treatment once he reached them.

That, or shoot me.

He gulped back a cough and plodded dizzily forward, the vast rusty patch at his feet going unnoticed.

* * *

"Is it on?" Darden called out.

"Affirmative," came Eily's reply.

Kella sat on her hands. Literally. They'd no ready means to tie her up, and Darden had an unexpected turn of imagination. Kella was on the hangar floor with her back to a packing case. Darden was four meters away next to the shield door that led to the rest of the complex. His blaster was level with Kella's chest. He was haggard, unkempt, and nervy. In deference to this, Kella kept still and studied what she could see of the hangar and its contents.

The ship wasn't special, a standard courier vessel large enough for a few people and a moderate cargo. Some of the present consignment littered the area in a haphazard way. Several monitoring units had been unpacked and jury-rigged together, their screens displaying empty corridors. Presumably, it was part of Eily's defense against Alard, whoever that might be.

One unit in particular held her attention. The top was off and the guts had been smashed by something heavy. A few undamaged plastic and metal pieces lay scattered over a worktable along with a variety of repair tools and replacement parts. Because of her conditioning, Kella couldn't be certain, but it might have been part of a comm-panel.

Eily slipped past the shield door, shut it, and sighed. She looked like a woman with too many headaches, with Kella accounting for at least five or six of them.

She checked the screens at length before turning her attention back to her prisoner. "How long have you been hiding here?"

Kella decided to answer; the truth would do well enough this time. Besides, her side still hurt. "Six or eight hours."

Darden glanced at Eily. The time meant something to them, though Eily gave nothing away. Kella had no idea how long she'd slept but made a conservative estimate in case they wanted to try linking her with the two-day-old bloodstains in the outer hall.

"Where have you been hiding?"

"In an officers' wing, presumably. There weren't any signs posted, but the food was good and the beds comfortable."

Eily tapped a few buttons below a screen and brought up a simple overview of the base with a dot marking their own location. "Show me. You may use one hand. The left, I think."

Kella flexed her fingers and pointed. "About there."

"And why did you venture into this area?"

"I wanted to be sure I was alone."

"Are you?"

"Not anymore." It seemed prudent to be vague on that point.

"How did you get inside?"

"I found a surface hatch. The lock wasn't difficult."

"Evidently, but they don't put mere lock-breakers in Riganth. Why were you there?"

"Something political. You wouldn't find it interesting."

"Treason?"

Kella shrugged with one shoulder. "Depends on your point of view, doesn't it?"

Darden scowled, shifting on his feet to express his revulsion. Apparently he was too well trained to spit. Treason was the worst crime you could commit, as far as the System was concerned, and he looked like he believed in the System.

"Trace the route you took from the officers' wing," said Eily, pointing at the map.

"If you want to know if I saw the bloodstain, the answer is yes. Was it this Alard's work?"

Eily was amused, Darden was not.

"Who is he?"

"A fellow officer until he went brainwarp and murdered our captain."

"How'd that happen?"

Eily ignored her. "The bastard's loose somewhere in this complex, probably not far away. You're lucky we found you first. At least you're still alive."

Kella's gratitude was thin at best. "Oh, yes. I'm so happy."

"Or have you met him already?"

"Obviously not. What caused this brainwarp?"

"Who knows?"

Kella watched Darden as though he made her uneasy, but her chief interest was to observe his reaction to what Eily was saying. She was lying about Alard's brainwarp; the glint in his eyes said as much.

"Why haven't you called for help?" Kella asked.

"We have, it's on the way."

His gaze flicked once at Eily.

Another lie.

"Notify Riganth you've found me," Kella suggested.

"Anxious to return?"

"My cell is preferable to being murdered by an armed brainwarp case. Call them, they'll lend aid."

"First we secure Alard. No need to have civilians on the base and getting in the way."

Kella had trouble keeping her face straight; that quick and ridiculous answer confirmed that they had no outside communications. She was careful not to let her gaze stray to the scattered pieces of the comm-panel.

There was a practical method to Alard's madness. He'd isolated the crew from immediate help, exactly what she would have done. Her next move would have been to take out the leader. Alard apparently accomplished that as well, though clumsily to judge by the mess. He must have hoped to get all three at once, but had missed. As she'd feared, the survivors were on high alert with defenses and warning systems in place.

"Put your hand back where it was," Darden ordered.

"What happened to your captain?" Kella asked, obeying.

"Why do you want to know?"

She shrugged. "There was so much blood, I wondered what kind of weapon would do that much damage."

He lifted his gun. "One exactly like this; the blast hit his neck artery. Like a demonstration?"

She shook her head, as if in sympathy. "The rest of the crew must be having fits."

"They're looking for Alard."

Kella grunted understanding, not trusting her voice. Eily would never have sent techs to hunt an ambush killer, but keep her people close and safe.

Right. Two survivors, both with combat training, with Darden as the greater threat. Eily was too distracted watching for Alard to keep her guard up all the time. She'd holstered her hand weapon and forgotten it. A bad move. Now if Darden's attention could be drawn away just long enough. . .

Eily watched one of the screens intently. "You said you were alone. Who the hell's that?"

Farron's unsteady figure—barefoot, wrapped in a blanket staggered into view. The idiot.

"He's a convict—one of your friends?"

"I wouldn't put it quite that way," Kella growled.

"What's the matter with him?"

"She said he was sick," Darden put in. "What's he got?"

Kella shrugged.

The cameras tracked Farron from one section to another. Kella's caution had been for nothing. They'd seen her long before the alarm went off.

"Darden, take the back way round again and bring him in, but careful, it might be an act, there could be more. Don't risk yourself."

He left with a brisk nod. Eily brought her gun out to cover Kella. Better odds, but she was too far away to try anything yet.

On the screen Farron took one step too many and tripped the motion sensor. He froze, looked down the hall he'd come from, and saw Darden step out.

"Hallo." He coughed pitifully. "D'ye mind if I give myself up?"

"Face the wall, put your arms out, and lean on them."

"If I can," he mumbled. He turned and raised them, groaning when his blanket slipped off.

Darden darted close enough to kick his feet apart.

"All right, I've got him," he called.

Eily motioned for Kella to stand, hands on her head, and go through the doors. Once in the hall she cut the alarm again and covered them both while Darden searched Farron for weapons. He found an auto-healer and dropped it on the blanket.

"Clean," he pronounced.

Farron looked deathly. "I don't feel at all well," he murmured in a subdued tone.

"Probably a hangover," Kella said acidly. She could smell his breath even at that distance.

"No, I mean I really don't. Who're these two? They with that other fellow?"

"You've met Alard?"

"Friendly sort. I think. No. I'm not sure. It's kind of fuzzy. . ."

"Where'd you see him?" Eily demanded.

"Back there." Farron half-heartedly indicated the way he'd come. "Only I thought he was ahead of me. Thought sure he was. Must have taken a wrong turn somewhere."

Or he let you get ahead to act as a decoy. Kella and Eily must have shared the same thought; as one, they looked back down the corridor, but it was empty.

"We're out of here," said Eily. "Move it."

"Give us a hand," Farron gasped. "I don't feel well. Don't. . . don't. . ." His head drooped and his legs caved. He slipped to the floor with a solid thud.

Darden jumped back in surprise, ready to trigger his blaster.

"What's the matter with him?" Eily snapped.

Kella knelt and felt for a neck pulse. "Fainted." Her eyes caught a peripheral movement at the first corner at the far end of the hall. She had a brief impression of a crouching shape.

Alard.

She dropped flat.

Darden yelled and spun as a blast struck his side. Diving against the wall, Eily sent a half-dozen wild shots into the ceiling. Kella took advantage of the distraction to scramble to the cover of the shield door and roll through, then was up and bolting for the ship. Eily shouted after her and sent two more blasts in her direction. Kella just made it up the ramp to the open side hatch when something heavy buffeted her arm, the force of the blow pushing her inside.

She stumbled, recovered, and raced forward to the bridge. Eily was aboard in seconds, but by then Kella ducked through the last door and cranked it shut.

Then she went hot-cold sick and ready to drop in her tracks like Farron. Her right arm hung useless and numb; blood dribbled down its length, spattering the scuffed deck with bright color. She listed away from the door, dizzy, her stomach upside down. Behind her there was a loud snap and a crack appeared where her head had been. That stupid tech bitch had her blaster up to full power.

"Eily!" she bellowed.

Another shot, lower. She was crazy, blasting away inside the ship like that. Crazy or shit-scared by Alard's killings.

"Eily—do that again and I'll set off the ship's weaponry!"

That bought a little time. Kella glanced at the controls, but the stress of the present situation brought on the old pattern again. Lights and buttons merged and danced, there was no time to sort them; finding the right one was impossible for now. Discarding that option, she looked for weapons. Nothing obvious offered itself, only a basic aid box and another fire extinguisher. She tore the box down and fumbled out a pressure bandage for her arm.

"Come out," Eily called through the door. "I know you've been hit, I don't want to have to hurt you again."

"I'm not that hurt," she lied, trying to ignore the terrible mess she was leaving all over the deck.

"You've nowhere to go."

"Exactly, but you do. Get off this ship or I'll destroy it. I've had the training; I know how to access the firing controls. One blast in the hangar bay and we're all cooked."

"You're not that desperate."

"Eily, think hard on this: I've been in a System political prison with only System interrogators for entertainment. I'm never going back to that, so believe me when I tell you *I am that desperate!*"

Hopefully, Eily would be put off by the convincingly shrill pitch in Kella's voice. Not all of it was bluff. Kella was shit-scared herself. No time to conjure mental images to keep the fear locked away, all she could do was shove it to one side and hope it didn't rush back and trip her.

She got the bandage on, more or less. The blood soaked through the dressing before the thing tightened around her arm and slowed the worst of it. The loose end dangled. Had to trim it before it caught on something. Wasn't there anything in this damned box with a sharp edge?

"All right," Eily called. "I'm backing off. Just take it easy."

A blunt-nosed cutter with a safety blade. Great for slicing away bandaging, worthless as a weapon. Kella dropped it back in the box and grabbed a packet of stimulant patches. She ripped it open with her blood-slicked fingers and slapped one on her throat. It'd take a minute to act.

"Listen to me," said Eily. "We need to help each other. Alard's a threat to us all. He will kill both of us. You're better off with me. Together we can stop him."

The tone and inflection were uneven as Eily moved around. What the hell was she up to?

"He got Darden, he's probably got your friend. We two have to cooperate!"

Kella took the fire extinguisher from the wall and held it ready. Compared to Eily's blaster it was useless, but she had to have some kind of weapon in hand. The solid weight of the chemicals inside provided a visceral comfort. She checked the ship's controls again. They weren't dancing so much. In fact, they were in sharp focus now. She hoped she hadn't overdone it with the stimulant.

"We've got to pool our resources in order to stay alive." Eily's voice was unnaturally loud, the words were running together. She wasn't thinking about what she was saying, yet there was a purpose to it.

Kella's arm burned. She was ready to fall down. Damn it all. Even if she got control of Eily and thus the ship, then what? Kella could force the woman to play pilot for only as long as the stimulants held. It wouldn't be long, either, not with this arm, not in the shape she was in.

From outside the door came more nonsense as Eily preached about their common enemy. Yes, she was a proper little System robot, mouthing fatuous nonsense. . .

That almost covered the faint hissing. . .

Gas.

Kella made a frantic grab for the aid box. She'd caught the first whiff of the stuff—something pungent—then stopped breathing. Heart pumping painfully, she clawed for a respirator mask, hastily fitting it over her nose and mouth, thumbing the flow valve open just in time. The seal wasn't perfect; some of what flooded the bridge seeped in, adding to her dizziness. She left the valve wide open and slowed her intake. That helped. Now air was escaping from the mask, reducing the chance of contamination.

What was that crap, anyway? Not tri-crynide or she'd be dead by now except for reflex twitching. Somose, maybe? No matter, as long as she could still move and think . . . which wouldn't be for long given the circumstances.

She put her back to a wall and sank to the floor. Bad move, that. Too tempting. She might shut her eyes and never open them again.

But she'd have to do just that. Only for a minute or two, or however long it took. . .

She jerked her head up, shaking it hard, blinking hard. The mask slipped a bit. Somose gas it was, then. Must be part of the bridge intruder defense control. Just the thing to subdue a dangerous Resistance terrorist; just the thing so the poor misguided creature could be humanely captured and ultimately rehabilitated into something more to the System's liking.

Not this one, she thought, *not today, not ever*.

Kella found another stimulant patch and slapped it against the other side of her neck. It wasn't the recommended thing to do, except for emergencies. This more than qualified, what with gas filling every corner of the compartment.

Her heart raced faster; blood hit the top of her skull and pounded there, burning for a moment before dispersing throughout the rest of her body. Tremors ran up and down her wounded arm. No need to worry about dropping off now; her nerves were galloping from the stim.

The next time her head jerked was in response to a minute change in the hissing. She stared at an air vent as though she could actually see the flow. Any more patches like the last and she just might. No need to look, though, Eily was flushing the place clean, preparing to come in.

Kella waited until the last second—when she actually heard Eily using the exterior manual to crank the door open—before taking away the mask and shoving it out of sight behind her. She bowed forward, protectively cradling the extinguisher in her good arm, hiding it with her body. Then came the hard part: sitting absolutely still.

The door folded open.

"All right, you." Eily's voice was thin, wavering, whether with relief or fear was hard to tell. She crept inside. Two slow, soft steps and she was standing over Kella's apparently unconscious form. The still-warm muzzle of a blaster nudged into an exposed part of her neck. Kella settled more firmly against the wall. The muzzle withdrew. Now a hand touched her shoulder. Pushing. Kella's slow topple had to look natural. . . right up to the last instant. . .when the extinguisher nozzle was clear and Kella made a convulsive move with her good hand.

The high-pressure spray hit Eily square in the face. She spasmed away, blind, choking. She triggered one wild shot. Kella gave her no time for a second, and slammed the cylinder into Eily's skull with all her strength. The shock went up her hand, her arm, instantly transmitting the sickening knowledge that it had been enough. More than enough. Eily dropped.

Kella's whole body shook, she had to brace her knees or fall; the stim and her own adrenaline were playing hell inside her, but it was better than being dead.

Her or me, she thought. *Better her than me*. She stared at Eily, at the bloodied depression in her temple, at her last, graceless collapse. No regrets for this enemy. One couldn't afford them.

Where the hell is her blaster?

Eily was on top of it. Kella pulled it clear. It was awkward in her left hand, but she'd be able to use it.

And how soon would that be? Alard was still a problem. Had Eily remembered to lock the shield door? Best to assume she'd forgotten. Assume that Alard was in the hangar and intending to board the ship.

A dull sound, more felt than heard, came through the deck.

Assume that he's *in* the ship.

Kella shoved the blaster into her belt, bent, and snaked an arm around Eily's waist, lifting. It should have been hard, but the drugs racing through her veins were doing their job. A wrench, a heave, and then Eily's body was in one of the command chairs. Kella unlocked the swivel mechanism and turned it so Eily faced away from the door, then she backed off, wedging flat against the right aft wall. She checked the blaster to be certain that it was charged and that the safety disengaged. She tried to thumb the power back to minimize collateral damage, but her hand froze.

The weapon was tech, just like all the other things that set off her reconditioning symptoms. Pulling the trigger on a non-lethal extinguisher was one thing, trying to use a true weapon was another.

Alard progressed toward the bridge; first she heard his footsteps, then his muted breathing. He paused outside the open door. From there he would see the mess on the deck: blood, scattered extinguisher spray. The stink of the latter was sharp in the air, like fresh vomit. He took his time. Kella breathed shallowly through her mouth and hoped that he couldn't hear her pounding heart.

He wouldn't be able to see anything more unless he came forward. It was a fifty-fifty chance who he'd spot first, Kella or Eily, depending on whether he looked left or right coming through the door.

Left, she willed at him. *Look left*.

Then he was in.

Fast bastard, she thought, having the time to think. He'd looked left.

And his attention had been caught and held by Eily for the critical instant that Kella needed. He must have realized it, too. He tensed as though to spin, then aborted the movement. It came out as a small jump throughout his whole body. Then he went still.

"Smart of you not to risk it," she said. She liked how her voice sounded. Cold. Measured. In charge. Quite the opposite of how she felt.

She couldn't shoot him. Her hand shook from the effort of trying. All the other stops they'd put into her brain were nothing compared to this one. Killing him was the most expedient way to end this—and she could not act.

Stall, then, restrain him now and kill him later.

"Put the blaster down and your hands behind your neck."

He obeyed.

"You're Alard?"

He nodded once.

"Are you brainwarp, Alard?"

"Is that what they told you?"

"They said you were killing everyone. You got a reason for that?"

He slowly turned, looking her up and down, his gaze resting briefly on her wounded arm and then on the twin stim-patches on her neck. "They're System. That's reason enough for me." There was contempt in his tone. He was untroubled over those deaths.

"Resistance?"

"Mercenary."

"What outfit?"

"I'm independent. They had a contract open so I took it."

The Resistance had no qualms about bringing in outside help, especially if the price was low. "Entailing what?"

His gaze darted from her face to the muzzle of her weapon and back. "I was hired to slip extra programming into the base computers."

"What kind of programming?"

"Nothing elaborate, but if and when it receives the proper signal, the reactor goes critical. The ship's my payment."

Interesting. If true, then the Resistance had made one hell of a bargain. For the price of a little forgery to get him assigned to the crew and one minor spacecraft they could remove the base as a threat anytime they wanted. Of course, the bang would take out Riganth Prison as well and too bad for the prisoners there. Maybe that was the reason behind the Resister raid. Free as many as they could, divert attention from the base . . . she liked the planning behind it. Hell, it was just the sort of thing she might have come up with herself.

But it took talent and training to command the kind of computer expertise needed to get past a reactor's safeguards. "You botched it."

"I did not," he protested. "I completed the job."

"You left a pile of bodies all over the place."

"When the captain found out what I was doing I had to shut him down. So?"

"So as soon as the next ship comes in, the first thing they'll do is check the computers for tampering."

"I'd have cleaned everything up before leaving. The logs would show all the work done with the tech crew leaving on schedule. Once off-world the ship goes missing."

Kella's mouth twitched.

"It's the truth!" he added sharply.

"But you can't prove any of it, can you?"

"No, but. . ."

"Go on."

"I could have shut you and your friend down at any time since you broke into the base, but didn't."

"Or maybe you were hoping we'd provide a distraction you could exploit—and we did."

"Your friend's alive, though. Darden is not. I can show you."

Moving cautiously, he backed toward a monitor and, one-fingered, tapped few buttons. The monitor came alive. It was linked to the same remotes as the ones jury-rigged in the hangar. The image hopped as he keyed in the corridor pickup. Kella saw two bodies on the floor. One was Darden's. There was a vast wash of blood around him and he wasn't moving. Farron lay exactly where he'd fainted.

Alard played with a control and the remote centered on Farron.

Numbers began to flow across the bottom of the screen.

"There's his heart rate, respiration, and temp," he said, pointing. "He's in bad shape, but fixable."

She was unimpressed. "All it means is that you were in too great a hurry to shoot an unconscious man."

"He could have been faking. If you were me, would you have taken that chance?"

Kella knew that she would not. But it still wasn't proof, and given the circumstances, there was no way Alard could offer any. The sensible thing at this point was to kill him, thus eliminating a liability she couldn't afford.

Once more, she tried to trigger the blaster. Her hand twitched.

He flinched, but otherwise stayed in place. "Look, you're hurt and need help. I'm no threat to you. We're on the same side in the end. All I want out of this is my skin and the ship. If you want a fast trip off-world, I'll pilot you there."

I'll pilot myself. Or get Farron to do it.

On the monitor, Farron sluggishly moved his arms, then pushed upright. He looked around, clearly confused, then yelped when he saw Darden's body. Farron backed away on all fours, tangling in his blanket. Where'd he find one of those, anyway?

Focus, dammit. Her stims wouldn't last long. When they wore off she'd drop in her tracks.

"I can take you to the Resistance cell that hired me," said Alard. "They'll get you a new ID. You can report to them what I did here, corroborate it. My stake is that it would get me more work. Having a ship is a start, but I'm going to need help stripping the registry. . ."

All reasonable, perfectly reasonable.

"There's also the System to consider. I smashed the long-range comm-unit. Eily couldn't make routine reports for the last couple of days. They'll wonder why and send someone to investigate. They could be on their way right now. We have to get out of here."

We have to get out of here.

She jerked, shaking her head at the echo of agreement that had come from nowhere. His voice had fallen into a soothing monotone. It was a common interrogation technique, meant to be non-threatening, to lull the subject into a trusting state. Some responded better to that than to shouts. People were hard-wired to want an authority figure's approval.

I'm the one with the weapon. Therefore she was the authority here, but her wound and the reconditioning were swiftly eroding her control.

Another stim patch would have her bouncing off the bulkheads, but she was tempted. If her nerves were bad enough she could shoot Alard by accident.

"Whether you trust me or not doesn't matter," he pressed. "We can strike a deal. I'll hold up my side. You have my word on it."

Which, in Kella's line of work, was worthless.

Liability, logic insisted.

And just as insistently, her emotion-based instincts whispered *asset.*

"You said you were getting this ship?" she asked.

"It's my payment. I'm a damn good pilot-navigator."

That was one for the asset column. Until she got the neurons in her head unscrambled for good, she'd need someone in better shape than Farron to handle tech problems. She could run the rest herself, providing her instincts were still functioning and not jumbled up by the stim and wishful thinking.

No. They'd knocked things around a bit inside, but she wasn't that far gone. She would beat it. She'd beat them.

Had beaten them. So far.

How about just a little farther?

Her stomach fluttered. Damned drugs.

The monitor distracted her. Farron was no longer in view. The numbers at the bottom were zeros. So he was dead or out of range.

"Tell you what," said Alard, "there are restraints in the ship's med-unit. Lock me down with those for the time being. Then you can look after your partner and talk things over. We have anti-virals; he can be fine again in just a day or two."

Very well. Decision time. But when it came down to it, she really had none to make. Without help, she'd sooner or later collapse just like Farron, then Alard, the System, or some goon from Riganth Prison would finish her off. It was just a question of who got to her first. With Alard there was the slim chance he might be telling the truth. A chance for her to return to her unit, a chance to get crucial deprogramming, a chance to feel in control again, to turn the illusion she projected into reality.

There was a subtle shift in her. Alard went a fraction more alert, but she did nothing more than nod at the floor where she'd left the respirator. "Get that out to Farron. I'm sure he'll find it useful, too." She moved her gun muzzle away from him.

Alard picked it up. He turned the mask over, watching her. "Why did you need it?"

She gestured at Eily. "She was clever, but never really wanted to kill, not if she had to think about it first. She flooded the bridge with Somose gas to take me alive. If she'd had any sense, she'd have used tri-crynide instead. It's faster and more final."

Alard shook his head. "Not Eily. I knew her. She wasn't enough of a bitch to do it."

Kella looked him up and down in turn. Now was as good a time as any to make sure he fully understood her. She was almost smiling. "So very few of us are."

Alard smiled, nodding agreement. "I can see that."

Then he hurled the mask straight at her face. She swung the useless blaster back, but he was inside her guard, pushing, tackling, and they both hit the floor. The impact drove the breath from her, and he used his weight to pin her in place.

She still could not trigger to fire, and it didn't matter, he kept the muzzle shoved away and had a hand around her neck. He squeezed hard to cut the blood to her brain. Kella let go the blaster and clawed wildly at his eyes. He drew back and cracked his forehead against hers.

Lightning flashed behind her eyelids, and she seemed to spin out of her body. Her vision blurred and went dark. Alard's grip tightened. Desperate for air, she tried to break his hold, but her fingers had no strength. She slithered down into blackness. . .

Where Alard gave a strange grunting scream and began convulsing on top of her as if in some disgusting parody of an orgasm. The pressure on her neck ceased. His weight suddenly lifted.

She gasped and gagged and forced herself to take air, however much it hurt. Her blood-starved brain seemed to lurch inside her skull.

Hearing returned first. She'd not realized it had gone until the pounding in her ears subsided.

In its place was Farron's hoarse and tired voice.

"Answer me, woman," he snarled. "Are you all right?"

She blinked, trying to reclaim her vision. Some of the darkness ceded to blurs, and she recognized the shape of Farron's head and shoulders in the swimming chaos. She groaned, and he could put whatever meaning he liked to that.

Farron sat heavily down next to her. "Bloody hell, that's done it," he wheezed.

She coughed and retched, her throat an agony. "Is he dead?"

"For his sake he better be."

"Is he—"

"Yes! He's gone. You need a keeper, you know that? Didn't your mum warn you to never trust pretty strangers?"

"As opposed to homely friends?" she rasped. Where had *that* come from?

"Wound me, why don't you? I just saved your life, you silly bitch."

Right on all counts. What madness had taken her that she'd let her guard down so far? The stims, conditioning, wound, sheer fatigue or all four had turned her into an idiot.

"Oh, I feel sick," Farron moaned. "That was *horrible*. Don't ask me to do that again. I'm not built for it."

"What did you do?"

"Killed him of course. I'll need a dose of forget-me to get that out of my mind. I don't want to live with that."

"How?"

"Eh?"

"How did you kill him?" She'd not heard a blaster shot.

He held up the auto-healer. "These things are nasty on full power. Touched it to his head. Every nanite in his carcass shot there looking for something to fix. Must have hurt like blazes when they clotted."

She gaped at Farron, fighting several levels of surprise. Of all things for him to turn into a weapon. She'd never have thought of it herself. Out of nowhere came a laugh. It sounded rusty and hurt her throat, but she couldn't help herself.

"You going strange on me? What's so damn funny? There's a man dead."

"Good riddance to rubbish," she muttered.

"You'll join him if you don't let me patch that arm while I'm still able."

But Kella wasn't up to moving yet except for involuntary twitching from the stims and unspent adrenalin. The air was thick, tainted with death. She used to not mind that stench; it meant she'd kept herself alive for another day. Now she wanted to vomit.

Must be the drugs.

"What you say?" Farron asked.

Was she speaking aloud again? "I'm. . .tired."

"There's a shock."

Tired of running, fighting, killing. Even if we get away is there any safe haven to hide?

"Never you mind that," he urged. "Patch up and rest for now. Work on the big decisions later."

She clamped her jaw shut and shifted around so he could look at her arm. The sooner she was back on her feet the better.

He left the pressure bandage in place and waved the auto-healer over the area. "Feel anything?"

"Not sure."

"Well then," he adjusted the device and smiled, "we'll just take it slow, shall we?"

.

THE WIND BREATHES COLD

Author's Note: *This was my first professional short story sale, which went into Martin H. Greenberg's collection, DRACULA: PRINCE OF DARKNESS. It was always intended to be the first chapter for QUINCEY MORRIS: VAMPIRE, but I didn't get to write that book until some years later. It sold to Baen Books and is available as an e-download from baen-dot-com.*

And yes, I am writing a new Quincey novel: QUINCEY MORRIS AND THE WEST END RIPPER.

Transylvania, November 1893

No single sense returned first. They mobbed me.

The numbing cold, the soft whine of dogs, the rough jostling, all tumbled together in my dulled brain like seeds in a rattle. I slipped to and fro between awareness and nothing until a sharp lurch and bump caught my attention, holding me awake for longer than a few seconds. It was enough that I dimly comprehended something was very wrong. The next moment of consciousness I managed to keep hold of; the moments to follow had me wishing I'd done otherwise.

Things were strongly tugging at my feet and legs, which seemed to be bound up. So was the rest of my body. I was wrapped snug and tight in a blanket from head to toe, unable to move or see. It was right over my face, which I never could abide. I groaned, trying to get free of the annoyance.

At this feeble sound and movement the tugging abruptly stopped, and the things—which I dazedly grasped to be several dogs—snuffled at me. I couldn't tell how many, but to judge by their sounds several at the least seemed to hold me as the focus of their attention. It made no sense until with a raw shock tearing through my nerves I realized they weren't dogs, but wolves.

In that instant full alertness returned, mind and body hurtling awake. I froze utterly, in the full expectation that the wolves would start ripping into me as I lay helpless before them. After a few truly terrible moments when nothing happened I tried to swallow my heart back into place, but there wasn't spit enough in my mouth for the job.

With whines and growls, their strong jaws clamped firmly on my wrappings again, and they resumed dragging me along. I could only think that made bold by hunger they'd entered our camp and picked me to pull away to a safe distance where they could feed.

Panic would kill me. I dared not shout an alarm to my friends. The noise might spark the wolves to attack their prize. They'd held off—for the time being—so I gritted my teeth and waited and listened in the frail hope I might somehow find a way out of this alive.

There must have been dozens of them. I could hear their eager panting and the click of their claws against bare stone or crunching into the thick snow. Wolves usually shy away from men—such had been my experience when Art and I had been trailed by that pack in Siberia. Had they been more desperate they'd have made a real feast for themselves on us. Being normal wolves, they'd held off and we'd escaped. But this pack seemed anything but normal. We were in the wild deeps of Transylvania, a far different place, and I'd already seen grim proof that a tall tale in one part of the world was God's own awful truth in another.

The wolves pulled me along another few yards. My weight, and I was aware of every solid pound of it going over those rocks, was nothing to them. Once they felt secure, they'd go through my all too thin blanket and clothes like taking the hide off a deer. I'd seen that happen once. The deer had been alive when they'd started in, and though quick enough, it hadn't been an easy death.

But all men have a limit to their self-control and that dark thought was enough to finally break mine; fear surged in my throat like vomit. It choked off any cry for help I might have made. I thrashed around like one of the madmen in Seward's asylum, fighting against my bindings. The wolves at my feet let go. One of them snarled, stirring up the others. They moved all around me, excited, nipping at the blanket as though in play, their efforts ironically helping my struggles as they shredded the cloth. Fresh air suddenly slapped my face as the damned thing finally came loose.

Bright-eyes catching the moonlight in green flashes, with lolling tongues and rows of white teeth, they scampered about like puppies. Some darted close to snap at me, wagging their tails at the sport of it. I wrested my hands free, but had no weapon to use. Some blurred memory told me I carried no knife or gun. I scrabbled in the inches-deep snow and found a piece of fist-sized rock. Better than nothing.

Then a big black fellow, one that was obviously the pack leader, lifted his head to the wild gray sky and howled. Ever an eerie sound, but to be so alone in the forest, to hear it so close and loud, to watch the very breath of it streaming from the animal's muzzle—had the hair on my neck not already been raised to its limit, it would have gone that much higher. The other wolves instantly abandoned their game and crowded around him, tails tucked like fawning supplicants seeking a favor. One after another joined him, blending and weaving their many voices into a triumphant song only they could fully understand.

The leader broke off and focused his huge green eyes upon me as the others continued their hell's chorus. It's a mistake to ascribe human attributes to an animal, but I couldn't help myself. The thing looked not just interested in what he saw, but curious, in the way that a human is curious.

He snarled and snapped at those nearest him. The pack stopped howling and obediently scattered. After a sharp, low bark from him they formed themselves into a wide circle like trained circus dogs. I was at its exact center. Some stood, others sat, but all watched me attentively. Though I'd had more contact with wolves than most men, I'd never seen or heard *anything* like this before.

A few of them growled, no doubt scenting my fear.

Clutching the nearly useless rock with one hand, I frantically tore at the bindings around my ankles with the other. It was desperate work, made slow by my reluctance to take my eyes from the pack. Despite the distraction of their presence, I saw that for some reason I'd been wrapped like a bundle for the mail, first in the blanket, then by ropes to hold it in place. Why? Who had tied me up so? I cursed whoever had done me such an ill turn, the burst of anger giving me the strength to get free.

I got clear of the blanket and staggered upright, half-expecting the wolves to close in. But they remained in their great circle, watching. There were no trees within it to climb to safety, and if I tried to break through the line at any point they'd be on me, so I kept still and stared back. One of the wolves sneezed; another shook himself. They knew they had me.

A gust of winter wind sent the dry ground snow flying. Flakes skittered and drifted over the discarded blanket. I slowly picked it up and looped it around my left arm. The leader stepped forward, growling. I angled to face him, my powerless fear turning to fury that I should be brought to such a base fate.

"Come on, you big bastard. I'll take you first," I whispered, growling right back. I would sell myself dearly to them.

The wolf lowered his head and rocked back on his haunches, like a dog about to do a begging trick. A roiling darkness that seemed to come from within the thing's body blurred the details as bones and joints soundlessly shifted, muzzle and fur retreated, skin swelled. It rose on its hind legs and kept rising until it was a match for me in height. The crooked legs straightened, thickened, and became the legs of a man, a tall, lean man clothed all in black. Only his bright green eyes remained the same, and when his red lips thinned into a smile I clearly saw the hungry wolf lurking beneath the surface.

I knew his face. One can never forget such stern features. They were the stuff of nightmares, all the more so for my knowing, of my being *absolutely certain*, that he was *dead*—for I'd killed him myself.

Yet there he stood before me, stubbornly oblivious to the fact.

I was as afraid as I'd ever been in my life and could have expressed it, loudly, but there didn't seem much point. In a few minutes I'd either be dead or worse than dead, and making a lot of noise about it wouldn't help me one way or another.

"I can respect a brave man, Mr. Morris," said Vlad Dracula, pitching his deep voice to be heard above the wind. In it was the harsh tone I'd heard when he'd taunted us from the stable yard of his Piccadilly house. Now he clasped his hands behind him and continued to regard me with the same mixture of interest and curiosity that had manifested itself in his wolf form.

The wind buffeted against his body with little effect other than to whip at his dark clothes and gray-streaked hair. Black on white was the mark Harker had left on the pallid flesh of Dracula's brow; he bore the scar with little sign of healing, yet nearly a month had passed from the last time I'd seen that face. But since then, I'd . . . I'd . . .

Something very like the wind whirled sickeningly inside my skull. The creature before me, the circle of wolves, the snow, the cold, all faded for an instant of nothingness before asserting themselves again. It was like the focus of a poorly made telescope shifting in and out.

"I killed you," I said faintly. I recalled the impact of the strike going right up my arm when my Bowie knife slammed firmly into his chest.

"So you did," he admitted. "With some help from Jonathan Harker do not forget."

"Yes. . . ."

Harker had buried his Kukri knife in the monster's throat. We'd fought our way through the Szgany to get to the leiter-wagon and the great box on top of it. The Szgany had drawn their knives to defend it, and one of them had . . .

I looked down, my hand going to my side. The clothes there were thick and stiff with dried and frozen blood. I could smell it, sharp and compelling.

My blood. It had fairly poured from me as our enemies fled into the growing dusk. Harker caught me as I fell and sank back in his arms, my strength abruptly spent. Jack Seward and Van Helsing had tried their best to stop the flow, but the wound was too deep, the damage beyond any skill to heal. Thank God it hadn't been very painful. The last memory I had was of poor Mina Harker, her face twisted by bitter grief, but I'd been so happy, so at peace. The awful red mark on her own brow had vanished, and from that I knew I'd spared her soul from damnation. With such joy in my fast-beating heart did I slip contentedly away into what seemed like sleep.

Not sleep. Nothing so ordinary as that had taken me, changed me, turned me into . . .

"No need for such alarm, Mr. Morris," Dracula said, reading my face. "What you have become is not so dreadful as you've been led to believe."

Not knowing my own voice, a cry escaped me. Heedless of the wolves, I burst through their circle, running back down their trail. I crashed through snowdrifts, blundered against trees, and tripped on invisible snares, but kept going. Not far ahead would be the warm yellow light of our campfire. If I could just get there, if Van Helsing still had some of his Holy Wafer left, there might yet be some protection for us.

For *them*. At least for them.

I was close enough to make out their huddled forms far down in the clearing where they'd made camp: the Harkers lying together, Van Helsing and Seward each rolled up in their blankets, Art a little off from them by the horses, presumably taking his turn at watch. All were fast asleep, though, worn out by the hard travel and the chase, but just one shout from me would bring Art instantly awake—

A hand, colder and heavier than the ice, clapped over my mouth just as I drew breath. As though I were a child and not a grown man topping six feet, Dracula lifted me right from my tracks, hauling me swiftly back into the cover of the forest. I lashed out with the rock still in my hand, but couldn't connect solidly enough to slow him. He was quite indifferent to my struggles, though I managed a few solid kicks that made him grunt. Then he spun me suddenly, and cracked my head against one of the trees.

Lights brighter than the sun blinded me. Ungodly pain robbed me of speech. I collapsed. Quite helpless to stop him, he easily hoisted me over one shoulder like an old sack and hurried back up the way I'd run. The wolves had tagged along for the brief hunt and now bounded playfully all around us. I couldn't tell how far he went, only that it was beyond where I'd originally revived, and well out of the camp's earshot.

He eventually dropped me flat on my face into the snow, and all I could do was lie there for a time nearly paralyzed and miserably ill from the shock. It passed too slowly to suit, but did pass. When I felt ready for it I pushed the ground away and propped myself against a tree. Dracula loomed over me, his white face twisted with fury.

"Fool," he snarled. "Do you think they'll show you mercy once they know about you?"

"I'm counting on it," I snapped back. "I know what to expect and shall welcome it."

"Well, I do not. Give yourself away to them if you must, but not me. I've been to enough trouble over this matter and want no more."

"Go to hell."

I didn't think his eyes could hold more rage. I was wrong. He raised a hand as though to smash me like a fly. His anger beat against me, a physical thing like heat from a forge, but after a long and dreadful moment he lowered his arm, and visibly shook himself out of his threatening posture with a sneer.

"You're but an infant," he muttered with no little disgust. "You don't understand anything yet."

"I know enough."

"I think not. Come with me and I shall be of some help to that end."

"No."

"Stay behind and your friends will be food for my children." He gestured meaningfully at the forest around us. No need for him to explain who his "children" were; I could still hear and occasionally see them well enough as they ghosted in and out of the surrounding trees. "Come and your friends will be safe."

"For how long?"

"As long as you remain sensible. And that is entirely up to *you*."

He stepped back and waited, watching as his wolves had watched. He offered no help as I found my feet, leaning hard on the tree. Though dizzy, I was able to think straight, but no idea running through my mind could be remotely mistaken for a way out of this spot. I did not trust him, was utterly repulsed by him and all that he represented, but he was well in control of things and we both knew it.

"Where?" I asked grimly.

He pointed behind me. We were to go even deeper into the timber, climbing away from the camp. I didn't like that, but followed as he led the way along what looked like a deer trail. The wolves kept pace, panting and wagging their tails like dogs out for a walk. Glancing back, I saw more than a dozen of them padding almost at my heels and realized they were obliterating my tracks in the snow. Was it accidental or intentional? I made a step off to one side as a test and went on. The wolves sniffed the spot and blotted out my boot print as they swarmed over it, tongues hanging as if from laughter.

We began climbing in earnest. Rocks rose high on our left, forming a natural wall that cut the freezing wind. The snow underfoot thinned and vanished. Dracula waited until I was well upon this trackless surface and a little ahead. He turned toward the wolves, stretching his arms before him, then spreading them wide in a dismissive gesture. As though the pack were one animal and not many, his children silently retreated down the path into the trees below, and were lost to sight.

"Where are they going?" I demanded.

The question surprised him. "To hunt, to play, to run with the moon, whatever they desire. Your friends are quite safe from them, as are you. I have pledged my word."

"What do you want of me?"

"Nothing more than the answers to a few questions."

"What questions?"

He pointed to a knee-high boulder. "Please seat yourself, Mr. Morris."

He had a presence about him that could not be ignored. I sat. There was a similar rock not four feet away and he took it, facing me, and spent several minutes studying me intently.

"With your permission," he said, and held his hand out, palm upward, looking for all the world like some Gypsy ready to read my fortune if I but mirrored him. I hesitated only a little, for my own curiosity was awake and on the move by now. He minutely inspected my hands, finally comparing them to his own, which were broad and blunt. "Your fingers are of different lengths," he pronounced.

"What of it?"

"They are also quite bare, not at all like mine, as you see."

From Harker's journal I already knew about the sharp nails and the thin hair on his palms, so there was little need to gape in wonder.

"And when you speak, your teeth appear to be perfectly normal. The same may not be said for my own." He let them show in an almost wry smile. Not a pleasant sight.

"Have you a purpose to this?"

"To confirm to myself and prove to you that we are similar, but not too very alike."

"We are most certainly not alike!" I couldn't control my rising voice.

"I am so glad that we are in agreement," he said with a calm sarcasm that took all the wind out of me. "Such differences should reassure, rather than alarm you."

"What do you mean?"

"You know the truth of that well enough for yourself."

Indeed, but the agonizing terror inside made me consciously obtuse. To finally face the truth, to actually *speak* about what I'd hidden for so long. . . .

"As I told you," he said with a glimmer of sympathy I would have never otherwise ascribed to that hard, cruel face, "what we are is not as bad as you have been led to believe."

A short laugh burst from me, a laugh that might have turned to a sob had I not forcibly swallowed it back.

"You are *Nosferatu*, Mr. Morris, nothing more. I am *Nosferatu*, but much more, hence the visible differences." He opened his palms again, as though that explained everything. "I know how I became as I am, but I want to know your story. Who took your blood and gave it back? Who initiated the change in you? And when?"

I was speechless for many long moments as he waited expectantly for an answer. "Why do you want to know?"

"Those of *your* kind are rare. I would know more about you. You are the first I have ever met both before and after dying. Our encounters in London and in Seward's house were brief, but I sensed changes in you no one else could discern—not even yourself. For that I decided to spare you and consequently your friends. For that I planned a way to rid myself of their nuisance without killing them."

"You *spared* us?"

"Look not so surprised, Mr. Morris. At any time of my choosing I could have destroyed the lot of you. Knowing what you do about me, could you doubt my ability?"

Van Helsing had been thorough in his lectures to us about the near-boundless powers of the Un-Dead, and of Dracula's genius in particular. I'd held serious reservations about just how even the six of us together—three being experienced hunters—could defeat such a formidable creature. Van Helsing had assured us again and again that God was on our side, which is always a help. My faith on that never shook for a moment, for it struck me we'd need an Old Testament kind of miracle to succeed.

"Why forbear then?" I asked.

"Your deaths were unnecessary. I could likely disassociate myself from the demise of five respectable people in the heart of England and be safe enough, but Harker is quite the diarist. So are the others, I discovered. Despite my efforts on the one occasion in that asylum study I knew I could never be certain of destroying all evidence linking them to me. And then there was Van Helsing. His knowledge of the *Nosferatu* is thorough, if short on wisdom, and he is highly respected within his academic circles. His sudden and mysterious passing along with the others would not go unnoticed. I also considered your reaction. If I killed all your friends you'd not be of a mind to freely speak with me, quite the contrary. It was far better to have my hunters believe in my own destruction than for me to deal with the inconvenient consequences of theirs."

"But I saw you die. We all did."

"You saw me vanish into dust," he corrected, "that was eventually whirled away by the wind into the darkness. A very excellent escape for me, was it not? It was a risk—things might not have gone so well had you used wood instead of metal weapons, but I am content with the results. Now you see why I had to stop you from waking your friends: to do so would have eventually meant their deaths and yours as well. You'd not let my actions pass, and I would defend myself from you. Larger parties have disappeared before in these mountains. Accidents are easily managed, and here I would not shirk the risk—but I chose to avoid such an extreme action lest you . . . take offense."

"You set all this to going just for a talk with me?"

"Had I a choice and an opportunity, I'd have found some way to speak with you in England and then quietly departed. No such opportunity presented itself, so I left, thinking to return some years hence. What I did not expect was for any of you to follow me to the very threshold of my own castle. You and your friends were possessed with such a grim determination to kill me that it needed to be dealt with first before I could indulge my curiosity. You may believe or not, as you will."

And I did believe him. He was the unopposed master of the night with the strength of ten, able to change shape or turn into mist at will, able to beguile anyone to do his bidding. Whatever gave us the idea we could fight anything like that? Van Helsing had been so confident, though, and had a way of instilling confidence in others. But seeing things from this direction put a whole new understanding in me. We'd been like children shaking our fists at a cyclone.

"You did all that, spared them, and yet caused my death?"

Now he had a turn at looking surprised, and a remarkable expression it was to be sure. "On the honor of all my sires, I swear that your being killed was not part of my plan of escape. I told the Szgany to resist but a little and then depart—to make it look well. Is that the phrase?"

I hung my head, staring at my snow-crusted boots. "Close enough."

"As with the others, your death was unnecessary, and not what I desired at all. Should you die, how would I then be able to speak with you?"

"Because I'd be a vampire." There. I managed to get the word out without choking on it.

He was silent long enough to make me look up. He shook his head. "Your ignorance again. You don't know?"

"Know what?" I couldn't keep the irritation from my voice.

"Though you carried the blood of change within you not all who have such rise from death."

"Draw that out a little more slowly," I said, giving him a narrow stare.

He understood my meaning if not the slang itself. "Those of your kind do not always transform after dying. They remain dead. To make the change is a rare thing. That is why I did *not* want you killed. What happened with the Szgany was . . . an unhappy accident."

"Is that what you call it? My life cut off? Me turned into a devil on earth . . ."

He assumed a look a vast patience and crossed his arms, apparently prepared to wait through a long tirade from me. I shut things down fast, scowling at him.

"You are not a devil, Mr. Morris," he murmured. "You will eventually come to learn that—if not from me, then from your own experiences and actions."

Which I did not care to consider just then. I was still mad as hell about what had happened to me, but there wasn't much I could do with my anger except push it aside for the moment. If I'd judged things right, then we still had a mighty big piece of talking to get through. I needed his knowledge.

"Now, as for your change . . ." Dracula prompted when he saw I'd mastered myself.

I gave a mental shrug, deciding no harm could come from telling him. "It was a few years back, in South America," I said. "Arthur Holmwood—Lord Godalming now—and I were at an embassy ball. I met her there. I've traveled a fair part of this world and seen a thing or two, but hands down she was the most beautiful woman I'd ever clapped eyes on. She and I—"

"Her name?"

"Nora Jones. By her accent she was English, I think, though she had dark hair and eyes and that wonderful olive skin. . . ."

Which I'd been on fire to touch the moment I saw her. I hadn't been the only man trying to claim her attention at that gathering, but I was the one she picked as an escort for a walk in the embassy garden. I reveled in my good fortune and hoped to give her a favorable impression of myself in the short time we had, but it was she who took the lead in things. She'd made up her mind about me fast enough, though I wouldn't call her fast, just almighty charming and irresistible. That night, holding to a promise and plan made in the garden, she found her way to my room, and we fulfilled one another's expectations—exceeded them, I should say.

I'd been exhausted the next morning, of course, not from blood loss so much as the excess champagne and sheer physical activity. Her passionate biting into my throat had startled me only a little. It was different, but didn't trouble me much. Young as I was, I'd known more than one woman in my travels and came to know that each had her own path to pleasure, and it was my privilege to assist her there. It was always to my own advantage to be ready to learn something new, and Nora was a enchanting teacher. My body's explosive reaction to her lesson was like nothing I'd ever felt before.

I rested throughout the day, and the next night we resumed exploring mutual pleasures with one another. It was then, caught up in the lust of the moment, that she feverishly opened a vein in her own throat and invited me to drink in turn. Brain clouded and body trembling for release, I gladly did so, taking us to a climax that left us both unconscious. I woke a little before dawn in time to see her throw on a dressing gown and leave, then dropped back into my sweet oblivion.

The word *vampire* was not unfamiliar, but its context for me then had to do with a species of blood-drinking bat that plagued the livestock of the land. In our drowsy love talk during later encounters, the subject came up, but Nora told me not to worry about it, and, lost in the warmth of her dark eyes, I forgot any and all misgivings . . . until that day years later in the Westenra dining room when I volunteered my blood to save poor dear Lucy.

I had no mind for Nora then—she was long behind me, an exquisite and happy memory—and put myself forward without another thought. It was afterward, when I began to hear more from Jack and Van Helsing about Lucy's alarming condition that the doubts crept in. The fact that her illness was so unique with her constant blood loss happening each night that gave me my first qualm. I feared Lucy had fallen victim to someone like Nora, but a ravisher rather than a lover. From that point everything Van Helsing told us confirmed my growing fears. It was only after Lucy's death and the hideous proof of her return that I realized what horror was in store for me when I died.

Dracula took that moment to interject. "If by that you mean being staked through the heart by your well-meaning friends, then you have every right to be horrified."

"If it will free me to go to God, then so be it."

"I doubt that He would welcome such an enthusiastic suicide," he said dryly. "Do not look so amazed. You are still one of His children—yet another difference you may rejoice in."

"How is that possible? I am. . .*Nosferatu*, one of the Un-Dead."

"Exactly. Un-Dead and nothing more. Do you not see?" I didn't, and he raised his hands in exasperation. "Your so-sweet Nora Jones has much to answer for. She should have told you all this and saved me the trouble and you your anguish. You *do* understand that she was, and probably still is, *Nosferatu*?"

"Yes."

"And you must know by now that she was not as *I* am. Her offspring, which includes you, will be like her. I have already had much proof that my offspring, no matter how lovingly taken, will never be so tame. Mine to hers are as the wolf to the hunting hound. Now do you see?"

"We're two different kinds of vampire," I whispered. "How is that possible?"

He gave an expressive shrug. "I know not, only that it is—for here you are and here I am, both hunters in the wide world. We have similar freedoms and strengths, but there are differences. Perhaps those will come to assure you that this life—or this Un-Death, if you will—is not so terrible as you've been told."

"Such as?"

"You will learn without doubt that your soul is still your own . . . and His," he added, with a quirk of his heavy brows toward the sky. "You will find the truth of it when next you walk into a church, which is something you are still very much able to do."

Well, time alone would tell on that one, if Dracula allowed me the freedom to test it.

"With some small changes you are free to live as before, but as *you* choose, for good or ill, as all things will be judged in the end. For me, it is not so simple."

"What do you mean?"

"I can do that which you cannot. The wolf, the bat, the curling mist are natural forms to me, but not for you. I prefer the shadows, but may walk in the sun if necessary; you would die from it and must sleep in darkness while it rules the sky. You can influence people and to some extent certain animals to your will, which makes the hunting easier, but can no more command the weather now than you could as a human, but that is of no matter. I've read in your heart and by your manner that you are a man who would refuse to pay the price for such powers. Long ago I paid and still do. My body bears the signs of that payment, marking me as different from other men. And as for *my* soul . . . I think you would be more comfortable to remain ignorant of such fearful things."

From the look that crossed his face I silently agreed with him. "And what of Lucy? Am I supposed to approve of what you did to her?"

"The matter of your approval is of no import to me. I did nothing with her that was not a part of my nature, a part of any man's nature. She was beautiful and willing—no, do not gainsay me for you were not there and never knew her true heart. I loved her in the only way left to me."

"Until she died."

"We all die, but I will allow that her time had not yet come."

"You kept taking her blood. I watched her weaken horribly with each passing day. You were killing her!"

"Her body was merely adjusting to what we shared. Another few nights and she would have gradually regained her strength with no harm done."

"I find that hard to believe."

He made a curt waving gesture, indication that my believing him on this was also of no import. "If you wish to fix a blame for her death, then you need look no farther than her attending physicians. Had they left her alone she would still be walking in the sun. 'Twas their ignorance that finished her, not my love. Doctors, bah!" His ruddy lips curled with contempt.

"And what about my own tainted blood going into her—?"

"I do not know. The seeds of becoming Un-Dead were within you, but you were not Un-Dead then. It may have helped or made no difference to her health or worsened things. That is beyond my knowledge. I have heard of such transfusion operations, though, and they fail more often than succeed. Some patients are not able to tolerate anything put into their veins and die from it. No one knows why as yet. In my own heart I believe that is what really happened to her."

And were that to be true, then by trying to help her Jack Seward and Van Helsing had . . .

"The poor, sweet child never had a chance," Dracula said heavily.

A painful thing it was to hear him refer to her in that manner, for I had loved her myself as truly as a man could. I could not imagine a dark creature such as he being able to love anyone. It angered and sickened me to think of her giving herself to the likes of him, of his even touching her. He must have hypnotized or forced her, though it may have been as it had with me and Nora, with her surrendering from honest innocence, unaware of the consequences. Were that the case, then I certainly had not known Lucy's true heart. With difficulty, I pushed all my emotions to one side for later reflection. Right now I needed still more information.

"So my blood might not have changed her?"

"It is barely possible, of course. I rather think it more likely that to create your own offspring you must first take blood from your lover, then return it, just as Nora did with you."

"As you've done to Mrs. Harker."

His face went hard.

"What is to happen to her?" I demanded.

"Nothing. The miracle she prayed for" —he touched the mark on his forehead, for it nearly mirrored the one she'd carried— "came to pass. Seward and Van Helsing will not bother her now. That alone should suffice to guarantee her a long and fruitful life."

"But what you did to her—"

"As with Lucy, that which has passed between Mrs. Harker and myself is none of your business, Mr. Morris," he rumbled, his brows lowering.

"But that poor woman—"

"Is quite capable of making her own decisions. If you live long enough, you may come to see that women are far more formidable than you think. Like the rest of you gentlemen, I found myself quite enchanted by Madam Harker's grace, charm, heart, and mind. Unlike you, I decided to act upon my desires. I've lived long enough to have certain . . . perspectives on a few things, and so took the chance, knowing I'd regret passing it by. However, I came to see that which was once acceptable—or at least ignorable—behavior in my youth, was not so for an English lady in these times. All was sealed when the lot of you burst in on us, and I knew then it must end."

For a seducing adulterer he sounded quite smooth.

"I have since tendered my admittedly inadequate apologies to her, mind-to-mind, and severed all links between us. I would have also apologized to her husband, but given the circumstances it struck me as being inappropriate. Besides, he thinks he has killed me. That should be sufficient recompense for his wounded honor."

"What about the blood exchange you made with her?"

"That cannot be reversed."

"Then when she dies, she'll become like you."

"And to you that is yet a bad thing. Worry not. When her time comes she will have a . . . decision before her."

"Decision?"

"It—it is not an easy thing to make into words. My own memory of it is clear, but to describe in a way that you may understand is difficult. Let it suffice that she will have the choice to live as I live or to go to God. At death, each similarly touched soul has a moment of decision. I have told her as much, so did I tell Lucy, whose choice was to tarry on the earth."

"But I had no choice. I went to sleep and awoke to—" I spread my hands to indicate my situation.

"Another point of difference between us, between our kinds. And another question I have no adequate answer for. Why some of you rise and others do not is a mystery to me."

"Van Helsing said nothing of this choice of yours. Neither did Mrs.

Harker."

"He may not know of it, and you can hardly blame the lady for such an omission. It is a most personal thing. But she has a noble heart, a great spirit, and her faith is so strong as to have done such to her—" again he lightly touched the scar on his forehead. "I have no doubt when her time comes she will fly to the angels to seek her rest."

"Are you sure of that?"

"Wait twenty or thirty years and see for yourself. For now, the subject of Mrs. Harker and myself is closed." By the finality of his tone I knew that to pursue the matter would result in unhappy consequences to myself. And he was right. It was none of my business. Besides, to be sincerely selfish about it, I had problems of my own to face. To judge by the miraculous healing of the burn she'd taken from the touch of the Host, Mina Harker was well recovered from her ordeal, and Dracula planned to leave her alone; I felt I could move forward with a fairly clear conscience.

Now that my eyes were opened a little wider than before, I looked out into the night. Though all would have been murky blacks and grays to my friends, it was as day to me. The faint moonlight put a silver gleam upon everything it touched, beautiful, but marred in my perception by my many troubling questions.

"Must I do as you—as Nora—to. . .to. . ." The words refused to emerge.

"Sustain yourself? Hardly. To drink from a lover is one matter, but you'll find that the blood of animals is your real food. One may live upon love alone for awhile, but sooner or later one must come down from the clouds and take more practical nourishment. This is as true for vampires as it is for humans."

That was a great relief. If it was true.

"Do you hunger yet?"

I continued to stare out at nothing in particular, giving no reply.

He shrugged. "When you're ready, then tell me. Your first feeding should be a pleasing experience."

He'd have a hard task of proving that to me. Separated so far from memories of Nora by time and new knowledge, the idea of my drinking blood of *any* kind like downing a cup of coffee sickened me to the core. I tried to hide my grimace as my belly turned over. "What about my friends? When they wake—"

"They will be shocked, of course. They will eventually conclude you have been dragged off in the night by a pack of ravenous wolves and will never recover your body. So very tidy, is it not?"

"It's monstrous!"

"Far better that than to see your footprints in the snow trailing away from the torn blanket that was your shroud. Then you would never be safe from them. I suspected you might revive and rise tonight, so I made sure my children and I were there to disguise your escape."

"But they're my *friends*. I cannot put them through such grief!"

His face went hard again, the change swift as lightning. "You will and must. It is part of my pledge of their safety to you. Leave them alone and they live."

"But—"

"You will leave them. Better that they suffer a little distress than for you to undo all I have done. I will not be moved on this. Accept it, or they will pay."

There would be no return to my comrades, not for the present, anyway, certainly not while his wolves were within call. "Very well," I murmured. Perhaps later I might be able to talk to Art or Jack and persuade them to reason as I had been persuaded, but in the meantime I was feeling very lost and miserable without them. And cold. The icy November air, something I'd been able to ignore because of my changed condition, had seeped well into my bones. It would take more than the long coat I wore to dispel it. I shook out the torn blanket I still had wrapped around my arm and threw it around my shoulders.

Dracula nodded. "Yes, it is time to go inside. My castle is not far from this place. Your friends thought to seal me from it, but there are entrances that they found not."

"What about *your* friends?"

"Mine?"

"Harker wrote of your three . . . companions." I nearly said "mistresses" and diplomatically changed the word at the last moment. I wondered how they would receive me. "The ladies."

His eyes flashed green, and his lips drew into a knife-cut of a line. He released a long hiss of breath. There was a strange blaze of madness in his stare that made me instinctively reach for my missing Colt revolver, for all the good it would have done.

Dracula rose tall and quickly turned away; one hand shot out against the stone side of the mountain as though to steady himself. I'd stabbed right into a nerve it seemed, and couldn't guess what it might be.

With a terrible strength, his bare fingers curled right into the rock, ripping off a piece. I stood, readying myself in case he decided to make a problem, but he took no notice.

"Sir," I ventured after some moments. "What is it?"

His shoulders sagged. He slowly turned back to me. Now his eyes had gone dark, hooded over by those heavy brows. "They are no more," he said, his gaze dropping. "Van Helsing murdered them."

"Murdered?" Here was a shock. I'd long known that the professor had the idea of visiting the castle during the day, but it was news to me to learn he'd actually done so. But murder—?

"He served them as he served poor Lucy," Dracula said.

That told me all. Unbidden, the sight of her hideous second dying passed across my mind's eye as it had every day since. I'd been told—and had been thoroughly convinced—that what we'd done had freed her sweet soul from enslavement to pure evil. Now I was not so certain. God in heaven, had I helped to murder her?

Dracula flexed his fingers enough to let the stone fall, his voice a bleak drone. "Their deaths happened because Van Helsing was more careful and they too careless. In their minds, in their dreams, I gave them warning of what I knew must be his intent, but they would not heed. They thought him to be yet only a simple peasant, easily cowed by fear or seduced by lust for their beauty. I . . . felt each of them go and could do *nothing*." His face darkened, then cleared, like the shadow of a cloud running over the flanks of a mountain. He struck me as a man who felt things deep and felt things hard, but could hold control if he chose.

"What will you do to Van Helsing?"

"Nothing."

"How can you—I mean, if you cared for them—"

"I am pledged."

That simple statement took me aback.

He saw my disbelief. "My word, Mr. Morris, may be trusted."

"Sir, I—"

"There is more as well. You are not so old as I or you would understand the futility of certain kinds of retribution. To avenge my dear ones would put Van Helsing where he belongs—in hell!—but bring me no gain, and only reveal my deception to the others." He gave another shrug, this time with his hands. "What's done is done. I have pledged the lives of your friends to you on your sensible behavior. I will not recant."

I kept quiet, relieved, but still dealing with inner doubt. I had the suspicion that should my friends make themselves a nuisance to him again he might find a way of getting around his pledge.

He straightened, standing tall. "Come then, Quincey Morris. I will show you any number of dark places for you to shelter from the day, places much safer than that which my dear ones had."

"Won't I need my home earth as you do?" I suddenly felt frail and weary and very, very alone.

He turned slightly and motioned toward where the wolves had vanished, taking in the vast forest. "*This* land has become your home, Mr. Morris. When a brave man's blood strikes the ground where he fights he has purchased it for his own forever. You will find rest here and may carry away as much earth as you want when you are ready to depart."

Another surprise. Me being free to leave? I'd no notion he'd even suggest the idea that I could ever depart this oppressive place. It wouldn't be tonight. The hour was too late, to judge by the position of the stars. Dawn was coming, but on top of all that, I needed help, which Dracula seemed willing to give. I'd be a fool not to accept, since I was still trying to get my brain to take in what had happened to me and how to deal with it. Back in Texas when a tenderfoot turned up on the ranch we'd guide him through things until he learned how to survive on his own. Now I was the tenderfoot.

"I'd appreciate that," I said.

Dracula grunted once and continued to stare away into the distance. His gaze and his mind must have been very much elsewhere, for he remained silent and unnaturally still for quite a long time.

I tried not to shiver, waiting, reluctant to intrude on whatever dark thoughts possessed him.

"But perhaps," he finally whispered, his voice so soft I barely heard, "perhaps you will tarry awhile? The wind breathes cold through the broken battlements and casements of my castle, but you will find more comfort there than in these wastes. We two have many griefs to settle in our hearts, and though I would be alone with my thoughts, in such a time of mourning it is better to have company."

My answer was to follow him. As we picked our way over the rocks and up the narrow path, his children began to sing again..

About the Author:

P.N. Elrod is best known for her ongoing urban fantasy series, *The Vampire Files*, and continues to write new adventures and mysteries for her undead detective, Jack Fleming.

In 2011, she was presented with the prestigious Romantic Times Book Reviews Award for *VAMPIRE FICTION PIONEER* for her work in the genre since 1990.

She's written and edited many short stories, novels, and non-fiction for Ace Science Fiction, Baen Books, Benbella Books, DarkStar Books, and DAW. The paranormal and urban fantasy collections she edited for St. Martin's Griffin have allowed her to work with the best writers in the industry. Her books have won awards and made it to the extended bestseller list of the *New York Times*.

Elrod ventures into new territory with a steampunk series for Tor Books and in 2008 began her own publishing imprint, Vampwriter Books, featuring reprints and new novels. She is embracing digital tech to make her works instantly available for ebook readers.

For the most up-to-date information on her toothy titles, friend her on FaceBook and check out her website at:

www.vampwriter.com.

This omnibus is available as a digital download through Kindle, Nook and Smashwords.

Made in the USA
Middletown, DE
09 September 2016